DAUGHTERS
of
NANTUCKET

Center Point
Large Print

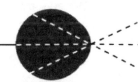

**This Large Print Book carries the
Seal of Approval of N.A.V.H.**

DAUGHTERS

of

NANTUCKET

Julie Gerstenblatt

CENTER POINT LARGE PRINT
THORNDIKE, MAINE

For Brett, Andrew and Zoe:
I love you
even more than I love Nantucket.

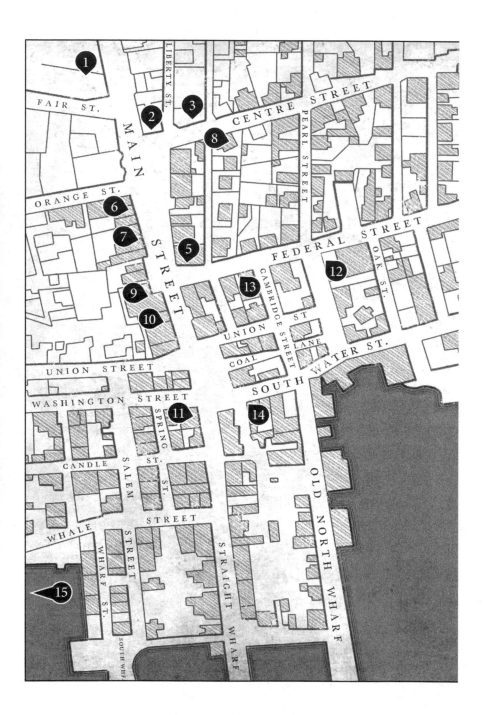

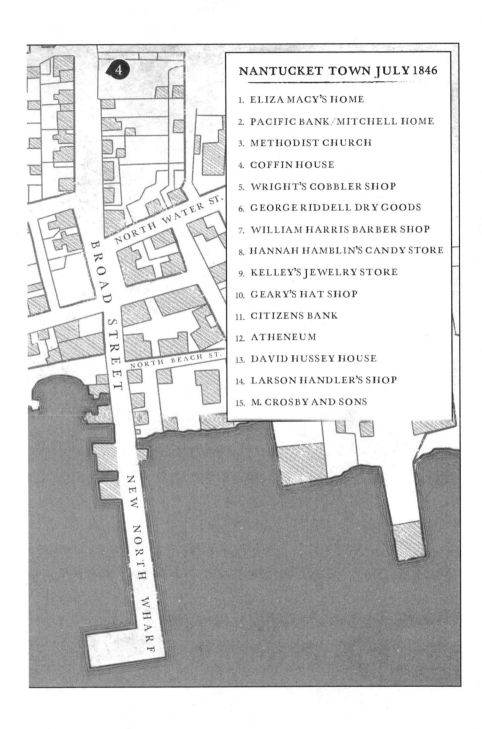

NANTUCKET TOWN JULY 1846

1. ELIZA MACY'S HOME
2. PACIFIC BANK/MITCHELL HOME
3. METHODIST CHURCH
4. COFFIN HOUSE
5. WRIGHT'S COBBLER SHOP
6. GEORGE RIDDELL DRY GOODS
7. WILLIAM HARRIS BARBER SHOP
8. HANNAH HAMBLIN'S CANDY STORE
9. KELLEY'S JEWELRY STORE
10. GEARY'S HAT SHOP
11. CITIZENS BANK
12. ATHENEUM
13. DAVID HUSSEY HOUSE
14. LARSON HANDLER'S SHOP
15. M. CROSBY AND SONS

One third of our town is in ashes.
There is not food enough to keep
widespread suffering from
hunger at bay a single week.
We are in deep trouble.
We need help—liberal and immediate.

—The Selectmen of Nantucket to
mainland America,
July 15, 1846

PROLOGUE

Nantucket Island

Before you begin this tale, you must go back. Not so far back; not to the beginning, when Natives were first naming names, claiming territories that they would eventually be stripped of—*Pocomo* for a clear fishing place, *Sankaty* meaning cool hill—but far still. Back to 1659, perhaps, to when European settlers with names like Starbuck and Macy, Coffin and Hussey, landed at the tip of Madaket and then moved across the island, where they founded a town.

But what to do in this town on this faraway island? The land, you see—fourteen miles of it, five miles wide at its broadest—was too wind-swept and sandy to cultivate, and so these men learned from the Wampanoag how to spear whales off the southern coast, along the strip of beach you now call Surfside. Just offshore, right there. Imagine their humped backs rising from the Melville-deep sea, shield your eyes from the sun and look. Squint back in time. Smell the rankness as each carcass is hacked into blubbery pieces, boiled down and rendered into profitable oil. Oil

11

for wax and candles, oil to spark a flame. Oil to light the entire world.

But that is old news. Old even to the townspeople of 1846. By now, the men have killed all the whales and, through diseases, all the Natives, too. The families of those founding settlers have multiplied and gotten wealthy. So very rich. They have built up their small town on a gentle slope, wooden house next to wooden house next to wooden house, structures that grow from modest to grand and grander still, a tightly packed, densely populated and busy commercial port anchored at its piers by hundreds of barrels of oil.

Nantucket is now the whaling capital of the world. Only where are the whales? Sailors can no longer find such creatures within a day's journey, within a week's journey, even within a year or two. They must now venture for four years at a time to hunt in the Pacific, rounding Cape Horn and crossing the globe, leaving their families behind.

And who is left, on this windswept, sandy island thirty miles out to sea?

Women and girls. Sisters. Mothers and daughters.

Women keep the island sailing smoothly. Women maintain the shops as owners and store clerks, manage the bank accounts, and run the homes, feeding the little ones and the aged alike, churning butter and politics as well as the tide of gossip. Thanks to their progressive and equality-based Quaker ancestors, they are educated and outspoken, these women, living in a way that is decades ahead of their female counterparts on the mainland.

Thanks also to Quaker ideals, abolitionist fervor thrives on Nantucket, making the island a safe haven for escaped slaves running from the South. Those slaves are free here, marrying one another and the few remaining Wampanoag, and have children born free. They, too, are educated. They, too, are free to go to sea and return rich. But, as we well know, there are degrees of freedom.

Certainly, men other than whalers live on this island, too. Retired merchants and captains of whaleships, men with professions on land that help those to profit at sea, boys who are not yet men. Men who want to see society advance as well as those who wish to protect the status quo. But how to prove your worth without a harpoon?

There are other ways to wound, and other ways to win.

This close-knit community is on the brink of something historic, you see. Devout Quakers, bigots, old flames, new loves, abolitionists, titans of industry, close friends, neighbors and acquaintances, an island of cousins all living in homes that practically touch.

And, of course, the presence of all of that oil.

Surrounded by other combustible material: rope walks, haylofts, candle factories, giant barns where sails are made.

They are aware, of course, of the flammable nature of their island home, having been tested before by the Great Fires of 1836 and '38. This well-read and well-bred community likes to think they are prepared for anything. But do they know enough?

It's July 1846 on Nantucket, and it hasn't rained for weeks.

Every great fire begins with a tiny spark. All Nantucket needs now is for someone to light the fuse.

PART I

HEAT

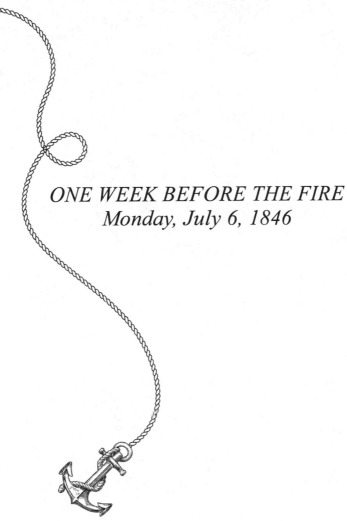

ONE WEEK BEFORE THE FIRE
Monday, July 6, 1846

1

ELIZA

In the heat of summer, gossip spreads through Nantucket town like wildfire.

Everyone on the island knows that, including Eliza Macy. Usually, Eliza enjoys the chatter of the women in town, the way her neighbors walk and talk with baskets of goods on their arms as they exchange tales along the busy, brick-paved and cobbled streets that lead to the harbor, where thousands of kegs of oil wait to be processed and shipped. Usually, she's very much a part of that very chitchat. On any given Monday, she might lean in close over a barrel of grain at Adams and Parker as so-and-so says such-and-such about you-know-who. And although she's not proud of it, Eliza has been known to follow a small cluster of ladies out of Hannah Hamblin's candy store on Petticoat Row just to catch the end of a particularly juicy tidbit about a Starbuck or a Coffin, prominent families on the island, even if she hasn't yet purchased the black licorice whips she came in for. But today turns out to be anything but an ordinary Monday, which is why Eliza isn't out socializing in town.

The morning begins with a vexing conversation with her husband Henry in the kitchen of their stately Colonial home on Upper Main Street.

"But, what do you mean, Henry? How can you possibly stay out at sea when we need you here at home?" Eliza asks. There is no answer. Eliza continues. "I just wish you would be clearer in your intentions. Less obtuse. It can be so very frustrating to be married to you!"

Well, not a "conversation," exactly. How can one possibly be speaking with one's husband when he has been off at sea for almost four years? Conversations exist mostly in her mind—and when she's really annoyed, aloud—in a pretend dialogue with an absentee man. In reality, these conversations are monologues, long letters sent back and forth across the globe. Delayed worries and emotions so stale that by the time they get a response, Eliza's concerns have moved on to something else entirely. In a letter, Henry will present a solution to a problem three months old—the leak in the roof Eliza has since gotten fixed, the seasonal cold that one of their twin daughters Mattie has recovered from—and think he is being helpful! And so Eliza thanks her husband of twenty years for his thoughtful ideas and lets him believe anything he says from the Pacific Ocean is meaningful to her everyday existence. Then she tells him what she *really* thinks from her kitchen. Alone.

The letter from Henry she receives this morning, by way of a sailor passing through to

Nova Scotia, is one such missive. On folded parchment, in his slanting script, Henry informs Eliza of his new plans. She reads the line aloud to herself, imagining Henry's deep baritone filling their home. "Although I promised to be back on Nantucket this summer, my love, this trip has been delayed due to unforeseen complications," his letter says.

Eliza is trying to enjoy a cup of tea, while sitting at the small table tucked under the windows in a corner of their bright kitchen. The tea tastes bland and watery, for she is trying to conserve sugar. And tea leaves. She reaches to the wooden shelf on the wall beside her, locating the dark glass bottle of laudanum, and adds a dash or two of the powder into her china cup. She closes her eyes and holds the bitter liquid in her mouth for a second to let it cool before swallowing. There. The hot tea is surprisingly refreshing as she gulps it down, one quick sip after another, knowing the medicine will do the trick and ease whatever ails her. Nerves. Loneliness. Headache. Heartburn. Three to four times a day, the dosage on the vial suggests. Better to take more than less, to ensure effectiveness. It's readily available on the island, so Eliza can always get more at the apothecary when she runs out.

She reads the letter again.

"What unforeseen complications, Henry? Please do tell!"

Henry doesn't specify, leaving her confused. What else is there possibly *to do* at sea but catch and kill whales, dismantle them by means of stinking, gory masculinity, and turn the massive mammals into profits? Isn't that what the captain of a whaling ship *does,* for goodness' sake? Grow his whiskers long and bark at his crew and risk life and limb in pursuit of oil?

He says only that he's reached the port of New Orleans and not to worry.

A puzzle. Apart from the obvious annoyances this letter implies—that she and her children, who haven't seen Henry for forty-plus months, will have to wait even longer for his presence— is the practical impact that delayed return will have. For Eliza Macy, on dry land, is out of household money. And, until Henry's ship comes in, weighed down with its hundreds of barrels of oil, albeit liquid gold (God willing!), no more money is to be found. She has gotten used to trading candles for goods and services, but now she is even running low on them.

Eliza takes a break from her worries by calling out to her twins, getting ready for the day in their bedroom above the kitchen. "Girls! Breakfast! School!"

"Five more minutes, Mother!" one daughter calls down the stairs.

"Where is my satin hair ribbon?" the other yell-asks.

Sixteen-year-old identical twin girls. Eliza goes to the front hall where the acoustics are better for shouting, and aims her voice up the grand staircase. "Girls, you know I cannot tell your voices apart unless you are standing before me. I found a hair ribbon on the floor last night, but couldn't see the color. It's on my nightstand."

Footfalls above. Then, "I don't see it. Let's just go to Jones's Mercantile after school and buy new bows." It's Rachel. The girl peeks her head through the spindles in the banister.

"*Oooo,* that's a lovely idea!" Mattie says, right beside her sister. "And then we can shop for summer dresses. Maybe something new for our upcoming birthday?"

"Maybe," Eliza concedes. Although she knows there's no way they'll be doing that. She must keep her entitled daughters away from the mercantile! As the girls finish getting ready upstairs, Eliza heads into the kitchen to avoid hearing them. With a small knife, Eliza cuts an apple into very thin slices and divides them onto two china plates with a slice of buttered bread.

Until Henry's ship comes in, their wealth is all theoretical, their profits floating in wooden barrels at sea. Eliza has no money on hand with which to pay for flour or cornmeal or music lessons. No coins for bolts of silk and wool to make party dresses for their sixteen-year-old twin daughters about to enter society. Just ink and a quill to write Henry's name on a black line in a leather-bound book at the dry goods store and the doctor's office, to record what the Macys owe and what they will pay back when his ship the *Ithaca* returns.

But when will the *Ithaca* return?

The rant that follows is also one-sided, as Eliza paces the kitchen alone, letter in hand, responding to Henry, her frustration causing her to speak much louder than she should. *Keep your voice down, Eliza,* she scolds herself, a reminder that Rachel and Mattie are probably listening in from the grand staircase in the hall.

Eliza takes a last sip of tea, her arms tingling with vague numbness caused by the powder she's added, as her mind fills with a pleasant fog. She pops the apple core into her mouth and chews. The twin girls enter the kitchen, both starving, not understanding why they can't have eggs *and* hash *and* corn fritters for their breakfast. After all, they have to walk to school, and they can't very well learn while their stomachs grumble, can they? Eliza does her best to appease their appetites while not arousing their suspicion that something might be amiss.

But one quick glance between the twins—with identical pale blue eyes like their father's—is all it takes for Eliza to know that they are alert to her every move. It's probably too late for her to continue pretending all is fine when it isn't. But keeping the girls calm and happy while their father is Lord Knows Where with a harpoon in his grasp has been her job for their entire lives, and she's not about to shirk her responsibilities now. Better her girls be left in quiet darkness than to deal with the harsh light of day, that's Eliza's parenting motto. There's only so much a girl needs to know.

And so Eliza lies. "I'm just so busy with house chores, I haven't had a moment to get to the grocer. You'll help me later with the last of the housework after school, won't you? Then maybe we can talk about the mercantile for another day."

The girls roll their eyes but nod that yes, they will. Then up and out they go. How Eliza has managed to raise such idle creatures, she'll never know. At least Alice, the oldest of the three Macy daughters, has some ambition. But then again, Alice isn't actually hers. She is Henry's daughter with his first wife.

Eliza gathers together items for a package she's been planning to send to Henry, adding a new note to the parcel. She tries to be measured in her response, although the point of her quill scratches through the parchment twice. She is frustrated by the miles and miles of time, oceans of time, between his words and her retort.

Eliza then spends the rest of the morning alone, washing dishes, changing and cleaning bed linens, dusting the wooden staircase, darning old stockings, and polishing the silver set that belonged to Henry's mother in anticipation of having to sell it. It used to sit atop a beautiful mahogany sideboard, but Eliza sold that piece six months ago for cash to run the house. Now she keeps the silver in a cupboard. Out of sight, out of mind, as the saying goes. That way, when she sells it soon, she won't miss it.

A sparse and unfulfilling lunch follows, stale brown bread with thin jam in the silence of her now clean kitchen. In these moments she misses her former housekeeper, Mrs. Charles, terribly. For her elbow grease, certainly, but even more so for the pleasant conversation. Eliza reads Henry's letter again over a second cup of tea. Then she sees clearly what she must do next, in response to Henry's delay. She has no choice.

She coils her long brown hair into a bun and tucks it under a gray bonnet that matches her silk dress. As briskly as her full silk skirt allows, Eliza marches out her front door and down the gently sloping Main Street, the shops and passersby passing by in a blur. Town is a bustling hive of activity this Monday afternoon, but she has no time or inclination to look at the fine baubles in the windows of Kelly's jewelry store or to say hello to William Geary as she passes him standing sentinel in front of his hat shop near the corner of Union Street.

Main Street's brick sidewalks are not particularly wide, but the street itself is still grand in comparison to the dirt paths that make up the rest of town. Flanked on both sides by white-washed clapboard buildings two and three stories high, each contains multiple places of business, from shops for clothing, food, and wares to a barbershop and a printing press. On the floors above the street level, behind large, glass-paned windows are halls for gathering, private offices for lawyers and other businesspeople, and a free anti-slavery library and reading room located over Obed Macy's store for anyone who wants to keep up with the latest news in national abolitionist activities. Horse-drawn calashes jostle over the stones while traveling merchants call out their global products for sale. The street is an energetic hub.

Eliza, a Nantucket native, has never been off the island, so she cannot truly compare, but she feels quite certain that *her* Main Street—the main artery of her family home for almost two hundred years—can rival that of any other town in New England. In their petticoats and bonnets, the womenfolk meander in small clusters, smelling spices from India and testing pears for their firmness. They raise funds for abolitionist causes and champion women's suffrage while tatting lace and playing whist in one another's lavish parlors. If any of Eliza's friends from the women's auxiliary are out and about today, she pays no mind to them. She pulls her gray bonnet down more securely, tucking in one stray curl at the back of her neck and hoping not to be noticed, just one of the crowd.

She must go to Citizens Bank. But first, to Old South Wharf.

At the bottom of busy Main Street, Eliza crosses the cobblestoned road and heads toward the harbor.

Here, in the lower part of town, the stench of whale oil is particularly ripe—a fermented odor that haunts Eliza hours after she has left the port, even when she escapes to 'Sconset for a picnic, enveloped by the fresh, salty-sea air. "That oil is the scent of our riches," Henry teases whenever she complains. "It is the odor of my success."

Today the wharf reeks of failure.

Rumor has it that the vessel *Atlantic* is about to launch, bound for the Pacific. Eliza must reach it before it departs tonight. The lanes down here are dry-packed earth that coat Eliza's pale gray silk skirt with dust. She passes a tight cluster of barnlike, cedar-shingled buildings that serve as rope walks and candle makers, plus smaller taverns and inns for sailors, and her distant cousin Peleg Macy's warehouse, all thriving businesses tied to the prosperous industry of whaling. She sidesteps hundreds of barrels of spermaceti and baleen whale oil being unloaded from the hull of a ship and stored on their side. There they will wait, lined up on the wharf until processed and sold.

Peeking through the wooden-roofed skyline, over the sail lofts and lumberyards, Eliza can see the topmast of a huge whaling vessel rising toward the hazy blue sky. The *Atlantic*. How she wishes it was the *Ithaca*.

"Pardon me," a young man says, accidentally brushing Eliza's side with an overstuffed cloth sack. He walks slowly along the wood-planked pier, head bent toward the fresh-faced girl beside him. They are hand in hand. The girl weeps inconsolably.

A sailor and his beloved, no doubt.

Eliza recalls those days twenty years ago, when she was eighteen, newly wedded to Henry Macy, eight years her senior. Through marriage, Eliza had become a sudden mother to Alice and—although she didn't know it at the time—pregnant with the twins. One chilly day at the end of April in 1826, Eliza wrapped herself in layers of knitted wool, left Alice with her mother in the house she grew up in on Union Street, and walked to the Straight Wharf to bid Henry farewell. As returning captain of a famously lucky Nantucket whaling vessel, Henry was eager to meet his crew. For weeks before the journey, he studied maps by candlelight and made several visits to William Mitchell's house to ensure that his compasses and chronometer were in fine working order. When Eliza arrived at the dock that day, he stood in a new suit, shaking hands with both Mr. Hadwen and Mr. Barney, owners of the *Alpha*. Eliza tried to hide her tears, but Henry read the distress on her face and excused himself from the men to talk quietly with her.

"Thirty months is a jiffy," he said, holding her chin in his hand. "You won't even miss me," he joked. He bent closer and whispered, his soft brown hair tickling her jaw, "and, if and when you do, remember my gift to you. Because there's a cure for that wanting." She looked into his gray-blue eyes and blushed, unable to treat the moment with levity the way he pretended to with such skill and ease.

The present he was referring to was hidden in a wooden box at the back of the tall bureau in their bedroom, where Eliza hoped to forget about its existence entirely. What a surprise it was: a carved phallus fashioned from the tusk of a whale! Ivory that was supposed to keep a wife company while her husband was at sea! She couldn't imagine possessing such an intimate object, much less using it, and she had tried to hide her shock when Henry presented it to her in their bedchamber the evening before his journey. Holding it made her uncomfortable, the weight and strangeness of it, so she had hastily wrapped it back into the cotton cloth, shut the mahogany lid on the box, and tucked the entire parcel in a drawer behind her wool stockings.

Although, over the years, Eliza has grown more comfortable with it, the object less foreign, more friend.

"I will miss you terribly," she had said that day to Henry, her voice catching with emotion.

He had kissed her softly on the lips, sealing the feeling between them.

"Captain!" his second mate had called. "Pardon my interruption, but we need you to meet with the cook and check over the food storage. Mr. Parsons thinks we might load in more grain and hardtack, but we're already over capacity down there."

"Right!" he called out to the man on the dock. "On my way." He smiled at Eliza and tipped his hat. "So long for now, my love."

"So long but never goodbye," Eliza answered, which would become their parting words before every journey for the next twenty years.

"Never goodbye," he echoed. Henry walked down the dock, stepped into a small rowboat with the first mate holding the oars, and glided out to a mooring where the imposing form of the *Alpha* was docked and ready to sail.

She watched as he gave a final wave and climbed up the rope ladder into the ship's hull. Eliza supposed that Henry's steadiness and confidence, coupled with that innate good humor despite life's tragedies, made him into a fine captain. The qualities had surely fashioned him into a fine husband.

A fine and wealthy one.

Until recently.

Eliza snaps out of her reverie and realizes she is staring, not quite at the heartbroken couple, but through them and through time. Certainly, though, the couple believes that she is eavesdropping on their final moments together.

"Are you sailing on the *Atlantic*?" Eliza asks the man pointedly.

"Why, yes, ma'am, I am," he says. "Part of the crew." He rocks back and forth on his heels, celebrating the fact.

The crew! Poor thing. The lowest-paying and hardest-working men onboard a whaleship. Henry had begun his career as harpooner and then a mate, and so she has mistaken this man for a person with a bit more skill and clout; a cooper, perhaps, or a blacksmith like her own father. The sailor smiles wide, excited for an adventure that he romanticized in his mind.

"How wonderful," Eliza says. She glances at the young wife, who, in her silent sniffles, seems infinitely wiser.

"Will you do me a favor?" Eliza asks the boy-man, extending the small parcel in her hand. "My husband is Captain Henry Macy of the whaleship

Ithaca. He has been gone many months and is now in the Gulf of Mexico. Your ship, as I understand it, plans to hold a gam with it and share news of home. I need this package to be delivered to Henry. Him, and no one else." She fishes in her dress pocket for a coin. Perhaps he will buy some tobacco with it onboard the ship. Instead, he hands it to his young wife. Smart, at least, in one way.

"It would be my honor," the young man says, smiling as he takes the package. He tilts his torso and bows slightly, reminding Eliza of how Henry always made that sweet, formal gesture to her when they were courting. Her heart suddenly aches uncharacteristically. Perhaps this is the true reason she never ventures to the port; it is all too real here. As they stand on the long pier, she pretends to study the ship out in the sparkling blue harbor, the scale and mass of it, the way it rises from the water like a mammal from the depths of the sea.

The bigger the ship, the longer the journey. This leviathan will be gone for over four years, Eliza suspects.

Her parcel will now begin its journey. It is, in many ways, no more or less remarkable than any of the others she sent out to Henry. Like those, this one contains a tiny cake soaked in rum, several detailed letters from the girls, a drawing in pencil made by Mattie (this one of a bluebird), and a long letter from Eliza wrapped together into a loaf of paper and twine.

What's different this time, besides Eliza's slightly chilly tone after being told Henry won't be back as scheduled this summer? Tucked inside her words, folded small and tight, is another warning, bolder than the last two: a third statement from Citizens Bank concerning Henry's impending bankruptcy, should his ship not return profitable, every casket filled to the brim with liquid gold.

The young wife of the greenhand sailor rushes past, head down. She has said her farewell. When this man returns to Nantucket—if this man returns—the wife will be a different person. As, of course, will the husband.

Although not impulsive by nature, Eliza suddenly has the urge to run after the young matron, to call out for her to stop so she can embrace her. Once the tears have dried and the woman's heartbeat settled from its gallop, she will tell her this:

You are married to a soldier gone off to fight an infinite war. You will miss him at first so fiercely that it will feel as if you have reached the brink of madness. The seasons will change and your loneliness will turn to despair, just as winter fog settles over this island.

She will say, *I once became disoriented as a girl, led past the safety of the town's gates and into the moors by an older boy. He charmed me with wondrous stories, but when I refused his kiss, he left me alone as dusk fell. Clouds covered the stars and blocked the moon and I could not find my way back to town and home. I wandered in a silent panic, imagining hungry beasts beyond my vision, until my father came for me, his voice cutting through the syrupy darkness like a beacon.*

The first year without your husband's company will be much like that.

Eliza will press on: *You will miss his birthday, and he yours. Easter will come and go as will the sheep-shearing festival, the Fourth of July. You will spend a summer day at the beach, gazing out across the sea and wondering where he is, if he is. At Christmas, you will not feel the light of the season inside your heart.*

You will give birth, and your child will have his eyes.

You will be wedded to a ghost.

Eliza imagines the woman pulling away from her—who wouldn't, upon hearing such a cataclysmic fate? But Eliza will reach for the stranger's elbow, and tighten her grasp. *Eventually,* she'll say, *the grief will fade. Your heart will toughen and you will grow strong. You will raise your child and teach her well, and control the household as you see fit and celebrate birthdays and make important decisions independently for all of you every day.*

35

Your marriage will be made up of three beings: a wife, her husband, and the sea between them. And because of that, you will—for better or worse—be free.

But instead of uttering a word, Eliza simply watches the young wife disappear into the crowd.

Now back on Main Street, Eliza enters the cool dark of Citizens Bank and tries not to let the imposing building filled with men intimidate her. Aiming for a calm she doesn't feel, she heads straight to the bank manager's desk.

"Ah, Mrs. Macy," the bank manager Mr. Edmunds says, not at all surprised to see her. "Would you like a seat?"

"No, thank you," Eliza says. The banker merely raises his eyebrows and waits for her to continue. The manager is lanky, his defining feature a protruding Adam's apple. She tries to focus on this. "I'm here to ask for another loan."

"I'm afraid that's impossible, Mrs. Macy. You've taken out three already. The bank won't allow me to approve any more."

Three. *Like her children,* she thinks. Expensive creatures. "Then more time perhaps, to pay off Henry's and my debt?" Darn. She didn't mean for it to come out as a question.

"Need I remind you—which I don't think I do, since we send you new statements every month—

36

that your line of credit ran out several months back," he says, nodding with false sympathy. "And, to avoid foreclosure and loss of your house, Mrs. Macy, you must begin to repay—at least in part—by the end of the month." He then checks his giant ledger, writes something down, and hands it to her.

The amount scrawled on the piece of paper is enormous. She has an urge to curse at him, say something unkind about his ugly Adam's apple, then storm out past the other bankers' desks and slam the giant wrought-iron door behind her. Instead she turns and quietly leaves.

What now? Eliza slowly skulks away from the bank, the heat of afternoon oppressive, a fierce combination of humiliation and anger building inside. How will she, who has over the years used up all of her own savings from her parents' small dowry, make ends meet until Henry's return? And when will that return come?

Her husband's last trip—from 1839 to '42— was not profitable, thus getting the Macys into this tenuous situation in the first place, and causing Henry to turn right around and head back out to sea. This current voyage needs to be a success. For all of them.

The small piece of parchment with the large sum is crumpled in her damp palm, black ink staining her hands. She crosses town at the corner of Main Street and Federal, stops for a passing horse and buggy, and drops the note in the gutter, right into a steaming pile of dung.

And that's when she notices the new storefront. Well, it's an old storefront, but it is vacant and seems to have a new tenant inside. Right there. On the corner of Main and Federal. In the heart of town. Nantucket's best cobbler—the Black man named Benjamin Wright who has the shoe shop out on Fair Street—stands inside the large glass windows with Mr. Landry from the town council, the pair of them holding up papers as they point around the space and nod at one another like old friends.

This is a terrible development, an unwelcome addition to all the bad news Eliza has already received today. Because Eliza's one last hope in all of this financial mess is to ensure that her daughter Alice and son-in-law Larson's men's shop, Handler's Clothing, only two blocks away from this very location, does well and turns a profit. They are currently the only store on Main Street that sells men's shoes. And right now Alice and Larson aren't making ends meet.

Eliza is doing everything she can to help their business stay afloat. She manages the accounting and purchase orders herself and even works in the shop in her free time whenever Larson allows her to. The last thing they need now is nearby business competition on Main Street. She had tried once before unsuccessfully to stop Benjamin

Wright from encroaching on their territory, but the cobbler keeps turning up.

"Mr. Wright, I shall see you at the town council meeting tonight at seven o'clock," Eliza hears Mr. Landry say as he exits the building with the cobbler. To avoid staring right at them, Eliza glances down. She bends over her skirts and pretends to tie the laces on her left boot, noticing with some irony that the top fastening on the old leather shoe needs replacing. "Bring all of your paperwork, including a bank note and letters of support, and be prepared to explain to the council your plans for buying the property and running your cobbler shop from the first floor."

"With a small inn and grogshop above, don't forget," Mr. Wright added.

"Yes, indeed. A nice little business proposition."

Not just rent, but *own?* Not even her Larson owns his shop. Eliza's neck cramps as she tilts her head up toward the men. She can't possibly stay hunched over her shoe any longer, so she stands and pretends to study the parchment nailed to a wooden pole announcing the time and date of the next abolitionist meeting.

"The councilmen will vote immediately?" Benjamin Wright asks. "Meg and I will have our answer tonight?"

"Yes. You'll know by the end of the evening. We'll open the floor for discussion, let the community speak their piece. Then we'll consider their perspectives and vote."

A new plan begins to form in Eliza's mind. Suddenly, this long, hot Monday is not long enough. So much to do! She must stop at Handler's Clothing and have a little chat with Larson and Alice. See what they are doing later on tonight. Then she must get home to supervise the twins in their afternoon chores and make sure they weed the garden and prune carefully around her few successful tomato plants. Finally, she will prepare a nice supper for her family. One of their favorite dishes. In fact, Eliza should stop in at the butcher's! Splurge on something fresh, writing Henry's name once more in the credit ledger—and then she will get dressed in her finest and prepare some words for tonight's town council meeting.

If anyone in town is gossiping about her, Eliza hardly even notices.

2

MARIA

Maria Mitchell stands in the center of the first-floor lecture hall of the Nantucket Atheneum, this former-church-turned-library and museum, directly under a ray of late afternoon sun shining through the large cathedral windows. Her arms are thrust out in front of her as her fingers pinch the top of a well-preserved creature while the rest of its small body dangles freely as if still alive. Oh, how Maria loves the natural world!

"What is it?" little Joseph Allen whisper-asks behind her, completely entranced. Joseph is one of her Atheneum Boys, who Maria trains in astronomy and map-reading skills in exchange for their help in her library. Although Maria isn't supposed to have favorites, Joseph Allen is a current pet.

"A bat from Madagascar," Maria beams.

"May I touch it?" He is slight for thirteen, giving off the impression of a much younger boy. But he's intelligent and curious, with a pug nose, light brown eyes, and a cowlick like a question mark in his sandy hair. Spunky and wiry, Joseph's body is always in motion, which should serve him well when he goes off to sea in a few years. Although restless by nature, Joseph has a sharp mind and a strong capacity for creating order from chaos, which is exactly what Maria needs in a library volunteer.

"Be gentle," Maria says, letting the boy stroke the bat's mottled fur. He circles the creature to examine its back, something most children wouldn't think of doing. "The scientific name is *Taphozous mauritianus*, or Mauritian Tomb bat. See the all-white ventral surface?"

"You mean like a belly?" Joseph asks, stepping back around to study it from the front.

"Yes, that center region there."

Although Maria, now twenty-seven, has left behind the formal profession of teaching children, educating others will always be a love of hers, as she doles out information all day to volunteers and patrons alike at the Atheneum. Not only did Maria teach at the local grammar school, but she also opened and ran successfully her own school for a year before being offered the position here at the Atheneum. Using her best instructor's voice, she quizzes Joseph about the location of Madagascar, pressing for specifics about the climate. He's ripe for more information, but it's almost closing time, so she shoos him along. "Enough staring for now, Joseph. You still have to shelve the new shipment of books from London. They are stacked on my desk for you upstairs."

"Yes, ma'am," Joseph says. "Thank you for

teaching me about the Taphozous mauritianus!" And he's off, around the corner and up the stairs to the library on the second floor.

On the first floor, rows of benches—once pews—line up neatly behind Maria, awaiting the next visiting speaker. From Ralph Waldo Emerson, to Horace Mann and Maria's personal favorite, Frederick Douglass, who gave his first speech to a mixed race crowd standing right here, this space has been graced by the voices of inspired and inspiring public figures. And, in the late afternoon, this happens to be the best spot from which to view a new item for the museum's collection. Natural light is not good for preserving unique and splendid curiosities, certainly, but it works for initial viewing, before cataloging the artifact and displaying it in the rear of the hall, where she has set up a small museum. Maria refers to it as her Cabinet of Curiosities.

Over the years, whalers and merchants have brought her incredible treasures, including minerals and shells from Polynesia, silks from the Orient, porcelain and onyx figurines, a variety of spears and other weapons, flora and fauna from India, ivory and bone carved with scrimshaw, the jaw of a sperm whale, two sword-fish swords, and, just last month, the skin of a python. Maria carefully catalogs each item's history along with the name of its donor, a task for which she receives extra compensation from the Atheneum's trustees.

Maria turns her attention back to the winged creature before her. It is a black-and-white mix, with beady eyes, pointy little ears and the furry body of a squirrel. *Fascinating.* She brings it over to a lecture table covered with white cloth and begins to take measurements, first of its wingspan, and then of its body length. She makes other notes about the small mammal on a card, carefully paying attention to every detail. Tonight she'll be presenting an update on the full Cabinet of Curiosities at the town council meeting, and she wants to make certain to highlight all of the best and newest items with accurate and specific descriptions. The more positive attention Maria can bring to this Atheneum and museum, the better. As its reputation grows, Maria hopes to attract even more visitors, both national and international, patrons with deep pockets, and public speakers through its stately doors. Already the Atheneum is the cultural center of the island. Why not the whole world?

Maria is excited for tonight's meeting, reveling in any opportunity to share her mostly solitary work with a wider audience. She carefully wraps up the bat in cloth and returns it to a crate lined with straw by her feet. She seals the top of the box and leaves it there for later. For she's just had the most wonderfully inspired idea: why try to describe this latest curiosity to the town council when she can bring the preserved mammal and display it for everyone to see. Now *that* should garner some attention. The community will be talking about it for days and beyond. She'll become a legend! *Remember the time Maria Mitchell brought a bat from Madagascar to the town council meeting? Oh, Maria, you rabble-rouser.* She can't help but chuckle to herself as she climbs the curved staircase to the second floor and the actual library itself.

She walks past the neat rows of wooden farm tables, straightening piles of books as she goes, and saying hello to patrons bent over small texts. Between the big windows, the walls are lined with floor-to-ceiling mahogany bookshelves, each alcove organized loosely by subject matter, from natural history to encyclopedias and poetry. Maria's most recent catalog of the library's 3000 volumes has just reached 120 pages, and it is growing each week.

"Maria, dear," an old woman named Mrs. Hodges says, looking up from her favorite spot by one of the tall windows. She has a strong, upper-crust Boston accent, putting much emphasis on the middle syllable of Maria's name, Ma-*rye*-ya. At least she pronounces it correctly. "Come sit," Mrs. Hodges says, a glint in her eye. "You work too hard."

Oh no. Maria recognizes that look. Of course

she does, since she receives it several times a week from the married women of this small island town. Their fevered need for matchmaking would almost be humorous if it weren't so cloyingly desperate. She sighs and resigns herself to be patient.

"Yes?" Maria asks.

"I saw you seated next to John Talbot at church Sunday last," Mrs. Hodges says.

"I arrived too late to sit in my usual spot," Maria says.

Her parents and younger siblings are still Quakers, attending church on Fair Street, but Maria left the Friends to join the much more open-minded Unitarians on Orange Street several years ago. She usually sits with her older sister and her husband, both also Unitarians, but by the time she arrived last week, the minister had already begun the service and Maria didn't want to be disruptive. She thought no one would notice her in the back pew, but now she concedes the truth: that everyone notices everything about their neighbors on Nantucket.

"Is that the only reason?" the old woman says, peering at Maria over the top of her spectacles. "Because last I heard, Mr. Talbot stopped courting Winifred Hicks."

Stopped courting! That is certainly a delicate way of presenting the story. "Yes, well, it's hard to court someone once she's run off with a sailor, wouldn't you say?" Maria says, standing and moving some stray books from the table between them. She pictures raven-haired Winnie waving theatrically from the bow of a ship as she and her companion make their way to New Bedford and beyond. Rumor has it they were married once they arrived in that port city, but no one has heard from the couple since.

"However it happened that Mr. Talbot became eligible once again, he is Oxford-educated, tall, and from a family of successful merchants."

Well-bred like a fine horse! Maria thinks. "Quite eligible, yes," she says, stifling a laugh. Not wanting to appear rude, she turns sideways and deposits the books into a pile in need of careful refiling. She will have Joseph put them back where they belong.

And then she spies a small note, wrapped in crisp newsprint and tied with red string, tucked carefully between the piles, and her heart skips a beat.

Linley.

Linley was here.

Maria scans the room for a trace of her friend among the other patrons, between the piles of volumes, but there is none. She smiles softly to herself when she realizes that she missed her yet again.

"Miss Mitchell? Can you assist us, please?" a woman asks, breaking Maria's spell.

47

Mrs. Jones approaches Maria's desk with her daughter, a girl who dislikes reading because, she says, the words jump on the page. How Maria longs to pore over the letter from Linley right now, unfold it here in the open and laugh and imagine the conversation. But that's impossible. She pockets the note in her full skirt and nods as she walks toward Mrs. Jones to help her daughter find just the right book. She will make time later.

"Can we look at the giant bird book, again, Mother? Like we did yesterday?" a young boy asks as he climbs the steps, and Maria can tell from the excited voice that it is little David Hallett, on his daily visit to the two-hundred-page, fully illustrated Audubon guide, *Birds of America*, bought directly by Maria from the naturalist himself.

She may never get to the note at this rate, although the anticipation is in itself a delight. Maria glances back to her desk and realizes she must finish composing a letter to Horace Mann, the secretary of education for Massachusetts, inviting him to return as a guest speaker. Her hands linger on a newspaper clipping from last month. A local resident wrote another scathing letter to the editor stating that colored children carry diseases like malaria and, therefore, they put white children at risk by attending school together. Nantucket, while progressive in its leanings, still harbors people afraid of change, some of whom are even willing to scapegoat people of color. Should she send the upsetting article along to Mr. Horace Mann to show him the real level of prejudice they are facing here? Or would it scare him off?

During the other seasons of the year, when the island is quiet, Maria pores over the library's academic texts in the sacred silence of this holy building, a cathedral of learning where she is free to study and create her own life's syllabus. She challenges and delights herself by deciphering astronomy textbooks in Latin, struggling through difficult mathematical calculations until night falls and she is needed at home. The Atheneum—with its museum, lecture hall, and compendium of books—is her college.

In summer, however, with the Atheneum abuzz, she must put her personal education (as well as personal relationships) aside for a time. It is a shame since the latest edition of *Silliman's Journal* arrived from Yale yesterday. Maria's meteorological observations on the average cloudiness of Nantucket from 1843 to 1845 were published in that journal just last year. To see her name printed there, in *The American Journal of Science and Arts*, still gives her a jolt of pride, and she looks forward to each new edition, learning about the work of other scientists and hoping someday her work might be once again included. *Ego stadium voluntas cras*, she tells herself. *I will have to wait until tomorrow.*

And always, always there is the matter of discovering a comet. As an amateur astronomer himself, the King of Denmark announced years ago that he would award a prize to the first person to discover a new comet. When the king died in 1839, his son took the throne and kept the contest alive. Originally, Maria was not motivated by competition, but by the joys of discovery for its own sake. But, as the years have marched on without a winner, Maria's competitive spirit has grown along with her astronomical abilities. Maybe this will be the year.

Before she knows it, it's half past five. Maria gently nudges the dozen or so patrons out of their intellectual trances brought on by their collective quiet study. She cannot blame them for getting so lost in thought—this serene building has a mesmerizing quality, one Maria herself helps to cultivate—but she has a busy evening ahead of her. She waves goodbye to them all and almost leaves the premise herself before remembering to take the wooden crate with her.

And then, once everyone exits the building, Maria locks the door behind her and sits on the steps of the Atheneum, her dark dress fanning out around her. She unfolds Linley's note in the fading daylight, her mind soaring toward the heavens.

3

MEG

Meg Wright looks around her kitchen, mostly satisfied. Dinner is cleared away, the dishes are done, and her daughter Lucy has had her bath. Cinnamon buns—a special treat for a special night—are cooling on the butcher block. Meg wipes her sticky hands on a damp rag and dries them on her apron, checking the time on the small clock on the wall by the kitchen table. It's just after six. She and Benjamin have to get going. They can't be late for tonight's town council meeting.

"Hello, Mrs. Wright!" a little voice says. Jenny Cole knocks on the screen door while simultaneously opening it and letting herself in. Her hair is braided in two neat plaits, matching the cloth doll in her hand. "I can smell your baking all the way down the street!"

Meg laughs. "I hope that's a compliment, Jenny! I'd invite you inside, but you're already here."

"Best friends don't have to knock, Mama says," Jenny smiles.

"Yoo-hoo!" a voice sings out.

"And speaking of your mother," Meg says, not needing to finish the rest of the sentence.

The next one through the door is Daniel, Faithful Cole's three-year-old, who dashes in and lets the door slam behind before his mother reaches it. He's got a wide grin and the chubbiest legs sticking out from under his short pants. Meg wishes she could scoop him up into her arms and squeeze him, but she is nine months pregnant and her back is aching and her belly is just too big, so she settles for a pat on the head and asks if he'd like a cinnamon bun.

"Yes, peeze!" Daniel says, clapping his hands together. He scrambles up into a chair and takes the treat with wide-eyed delight, and Meg turns her attention to Faithful, coming toward the door.

"Need help, Faith?" Meg asks.

"No, I'm doing fine. Doesn't hurt. Just slow."

Although Faithful is around Meg's age of twenty-six, she's been plagued with arthritis in her hips since she was a girl, and she grimaces in pain as she climbs the two steps into Meg's shingled house. To add to this, Faithful recently put on quite a bit of weight, which also slows her down, especially in this heat, that hasn't let up even now, at dusk. Faith's hair is tied back in two braids like her daughter Jenny's, her skin a deeper dark than either of her children's. Meg pulls out a chair for her friend and pours her some water from a pewter pitcher on the table. Faithful drinks it down and Meg refills it.

"Thanks for keeping Lucy company tonight,"

Meg says. Although she feels a restlessness to get going, Meg knows that Faithful likes to chat and gossip. Meg doesn't mind indulging her friend for a few minutes while Benjamin changes out of his work clothes.

Faithful makes a gesture with her right hand as if shooing away a fly. "You know I love that little girl like my own. And you know we need your shop to get the town's approval tonight. Now more than ever, especially with everything that's going on in protest of the integration of the schools."

Meg passes her a nicely over-iced warm bun. "I know, believe me. I'm counting the days until school's out." Four more days, to be exact. They have made it through so much; they just need to hold on a little bit longer. On Friday, the island folk can celebrate their victory: that Nantucket made it through its first year of school integration without incident.

Daniel Cole jumps down from the wooden chair, his hands sticky and half the bun uneaten. Meg's baby Elias would have been about the same age as Daniel, had he lived. Would he have been a chubby thing like Daniel, she wonders, or more of a string bean, like Lucy? Would her son have liked raisins in his cinnamon rolls, even though his big sister picks them out? Meg blinks back tears—she's so emotional these days—as she feels the new baby in her belly kick: a good omen. No use in dwelling on the past, on the what-would-have-beens. Time to stay focused on the now and the future. Meg dabs at the corner of her eyes with a knuckle and sits back down at the table beside her friend.

Faithful licks some icing from her thumb and takes another bite of the pastry. "I do not know how you get the dough so flaky! I try for the life of me and mine never come out as good as yours."

Meg laughs good-naturedly but shakes her head no. Faithful's cinnamon buns are identical to her own. The only difference is in having someone else bake for you; that's what makes the food taste better. That act of love is the only special ingredient. Meg has explained her philosophy to Faith, but she won't hear of it. Her friend maintains it's something extraordinary about Meg's butter, or cinnamon, or sugar, when it's really about a friend doing the work so you don't have to.

"Got a letter this morning from Big Daniel, from a ship passing through on its way to Nova Scotia," Faithful says.

"Yes? And?" Faithful is Meg's main source of information, but she doles out her knowledge like she expects a penny for each piece. Meg wants to hand her friend a dime and say, *Out with it!*

"All's the same this trip. Hunt whales and pass the other time carving designs into whalebone as they weigh down the ship with barrels of oil."

"When's he due back?"

"They made it safely back round the horn, so he's inching closer. But he says Captain Macy is making them delay their return. *We got more to do,* the captain says. Daniel said he's been sworn to secrecy, but he said they were docked in the port of New Orleans and I think—"

"What?" Meg asks.

Faithful shuts her mouth, shakes her head no.

"Something bad, then?" Meg adds, a shapeless worry creeping up her spine. The South is not a safe place for any Black man. Even a freeborn person on a Nantucket whaling ship can be kidnapped and sold into slavery, although Meg hasn't ever heard of it happening to someone she knows. "Do you think Daniel and the others are in physical danger? Or is the issue more financial, that they haven't secured enough oil?"

Meg recalls that the last trip wasn't profitable, that something had gone terribly wrong. The men of New Guinea refused to discuss it when they came home, every single one tight-lipped even when plied with liquor at Absalom Boston's alehouse down the street. They stayed in Nantucket for only one month, that crew. Turned right back around and went out with Captain Macy again, no questions asked, Big Daniel included. They all seem to trust and admire that man, but so much can go wrong on a whaling

55

expedition, even when it is in capable hands.

Meg scoots her chair closer to her friend's and takes Faithful's hands in her own. "You can tell me anything, you know that."

"Big Daniel hinted at—well, more like suggested that Captain Macy was trying to—"

But here she stops. Faithful is clearly distressed, so Meg doesn't press her any further. She'll let her know in good time, if there ever is such a time.

"Stop being such a bully!" Lucy calls out from the bedroom.

"I'm not the bully!" Jenny yells back. "You are!"

Meg and Faithful exchange a look, both at first worried a little about the content of their daughters' exchange. But, while the pair of seven-year-olds try to sound menacing, their voices are raised in a playacting tone, eventually dissolving into a fit of giggles.

"They never really argue," Faithful says.

Meg nods. "But Lucy does keep talking about this school bully. Any idea who it might be?"

Faithful shakes her head no. "I keep trying to get Jenny to say, but she won't."

"Maybe we should go by the schoolhouse, ask Mr. Hart if he's witnessed anything."

Faithful raises her eyebrows. "And what would your husband have to say about that?"

Benjamin, so focused on trying to purchase

the cobbler shop, would not be happy if his wife caused trouble at the South Grammar School. But causing trouble is what Meg thinks democracy is supposed to be about. It's her family's legacy. Meg's grandfather, Giddeon Lewis, sued the state of Massachusetts for his freedom in 1775 and won back the money he earned working on a whaling ship. Because of that lawsuit, Meg's father, Captain Wendell Lewis, was born free— becoming wealthy as one of the first Black whaling captains with an all-Black crew—and Meg Lewis was born free. It's a story she tells any and every chance she gets.

Imagine it. Suing your way to freedom.

But that was just the start of what her Lewis family had endured, and had done here on this small island. The battle for school desegregation on Nantucket has been going on since Meg and Faith both were in public school. More precisely, since 1837, when Meg herself passed the high school entrance exam but was denied actual admittance to the high school. Oh, all the studying she did to prepare. Months and months of mathematics and reading, of being quizzed by her father, who hired Quaker tutors like Anna Gardner—an educator and ardent abolitionist besides—to help Meg study for the examinations.

Wendell Lewis's philosophy about his daughter Meg entering the high school was simple, and thus he stated it simply for Nantucketers to understand: Since our whaling ships have been successfully integrated for the past 150 years, why haven't our school buildings in the same port done the same?

Oh yes, Meg is used to watching the tide turn quickly on matters of race on her island; she is, in fact, caught up very much in its current.

Thinking back on her family reminds her of her goals. She wants, needs both her and Benjamin to be the first Black shop owners on Main Street, and to have her daughter Lucy be part of the first integrated class in Nantucket's history.

Four more days, that's it.

She needs a decision in their favor tonight.

And then, if she dares to let herself think it, she needs to deliver a healthy child in a few weeks' time. Her last baby, Elias, didn't survive ten days. Meg isn't sure she could herself survive a loss like that again.

"Ready, my dear?" Benjamin says, coming down the steps from their two-story saltbox, his hair combed back and his beautiful leather shoes shined to a high gloss. He holds a neatly folded stack of papers. Benjamin needs her to be strong.

Meg pushes away her worries and doubts.

"Well," Faithful says, rising from her chair. "Don't the two of you look like important people."

How Meg wants to believe it.

She and Benjamin walk from their home on

Atlantic Avenue toward the main intersection at Prospect Street, the lively center of life in Nantucket's New Guinea neighborhood—comprised of a vibrant mix of cultures, including those of African, Wampanoag, Pacific Islander and Cape Verdean descent—and they pass the barbershop closing up for the night. They give Mr. Thomas a wave, then pass the rope walk, the dance hall and the general store before turning onto York Street, where the gray-shingled African Meeting House stands on the corner. Just past there is the York Street School.

The York Street School was previously the only school on the island for Black children. Lucy attended school there with Jenny Cole for the last two years, and it is where Meg herself was educated, after they moved the school out of the African Meeting House. But now an invisible line has been drawn straight through New Guinea, redistricting some children, including Lucy. Jenny Cole lives on Orange Street, so for her, that newly integrated school is actually closer. For Lucy, it's a bit of a walk, especially on a hot, blustery, or rainy day, which is basically any day on Nantucket.

The couple stop at Absalom Boston's tavern and inn. A horse-drawn, two-wheeled calash is waiting there to take them to the town hall, a large clapboard-fronted building on Orange Street that, during the day, is Lucy's grammar school.

The same structure also serves as the courthouse, not that Meg or Benjamin has ever been there for any legal reason. Like many people on Nantucket who often hold two or more jobs—the barber is also a woodworker, the farmer dabbles in coopering—the buildings also work morning to night to serve different capacities, depending on who needs to use them.

Given Meg's back pain, Benjamin doesn't want Meg to walk, especially at night when she can't quite see the uneven ground beneath her feet. But they must both attend the meeting, so Benjamin was thoughtful enough to ask Absalom to borrow his horse and buggy.

A famous Black whaling captain in his own right, Absalom Boston, who in 1822 was the first Black man to captain an all-Black crew, was friendly with Meg's father and dotes on her like an uncle. Men's laughter punctuates the night along with the glow of candles from inside the first-floor alehouse attached to the inn, and, as the couple prepares to go, Absalom comes to the open door, barrel-chested and full of vitality. He scratches his beard, lifts his eyebrows, and raises the mug in his right hand to them. "Best wishes to you in town tonight. You have every right to own that property on Main Street, Ben and Meggie. Don't let them insinuate otherwise. Stand firm and, if they start to waver, show them your cash."

Benjamin laughs. "I thought you were going

to advise us to show them your letter of recommendation," he says.

"That, too. But on Nantucket, thank goodness, money is king. I have found the dividing line between Black and white can be significantly blurred by green."

Meg smiles and thanks Absalom, who steps forward and plants a small kiss on her cheek. "Your parents are looking out for you, Meg," he whispers. Rum lingers on her skin, which does remind her a bit of her father, and so the scent brings Meg comfort more than the words. "The situation will work out fine, you'll see," he says, waving and heading back into the alehouse.

Oh, how Meg despises that word *fine*. There's nothing fine about this. Every time Meg thinks of walking into that stuffy, dark hall filled with people judging her worth, butterflies of nerves flap their wings under her rib cage. And didn't Absalom run for school committee this year— one of forty-four candidates—and lose? What makes him so sure things will be fine in this town?

Benjamin has readied the horse, and now he helps Meg step up into the open cart. She sits and runs one hand nervously over her dress skirt, which puffs up around her. She wishes she could have worn her best summer dress, a pale yellow frock with lace around the collar, but it doesn't fit her anymore, even after letting the waist out twice, so she has to make do in a flower-print sack hastily stitched together from an extra bolt of fabric she found in the back of Jones's Mercantile on the wharf. After losing Elias, Meg had given away her maternity dress because the sight of it left her bereft. Now she almost wishes she had kept it.

"You look pretty," Benjamin says, putting his foot in a stirrup and settling on the wide brown mare.

He means it as a compliment, but she wants to look fierce. Menacing. Strong. All those daisies and roses dancing around: too much pattern for her liking, and too much like a little girls' dress to be taken seriously as a businesswoman. "I look like a tea cozy," Meg says to the horse's backside, her words lost to her husband. Benjamin clicks his tongue and grabs the reins, and off they go, down Prospect Street and toward town hall as dusk settles over the gray-shingled homes, the air heavy with the scent of roses, which cling and climb up the town's cottages and decorate their roofs like party hats.

Benjamin stops the horse on Orange Street in front of the South Grammar School and Town Hall, dismounts, and hitches the reins to a nearby iron post. A small crowd has gathered on the lawn leading up and into the clapboard building, people milling about trying to enjoy whatever fresh air they can get before entering the cloying humidity of an enclosed space in July. Meg quickly scans the mostly white crowd. Are they a friendly or hostile bunch? Right now, they just seem worn down by the heat.

Benjamin helps Meg out of the calash. It takes a bit of balance and is not the prettiest of exits from a buggy ever seen, although Meg tries to make it look natural. Once she's out, Benjamin squeezes her hand twice. She pumps his hand twice in return. It's their quick signal in a crowd, a way to send a small conversation back and forth between themselves without using words. *You okay? Yes, I am.* Or, *I'm frightened. Me too.* Mostly, it means an echo, of *Here I am. And here am I.*

David Joy, staunch supporter of abolition and Black rights and one of the co-founders of the Atheneum, is here, shaking hands with another man and heading into the meeting hall. Anna Gardner, Meg's former teacher, waves. And William Hadwen and his wife are here, too. They're the ones building that huge white mansion on Upper Main Street. Maria Mitchell, too, who gives Meg a wave hello. Everyone holds lanterns; Meg can see the glow of them from inside the wood building as more and more people enter. Although these are only candles, the smell of so many lanterns in the dense night air reminds Meg of the charred scent hanging over town after the Great Fire of 1838, and she hopes it isn't a precursor of bad news tonight.

And then, some bad news indeed: walking directly toward her down the dusty street is none other than that insufferable Macy woman who tried to prevent Meg and Benjamin from opening their first shop two years ago. She said that it was too close to downtown and her son-in-law's shop, and therefore unfair for business. Mrs. Eliza Macy. Wearing a wide-brimmed blue silk bonnet with colorful rosettes, more appropriate for a formal wedding than a town hall meeting, and on the arm of that very son-in-law, the one who owns that almost-failing men's shop. Beside her on the other arm is a young woman, who must be the man's wife and Eliza's grown daughter, although they look nothing like mother and child. Meg hasn't heard a peep of negativity since opening the shop on Fair Street, though, and had assumed that all of that nastiness was behind them, and, that the woman would have moved on by now to fight other misguided battles against other unsuspecting competitors with stores closer to her son-in-law's.

"Maybe she's here for another reason," Benjamin whispers, as they file into the hall directly behind the woman.

Maybe, Meg concedes. Perhaps Eliza Macy's son-in-law wants to expand his business in some other way. Perhaps they are here about something else entirely, not having to do with them.

Maybe to announce some news of her husband's whaling expedition, or the fledgling women's suffrage movement, or to support another in the crowd trying to secure a new office space or shop headquarters. There are about thirty townspeople in total gathered tonight, plus the six or seven on the council itself. Eliza Macy could be here for any number of reasons.

But as they settle into the wooden benches lining the hall, Meg decides that Mrs. Macy's presence at tonight's meeting is personal. Benjamin might call it unreasonable, but as Meg stares at the back of the woman's neck, where a light brown curl has escaped from the coiled bun under her cap, Meg knows it's the most reasonable of all things: her woman's intuition kicking in.

The loud rapping of a gavel on the wooden table shocks Meg back into time and place. "Ladies and gentlemen, this meeting is now called to order!" a white-bearded man announces from the front, and Meg sits up as tall as she can in her seat, trying to be seen over that woman's damnable silk hat, and linking her arm with her husband's.

4

ELIZA

The meeting is called to order, and Eliza gets a nervous flutter in her stomach. She was taught the art of public speaking as part of her schooling, with teachers who believed that girls' opinions were as valuable as boys'. The teachers were almost all local Quaker women, who worked hard to take the best of their religious beliefs, scrub them clean of any worry over Church and State, and distill them into elocution and speech lessons fit for a Unitarian like Eliza.

Eliza had not minded these public-speaking tutorials until the sixth grade, when she was asked to stand and defend her position on the Second Amendment of the Constitution and fiercely started defending the Third, until snickers from around the room made her take pause. Once corrected by her teacher, Eliza's skin flushed hot and she ran from the room as the laughter grew in intensity. Long after the incident, the ramifications of such a humiliation reverberate within her. Even now, every time she stands while others are seated around her, Eliza feels a momentary shock of extreme loss.

Still, she knows she must speak publicly tonight to help Alice and Larson with their failing business by keeping competitors from moving too close to their shop. Without knowing when Henry might be back from sea, the entire Macy livelihood depends on it. Her daughter and son-in-law both protested it when Eliza suggested she attend the meeting tonight and contest the new cobbler shop, but Eliza would not back down. Now Alice and Larson sit quietly next to her, both with arms folded and heads bowed, as they wait for the meeting to begin.

The minutes from last month's meeting are read and accepted with a hearty aye. Then the lead councilman directs his comments to the room at large. "Tonight's order of business includes sharing the town's financial report, which will be explained by our treasurer; followed by the School Committee report, read by the new committee leader Samuel Jenks; discussion of several propositions for businesses; and finally an update on the growing collection of ephemera at the Atheneum presented by curator and librarian Miss Mitchell. Lastly, there will be a call for any comments by town members, which will be recorded for discussion at the next town meeting in one month's time. Mr. Landry, if you will," the town council leader says, motioning to a man on his direct left at the table where all the male leaders of Nantucket town are seated in a neat line, each with his stovepipe hat removed.

"Thank you," Mr. Landry says, running his

palm flat over his head to smooth the few light brown hairs he has remaining. Then he begins to discuss the town finances at great length from where he sits. Eliza tries to stay focused on the man's words, but his voice is almost lulling as he drones on in a monotonous hum, and the room is warm, and the day was so busy, and quite upsetting.

Eliza thinks about how she had finally confronted the banker, and how her courage alone should have been rewarded in some way. But apparently no consolation prize exists for facing one's impending bankruptcy.

At this point, swallowing her pride, Eliza would have told her parents, who once lived near her in town on Union Street. But they recently moved to New York, to live with her younger sister Charlotte and help with her four children. Eliza didn't want to alarm them in a letter, but she truly thought she might go mad keeping her financial worries a secret. Before their departure, Eliza delicately asked her parents if she could borrow some money until Captain Macy returned home, but, having put aside little for their elder years, and shocked that the wife of a whaling captain would turn to them for financial support, they had declined. A quick and decisive "no" was uttered before Eliza's request had been fully stated, if she recalls correctly.

"I'd like now to relay the financial situation

with regard to imports and exports, and taxes collected at our docks. The whaleship *Atlantic* . . ." Mr. Landry drones on, and women around her begin to cool themselves with paper fans. Eliza has forgotten to bring hers.

The clawing heat. The boring tone of the town councilman. Eliza finds herself wanting to doze, her eyelids closing slightly, and then slightly more, as if pulled by an invisible string.

Yes, a summer town meeting is very much like a summer suffragist meeting.

A jab by a sharp elbow jerks Eliza awake. "Mother, your turn is coming soon," Larson whispers.

Although she wishes Larson was a bit more of an adult when it comes to running his own household and business, the term "mother" fills Eliza with warmth. She loves how doting and sweet Larson is, like a big child. And although Alice is not her own child by birth, Eliza has always felt immense pride in her, calling her daughter and enjoying being called mother in return.

Henry's first wife, Augustine, died of sepsis when Alice was two years old. Everyone in town heard the story when it happened, of the wealthy whaling captain, now widower with a baby daughter. Eighteen-year-old Eliza knew it, too, as it was all her parents would talk about at mealtime, but she was too absorbed with her own recent tragedy to worry much about someone

69

else's, especially a man eight years her senior. That's because Eliza was trying to mend her own broken heart.

But, apparently, their different types of grief brought them to the same location: Hannah Hamblin's candy store on Petticoat Row. Eliza always headed straight to Hamblin's whenever she was sad or angry—or in this case both—and treated herself to black licorice. When she opened the glass-and-wooden door that day, she heard a child wailing in frustration and pain, and thought, *this child understands me. And I understand this child.*

Henry Macy stood in the middle of the store, rocking the toddler. He was gently bouncing her up and down and saying *shhhhhh.*

"I'm trying to console Alice with a honey stick," Henry Macy said, looking at Eliza with such deep sadness and loss that it moved Eliza out of her own grief.

She blinked.

She could help another. This baby, this man.

"Give me that honey stick," Eliza said to Henry Macy.

Confused, he did. Eliza then crossed to the front counter and pulled her favorite candy from a glass-topped jar, discarding the honey stick in a barrel behind the counter. She marched back to the middle of the store and handed him a thick braid of black licorice.

Henry Macy's eyebrows raised.

"Some have a sweet tooth, some have a sharp tongue, my mother always says." Eliza shrugged, smiling.

"I'm guessing you have the latter," Henry said.

"Maybe so," Eliza said.

Alice smelled the candy and opened her mouth. Liking the taste, she grabbed the trunk of licorice and held on tight. Alice gummed it with satisfaction while studying Eliza out of her clear green eyes. Henry, too, studied Eliza, his eyes as palc as a dusty blue sky.

"She may be teething, too," Eliza added, feeling suddenly warm. "And licorice settles stomachs."

"A cure-all," Henry said, thanking her. Then he bought her licorice whips and invited her to dinner. Within the year, they were married. It was, as Henry said, perfect timing, because his ship was due to head out in the spring and he certainly couldn't travel with a young daughter. Eliza had saved him from a life on dry land! He joked, but Eliza never found it funny. Instead, she found that she had suddenly fallen completely in love with little Alice, and a bit less so with Alice's father.

Alice, once such a pudgy baby, is now rail-thin and delicate. Tiny wrists, perfect little sloped nose. But her porcelain doll exterior belies a very strong core, Eliza knows that. Seated on the other side of Larson, Alice smiles tightly at Eliza.

71

She clearly wants her mother to keep her mouth shut . . . and maybe her eyes closed as well.

"I'm perfectly alert," Eliza says, stifling a yawn.

And now, with the twins almost grown but still under her roof, and Alice and Larson not making ends meet, and Henry of no help whatsoever, Eliza must save the day once again.

She has a feeling licorice won't do the trick this time around.

Larson—despite his handsome face and usually pleasant demeanor, both of which no doubt enticed Alice to fall for him—is a lackluster entrepreneur. He is kind, and he is patient, and, above all, he is ever-present, a quality Alice no doubt looked for in a husband after having such an absentee father, and, at twenty-one, he is very much besotted with twenty-year-old Alice. They met in grade school and have been inseparable ever since. Ah, well. This is exactly why Eliza will do her best to help them, the beautiful, hopeless couple. She gave Larson a loan when he and Alice married two years ago, to try and bolster the shop, but like sand through a sieve it went! Since she cannot provide them any more money for their business—in fact she needs them to be successful on their own, Eliza will support them through her strong action. After all she may need *them* to support *her* before long because, should she need to sell the house and all the contents inside to have money to live on, Eliza and the girls may in fact have to move in with Alice and Larson. She needs this to work out for them. For her.

"Now, to the next order of business, an update on the school committee, which met last week and voted in new members. Mr. Jenks, we understand that much has come into question about the plan for school integration under the newly elected, or perhaps more like reinstated, gentlemen on the committee. Please, inform us."

Samuel Jenks, an older gentleman with pale skin and sandy-blond hair, approaches the front podium. He is the editor of one of the town newspapers. As a journalist, he likes to stick his long, thin nose into everything happening politically in town. This is going to take a while, Eliza fears.

"Thank you, sirs," Jenks says, clearing phlegm from his throat. "As mentioned, at the annual town meeting last month, the new school committee was elected and promptly voted in favor of resegregation, reversing the previous rule that integrated schools. A plan is being drawn up to return the Black children to the York Street School where they belong. Like generations before, these children will get a fine education."

"I have a question about that plan," a voice says from right behind Eliza. She turns. Meg Wright, the one who wants to open a shoe store on Main Street, waves her hand in the air.

"We are not taking questions on the school matter at this meeting tonight," the councilman says.

"But, quickly, when is the school move going to take place?"

Jenks looks directly at Eliza with a fierce, hot stare—no, she realizes, past Eliza and to the woman behind her—and says, "As soon as is possible."

Then with a heavy silence draped over the room, he returns to his seat in the crowd.

5

MEG

Jenks stares Meg down, and Meg stares right back, her heart beating so loud that she's sure everyone in town hall can hear its gallop. She sits as still as she can, her spine rigid, her left hand in Benjamin's right. He squeezes, she squeezes back. *Don't say anything,* his grip signals. *Wait for our turn.* And she knows her husband is right. They aren't here to fight over school segregation. It just surprised her, that man's grand plans for dismantling progress so rapidly.

And the look that Jenks character gives her? It shocks her to her core.

"Moving on, to the next order of business: the applications for permits to purchase either land or property on the island of Nantucket," the council leader says, and Meg sits up even taller in her seat, getting ready for her turn. He calls upon a man who wishes to open a pub by the wharf and requires approval of a liquor license, which gets approved, and to a second man who asks for a liquor license as well, but that one is denied, with explanation from Mr. Landry. "While the town council understands the importance of alehouses to our local commerce, and that not every modern citizen is a teetotaler, we are still

75

governed by Quaker ideals and must not give off the impression that Nantucket encourages imbibing. You may reapply for that liquor license in six months. Everything in moderation. Next request."

Meg glances quickly at Benjamin, and he nods back to her. It's agreed then. Given what they've just heard, they won't mention plans for a grogshop above the cobbler store. Just stick to the most important issue: to own the property. They can always apply for more at a later date.

Someone wants to sell their land in Quiase to a neighboring sheep farmer, only he cannot provide a deed to prove he owns the land in the first place—a situation that gets rather confusing and is ultimately set aside for resolution at next month's meeting.

"Next, is the matter of Mr. and Mrs. Benjamin Wright, who wish to purchase 21 Main Street, the building on the northwest corner of Federal Street and Main," the councilman says.

Meg rises and the wooden bench scrapes the floor. That nosy Eliza Macy turns her head just as Meg's enormous belly rises before her, like a whale emerging from the depths of the sea. Eliza's eyes go wide and Meg looks away, embarrassed by her girth and the hideous print of flowers on her dress.

Benjamin places his hand on Meg's back, guiding and steadying her as they walk to the front of the hall. They approach the councilmen, and, as Benjamin begins to relay their interest in purchasing the building, Meg steadies herself at the wooden podium. Benjamin hands over several letters of support from well-known business leaders, both Black and white, and then together they face the crowd.

"My wife and I are proud Nantucketers," Benjamin says, speaking to the meeting attendees, as well as to the council leaders seated off to the left of the podium. Meg calms from his sure voice. "I am Wampanoag on my mother's side—making me half-native to this land—and African on my father's side. In fact, my great-grandfather arrived on Nantucket as part of the seafaring Underground Railroad, hidden on a merchant vessel. When slave-catchers from Virginia came looking for him, our island's community kept him safe. My wife Meg, as many of you know, is also a third-generation Nantucketer, as daughter of famous whaling captain Wendell Lewis, and granddaughter of the manumitted slave Giddeon Lewis."

Several people nod in acknowledgement, including Maria Mitchell and Anna Gardner. Meg knows she has support here. They are so close to getting what they want.

"Two years ago, thanks to your committee, we opened our first shop on Fair Street, about equidistant from New Guinea and Main Street.

It has been successful, serving all islanders and those traveling from far and wide as well." Here Benjamin stops, just as they rehearsed.

Meg clears her throat. "We stand before you tonight asking for your approval of our proposal to buy a building on Main Street. It has been vacant for over a month now, since Jessup Moore moved to New Bedford, and I know he's keen to sell. Not to mention, an empty shop on Main Street is a blight on the town. So, much like William Harris, the barber whom many of you know and patronize, did several years ago— and quite successfully, I might add—we wish to move our shop downtown."

"William Harris is Black, but he doesn't *own* his storefront," a man from the back calls, and the crowd turns toward the sound, rustling with the sudden anticipation of a fight.

"Please, hold your comments and questions until the Wrights have finished speaking," the head councilman says, and the man in the back nods and sits down.

Meg takes a deep breath and continues, the hall now taut with quiet tension. *That means they're listening,* Meg thinks, as she explains what the shop would look like and what services they offer, from both men's and women's shoe repairs to high quality, custom-made boots in the style preferred by Prince Albert. Benjamin then shares their plan for the shop's signage and discusses their ability to offer a cash down payment.

"Does anyone have objections to this application? Any questions they wish to ask the Wrights or the council?"

No, Meg wills the crowd. *No, you don't.*

Eliza Macy raises her hand. So does the man who spoke earlier from the back of the hall. Meg's heart sinks. She cannot look at Benjamin or she will crack open.

The councilman calls on him first. "Sir, please stand and speak your piece."

The man does. Dressed more casually than the rest of the men at the meeting, in loose tan pants held up by suspenders over a white shirt gone gray, he removes his cap and places it over his heart. He introduces himself as Jonathan Pyle, a carpenter and housewright who lives on the North shore. He gives his home address for the recording of the minutes. Meg feels a twinge up her leg from standing too long. She tries not to let the pain show on her face, which the attendees might view as disdain.

"While I think it is fine for William Harris the barber to work downtown, I do not believe a Black man should own property outright on Main Street. Why not have Jessup Moore rent them the storefront, I say, for a few years, and see how it works out. See if they are reliable and have a strong enough work ethic."

"Sir, with all due respect," Benjamin says,

speaking quickly and with emotion in his voice, "We have a letter here stating that Jessup Moore is happy to sell to us. Plus, we have proven we are reliable by renting for the past two years on Fair Street, paying on time each month and even making small repairs to the building to improve it at no cost to the landlord."

You tell him, Meg thinks, stepping a tiny bit closer to her husband behind the podium and almost knocking over the lantern placed atop it.

"But Main Street is different," the carpenter-and-housewright counters.

"How?" Benjamin asks. The room holds its breath.

"Because like your wife just mentioned, Main Street is the pride of Nantucket," the man says, shrugging. "It's bad enough to have social amalgamation happening right now in our schools. And, well, I know that in our newspapers, some people have been writing about the dangers of that very thing. Imagine the consequences of amalgamation in years to come: the races mixing in the most personal of ways. Unthinkable, some say. That's why schools are segregating again. Let's not sully our main thoroughfare of business, too."

A murmur of opinions echo around the room as everyone turns to their neighbor to share their dissent or agreement with this man's point of view. While they can't be heard, Benjamin turns to Meg and says, "It's okay. Just democracy at work. People are allowed to vent and have their say."

Just democracy! Meg thinks, with some irony. *Oh, that little thing, which has mostly been against us since we arrived on these shores by force.* That exact thing she's been leaning on and trying to use to her benefit ever since.

The room is full of chat and chatter, people excited by conflict. Meg wonders if these towns-people have any actual business to discuss tonight, or if they attend the open meeting on the first Monday of the month for the spectacle, for something to discuss on long, dull evenings: *Remember that night at the town council meeting last July, dearest? Why, indeed! That was a goodie!*

Voices die down. Another man stands and continues where the carpenter left off. He is a grocer on Main Street, who surely cares about what other businesses populate his corner of downtown. "As many of you know, I am Charles West, and I serve on the school committee, newly reinstated with Samuel Jenks after being voted out last year—"

"Mr. West, this is *not* a school board meeting—" the head councilman says.

But West, an old man with white hair, dressed impeccably, waves him off and continues to speak. "And I say, what a good thing it is to return to the way things were before, because they worked fine. Better than fine! Let the Blacks have their own schools, and the whites ours, and same with the stores. I agree with this carpenter—Mr. Pyle, was it?—about the real dangers of social amalgamation!"

Another gentleman rises next to Easton, standing and clapping. Oh, no. That same upstart Samuel Jenks. Meg fears that this meeting will get completely sidetracked now, with him speaking out of turn. "Hear, hear! I agree with these men wholeheartedly! Not just as a newly reelected member of the school board like my friend here, but also as editor of *The Inquirer*, and as a founder of the Coffin school, as well as a private citizen of this island!"

"Mr. Jenks, it is not your turn to speak!" the councilman says. "Please sit down."

The crowd erupts in calls and jeers, some cheering and some booing, while the two men wave to the crowd serenely, as if happy about the fire they've helped stoke, before sitting back down. Sensing danger, Benjamin tucks Meg as much as he can behind him, trying to bodily protect her with his own torso. He glances to the side. Meg follows his gaze, to where a door is propped open to let in some air. A quick exit, if need be.

But no. She can't leave. Meg must make her point heard before the room disintegrates into chaos. If they call the meeting over now, or if there's any violence, she'll lose her opportunity.

"Gentlemen!" a voice calls. It's female, but low and strong. Commanding. "Sirs! Please! If I may."

Meg knows that voice. Everyone in town knows that voice. It's the voice that hushes crowds before a large lecture at the Atheneum, the one that reminds you to keep your voice down when gathered with friends at the library.

And then from her seat on the left side of the hall, Maria Mitchell stands and faces the crowd.

6

MARIA

Maria is not planning to call out, but here she is, standing, facing an agitated but attentive group. All those important men on the town council letting their meeting run away from them like a spooked horse. Churning up anger and fear and worry! Someone has to pull on the reins. My goodness! Even with such power in their hands, men can be so useless.

"Sirs," she repeats, because Maria really doesn't know what to say next. She's reminded in this moment of the Brotherhood of Thieves riot from four years prior and knows she must tread lightly. Maria is certain that others in the room feel that same hot, negative charge of energy right now as well, the Wrights most of all.

During the Massachusetts Anti-Slavery Society convention in 1842, held in the Atheneum, discussions of abolition had gotten heated. Maria will never forget the moment when Stephen Foster called the clergy "pimps of Satan" for not coming to the aid of their Black neighbors, both in terms of Nantucket's school integration and the larger issue of abolition in the South. The next evening, an angry mob appeared outside the library, throwing rotten eggs, slurs, and other objects at the abolitionists. One woman in the crowd was hit with a brick.

Just last year, with the announcement that schools were to be integrated, there had been violence in New Guinea and someone had broken the glass windows at Zion's church.

She knows she must defuse the meeting.

Still standing from her seat in the second row of the hall, Maria shakes her head to clear the memory, her black curls wound as tight as her nerves. "Ladies and gentlemen," she begins. "Thank you for giving me your attention."

Maria would like to scold the town council for leaving the Wrights exposed and unprotected as they try to do what anyone else in town is allowed to do. For as Maria's mother, Lydia, would say—having raised nine children—there's nothing wrong with shaking a pointer finger in someone's face, a simple *shame on you* to remind people of their bad behavior.

But how to do so without adding fuel to the fire or chastening the crowd and thus alienating them? She looks down to gather her thoughts and notices the wooden crate by her feet. "I came here tonight to discuss the recent acquisition of books to the library and curiosities to the museum at the Atheneum."

"Thank you, Miss Mitchell," Mr. Landry says, clearly relieved that the conversation has shifted away from a verbal conflagration. "We all value the Atheneum very much. It truly is a one-of-a-kind destination, helping to make Nantucket an attraction for important speakers and scholars from far and wide. There truly is nothing else like it in the world."

Maria smiles. She's humbled by the admiration and the attention to her work. But even better, Mr. Landry unwittingly just set Maria up beautifully for her opening remarks. But if she crosses to the podium, she'll be pushing the Wrights out of the way, and she doesn't want to do that. So she scoops up the crate, carries it to the long table where the councilmen sit, and plunks the box loudly down in front of the last man in the row, as far from the podium as she can be while still having a platform from which to speak.

"Mr. Landry, I couldn't agree with you more. And you know," here she pauses for dramatic effect, looking around the room, from face to face to face, most of the complexions Caucasian, "that reminds me of something very important about the Atheneum. For two years, from 1838 to 1840, our Black community was barred from entering the esteemed space."

A murmur of dissent bubbles in the room. "Miss Mitchell, I don't think—" one of the other councilman says. *Silas Jones,* Maria thinks. Yes. The pig farmer.

She steps forward and continues, undeterred.

"But then Nantucket hosted Massachusetts' first Anti-Slavery Society convention—in the Atheneum, ironically—and someone realized the problematic nature of that. After all, how can we discuss our belief in abolition and freedom and equality if we aren't acting on that belief in our own town? If the Black members of our community cannot even enter to hear Frederick Douglass speak?"

"And so we rectified that situation, Miss Mitchell. As you well know. The Proprietors of the Atheneum changed their minds and began to let Black community members back in," Jones says. "They attended the convention that year, and have every year since. Plus, all of the other wonderful lectures you've helped curate."

"You're correct, Mr. Jones," Maria says. "Because, ultimately, we may falter, but Nantucketers know what's just." She nods to Benjamin and Meg Wright, still standing at the podium. Maria notices they are holding hands. "Like allowing all of our townspeople equal access to opportunity, whether that be entering a building, deciding which school to attend, or owning a shop."

This sparks instant murmurs as people turn in their seats to discuss, agree, dissent. Her island community is already politically and socially divided about the segregation of schools, making it a particularly difficult moment for the Wrights to garner the support they need for their shop. But what a huge moment it could be, will be, when Main Street—and all of Nantucket town—is truly integrated.

Maria thinks back to the year she opened her own school for girls. In 1835, she placed an advertisement in the *Nantucket Inquirer* and prepared lessons in everything from reading to grammar and geography, paying special attention, of course, to her favorite topics of math and science. Maria rented space at the Franklin Hall and charged three dollars for three months of instruction. Three Black girls showed up on that very first day. And what had Maria done? Let them in.

But hers had been a private school, which Maria only ran for a year before taking her current position at the Atheneum. Teaching them had been something, but it had not been enough.

So she tries to advocate in other ways. For instance, both Maria and her father William stood by the Black members of town at the annual meeting last week, hoping to keep the school board from reinstituting segregation in the public schools, but Jenks's minority report won out in favor of resegregating schools.

Maria believes in the goodness of her island, in the fairness of its people. She cannot let one bad apple spoil the barrel, as the saying goes, although science has proven this to be so; for mold to grow and spread, one rotten piece of fruit is all it takes. The current school committee may be rotten to its core, but Nantucket on the whole is not. "As a woman who has been taught to speak her mind, and as a daughter of Nantucket, I stand with the Wrights."

"That may be so, Miss Mitchell, and we will take your comments into consideration when voting. But we asked you here tonight for another reason entirely," Mr. Landry says. She can tell his patience for her is growing thin.

"I'd like to take just five minutes of your time for my presentation, at which point we can return to the matter at hand." Maria nods to the Wrights to let them know she'll be quick; she hates to think of pregnant Meg having to stand for any longer than necessary in this heat. Maria regales the crowd with educational facts—fifty new books have been added to the collection—and an entertaining story about how a Polynesian man traded a conch shell for hardtack. "I am proud to say that the shell, which is a beautiful specimen of goldish white with a pink belly, now lives in our museum. And the Tahitian man? Never got seasick again."

People chuckle good-naturedly and the mood shifts slightly.

"This shell and so much more can be viewed at the Atheneum. I've written notes next to most pieces so you can learn at your leisure, but if I'm not busy when you stop by, I'd be happy to give you a private tour." Maria is always busy and just made herself busier still, but it will all be worth it if she can encourage more people to donate to the museum . . . and to lessen the hot tension building around the Wrights.

"And, finally, I'd like to show you this."

Then she removes the bat from the straw casing and holds it high above her head.

7

ELIZA

The bat from Madagascar is disgusting and completely beside the point. Eliza sees what Maria Mitchell is doing, trying to distract from the real issue by waving a stuffed flying rodent before the crowd, like a magician doing sleight-of-hand and making a rabbit appear from a black hat. And oh, how the crowd responds! They are filled with *oohs* and *ahhs,* some actually applauding, others leaving their seats to come closer, some asking even to touch the dead creature. And Maria indulges them all while the Wrights patiently wait at the podium for the meeting to turn back to them.

Well, Eliza isn't impressed or bemused. In fact, she's getting quite vexed. She came here to achieve something beneficial for herself and her family, and she's going to state her case. She decides to get the meeting back on track.

"Sirs, if I may," Eliza says, her legs straightening and standing before her brain can tell her yes or no. The crowd hushes and all eyes turn to her, including those of the Wrights. Maria had just put the bat back into its crate. She raises her eyebrows at Eliza but makes her way back to her own seat.

On any other evening, the two women are friends and neighbors, living across the street from one another and spending much time visiting. In fact, since Eliza's best friend Nell Starbuck left last year to set sail on global adventures with her merchant husband, Eliza has spent even more of her free time with Maria. She's brilliant, of course, and devilishly funny to boot. And while she's no match for Nell Starbuck, and a decade younger than Eliza herself, Maria's been a decent sidekick and companion. Not to mention, a heck of a whist partner. But tonight Maria has chosen a side to support that isn't Eliza's, and so she doesn't need to be particularly polite.

Eliza feels exposed, naked, but pushes past that vulnerability and takes a deep breath in and out. "I am Mrs. Eliza Macy, of 80 Main Street. I think we should return to the discussion at hand, before Miss Mitchell's interruption. As you may recall, I attended the meeting two years ago when the Wrights first applied for a permit to rent a shop in the greater downtown business district, and spoke out against it. My son-in-law, Larson Handler, has a shop that also sells and repairs shoes, and, therefore, we are not in favor of there being a competing shop so close to his." Eliza gestures to him with her right hand, hoping the slight tremor there goes unnoticed, with people instead focusing on Larson's wide smile and perfectly handsome face. "Of course, Larson's shop sells clothing as well, and caters to men of all professions, not just the more menial ones. So his shop is more versatile than the Wrights'."

"Menial?" Meg Wright says, but her husband shushes her.

Eliza has struck a chord! Good. Eliza thinks on her feet: What else she can say that might work to undermine these cobblers, and bring more positive attention to Larson's shop?

"And their shoes are lacking true craftsmanship besides," she goes on. "Only people without discerning taste would buy from the Wrights."

"Mother!" Alice gasps.

"Mrs. Macy, if you will—" Mr. Landry begins, but Eliza is in her element now, rolling down a soft hill composed of her *fabrications.* Mustn't one shop always advertise bigger and better products than its competitors, to lure buyers to enter its storefront and bypass the others? She holds up her palm to stop Mr. Landry midsentence and continues on, the councilman's mouth gaping like a fish on a line.

"And I hear that they upcharge for the same, or lesser, leathers. They claim to use the softest hides . . . but who can be certain?" A murmur of voices simmers around the room.

"Untrue!" Meg Wright calls out from the front podium, and all eyes turn to her. "Anyone is welcome to come by our shop and touch the leather samples for themselves. We customize, so you can pick the hide before it's turned into a shoe. Handler's Clothing doesn't do that."

"Ladies, ladies, if I may—" Mr. Landry begins.

"Mrs. Macy is twisting all of the worries she has about her son-in-law's own store and placing them onto us!" Meg Wright says.

"Now who is speaking untruths?" Eliza says back.

"How is Handler's Clothing faring, Mrs. Macy?" Meg asks, staring straight at Eliza, her chin pointed out, eyes wide and accusing. "Are sales strong this summer?"

Eliza blinks. Larson moves to stand next to her and speak, but she gently pushes him back down. She started this; she can finish it, too. "I—" she stammers. "They are quite strong. Quite robust sales, indeed."

"Because our clients talk. They tell us things, bring us news as well as business. How curious that you would be fighting so hard here to block our storefront if Handler's Clothing was indeed having such strong—robust!—sales, as you suggest. Fair competition being good for business and all." Meg's husband leans toward her and whispers something, and Meg stops talking, although she keeps her gaze fixed on Eliza.

Eliza holds Meg's gaze. She cannot admit defeat, not yet. All she had wanted was to be able to help Larson run his shop at a profit, so that he can repay her the loan she gave when they got married. Then she can ease her own financial worries and begin to pay back Henry's debt to the bank. She married Henry for stability, for a lifestyle fueled by steady wealth that she would never have to question. So that their future children would never lack, like she did, and would want for nothing. Is that so terrible? To want what she was promised twenty years ago? There is no money left from Henry's expeditions, and now no money coming in from Larson's store. Creditors are trying to collect from Citizens Bank. Her heart hammers in her ears.

"Thank you, Mrs. Wright. And also Mrs. Macy," the councilman says, somewhat flustered. "I think it may be time to vote, unless either woman has anything else to add."

"Sir. It isn't fair for one person to dictate where another can purchase land, if one has the means to buy it," Meg says. "And we have the means. As my father Wendell Lewis always said, a fair society is one where commerce lives free—just like all the human beings in that same society."

Ugh, not the famous whaling captain father of hers again. *We are all descendants of someone of consequence on this island,* Eliza thinks. Why, Eliza's maternal great-grandfather was one of the first to circumnavigate the globe by going round Cape Horn! And her paternal grandfather traded in the Far East before the Silk Road was even known to most of Western world. She is a daughter of Nantucket as much as anyone else. Yet you don't see her automatically getting what she wants from—let's say—Citizens Bank by using her lineage as proof of worth! How uncouth. The world doesn't work that way, at least not according to what Mr. Edmunds at Citizens Bank told her this morning.

Eliza, still standing, looks away from the podium and scans the crowd, collecting herself. Fair! Who's to say what's fair in life and what isn't. This argument has gotten away from her, like seemingly every other conversation this past week. There is still so much more she wants to say, about working hard and showing promise, and getting help from one's community when one needs it. Eliza needs help. Larson needs help. The Wrights don't need help, don't need to move their shop—they just wish to. To make more and more money, to take from others getting less and less.

And then Eliza spots a man she recognizes, standing way off to the right, leaning casually against the wall of windows facing out onto Orange Street. It can't possibly be, but it is, like a bad dream come true: James Crosby is here.

He is dressed finely in a top hat and gray tweed coat. Broad-shouldered but not too tall. The man removes his hat and bows his head slightly in greeting, revealing wavy blond hair swept back from his high forehead, his sharp chin covered in stubble, and his eyes dark blue and sparkling with mischief. One lock of hair falls forward as he tilts his head, and he tucks it behind his left ear.

Like he always used to do when they were in their teen years.

He smiles at her. Is it merely a sign of recognition? Or is he trying to signal for Eliza to continue speaking?

Eliza clears her throat. Feels all the color drain from her face. "I have nothing further to say," she says, sinking down into her seat.

The vote is four to three in favor of the application, and the Wrights win.

8

MEG

The meeting is adjourned, and Meg and Benjamin are victorious. The mood in the hall is celebratory now, everyone siding with the winners even though they may have begun on the opposing side. Fickle. Small-minded. But allies, now, nonetheless. As the Wrights make their way through the crowd to the door, people stop them with congratulations and well-wishes. Meg knows most to be sincere, but she doubts the veracity of some. Well, they can show their support by shopping in the new shoe store. She lets herself smile a little bit, not wanting to gloat too much. Her pregnant belly helps move people out of the way. She doesn't see Jenks or the other bigoted naysayers anywhere. They were wise to skedaddle.

Meg gets down the stairs and out the front door with Benjamin's help, the glow of moving lanterns like fireflies in the night. Just as they reach their buggy at the bottom of the small hill, Meg's back seizes up in pain. She winces, closing her eyes against the sharp twinge.

Sure, she is happy that they won the right to purchase property on Main Street, but her body is sending her a different message. One more ominous, and always on the edge of her mind. *My destiny is to lose my other babies, like my mother did,* she thinks. *One is all I'm allowed.*

"Meg, are you okay?" Benjamin asks. "Are you having labor pains?"

Robbed of speech, Meg doesn't answer. Instead, she finds herself rocking back and forth slightly with the force of pain across her lower abdomen and back.

A cool hand on her arm steadies her. A young woman, petite with delicate bone structure and dressed finely in green silk, stares at Meg with startlingly bright, emerald-green eyes. "There you go. You're almost through it, looks like," she says kindly.

It's Eliza Macy's daughter.

Meg shakes her head, something between a yes and a no. She's stuck right in the middle of a sharp pain and doesn't have a moment to be thoroughly confused by this particular woman's show of kindness.

"When are you due?" the young woman asks.

Meg answers by putting up three fingers, just as Benjamin says, "Three weeks."

"Not your time, yet, I don't think." The young woman assesses her like a fine piece of sculpture, as she studies every angle. She seems young to have had children of her own, yet she speaks with a knowledgeable demeanor.

Benjamin listens in as he reties the horse's reins

to a post now that the woman is supporting Meg by the arm.

"You're still carrying high; the baby hasn't dropped yet. False pains," she says. "You're holding your breath like you're underwater, and that's only going to make it worse. Let yourself breathe normally." Then she shows Meg what she means as she holds firmly to Meg's left elbow and pretends to exaggerate blowing out a candle.

Meg imitates her. She feels silly—all these townspeople watching her, but also somehow better. Benjamin breathes deeply, too.

"Good. I know it seems strange, but I was taught this method by Sarah Penney, the well-known midwife in New Bedford, when she came to train women on Nantucket. I thought I might become a midwife myself, before I married two years ago. Now I help my husband run his shop. But I still recall learning how deep breathing helps a lot of pregnant women get through labor pains."

"Alice, what are you doing?" Eliza Macy's distinctly shrill voice punctuates the night air. "Who are you talking to?"

Alice doesn't seem bothered by her mother's sharp tone. She's probably used to being spoken to like that, Meg decides. "I'm helping Mrs. Wright, Mother."

"Well," Eliza says. She pulls her mouth tight,

holds her head high under her elaborate hat. She looks everywhere but directly at Meg. "That's generous of you."

"I'm feeling much better now, thanks," Meg says, and Alice releases her arm.

"You should lie down and rest," Alice says. "Perhaps take to your bed more often until the baby really does come. Save your strength."

"A good idea if ever I heard one," Eliza adds, again not looking at Meg. Of course Eliza Macy thinks that having Meg stay in bed is a good idea! It removes some of her competition.

Benjamin nods in favor of Alice's idea, too. Meg is incredulous. She won't do it. Can't. Stay in bed for the next three weeks? With a new store to open? Impossible. Once the baby comes, she'll want to spend all her time with him; she needs to use the time before to work and prepare. Men just don't understand. She'll call on her midwife, Jane Brown, in the morning. Jane will probably just give her some chamomile tea and send her on her merry way.

Alice's husband approaches the group. "Mother, why don't we walk you home," he says to Eliza. "It's been a long night. Perhaps we'll light a fire in the sitting room. Keep you company."

"I think she should apologize, Larson," Alice says.

"I'm perfectly fine on my own," Eliza bristles, turning from the group. "And there's no need for the Wrights to apologize for winning. Good night."

Larson and Alice exchange a surprised look, then Larson shrugs. "I tried, but she just doesn't understand—"

"I know," Alice says.

Having heard the exchange, Meg watches the woman walk alone into the darkness, feeling almost sorry for her.

9

ELIZA

She cannot stand there a moment longer with any of them. Not with the smug, self-satisfied Benjamin Wright who will surely take away much of the business Handler's Clothing still has. Not with Meg Wright his wife, who shouldn't even be out in her delicate condition, much less standing and speaking publicly. If something were to happen to that baby . . . well, Eliza wouldn't be surprised.

And most of all, Eliza cannot be near her daughter Alice for even another second. Alice! Betraying Eliza like that by helping the very woman who might threaten their livelihood. Alice is not even a true midwife, having only attended a lecture or two a few years ago. Talking about birthing is no match for the real thing. Alice is probably doing more harm than good by advising a pregnant woman about anything other than what to wear, and Lord knows, Meg could use some style advice.

All Eliza wants to do is be left alone to lick her wounds. She refuses Larson's offer to be walked home like some old ninny, and says good-night to her daughter and son-in-law, then turns up Martins Lane. She walks along Fair Street to avoid any others heading home from the town meeting on Orange or Main, like the Hadwens, politically minded community members and staunch abolitionists who attend every Nantucket town meeting. Eunice and William Hadwen have just built a new mansion on Upper Main Street that is the talk of the town; luckily, Eliza will get to see inside of it soon, since she's been invited to a grand wedding that the Hadwens are hosting this coming Saturday. Eliza waves to the couple and purses her lips into a tight smile as they walk past. Then she waits a few moments before heading out on Fair, once the coast is clear of neighbors and gossipmongers, which are really one and the same. But by choosing this street, Eliza finds herself walking past the Wrights' current cobbler shop, which only adds salt to the wound.

The wind gains force and sound, as the leaves on trees rustle overhead, like dried rice inside that old, silver baby rattle she keeps in a trunk with her children's keepsakes. The lantern at her side bounces back and forth with her steps.

For the first time in weeks, Eliza is chilled. There are no streetlamps on the island, but candles flicker in house windows, dotting the street with soft light that makes Eliza feel less alone. Windows are open to let in the welcomed cross breeze, and laughter blows from one gray-shingled home as the clinking of plates and cutlery chimes in another. Here's a person reading, and here's a family getting settled for the night, and here's another mother, worrying over something as she rocks in a kitchen chair and listens to the wind blow. While the image is indeed cozy, Eliza is simultaneously alert to the dangerous combination of candles and wind, especially on a dry summer night such as this. This thought comes unbidden and does not help to quell Eliza's growing sense of dread.

What will help her feel calmer is if she can be honest with her daughters about the state of their finances. Especially now that Larson's shop will have direct competition from the Wrights. Rachel and Mattie are certainly old enough to talk about such things. They know that Henry did not stay home long in the spring of '42 after his last voyage before turning around and heading out to the Pacific again . . . but do they know why? No, because even Eliza doesn't know why. Henry had been distracted upon his return from that failed trip, and, when she pressed, he evaded Eliza's questions about what exactly had gone wrong. Why go back out to sea so quickly after his return? And what had gone so wrong on the last voyage that he seemed determined to right it?

Something unavoidable, he had said.

Trust me, he had said.

This will be the last trip, he said. *I promise.*

Nothing more.

She felt like he was lying to her and she didn't like it one bit.

Why would Henry keep a secret from her? It made Eliza feel even more distant from him than usual, unmoored. She needed to feel in control of something; she needed to be industrious and independent of her husband's whaling expeditions. Which was why Eliza had turned to Henry in bed the night before he left again and told him her own plans to find employment.

"Outside of the home?" he had said, his eyes tired.

"Many wives do," Eliza said, conjuring up the names of women in her mind, lining them up like tin soldiers ready to do battle with her husband's provincial thinking. Anna Gardner, teaching at the African School, Louisa Hammond's bakery and Polly Burnell and the other women shopkeepers on Petticoat Row. Not to mention the many women working from within their homes, spinning wool or dressmaking or running a penny school to teach young children their letters and numbers.

"Of course they do. And we whaling men appreciate that support—and count on it, in many cases. But our daughters still need you."

"True," Eliza said. With husbands so often at sea, there wasn't time or opportunity for couples to have many children. Three girls was quite a bounty, and Eliza knew to be grateful, although it meant she had little time for gainful employment. She felt useful as a mother and wife, but useless, too, waiting for Henry to come back to shore with money when she could walk across the street to Petticoat Row, don an apron in a store there, and make some cash herself.

While Henry was home that month in '42, Eliza had hoped to take Henry visiting with her, to join in on the social circles and play cards with her and the other wives and other husbands home from sea. But, with this next journey imminent, they had spent the last few days together going over accounts, paying bills, and assessing their worth. Alice was still living at home, attending school with her sisters, and thus, still a part of the Macy finances. Henry's lay from the last trip, the failed one on the *North Star*, had been meager in terms of cash, but he had been given spermaceti oil and wax from his one kill while at sea. "And we still have money left over from the other voyages," Henry had said. "At the bank."

"No, we do not," Eliza said.

"How could that be?" Henry had sat up straighter against the headboard, pillow propped behind his back, his blue eyes flickering black in the candlelight. Eliza sighed. The bedroom was no place to be talking about real life, and yet, somehow that was where these conversations always seemed to take place. Downstairs, they were too busy with household chores and there

107

always seemed to be a child underfoot. There was never a moment to chat privately, except in Henry's office, but when Eliza had tried to broach the subject there the day before, she had found Captain Paul Cutler settled comfortably in a leather chair by the fire, smoking a pipe and laughing with Henry. Something about Polynesian women and their customs? An awkward silence had filled the space upon her entrance, and so she found herself apologizing and backing out of the room. She heard the lock catch as Henry shut the large oak door behind her retreating form.

The *Ithaca* was to set sail the next day and be gone for the next three years. Which is why she felt the need to bring up the topic of finances in bed on their last night together.

How could that be, her husband wanted to know. Because of the passage of time. Time, which is suspended in some way while on a whaling ship thousands of miles out to sea, kept moving forward at home. Henry measured the passage of time in the movement of the stars. When Cassiopeia was at its apex in the South Seas, he once wrote to her, it meant that his journey was nearly halfway over, for the next time he saw it like this would be when he was in this same spot two years from now, on his way home. He also measured time based on food supply; when little was left in the barrels of grain and corn and preserved meat, well, then time was running out and the ship better hit land soon. Henry also measured time in oil; the more he had onboard the ship, weighing it down with its importance, the sooner he could return home.

Back on land, time was measured in dwindling dollars, in savings spent day by day on new schoolbooks and new shoes and food. When she could, Eliza bartered goods she had for services she needed; Mr. Poole had fixed a leak in Eliza's roof in exchange for candles, and many a dry-goods bill had been repaid in the same way. For that was one thing Henry had left her with after each journey, not cash, but candles and wax from the captured whales. Eliza sometimes felt that most of her family's wealth was weighted in candles, and, at night, as she lit a small nub of white wax next to her bedside table and watched it burn down to nothing, it was as if she could see her financial security deplete before her very eyes. As her supply dwindled, she watched the wax drip, drip, drip down the side of a brass candlestick in Mattie's hand or along the dining room sideboard and felt a mounting fear in her chest.

"Don't fret," Henry had said, reaching for her hand under the soft cotton sheets and inter-twining his fingers with hers. "All the shops on Main Street will keep you on credit for as long as we need."

"I know," Eliza said.

Henry's voice turned softer, his head bent toward hers. Eliza felt slight panic, as she always did in the moments right before lying with Henry, knowing that her husband wanted to be intimate with her and pushing away this nagging thought that she did not. Eliza knew that she should want such a physical connection as well, crave it after so many years apart, but the distance and time apart only heightened Eliza's disinterest instead of her desire. She had figured out a way to pretend, to make her body and mind malleable to the possibility that this man touching her and kissing her and entering her was indeed desirable. She did this by exiting herself, by vacating her body and thinking only of her duty to her wedding vows. She also reminded herself that he was a good man. There was nothing to dislike about Henry, after all, and for this Eliza felt tremendous guilt, a sense of how she failed him as a wife, for not enjoying their lovemaking more.

Perhaps sensing Eliza's hesitation that evening, Henry had pulled his hand free of hers and propped himself up on an elbow, staring into her face as if trying to memorize it. He smelled like cedar and pine, like the hull of a brand-new ship about to leave the harbor. It was not an unpleasant scent. So why didn't Eliza welcome the invitation? She didn't quite understand how desire worked, and even after all these years of marriage, she felt like a young fool. "Write my name in George Riddell's book each time you go in for groceries. He knows we're good for it."

"I will," Eliza said, deciding not to say anything else. Thoughts and questions like, what if one of the girls burns herself in the kitchen and needs a salve? Will Dr. Swain take credit, too? And what if the roof starts to leak again, or my garden doesn't produce enough vegetables for us to can and save for the winter? What if, what if, what if?

Instead, she sighed, which Henry took to mean desire.

He reached his other hand across Eliza's body, brushing her nipples with his thumb. It was April, and she had swapped out her heavy flannel winter nightgown for her lighter spring one. Under her thin white nightgown, her body began to respond, and she was grateful for this. Henry kissed the nape of her neck. He paused there, breathing softly against her, and she thought of how alive they were.

Henry had only been home one month and now he'd be gone again. Tears upon one welcome-home party quickly followed with tears at a send-off gathering. This fleeting nature of their relationship, coupling followed by abandoning, kept their marriage precious. Eliza had time only to enjoy his company, not to tire of it, before he was off again. But it also meant that their marriage hardly ever felt like a real, true thing; more like a make-believe version of what one might be like, like something out of one of Rachel's beloved books.

"And Petticoat Row, too," Henry said. "They'll take you on credit." He kissed her mouth now, and ran his hand down her arm and up and under her nightgown, his fingers light and teasing. She relaxed her mind and let him touch her.

"Of course." She swallowed. "Petticoat Row."

"These shop owners understand. They support our way of life." He rolled on top of her, a hardness between her legs, needing her immediate response, and their conversation turned to more pressing matters.

Many years earlier, on their wedding night, Eliza had been so nervous that she couldn't manage to complete the act. But Henry had been patient with her, and his body had become more familiar and somewhat exciting to Eliza over time, especially if she dulled her mind with tea before bed.

If Eliza was to be honest with herself—which she wasn't wont to do, as it rarely served her well to do so—she had never felt as strongly for her husband as she once had for another man. A boy, really. A boy who she had grown up living next door to, a boy who made her heart seize in her chest every time she saw him, a boy who made her fingers tingle with the thought of holding his hand.

A boy named James Crosby.

Eliza turns left onto Main Street, careful as always to avoid piles of horse dung. At the Pacific Bank, a light flickers in the grand hall on the second floor, where the Mitchell clan gathers. Eliza cannot believe that Maria Mitchell had the nerve to lecture them all about civil rights of all things, when she was merely invited to talk about the Atheneum.

Maria left the Quaker faith a few years ago, over some small issue having to do with attendance at meetings or the like. But once a Quaker, always a Quaker: they feel the need to take perfectly good people and make them better. To teach, always. To be the moral compass for all. Maria's intentions are beneficial for the community, fine. But tonight Eliza feels like her personal rights were encroached on. *Stay out of my business, Maria,* she wanted to say. *This has nothing to do with you.*

The Mitchell home is chaos from dawn 'til dusk, with all of those growing and grown children running about, and William Mitchell's business besides. She used to feel sorry for Lydia Mitchell for having no time to herself, but now that Eliza's girls are almost grown and out of the house, she wishes she had been able to have more children, to fill the void of time with the company of others. But one needs to have a husband home frequently in order to do that, and, furthermore, a desire to be intimate with that husband.

Eliza's own house is dark when she arrives. Rachel and Mattie have gone to bed and blown out all the candles as she requested.

She is about to go around to the side entrance by the kitchen porch when a movement on her front steps startles her.

"Eliza, it's only me," a man says, rising from her stoop. "I'm sorry to have scared you."

Then it really had been him at the town council meeting. Eliza can't believe she is seeing James Crosby for the first time since he left the island abruptly twenty years ago. She tries to change her expression from shock to pleasure, as she tries somehow to look youthful and wise and attractive all at the same time. She's had no time tonight to prepare herself. It's unsettling, which, in itself, is an echo of their past relationship. James has always had a strong ability to disarm her.

She approaches the front landing. He has stepped down and meets her in the street, the wind moving a sweep of blond hair off his forehead. "Are you lost?" she asks. "I believe New York is in the other direction."

He chuckles. One dimple flashes in his left cheek. He's lopsidedly handsome, just a bit imperfect. Which of course makes him perfect.

114

"Perhaps. A little bit lost," James says. "Although I know where I am now. I'm with Eliza Cowan." His blue eyes are bright with a mischievous twinkle. "You mentioned your home address at the meeting."

"It's Macy now. As it's been for almost twenty years."

"I know. I just always think of you by your maiden name. And you look the same as always. Haven't aged a day."

"Only a lifetime!" Eliza says, aiming for a levity she doesn't feel. She tilts her head sideways, glad for the darkness and her giant hat.

"I'm sorry—I thought you knew I was on Nantucket. One of the Mitchell cousins is getting married on Saturday. I sent you an invitation last week."

"You sent it? Ah, that explains it," Eliza says. The Mitchell cousins. Eliza almost forgot that Maria Mitchell and James Crosby were related. Second or third cousins once removed sort of a thing, like most everyone on the island.

Although delighted to be included in the huge wedding that was to happen at Hadwen House, Eliza didn't know the groom very well or the bride at all. She had assumed Maria Mitchell had extended an invitation on behalf of herself. The two women had certainly grown close enough as friends. Lydia Mitchell would invite Eliza and the girls over for dinner frequently, knowing

Henry was away, and other times Maria would come across the street to spend time with Eliza in a spacious house filled with peace and quiet.

And of course Maria and Eliza spent time together also because of Eliza's roles on the women's auxiliary committee and Anti-Slavery Society. Although Eliza didn't care very much about politics, she liked to be socially active, and on Nantucket, the two activities were very much intertwined. Especially for women.

"Well, thank you for including me. I am looking forward to it." Although she has absolutely nothing to wear and no money to purchase something new. And to think she has to face Maria so soon after tonight's failure, and act like her friend's betrayal didn't sting.

"I attended the meeting to hear Maria speak," James says.

"I see," she says, turning her head sideways toward the house and wishing the sky would open up and swallow her whole.

"But, as is typical of these small town meetings, I heard a lot more. The vote didn't go your way."

"So I noticed," she says.

"I'm sure that wasn't easy for you," he says, stepping slightly closer and trying to catch Eliza's gaze.

James chuckles again and so she turns to face him in the darkness, the glow of his lantern between them, watching as he scratches at the blond stubble of a shallow beard growing in. A nervous habit he always had, and apparently still does, to scratch absentmindedly at his jaw while trying to find the right words to say. Unlike other boys who tried to charm Eliza with long, wearying tales, James always spoke deliberately, figuring out exactly the correct turn of phrase. Something honest and true, that cut through the pretense and silliness.

"Your speech reminded me of that time you stood up to Caroline Posey at the sheep-shearing festival. You accused her of starting the sack races before the whistle was blown."

"I recall it well. Not my finest hour," Eliza says. She pictures little Caroline weeping in frustration for being disqualified when she had only sneezed, causing her head to pull out over the starting line. Her feet hadn't moved, but Eliza had the sun in her eyes and the spirit of competition in her heart. "I was wrong that time."

"Yes," James says, "that you were."

But I wasn't wrong this time, Eliza wants to add, only the words get stuck in her throat. How could she possibly explain or admit to James Crosby her financial woes and worries? What must her comments have seemed like to an outsider, with no knowledge of what truly motivated her?

"I have no problem with them opening some *other* type of store if they wish, or at the very least, keeping theirs as far away from the town harbor—and Larson's shop—as possible."

"Your face takes on a determined quality when you think you're right," James says.

Eliza doesn't quite know what to make of his comment.

"You're doing it again now. Deep stare, faraway look. You pull your lips in a bit."

And what is she to say to that, exactly? It doesn't sound like a compliment, nor a criticism. Mere fact. While she's thinking of an appropriate retort, a strong wind pulls the hat right off her head, ribbon and all.

"Oh no!" Eliza cries, more from surprise than any fondness for the accessory itself. She and James chase after the colorful, airborne object, James grabbing it after a few paces.

"Got it!" he says, clutching it in his grasp and raising it overhead like a trophy.

Eliza claps, trying to catch her breath.

James smiles and hands over her hat, then pulls it away from her teasingly the moment she reaches for it. He does it again and again. She keeps snatching at the silk, but it keeps slipping through her fingers.

"No games!" she insists, growing impatient.

"No games," he agrees, handing the hat over to her with a bow and a sheepish grin, looking more boy than man under the moonlight, as the wind whips around them.

"A change of weather, finally. Perhaps the heat will break tomorrow," Eliza says.

Lightning flashes overhead, a quick spark. "Looks like a storm," James says. The wind shifts abruptly, and they both look up, expecting rain to fall, but none does.

Another flash of light brightens the sky. "We're not safe out of doors right now," Eliza says.

"I should probably—" James says, signaling toward town and wherever it is he's staying.

"Would you—" Eliza begins, her words stepping on his.

James doesn't finish his previous thought. Instead, his head tilts sideways, looking at Eliza curiously. "Would I . . . what?" he asks.

Eliza blinks, thinks. The girls will be asleep by now, their bedroom door shut. School begins bright and early tomorrow, and they like their beauty sleep. "Like to come inside for some tea?" The question is a quarter of what she is thinking, and the only part rational enough to say aloud. James nods and follows Eliza up the stairs, the wind picking up around them.

10

MARIA

Maria walks home from the town council meeting feeling physically exhausted but with her spirit energized from the outcome of events. She initially wasn't sure about her decision to add a show-and-tell lecture to her evening's discussion of the Atheneum. And then she found herself speaking out against the bigotry faced by the Wrights. As a former teacher, she knows she has the tendency to teach—but she is an activist at heart, and feels compelled to share her knowledge whenever an attentive crowd is gathered. Most people aren't really evil, just unenlightened. When headed toward darkness, they just need to be led back into a well-lit room.

After witnessing Eliza's harsh and defensive speech, Maria was pleasantly surprised to see the Macy family talking amicably with the Wrights outside the schoolhouse. Maybe there's room in this town for differing opinions to thrive after all. But then Eliza walked away agitated, so perhaps only some of the Macys hold more liberal views.

With her swift and purposeful stride, Maria passes large captain's homes, neat-looking, perfectly proportioned colonial-style houses and some older saltboxes on Orange Street. She turns left onto Main Street, and sees her family home: the Pacific Bank. The large, redbrick building anchoring the top of town is where Maria's father works as the head cashier. She goes around to the private, side entrance. This door leads to the two-floor apartment where she lives with her parents and her three siblings—Phebe, Kate, and Harry—who are still living at home. Maria is the oldest. The rest of the nine Mitchell children have married and all but one moved off island. Or *flown the nest,* as her mother likes to say. All except for poor little Eliza, Harry's twin, who died at age three and will live forever in Maria's heart.

As she enters the home, Maria hears singing. Specifically, Phebe and Kate. Oh, no. They are trying to harmonize. *"We have come from the mountains of the old granite state . . . we're a band of brothers, we're a band of brothers . . ."*

"No, Phebe, you need to do the low harmony, like this—*we're a band of broh-thers,* and I'll do the higher one, like this—" Kate says. The Hutchinson Family Singers visited the island last summer and now the Mitchell sisters think they are the next great act.

"Hell-o!" Maria calls from the front hall. She unties her bonnet and places it on the wooden hat rack in the hall before stepping into the parlor.

"Hell-o!" Kate sings back.

"Hell-o!" Phebe harmonizes.

121

"Please, make them stop," Harry says from the dining room table, where he is—as usual—hunched over a book.

Maria smiles sympathetically at Harry and suggests he remove himself to the library room next door, which he does not. She suggests next that her younger sisters go upstairs to the hall, and play music on the spinet. Quakers are not allowed to participate in music-making or merriment of any type, from singing to dancing to playing an instrument. One could even get disciplined for humming, of all things. Maria is happy to be personally free from these stringent rules, but her family still belongs to the Society of Friends. "Why did we risk sneaking a small piano into our home if not to use it?" Maria asks.

"Because we'd have to move it out of the back corner and uncover it, and Father wants it to stay hidden during evenings, when visitors are most likely to come by."

Maria says nothing to this. She allows the girls to continue harmonizing, for they clearly enjoy it greatly, but the curmudgeon in her wishes they would quiet down.

Or perhaps momentarily disappear. She adores her family, but they are everywhere tonight and she wishes to be alone after a long day of work, and after the long, hot, and heated town meeting.

Her job requires her to be outgoing and gregarious, interacting with people all day, teaching celestial navigation to her young volunteers before they set off to sea, and speaking in public like she did tonight to share news of the Atheneum's ever-growing library and museum collections. Maria loves working, relishes the pride and independence of making her own wages. But she is, at her core, a quiet person, studious and solitary. Happy in herself, content with her own company. And although she loves the work she's done at the library over the past decade, and the years of teaching she did before that, these days force her to be *other,* to push herself outside of her normal ways of being, which she finds incredibly draining. Like today.

And after the hot summer days at work, there are the long summer nights.

For the only time she can help her father with his work—*their* work, really—is in the darkness. On every clear night, Maria and William Mitchell observe the sky, making meteorological notations in relation to the weather, observing the planets in their orbit, and studying aural clouds and meteors. One of her favorite tasks is to sweep the sky for comets, and, once found, to map their movements. Last year, Maria and her father began searching for double stars together, which required setting up two telescopes side-by-side for precise observation.

It's growing dark now, close to 9:00 p.m. With everything else, Maria has hardly had a moment in the day to herself to think about Linley's letter. In it, Linley said she is going to come by tonight to help Maria with her astronomical calculations on the roof. Maria isn't sure how to respond.

Linley Blake walked into Maria's life several months ago, when the young woman arrived at the Atheneum to seek out Maria and learn more about astronomy. She had studied it a bit with her tutors when she was younger. "I've never lost my early passion for the stars," Linley said. "The cosmos travel with me wherever I go."

It was past five o'clock one frigid winter night and with everyone at home stoking their fireplaces and settling in for an early evening, the library was not crowded. "I assure you, the novelty of us being left alone here to peruse and converse like this is quite astounding!" Maria had said, as she walked between the shelves with Linley and introduced her to the entirety of the collection uninterrupted. Even Joseph Allen and the other volunteers had gone home early. Maria was instantly taken by this woman's intelligence—and her violet eyes—as the pair discussed first astronomy, then the business dealings and religious connections that had brought Linley and her parents from Philadelphia to Nantucket.

Like the Mitchells, the Blakes were Quakers, and like Maria, Linley had left the faith. "About two years ago, when I was twenty-three," Linley said. Which meant Linley was twenty-five, only two years younger than Maria herself. "It wasn't anything in particular that I had done or not done that prompted me to leave," she had explained. "I could no longer abide the strict rules for attendance and the long list of benign offenses the Friends kept on one another," she said, as she looked off somewhere above the bookshelves to a remembered moment. It must have been a painful one because suddenly Linley's lovely eyes filled with tears.

"It is a devastating experience, to be alienated from one's faith," Maria had said, reaching out to take Linley's hand in hers. "One I recall with such sorrow. Like a death."

"Yes," Linley had said, recognition dawning in her eyes, her focus now completely on Maria. "I hadn't thought of it as that until just now, but you are quite right. I experienced it like a death. Like a death of myself."

Maria had nodded with deep knowing. "I mourned that loss for some time," she said. "Though it was a choice on my part to approach the elders and ask to leave, as it was with you. My parents did not take the news well. They are *still* in mourning for me, I think."

Linley had laughed. It was not exactly a merry sound, but it still sounded pleasant to Maria, for it held a tone of recognition, of understanding. Of being seen and known by another.

And so, a fast friendship formed between the two women. Maria invited Linley into her social circles, with a bevy of activities offered by the women of society who rotated from home to home: playing whist one evening, knitting the following night, lacemaking one Saturday, and joining important meetings about women's suffrage and the abolition of slavery led by the Women's Anti-Slavery Society. A few weeks back, Linley started sending Maria the most wonderful notes, filled with humor and conversation, intellectual theories and schoolgirl gossip alike.

And Maria began to write back. Only recently, as her heart leaps with each new correspondence's arrival, has Maria started to wonder if this relationship is becoming something more. Linley has, of late, been asking to see Maria alone. And Maria is concerned that these actions can hint at something more.

And now she's invited herself to Maria's rooftop.

Tonight Maria will have to make it perfectly clear that their friendship is strictly platonic.

The house smells yeasty and sweet-sour, like rising dough. There will be bread with tomorrow's breakfast, which Maria will slather with honey and butter. Her stomach grumbles in anticipation. Maria should say hello to her mother in the kitchen, but instead, she goes over to one of the sofas in the parlor, sinks down onto it, and closes her eyes. For just a moment she lets the swirling chatter in her mind hush. There. A heaviness in her limbs. Calmness creeps into her spine.

But her sisters pipe up again. Kate, though five years younger than Phebe, is bossing her poor eighteen-year-old sister around. "Try to sing this part here with me, the chorus. I'll take the soprano and you take the alto. Look, Phebe. On the bottom of the sheet music."

"We have eight other brothers,
And of sisters, just another,
Besides our Father, and our Mother.
In the Old Granite State . . ."

"Kate! Phebe!" their mother calls sharply, an admonishment. "You know how I feel about your singing."

"That they are off key," Harry jokes again, standing and stretching. He grabs an apple from the wooden bowl on the table, rubbing it on his sleeve until it shines, and takes a juicy bite. As the only male child still at home, Harry likes to use his Important-Sounding Voice when speaking with Phebe and Kate, though he's only fifteen. With his much-elder sister Maria, Harry is less obnoxious. Maria sighs and wishes for a quiet the Mitchell home will never have.

Kate pulls her pretty face into an exaggerated pout. "Well, we wouldn't be off-key if we could move the spinet right here into the parlor, where

I could pluck a middle C and hum along to make sure our voices were aligned."

"Or not sing at all, in the way of our Society of Friends," Maria's mother says, coming out from the kitchen, eyes fixed, her voice as hard as the New Hampshire granite her daughters have been singing about. She brushes the flour from her hands onto her apron and crosses her arms defiantly in what Maria thinks of as her mother's commanding pose. The Mitchells are not a seafaring family, but if they were, Lydia—black-eyed, with her mouth almost always set in a straight, thin line—would be captain of their ship.

"Now you've done it," Harry says as he chews, eyebrows raised in perverse delight.

"But, Mother, I've come of age," Phebe says. "Let the elders discipline me, if they must. I can make my own decisions now. I can sing all I want, and play music."

"And dance!" Kate says, swinging her arms wide in a grand gesture.

"Please don't dance," Harry adds.

"You see? You've offended Harry. He's still proudly Quaker, after all," Lydia says.

"Although that's not why your dancing would offend me," Harry adds.

But their mother doesn't pause, not even for the joke. "You may be eighteen, but Kate is just thirteen. And, most importantly, your father and I remain in the faith. So, girls, whether you're two or twenty-two years old, as long as you are our children living under our roof, you must honor our wishes."

"Our wishes about what, Lydia?" Maria's father asks, entering the parlor.

"Music," Maria says, giving her father a sideways glance.

"Ah, yes. The nightly exchange of opinions has begun!" Maria's father says, rubbing his hands together. "No matter how clear your mother is about this issue, we shall never tire of debating it with her."

"William . . ." Lydia says, trailing off. They all know where he stands on the matter of music (staunchly in favor) and that his leniency in indulging this interest of his children has the potential to get him disciplined by the Quaker elders as well as his adoring—albeit strict—wife.

"Why don't we discuss it tomorrow over breakfast," William suggests. Lydia sighs, mollified for the moment, steps toward her husband to kiss him on the cheek. She goes to the open-shelved hutch against the far wall and sets a clean stack of plates down for the morning.

William turns to his daughters. "For now, sing softly," he says, winking and heading toward the staircase leading up to the second-floor bedrooms and the grand hall where he keeps his chronometers. "Very, very softly."

A knock at the door interrupts them just as William reaches the first stair. Maria's heart jumps to her throat, thinking perhaps Linley has arrived earlier than expected. She touches her hair to make sure no curl is out of place and turns toward the door that her father goes to answer. Then she chides herself for making such a silly gesture: after all, she and Linley are just friends. Nothing more. But she could use a few moments of solitude to gather her thoughts and mentally rehearse what she wants to say.

"Captain Matthews!" William greets the visitor and the man's low voice follows.

Not Linley yet; her heart settles back in place.

Her father opens the door wider, ushers the person inside. "No, no, you're not disturbing us at all. Come in! Let's have a look at that chronometer."

A redheaded man carries a mahogany box tucked under his arm and follows William to the upstairs hall, greeting the family along the way.

In the dining room, Lydia shakes her head knowingly and addresses her children as if they are still in grammar school. "Always remember: this house is busier than a market day at Old South Wharf, with merchants and whalers coming and going at all hours. Kate, Phebe! Imagine if Captain Matthews had heard your voices raised in song! The trouble your father would get into."

Chastened, the singers keep their mouths shut.

"Now off to bed, all of you," Lydia adds. The girls nod and climb the stairs to their bedrooms. Henry stands and stretches over the long table where he conducts his evening studies of geography. He closes his book and gathers together scraps of paper while Lydia sweeps around him.

The note from Linley is still secure in Maria's dress pocket. *These past months have been some of the happiest in my life, because of you, and the stars and Tennyson. If you are amenable, I wish to view these stars with you and see what you see through your telescope. I know that tonight will be clear, so I will be so forward as to invite myself, unless I hear otherwise from you. If I do not get a response by 5:00 today, I shall take your silence as a yes.*

This idea is wonderful and terrible, for of course Maria would like to show Linley her particular view of the sky. But is this the mere pursuit of science? Or will being alone together on the roof's observational platform, the star-flecked night unfurled before them, further complicate the dynamic between the two friends?

Because Maria knows who she is, what she is. She is a woman who enjoys the company of other women, who is attracted both bodily and emotionally to the female sex. And so she lives as an old maid by choice, for she has no desire to be with a man, and no opportunity to be with a woman. Maria had tried once before,

131

and her heart had been shattered by the relation-ship's abrupt end. Years later, Maria experi-enced a similar feeling of loss when she was excommunicated by the Quakers. So no, opening herself up only to have her heart broken is not something Maria has any interest in. She will not—cannot—go through that again.

She tells her mother that an astronomy helper is to be expected this evening, and Lydia says she'll send them up upon arrival.

Maria lights her glass lantern and dismisses herself to the roof.

All that fuss over music! Imagine if Maria's family—or her community at large—knew the tremendous secret she is carrying in her heart.

11

ELIZA

There is nothing wrong with having a childhood friend visit, Eliza tells herself, scooping fragrant black leaves into a silver tea ball and steeping it inside a pot of hot water. *Nothing at all.* And yet she is nervous, giddy as a girl: James Crosby is in her parlor! She lights a candle, places a glass hurricane lamp over it, adds it to the tray, and carries the set up into the formal sitting room. If her children hear her and come downstairs to inquire, she can merely introduce him as an old friend and Mitchell cousin. Yes.

James is standing by the dark fireplace. Eliza places the tray on a small wooden table by the sofa and uses the candle to light several others also set inside glass holders around the room.

"It is a lovely home you have made here, Eliza," James says.

"Thank you," she says.

"You married a widower, Maria tells me."

Eliza wonders what else Maria has told him, but chooses not to think about it. Maria's a scholar and a community leader, yes, but also a bit of a talker. "Yes," she says, keeping herself occupied by pouring out the tea. In the kitchen, she had added laudanum to her cup, and now she's glad for the dose of medication.

"A man with a child." James looks at the portrait of the girls over the fireplace, commissioned by Henry when the twins were five and Alice nine years old. They were so precious. Precious and loud.

"Yes," Eliza says, offering a cup and saucer to James and taking one herself. "Alice is the one standing in the portrait in the pink dress, behind the twins seated on the divan. She and her husband were at the meeting with me tonight. What a delight Alice was as a baby. She needed a mother. One look at her and I was smitten." Eliza smiles, thinking of that green-eyed, chubby baby girl, and how pleasantly weighty she was in Eliza's arms. "I carried her everywhere for the better part of two years. She hardly ever let me put her down! Tucking her feet up whenever I tried."

James smiles. "And then you had these two of your own?" He points to them with his chin. The portrait is dark in the dim candlelight, but one can still see three figures.

"Yes. Mattie and Rachel are sixteen. Soon enough to be married themselves, I suppose. Like Alice, who married two years ago at eighteen." She tries to keep her tone light, her mind free of the emptiness that fills her whenever she thinks of living in this big quiet house alone. Eliza loves

134

her children, even when she is irked by them. She takes a sip of hot tea and scalds her tongue.

"I remember you at that age," James says, surprising Eliza with his candor.

"And I you," she says, surprising herself more. Her eyes hold his for a moment, so deep, dark and dancing-blue, and she wonders, for the first time in a long time, what would have happened to her life if she had kissed James Crosby all those years ago.

But he had left Nantucket before she had gotten the chance.

Where has he been? Why does he look like he hasn't aged a day, while Eliza herself feels like she's grown practically ancient, dressing like her mother-in-law once did, living in this stuffy old house with cranky old children, worrying over the future more than enjoying the present? She's practically unrecognizable to herself anymore. "Why invite me to the wedding?"

"Because I was nostalgic, I suppose, being back on the island for the first time since that long-ago time. And then I spotted you in town one day last week, rushing to and fro doing your errands. You were coming out of the chemist's. I wanted to slow that moment down and talk to you and see what the years have brought. You look so much like the girl I remember, although I know much has changed. Inviting you to a public event seemed like the only proper way to have you in my company." He pauses and brings the china cup to his lips. "Although I suppose we are in each other's company now."

Eliza doesn't want to acknowledge James's nod toward their possible impropriety, so she changes the subject. "I wouldn't drink that if I were you."

James looks at her curiously over the rim of his teacup. "Trying to drug me?"

Eliza smiles; James always was quick-witted. "Either I poisoned your drink or I'm all out of sugar. You decide."

"Well. I do like having options, and I'm not averse to taking risks. It makes life much more interesting." And with that he raises his cup and drinks the liquid down in one gulp.

"So?" Eliza asks, moving to the couch.

"Hot, for one thing." James says, sitting beside her. "Black tea with a hint of something smoky?"

"Cloves." Eliza nods. "A homemade blend." Although they are seated apart, James angles his knees toward hers, so they are practically bumping against one another. Eliza tries to be as still as the porcelain urn in the corner. She doesn't dare move.

"Cloves! Exactly. And definitely no sugar." Knee bump. Smile.

Eliza doesn't know what exactly is happening in this moment, if anything at all is. Who is this man in her living room, really? His voice, his

136

face, his easy conversation—it is as familiar to her as a favorite knit shawl. But it also teeters on the precipice of something else, something more intimate, like flirting. She clutches her own kneecap with her palm, hoping this will keep her hands from reaching out to touch him, grip tight, and never let go.

She must get ahold of herself; her thinking is ridiculous. James had always been like this with her. And not just her, but everyone. A convivial manner, a naturally relaxed demeanor that Eliza's own parents took to mean he wasn't a serious boy, that he lacked drive and ambition. And that, though his family had a solid business in town, James Crosby himself wasn't the marriageable type.

"Why, his own father thinks he's in need of maturing! Sending him off island for college, instead of putting him right to work!"

Eliza remembers clearly her father saying this one night when she was eighteen. He leaned over the kitchen table at dinnertime, his eyes bulging in anger at the very idea that Eliza might harbor thoughts of James Crosby. Eliza's mother and little sister Charlotte stared down at their plates while Eliza looked directly at her father, whose thin lips were drawn into a tight line. She and James had been caught alone together in his back garden, and while the Crosbys didn't mind, the Cowans did.

"James is so lazy that his father refuses to take him out to sea with him! That young man will amount to nothing, I tell you, Eliza Ruth Cowan. His own father thinks so. Even his two older brothers think it! I forbid you from ever stepping out with him again."

Later, she remembers lying in the dark next to ten-year-old Charlotte, consoling her little sister in the bed they shared. Charlotte was more distraught and heartbroken than Eliza herself. Eliza rubbed small circles on the girl's back while Charlotte kept weeping softly, saying, "But I thought we were going to marry him, Liza. We wanted to marry him, right?"

Indeed she had. Eliza had thought James might go so far as to ask her father for her hand, but obviously that wouldn't happen now.

That night their mother came in to blow out the candle on the dresser, but before she left, she paused with her hand on the door. A white cloud of smoke from the extinguished candle hung in the air. Mother—like her father—was not a sentimental person, and her nature over the years had only hardened. "You want to marry a wealthy man, Eliza. Remember that. Not a third son, a dreamer with his head in the clouds. We'll find you a steady, rich man. Perhaps even a whaling captain. Someone hardly ever home, but whose money will be a warm and constant companion to you and your children. Otherwise we'll do second-best, and find someone like your father for you to marry."

A whaling captain? Weren't those men . . . old? But, as her mother closed the door to their dark room, the sulfur of the extinguished candle wick tainting the air, Eliza made a vow to herself: *If I cannot have James, then I must find a whaling captain, for who in their right mind would want to marry a man like my father?*

And then Eliza had walked into Hamblin's candy store. Had she consoled wailing baby Alice Macy that day, or had she been consoled by her? At some point, it didn't matter: the outcome was the same. She married Henry Macy.

Her parents always thought nothing good could possibly become of James Crosby, the love of Eliza's life. Yet this very man in her parlor, *this* James Crosby, appears to have made something quite fine of his life while retaining his easy manner. Where has life taken him with this casual stance? Did he really make something of himself, or, like Eliza's parents feared, did he merely move on from cloud to cloud, a dreamer who never quite landed on steady ground?

And so, Eliza inquires. Question after question, story by story, the clock ticking out the minutes before them, while her daughters sleep upstairs in their shared bedroom as she discovers who James Crosby the man is.

139

He is a person who knows how generations of Nantucketers have lived—by conquering the oceans, pilfering the sea for profit—and has the vision to apply the same sort of entrepreneurial spirit off island. Eliza is amazed by this notion, that James could be as successful as his own father and his family and seemingly all of Nantucket by taking the same world view and transferring it onshore.

"Land is where the money is to be made these days," he says. "Building railways, creating new towns and cities, and expanding the United States territories in a decidedly westward trajectory. Forget the sea. You know, too, that whales are getting harder and harder to find—we've fished the oceans too much. The industry has been shrinking year by year, journeys are taking much longer, making it harder to profit. As I'm sure you are aware."

James is careful, Eliza senses, to never make direct reference to her husband Henry, though his words skate close to the truth.

"So is that why you didn't join a whaling crew? Or own a fleet of ships and join your family's candlery with your father and brothers?" Crosby and Sons specializes in spermaceti candles, those made from the clear oil inside the head of the sperm whale and prized for its clean, near-odorless burn. Sperm whales are now hard to find; scarcity of high-quality oil means their high-quality candles earn a premium. The Crosbys are rich indeed.

"Truth?"

"I'd prefer if you'd lie to me, please," Eliza jokes.

James scoots an inch closer to her on the velvet cushions and lowers his voice. "I get horribly, violently seasick."

"No!" Eliza exclaims loudly, covering her mouth with her hands, trying to contain her laughter. "The girls," she whispers, pointing above.

"Yes, even pampered girls have stronger sea legs than I."

"Shhhhh . . ." Eliza says, the sound half laughter, half actual shushing.

"So, you see, I needed an artful solution to this ugly problem. I could have stayed in the candle shop in Nantucket, but I craved adventure like so many of my childhood friends. I could not pursue what they had achieved on the ocean, for obvious reasons. And there wasn't any . . . *personal* . . . reason for me to stay. So. I went away to Harvard."

"I recall," Eliza says, contemplating those "personal reasons." Thinking of that day now, Eliza is filled with a strange sort of homesickness, although she wasn't traveling anywhere, safe in her parents' house on Union Street. And yet there was a churning in her gut as she watched James depart from the Crosby home, a whitewashed, clapboard-sided Colonial so close to hers it practically touched the house where she'd always lived. And to think she believed her father's gossip, that James's father wouldn't let him go to sea or work in the candlery, when it was really James himself who made that choice.

"It was my friend Marcus Abelman who first suggested it," James says, scratching the blond stubble of his short beard. "A few days before graduation. I was without a plan at that point, and my parents were pressuring me to return to Nantucket. But I had kept up occasional correspondences with Charlotte and—"

"Charlotte who? Not my sister?" Eliza asks, startled.

"Yes, once or twice a year. She wrote of her school and life on the island, and, once she grew up, of her marriage, their move to New York, and sometimes, when I was lucky, of you."

"Charlotte never told me a thing about this," Eliza says, replaying the years backward, composing a not-very-kind letter in her head right now to her dear, deceitful younger sister.

"Then she's a woman of her word. With you married, Nantucket had nothing for me to return to, and so Marcus and I headed west. We connected cattle ranchers and corn farmers with the trains and helped them make business deals, distributing their goods far and wide, marking up the products and earning profits as middlemen."

"Exactly like your family did with whale oil and candles, shipping them around the globe," Eliza says. "Only on land."

"Exactly like it, yes."

Eliza nods in agreement with the steady pride in James's voice, for he has a right to feel this way. His self-assurance is contagious. "The Crosby-Smythe Freight Company."

Such accomplishment, and such ingenuity. Eliza is even a little bit more awed by James Crosby than she had been before. But that wonder is tinged with a certain sadness, for she is wistful as she wonders what might have been. What if she had stood up to her father that night, stormed out of the house, and . . . what? Run off with James Crosby? Here the story ends. She would never have disobeyed her father in such a blatantly disrespectful way. Nor would she have so boldly followed her own passions at eighteen. There was duty and honor and respectability. There was Nantucket as her home.

James is looking at her strangely, and she realizes that she's lost the thread of their conversation. She tugs, and it comes back to her: The Crosby-Smythe Freight Company.

"But what about the natives already on those lands?" Eliza asks. "And the new states being formed that claim their right to slavery?"

She has no firsthand knowledge of such

political questions, but she's been made aware of these issues by attending local meetings, from the women's auxiliary to the Anti-Slavery Society. There is much debate about who rightfully owns the land, who can lay claim to it and use it, and for what purposes.

"Says the woman who doesn't want a Black couple to own property on Main Street!" James says, raising his eyebrows.

"Apples and oranges," Eliza says. "Besides that's not what I said at all." But now she wonders aloud, "Do you think people thought that of me? Because I'm certainly not prejudiced."

"I think you're more . . . territorial. Striving. Trying to claim what you believe you have a right to. Even if perhaps you don't."

"Well," Eliza says, not sure how to take what he said. It's true she had begun the meeting on the offensive, lashing out at the Wrights to save face in front of the town. "I suppose the way I acted was not very nice."

"Out West we know that nice doesn't pay the bills," James says. "But manifest destiny does."

His eyes are dark and serious in the candlelight, as if he believes firmly in his conviction to claim what's his.

The clock strikes eleven, and James stands and stretches, his torso lean and lithe in his well-made gray wool suit flecked with blue that matches his eyes. "I've overstayed my welcome," James says.

Curse that clock! How lonely she's been, and how wonderful it is to be back in James's company. Eliza wants him to continue talking to her and listening to her with his attentive eyes and the corners of his mouth turned upward in a smile. She forgot how much she enjoys his sharp mind. But she cannot ask him to stay. "You're welcome here any time, James. As an old friend."

James nods but says nothing. She follows him to the front hall, hands him his hat from the carved wooden coatrack. She longs to touch his arm, lean her body full against his, kiss him. But she resists the urge.

"Good night, Eliza Cowan," James says.

"Good night, James Crosby," she says back.

Upstairs, Eliza undresses fully, feeling the warm night air from the open window against her body. She makes sure the lock is fixed in place on her bedroom door before she blows out the candle nub and all is darkness. Then she turns toward the long mirror next to the bureau and studies her form by the moonlight streaming in the window. Her body has changed since giving birth to the twins, her belly softening and her bosom heavier. But she is still small-boned at thirty-eight, her waist narrow. Eliza believes she might fit into that simple cotton dress from when she was eighteen, should it exist somewhere in the world. She touches her hair, releasing it from two decorative pins, and shakes the long dark waves over her shoulders. Turns slightly sideways. There. The dark is forgiving, and she can trick herself into thinking herself young again.

A long time has passed since she has last gone poking around in a particular dresser drawer, the one that contains her woolen socks and knit stockings, where no one would think to look for anything out of the ordinary. But out of the ordinary the coveted object is. Using the moon's glow as her only light, Eliza creaks open the topmost drawer of the tall bureau with its ornate brass pulls, then stands on tiptoes and searches around until her hands land on the wooden box. She lifts it out, shuts the drawer, and brings the box to the four-poster bed with her.

A special gift from Henry, a carved phallus fashioned from the tusk of a whale. Ivory to keep a wife company while her husband was at sea, a cure for the wanting, for the loneliness.

Her hands explore the "he's-at-home" inside the box, unwrapping it from its linen sheath and running her hands up and down the length of its smooth ivory. It is carved to resemble a man in an almost humorous way, for only a man would think of honoring himself like this. Scrimshaw lettering circles the base of the object, a simple rhyme that she cannot see now but that she knows by heart: *Think of me / Whenever this you see.* What would a true poet, like that Poe fellow everyone reads, think of this ironic little turn of phrase?

And what would Henry think of Eliza now? If he knew that after years of being prudish and not using the he's-at-home, she finally tried it in a moment of longing several years ago . . . and has now found that this false twin satisfies her better than the man who gifted it? She pushes the unkind notion away as she moves to the bed.

Instead Eliza thinks of James earlier tonight and holds the phallus against her pelvis. She tests the feeling, as if a man were rubbing up against her playfully before the act of lovemaking, as a way to signal that he's ready. It has always felt rather animalistic and unappealing, Henry's insistent rub, but when Eliza is in control of the movement now, the feeling becomes much more like desire. Eliza realizes she has limited carnal knowledge even after twenty years of marriage, for she has only been with one man, her husband.

Usually, Eliza must touch herself first to excite her body before using this piece of ivory. Usually, she must conjure James Crosby from the great depths of her memory, making him rise before her like a phantom shipwreck from the bottom of the sea. But tonight he's fresh in her mind, just moments ago, in her parlor, smelling of wood shavings and vetiver, with new laugh lines around his eyes and the same wit and honesty she remembers. It has been so long since

Eliza has felt truly seen and known by a man, drawn in by the chemistry between them, and as she moves her hand along the shaft of ivory, she imagines turning the ivory phallus magically into the warm, pulsating reality of James. Right here, in her bed, where she now lays. She touches her nipples, caresses her own hips, and finds that, without much work at all, she is able to insert the member into her body and cause ripples of shocking delight.

Usually, Henry is in the space between them. Tonight, there is only Eliza and James Crosby.

12

MARIA

Which is harder on her body and mind: the short, frigid nights of winter, when the tips of her fingers turn numb as she steadies the telescope, white breath against the black sky; or the long, late nights of summer, when dusk stretches out in an endless sapphire and the heavens never grow inky enough to take measurements?

Cold nights at least keep Maria's body alert, her mind sharp. The warm, honeyed evenings of July lull her into sleep if she's not careful, especially after a long day at work.

But tonight's stargazing will be different. Because tonight Linley will be here.

Still a bit too early to begin her nightly calculations, and no sign yet of Linley. It is a good moment to add Linley's latest note to her collection, stashed away under the floorboards of this raised platform on the roof. Maria keeps her leather-bound journal there as well. On her hands and knees, by the glow of her lantern, she locates the loose board, pries it up, and brings out the small wooden keepsake box that her grandmother had given her for her tenth birthday. It has curved sides and a hinged top with her etched initials. Maria adds the new note to the box, which now holds four total correspondences, and places it back in its hiding spot. She removes the journal, an inkwell and a quill, and moves to her small chair.

At last, she gets to air her concerns in the privacy of her journal, propped open on her lap. The lantern by her feet provides enough flickering light for her to make out the page before her, and a soft breeze blows back the pages, opening it on an entry from September of the year before. *Hoorah!* She reads back her own script, written bold and large, with an exclamation point. She must have really been in a celebratory mood that day. Ah, yes: penned after the town council finally voted to integrate the high school, after years of protracted battle. *Liberty has triumphed! The small-minded, narrow-thinking persons on this island will have to learn how to live with civility among their fellow man, no matter their skin color . . .*

Strong words, Maria, she chides herself. She tries never to speak ill of people . . . except in her journal. Because she must have a safe place to be, to think through what she feels and believes. She can trust her family with most of those matters, but there are so many Mitchells and, well, they talk back. A lively household conversation will ensue over any and every issue raised, each family member angling to make his or her opinion known. Maria values these discussions greatly, for they have molded her into who she is. But there are many moments when she craves the solitude of her own thoughts on pen and paper, when she allows her mind to speak its truth without the worry of judgment from any other human soul.

Plus, her parents are still Quakers, which means they are both liberal-minded and yet, at the same time, afraid that any small action outside the religion's strict rules will cause them to be disciplined, or worse, excommunicated. *Living in fear is not living fully,* Maria thinks.

She realizes this with some irony, her mind on the notes to and from Linley.

She picks up her pen and begins to write, documenting her thoughts on the meeting—and in particular, Eliza Macy's harsh stance on the Wrights' desire to own the Main Street property for their cobbler shop. She knew that issue would get territorial and competitive, but really, wasn't this display tonight a bigoted act? She'd never known her friend Eliza to be quite so narrow-minded and was disturbed by it. Maria will have to work on her, enlighten her, make her see her faulty ways. Eliza is stubborn and won't like that one bit. But if Maria cannot be honest with her friend and change her mind about this important issue of race, then perhaps they shouldn't be friends at all.

Fifteen or twenty minutes later, Maria's hand

cramps up and she stops writing. She drops the fountain pen between the pages and rolls her wrist around to loosen the tightness. Her eyes drift heavenward: yes, the darkness is deepening, and with it comes her opportunity to work. She puts the journal away feeling revived, and takes out her father's observational notebook, used nightly to record what they see in the sky.

Maria checks the time again: 10:22. Father must still be downstairs with Captain Matthews. She pictures them working in Maria's favorite room of the two-story home: the hall, a giant parlor with large windows overlooking Market Square.

If Nantucket town is the stage for life's dramas, then the Pacific Bank and the Mitchell home atop it has front row, balcony seats to the performance. Perfectly centered and raised to view all, the hall has hosted many a lovely affair. The room is grand and has multiple uses, from a wonderful entertaining space to a serene, light-filled spot for sewing. Her father keeps his chronometers there as well.

With over seventy ships calling Nantucket harbor their home, and many others passing through from the south of America and the South Seas, the Mitchells often find someone knocking at their door for assistance with one ship's navigational instrument or another. Sextants and chronometers are the most common, but occasionally, Maria has seen a man yielding an ailing telescope. William Mitchell fixes them all, like a doctor on call helping babies with croup, their mothers concerned about survival in the wee hours.

Because so many whaling captains and sea merchants use her father's services, Maria learned how to rate a chronometer when she was fourteen, thus expanding the capacity for her father's business and earning some extra—and always needed—money for the large Mitchell clan. A chronometer stays steady at sea, which allows sailors to properly calculate their longitude, and it can mean the difference between life and death, between floating aimlessly in the Pacific with your crew or finding your way back home to your family.

No wonder sailors are anxious when they appear at the Mitchells' door.

Maria sits and stares at the clear night sky, her lantern propped beside her feet. Everything in her orbit depends on the movement of the stars. Her father's three jobs—bank telling, the rating of chronometers, and astronomy—are braided together with the whaling industry the way thin pieces of twine become thick cords of rope.

The gibbous moon now glows from the cerulean sky and signals to Maria that it's time to get to work. But first, Maria picks out the softly glowing stars of the Milky Way, imagining each one a sailor's knot in an ever-expanding, infinite cable connecting sea to sky. Maria is not religious in the traditional sense. Nature is her church. But after leaving Quaker Meeting, she joined the Unitarian church, for she still likes the silence of prayers, the connection it brings to oneself. It is with nature that she finds holiness. What is it that Emerson writes? *But if a man would be alone, let him look at the stars.* Maria thinks of that each night, adjusting the pronouns in her mind to suit her world view.

"Maria?" a woman's voice asks from the darkness, startling her so that she almost knocks over the lantern at her feet.

"Oh!" Maria says, hand at heart. "Linley!"

"I didn't mean to scare you," Linley laughs, eyes dancing with both apology and amusement. "I knocked on the hatch door before opening."

"I wasn't paying attention," Maria says, standing and straightening her skirt.

"Did you get my note? I hope you knew to expect me." Linley is almost as tall as she herself, Maria realizes, standing next to her.

"I did! And I am . . . delighted."

"You don't seem so," Linley says, stepping closer to her friend, evaluating her mood. "When I saw your father in the hall, he had just said goodbye to a redheaded captain. I suggested that he stay to work on nautical matters in the comfort of that beautiful room, while I assisted you on the roof! In that way, I get to keep you all to myself."

Trying to avoid looking straight at Linley, Maria considers the sky above.

"I—well." Her heart soars, her heart tumbles; she both welcomes this preciousness and simultaneously pushes it away. Maria doesn't know whether Linley desires women the way she herself does, and she finds strange consolation in this notion about their relationship: that she, and she alone, is inventing something from nothing here—a mad scientist, like Mary Shelley's Dr. Frankenstein!

Being alone together like this tonight, with Linley's attention and focus absolute, is fortuitous. Their privacy will allow Maria to gauge Linley's interests and make clear on Maria's side that this relationship is a friendship and nothing more. It is not a conversation she's ever had before, and she doesn't quite know how to broach the subject. After all, the last time, with her friend Helen, they had acted on their adolescent desires without naming it first. But Linley is an adult. The costs are much higher.

"Yes?" Linley prods. "Maria, that was not quite a complete sentence, you know."

Maria nods. She sits back down and invites Linley to sit in the other wooden chair on the roof. They are side by side now, not facing one another but looking out over town, and toward the dark harbor where boats of all sizes are anchored in the moonlit water. It is easier this way, having a frank conversation by gazing together at something else, and Maria is thankful for the darkness.

She points out Cassiopeia and the vain queen's mother, Andromeda, the chained lady. She uses her pointer finger to trace other constellations, the big and little dippers, the glowing orb of Jupiter, the gibbous moon. Then she drops her hand in her lap and settles in to tell Linley a story. For aren't stories how the ancient Greeks and Romans made sense of the stars?

"When I was fifteen, I had a friend." Maria swallows. "A best friend. Her name was Helen Albright, and we attended Cyrus Pierce's Quaker school together. We were students of his and also teachers to the younger ones."

"I'm listening," Linley says. The silence around them draws nearer, and Maria continues on.

"Helen and I used to study together each afternoon until dark, almost always at Helen's house, which was quieter than mine, as she was an only child. One afternoon, she and I built a fort, pulling Helen's yellow and blue calico coverlet down to the end of the bed and stretching it over to the dresser, weighing it down with a porcelain pitcher and bowl. We dragged the round rag rug to cover the wooden floorboards and crawled underneath the tarp, giggling with excitement. The soft light through the window created shadows under our hideaway, I remember, dappled buttercup and cornflower dancing across our skin and clothing. Then I closed my eyes and kissed Helen softly on the lips, and all the colors melted into one."

Maria stops. Clears her throat.

"Go on," Linley says, her focus somewhere in the heavens.

"So. This became a ritual, one we performed many times. Helen called it a game, and said we were practicing for marriage. 'Who do you picture?' Helen would ask me, whispering as she closed her eyes and presented her mouth to mine. 'I am thinking today that I will marry Thomas Crane. That you are Thomas Crane.'

"'He's a good Quaker,' I would say. You see, I would say anything to begin the game, anything except the truth: that I was only picturing marrying Helen."

Linley turns her head quickly toward Maria, who has paused in her tale. Maria doesn't look at Linley but feels the woman's eyes roving over her face, searching. "Certainly, that's not the end of the story?"

"No," Maria says, taking a deep breath. She never said so aloud, and cannot bring herself to say it now, but at the time, Maria wrote in her journal—often—that she believed she was in love with Helen Albright.

"Time passed and we each celebrated a

157

birthday. One night when we were sixteen, Helen's parents came home early and caught us in a not quite chaste but not quite guilty moment. Helen lied about what we were doing, why exactly I was lying on Helen's bed with the sleeve of my modest Quaker dress raised all the way past the elbow. 'We are pretending she's been wounded and that I'm her nursemaid,' Helen said, her voice shaking with worry. I kept my eyes closed the entire time—both to hide my fear and to stay in character, I suppose, as an injured soldier. But I could hear Mr. Albright breathing in the doorway of Helen's room."

Maria finishes the story. "The Albrights moved off island the next month, and I never heard from Helen again. My heart ached from the separation, and, although I knew who I was and was not ashamed by it—*am* not ashamed by it—I vowed never to let myself connect so deeply again. It was all too painful, too messy. From then on, I'd only allow room in my heart for academics, for the love of knowledge."

"And now?" Linley asks, turning to Maria in the dark. "Why are you sharing this story with me?"

"Because I wonder . . . I believe that *you* . . . I am not certain, but . . ." She ends her words there, because how could she name another person in this way, if they haven't admitted the same to themselves? That is not something she

158

would ever be comfortable doing. "It doesn't matter. Since I have no interest in loving anyone, you see," Maria says.

Linley leans in and kisses Maria softly on the lips. So softly and swiftly Maria wonders if she imagined it. Her body floods with desire, and she kisses Linley back. It is the best kind of confirmation of her hunches, to kiss as they do, with pulsating understanding and shared want. Maria pulls back, stunned in the best possible way.

"No interest, hmm?" Linley jokes. "Even in someone as lovely as myself?"

Maria rises and moves toward the telescope, so it stands between her body and Linley's. "I prefer the romance of science."

"I don't believe you."

"With its rules and structure, science cannot break your heart."

"I will not break your heart, Maria," Linley says, standing now, too, and moving to the other side of the Dollond, the small telescope she prizes above all the wondrous instruments she and her father have for their astronomical work. In the relative dark, Linley's eyes up close are more purple than blue, wide and wet. Maria has never seen anything quite like them.

"You do not know that," Maria says.

"And you do not know that you will discover a comet, and yet every night you continue to try."

Maria lacks a compelling retort.

Linley looks eminently satisfied. "Ha! See?" Linley says. "All I'm asking is to court you."

Maria's rational mind wants to decline, but she finds herself excited by Linley's offer. She doesn't want to lose her ties to this wonderful friend. "Fine," she says.

Linley arches her blond eyebrows. "Fine with me, too. Let's shake on it, like men do to seal a bet."

"Am I the bet?" Maria laughs.

"I challenge that, by this time next year, we shall both have found our comets."

Maria cannot believe herself, but over the telescope, she shakes Linley's hand. Linley holds on a moment longer than necessary.

"Now we must get to work," Maria says, exhaling, glad to be moving back to the familiar world of astronomy.

Pleased with the outcome of their talk, Linley awaits her orders.

Stars move at fifteen degrees per hour. So, throughout this conversation, the sky has already altered slightly. The stars' movements over such a short period of time are imperceptible to the human eye, yes, but Maria's expert gaze can sense the shift from their initial coordinates earlier this evening. Maria fiddles with the Dollond. She finds Polaris. They work for several hours, Linley proving to be a quick study and a companionable partner. The sky's edges begin to lighten, their cue to put the instruments away.

"Will you attend your cousin's wedding with me on Saturday?" Linley asks before departing, stretching her arms overhead and bending sideways to release tension from her back. "We can sit together at the ceremony and at the dinner reception, like a proper couple." Maria hems and haws for a bit before finally agreeing. She is being "courted," after all.

"You cannot hide behind that telescope for your entire life, you know," Linley says, looking pleased as punch. But Maria believes that she can.

All she has to do is convince herself that she doesn't have feelings for the wonderful woman by her side, who she leads down the roof hatch ladder with a gentle hand.

FOUR DAYS BEFORE THE FIRE
Thursday, July 9, 1846

13

MEG

Meg Wright shouldn't gloat, but ever since that meeting three days ago, when she and Benjamin won the right to purchase the building on Main Street, she finds herself grinning.

Oh, yes, they showed up Samuel Jenks and Eliza Macy, and anyone else harboring bigoted notions of fairness and equality. They showed them that, although prejudice may try to prosper here on Nantucket, commerce will always thrive.

That night Meg's back pains subsided a bit, and Benjamin had carried her into the house and laid her on their bed so gently she almost wept from the love she felt.

"Don't you want to go back out to Absalom's tavern?" Meg asked. She was certain the word had spread through New Guinea, this being Nantucket, and she didn't want Benjamin to miss the cheers. "Have a mug of ale in celebration and tell the whole world about what we've accomplished."

"You are my whole world," he said to her, falling asleep with one hand draped over her belly.

Jane Brown the midwife came by the next morning, making the definitive proclamation that

Meg was fearing: bed rest for the duration of the pregnancy. And so Meg had stayed in bed . . . for two whole days at least. Benjamin went to town hall without her on Tuesday to sign paperwork transferring ownership of the property at 21 Main Street, returning with a copy of the document for their records. Meg showed the bill of sale to her parents' portraits before tucking it safely in a fireproof metal can. After the Great Fires of '36 and '38, Meg started keeping her important papers tucked away like this, even though neither fire had reached New Guinea.

She sent Lucy to Jenny Cole's house after school on Tuesday, where the pair made berry hand pies and sold them to sailors and merchants at the docks, under Faithful's supervision of course. The wharf was the commercial center of town, yes, but also had its fair share of seedy taverns filled with drunk men seeking companionship. It was no place for little girls.

Lucy came back with an entertaining report, which at least had made Meg feel like she herself had momentarily escaped the confines of her bedroom. "It was so crowded down at the docks, Mama! Merchants from everywhere were pushing carts of goods up toward Main Street. And it was so hot out and dusty! And stinky! The smell burned my eyes!"

"Dusty since we've had no rain for weeks, and stinky from the whale oil, you know that," Meg said. The wharf always smelled ripe and dank like a thousand dead fish, which, she supposed, was exactly what the smell was composed of. In summer, the odor hung thick in the air like fog over the island. Meg hadn't been down to the wharf at all since getting pregnant, knowing the stench would overwhelm her.

Lucy nodded her head furiously, waiting for her chance to say more. "Oil! Which reminds me, I saw men unloading barrels of it from a giant ship! So many barrels of it! They brought them off with a rope and pulley system and then stored them on their sides along the pier. There was hardly any room to walk on our way back up to Main Street after we sold the pies." Lucy's brown eyes were wide with delight. She had her father Benjamin's eyes, almond-shaped and flecked with gold. But Lucy's face itself was Meg's in miniature, same high forehead, same pointed chin. A heart-shaped face, Benjamin called it, with love written all over it. Lucy's childhood-plump cheeks were now matched by Meg's bloated-from-pregnancy ones.

"One man lit a pipe and another one yelled at him for doing it near the casks of oil! Said he could accidentally blow us all sky high!" Lucy adds.

"Well," Meg swallows, "that certainly was bad judgment on his part." She does not add that their island home is precarious in that way, and

167

while a huge conflagration is not probable, it's always possible. Meg and Benjamin constantly work hard to improve their standing, when really, so much of life is just about avoiding others' stupidity.

"And here's the money," Lucy said, fishing coins out of her dress pocket and handing them over to Meg.

"You made quite a nice little profit!" Meg said, handing the coins back to Lucy and making her count and add them up in her head.

"Twenty-seven cents." Lucy smiled. Meg gave her a big, sloppy kiss and then told Lucy to add the change to the tin canister under the washboard sink.

But the next day, after sending Lucy off to school, Meg had grown restless. And, when Faithful came by with lunch for them, she felt useless, too. She had been itching to get into the new storefront and make it her own, sweep the floors and polish the brass doorknobs, paint the front door light blue, just like at the old store, but all she could do was lie in bed and watch the world go by outside the window of her saltbox home. A man called for his horse, and another yelled at his horse (or wife? Or pig? Bess being a common enough name), and she watched as the sun moved across the sky in a bleary arc of heat.

Meg, who was usually so fearful of doing anything to upset this delicate pregnancy, was going to go stark raving mad if she had to stay in bed another minute. Benjamin and Lucy would have to take her out to the asylum in Quaise after another twenty-four hours and leave her there to rot. And so she got out of bed for an hour on Wednesday after Faithful left, just to clean the house and prepare a dough that she let rise under a cloth in the corner, and back to bed she almost went. But then one hour turned into two, which turned into three.

When she wakes up on Thursday morning, she decides to walk—at a leisurely stroll, nothing taxing—to the new shop. Just a fifteen-minute amble. Good for the body and soul. Just to see the new storefront. Not to do any physical labor.

Meg is slowly making her way into town along Orange Street when two older, distinguished-looking men walk briskly by her—one passing physically so close on the narrow brick path that he brushes her skirt with his cane. She looks up in surprise, but the men do not pause their intense conversation to utter an *excuse me* or *pardon us, ma'am.*

They look familiar, even from behind. Both white men have perfectly starched stovepipe hats atop their hair; both are clad in fine, black suits that speak to their easy wealth. Darn. Meg recognizes the pair as those outspoken, bigoted men from the school committee who came to the town council meeting on Monday night. They were the ones who argued against the Wrights owning a store on Main and who had voted at the meeting prior for Nantucket to return to its former educational system, to the so-called norms of segregation. The man with the spectacles and blond hair is Samuel Jenks. The other, older gentleman is Charles West, the grocer with a store just up the street from where the new cobbler shop will be.

A tingle of curiosity dances up Meg's spine, and she begins to follow them.

The men walk briskly down Orange Street. With purpose, they turn left, past the iron gate and into the schoolyard. Meg's heart leaps to her throat, for they are marching directly toward the South Grammar School that her precious Lucy attends.

Meg hurries her steps, which is not easy given the fact that she's nine months pregnant and supposed to be on bed rest, especially in the incessant July heat. For two older gentlemen, these men certainly do have a spring in their step! Meg huffs along from a safe distance behind.

The school sits atop a grassy slope, shutters open wide to let in cross breezes. She hears singing from inside the schoolhouse, with piano accompaniment carried lightly on the air—*baa, baa, black sheep, have you any wool? Yessir, yessir, three bags full*—the voices so high and clear and innocent that tears come unbidden to

Meg's eyes. Crying over nursery rhymes! Too soft. And yelling this morning at Benjamin, over what? The coffee beans getting burnt? Too hard. And letting herself be helped the other evening by Eliza Macy's daughter, Alice? Too vulnerable. Wildly emotional and unpredictable, even to herself. She never did this with her last two pregnancies, oh no, didn't believe in the tales of crazed-women-with-child, because Meg's state had remained constant, her mood had remained true to her strong, steady nature month after month. But something fierce has taken hold of her this time, and she hopes that her emotional instability is, in some strange way, a good omen of a healthy, strong baby boy.

Now, as the children in the schoolhouse sing, she wipes her eyes with the back of her hand and pulls her shoulders up straight. Better.

The men enter the building. A moment later, the music stops midchord, although children's voices linger a beat beyond. As Meg waits outside, trying to decide what to do, several onlookers gather near Meg. Some she recognizes as parents, both Black and white. Others might just be nosy neighbors. Meg is not surprised when Faithful, who lives on Orange Street not far from the schoolhouse, sidles up beside her and sighs audibly, putting her toddler, Daniel, down beside her.

"I heard a rumor that there might be some

trouble here today, concerning those men's plans for desegregating the schools again," Faith says. She takes Meg's hand in hers. "I guess that rumor got you up and out of bed."

Rather than correct her, Meg accepts the close contact with Faith, suddenly stronger with her friend by her side.

What to do now? Meg thinks of Benjamin's poise the other night at the town council meeting, speaking softly in her ear when she wanted to shout or scream or punch a wall. But she didn't act out, and by remaining calm and speaking clearly—and with the help of Maria Mitchell—she helped convince enough voting members to grant her and Benjamin what they wanted—the right to buy the building. Her father would also have handled a tense moment like that by stating his opinion clearly, yes, but also with measured calm. No good can come of interfering with school business, not at a precarious time like this when Meg is worried about her unborn child as well as the success of her new store. She doesn't need or want to draw negative attention.

But then her daughter's earnest face comes into her mind, Lucy's eyes closed in song the way they are during the hymns at church. In contrast, Meg thinks about Samuel Jenks's face the night of the town council meeting, cold-eyed and hard, threatening to end desegregation as soon as possible.

Meg lets go of Faithful's hand, hikes her skirts, and climbs the small hill.

"Meg! Wait—" Faithful says behind her. Several others begin talking, weighing in about whether they should join Meg or watch from the street. But Meg doesn't need them. All she needs is Lucy.

Winded, she pushes open the wooden doors to the large schoolhouse.

There's a time for decorum, yes. And also a time for action.

The door bangs shut behind her. "Must leave at once!" Jenks is saying, pointing the bottom of his ivory cane at the bewildered teacher, Mr. Hart, hired just this year from some Quaker school on Cape Cod. Not native to Nantucket, some parents have unkindly called him a *coof* behind his back. He stands with sheet music limp in his hand, his mouth an O of shock as Jenks continues speaking. "These children cannot stay here in this school a moment longer."

These children? Which children? Meg wonders. *All of them?* There must be thirty or forty, ranging in ages from six to about ten, standing around the teacher or clustered near the piano, the heat in the day-dark room heavy around them.

Meg scans the crowd for Lucy, but cannot find her. Nor can she see Jenny Cole.

"Mama," Lucy says, in a soft, pleading voice from somewhere behind Meg. Meg turns toward

173

the sound, where her daughter sits on a bench along the far wall. Hands folded in her lap, in a line along with eight other children. Each with one particular trait in common: the dark color of their skin.

Meg looks back at the children clustered around the piano: only white faces. One tall, thin boy looks sheepishly away. *That's right,* Meg thinks, *you should all be ashamed.*

Mr. Hart composes himself and speaks. "As the head of this school, hired by these very men on the school committee here, I suggest that we should talk after dismissal at lunchtime. Not involve the children."

"Yes," Meg says, swallowing, finding her voice. "The school day is almost over. In fact, the school *year* is almost over. Just one more day! Perhaps the summer months can be spent in deliberations about the best way to continue educating our children."

"A new plan is in order," Jenks says, taking a step closer to the bench of Black children. "This experiment has failed."

An experiment, he calls it. As if equality is nothing more than folly, a game to try out and modify as needed. These same men who speak out against slavery in the South fight so mightily against integration in their own community. You can be free, they are saying, but you'll never be equal to us.

174

Yes. Meg can see it all now. Eight years of talking and voting and petitioning, of building something great and meaningful as a town, and in eight minutes in one hot and dusty schoolhouse, these men have the power to burn it all down. It's as if she's watching Jenks and West light a match and hold it over kindling. She can't let them drop it.

"Mama, let's go," Lucy says again.

Oh, my baby girl, Meg thinks. How she wishes she could scoop her right up and fly her away, over the salt marsh pond and the sheep meadow, past the church spires and on toward their home, safely nestled together into Meg's wrought iron bed.

But then this so-called experiment would surely fail, and Meg cannot be the first to let such a hard-won victory go. She breathes in and out, clear, clean air. Not fire. "Lucy, stay right there."

"But Mama—this man says we're being spelled from this school."

"Expelled. With an 'e-x.' And no, you are not."

Charles West clears his throat, addresses his comments to Meg. "Your daughter is correct. We're resegregating the schools, effective immediately. The Black children must leave at once."

Lucy rocks forward tentatively, locking eyes with Meg. One foot in its soft black leather shoe extends out from the bench, toward Meg. But Meg pushes her back with a single shake of her head *no,* and Lucy—obedient child that she is—returns to her seat. Jenny Cole, seated next to Lucy at the end of the row, scoots her bottom closer to Lucy, takes her hand, and slips it inside her friend's. *A faithful friend, just like her mother,* Meg thinks. Several others begin to cry softly, and one little boy moans for his papa.

"I don't want to stay here anymore," Lucy says. The world outside disappears: birds stop chirping in the trees, the wind stops blowing, townspeople stop gossiping, and no one in the schoolhouse dares move. There is only a mother and daughter, in fraught dispute, in close connection.

"It doesn't matter right now what you want," Meg says.

"But *they* don't want me to stay," Lucy adds, her brown eyes flicking quickly toward Jenks and West.

"It doesn't matter right now what they want, either, I'm afraid," Meg adds, ignoring West and stepping closer to Lucy, her voice soft as a lullaby. "The state of Massachusetts has passed a bill prohibiting discrimination and allowing you to get an equal education in public school no matter your race. Now, you wouldn't want to break the law, baby girl, would you?"

Lucy's big eyes well with tears. She's confused. Afraid. And so is Meg.

There is a silent beat—a stalemate.

Meg doesn't know what to do next. A chess

game. Maybe the men are waiting for her to react negatively, so they can trap her, say she caused a disturbance. A pregnant Black woman in a highly emotional state! Which she is, of course, but they cannot know that. She cannot let them see that.

Meg scans the room for allies, and looks to the teacher, Mr. Hart, for further guidance. But he offers none. If only there were another woman in the room, another mother! Surely there would be something they could do together.

Meg needs to stop these men from dropping that lit match onto a pyre. She needs power. She needs to maneuver these men away from her daughter.

"Shall we go outside?" Meg asks, addressing the three white male adults in the room.

"Yes," Jenks says. "Let's."

Realizing she's been holding her breath, Meg begins to sigh it out.

But then Jenks picks up Jenny Cole from the end of the row. Picks her up sideways, under his arm like a sack of grain. Jenny cries out, kicks her feet. Reaches her hands out toward Lucy, who cries out *No!* and reaches her hands out to grasp the empty space where Jenny's fingers just were. A chorus of voices suddenly fill the room, as if singing again, a mad song's refrain—a mix of cheer, protest, and sob. One of those voices is Meg's.

"No!" Meg says, lunging for Jenks, who side-steps her easily.

Unfazed, Jenks marches Jenny to the entrance of the schoolhouse, sets her on her feet and deposits her onto the burnt grass right outside the front door. Dropped so quickly, Jenny loses her balance and falls on her rear, eyes wide.

"Children, you are no longer members of this school, but have been dismissed entirely. A school has been provided for you on York Street. You must go there," Jenks says, speaking directly to Jenny but raising his voice to acknowledge the crowd.

"Jenny!" Faithful calls from the street. Meg imagines her friend moving as quickly as her arthritis will allow, scooping her daughter into her arms.

Inside the building, Meg looks for assistance from the other two men. Hart does not move, does not act. *That's what you get for hiring a coof,* Meg thinks: *no loyalty, and a whole lot of ineptness.*

And West? He stands sentinel, crossing his arms in front of his chest, daring anyone to question his right to watch another man forcibly remove children from a schoolhouse. Not that he'd sully his own hands, tucked tightly under his armpits.

Mr. Hart, the teacher, starts to speak. "I don't think we really need to—"

Jenks cuts him off. "Oh, but I very much *do* think we need to! To keep the races from mixing." Panting from physical exertion, Jenks turns to Meg with fire in his eyes. "Don't talk to me about laws! There's thirty miles of sea between us and the mainland; we make our own laws here. So, are you going to remove your daughter, or am I?"

Oh, how Meg would love to form her right hand into a hard fist and punch Jenks in the face, breaking both his glasses and his already-crooked nose and watch him fall. Her blood pumps with rage, perhaps fueled by the extra heartbeat living inside of her. Meg shakes violently with the injustice of this scene, of one man's audacity not to see her child as the beautiful being she is. *Lucy. What am I teaching you in this schoolhouse right now?* Meg wonders as she reaches out a hand to her daughter. A legacy that Meg's father could not outrun, nor can Meg, nor Lucy: we are not welcome here. Here we must always feel shame.

"Come, baby girl," Meg says.

A mother reaches out her hand, and her child holds on tight.

They walk in silence out the door.

A larger crowd is now assembled in front of the South Grammar School. Atop the hill, just outside the school doors, Faithful and Jenny Cole hold each other tightly and sob.

"Mama, *that* was the bully," Lucy whispers,

looking up at Meg with wild eyes. "That old man. The one who threw Jenny out."

Meg blinks in the sun, breathes in the honey-suckle air, and vomits in the grass by her feet.

14

MEG

There is only one more day of school remaining. One. More. Day.

Jenks and West can't let the Black children stay in the classroom for even one more day? Is that how threatened they—and who knows how many others—feel? How angry they are that they pick up Jenny Cole and haul her out like a sack of grain. How utterly horrified Meg is to witness such brutality.

These are children!

What kind of community allows that kind of behavior to occur under their watch? Especially for a place that prides itself on abolitionist ideals and progressive notions for all. An island of Quakers, pacifists who stayed neutral during the War of 1812 and who expound upon the virtues of loving thy neighbor as thyself! And yet, leaving that schoolhouse, Meg feels Nantucket's bigotry as the loudest proclamation of all those extolled, as if it were ringing from the church bells throughout town.

Quite a crowd had gathered outside the schoolhouse by now, with people shouting terrible things at one another on both sides of the divide. After Meg gets sick outside the school doors,

Faithful leads her and Lucy back to Faith's house and helps clean Meg up.

Meg feels safer there, inside Faithful's cozy home, with its low ceilings and large wood beams. Physically, Meg is exhausted, but her mind races ahead, trying to walk a clear path. And Faithful's questions, over and over, become a hymn of sorts, asking What should we do next? and What would your parents say now, Meg? And so she chews on those questions, over and over, round and round, while everyone else chews on their midday meal.

Faithful calms the children—including little Daniel, who started crying the minute he saw his sister being ejected from the schoolhouse and doesn't stop until a warm biscuit is placed in his hand. She soothes them all with a hearty lunch. Everyone except Meg, that is, who has heartburn.

Then Faithful clears the dishes and shoos everyone—including Meg—out to the back garden. Meg moves slowly and drops heavily onto a whitewashed wooden bench while the children play ring-around-the-rosie around her. The bench sits under a large maple, and the leaves provide a cooling dappled shade.

Then Faithful sends Jenny and Lucy to fetch Benjamin from the new shop.

The moment their daughters are out of earshot, Faithful begins to speak, her voice halting. "I've got to tell you something, Meg. You deserve to know," Faithful says. "And I think it might help you, in some way, although I don't know how exactly. I'm sorry I didn't tell you before. The other day. I just—"

"Faith, you are a terrible storyteller!" Meg says, losing patience and then immediately apologizing.

Faith smiles and shakes her head. "You're right. Big Daniel says it to me all the time." She picks up another small bench from the far side of the yard and drags it under the shady tree to sit by Meg.

"So let me just tell it to you plain, Meg: I know where Captain Macy is. And I know what Daniel's been doing."

"What does that have to do with me? With us?" Meg asks. "Or with desegregation?"

"You'll understand in a minute," Faith says, beginning her story. "Because it has everything to do with helping Black people."

The news—the most interesting and intriguing bit of gossip ever to cross Faithful's lips—fills Meg with an awe tinged with fear, as if she is standing before God on judgment day. A ship, a crew, a passage out, following the North star, smuggling precious cargo. Imagining it, Meg is filled with a deep reverence, something almost holy. And more than that: Faithful's tale has its intended effect. For if those men can risk their lives to do what they are doing at sea—something that would make Meg's father Captain Wendell Lewis so very proud indeed, not to mention what her once enslaved grandfather, Giddeon Lewis, might think—well then, Meg knows she better come up with an equally powerful plan on land.

The tree she's sitting under is old, with roots that spread far and wide and deep. The roots cling to the soil and grow underground, so far underground.

Meg hears a door creak on its hinges and turns to see Benjamin. "How are you?" he asks, kneeling at Meg's feet in the Coles' back garden, his chest heaving from running three blocks. His soft hazel eyes look up at hers with anxious worry.

"Better," Meg says, calmer now that her husband is here with her, that her family is together and out of harm's way, for the moment at least.

"This damned town. Those bigoted men. Lucy seems shaken, but okay. How's the baby?" Benjamin asks.

"He's good." Meg nods. She feels no back pain, no cramping, but instead a sudden jolt of energy and an invigorating clarity of mind that fills her with strength. She cradles her round middle with her right hand. "I actually feel the best I have in days."

"I didn't expect that, but I'm glad," Benjamin says, straightening up next to Meg's chair. "Now

184

you need to rest. I'll help you home so you can stay in bed, like the midwife says."

"No, Benjamin. Now I have to act," Meg says, startling herself almost as much as her husband.

Benjamin looks wary; Faithful excited.

"No, you really don't," Benjamin says emphatically. "There's time for that. We have all summer before school starts up again—"

"We have to act now," Meg says. "While everyone is heated over these issues. Before it's too late and we return to the status quo."

"We have to protect our daughters," Faithful adds.

Meg nods her head in agreement. "More than that, we have to continue to advocate for them." Because, years earlier, Meg had been one of those very daughters. She hadn't been physically pulled from a schoolhouse like Lucy had been today, no, but that's because she hadn't been allowed to step foot in the building in the first place. In the late 1830s, Meg had been completely denied access to a public high school education. And today, in addition to this hateful resegregation of the elementary schools, the Black children of the island are still being denied that right to attend high school at all. But time has passed and, due in large part to petitions filed by Nantucketers over the years, the state laws have changed in their favor.

"Advocate how? Something that your father

did?" Faithful asks, her eyes glowing with fiery excitement. "Sign a petition. Boycott the schools."

"No, bigger than that. Something that my grandfather Giddeon Lewis did." Meg nods thinking of the soundness of this action and pulls herself up from the little bench she's sitting on. "The best kind of American something." She looks back and forth between Benjamin and Faithful, husband and friend, knowing her plan is going to surprise the devil out of them both. The girls look up at her with hope, while Daniel picks fistfuls of grass.

"It's simple, really. We're going to sue the town of Nantucket, Massachusetts," Meg says.

15

ELIZA

Eliza has seen James a total of three times since James first visited her the night of the town council meeting. The first was an accidental run-in, passing one another in town on Tuesday, a quick hello as Eliza was, as usual, headed to the harbor to see if there had been any new word from Henry. There hadn't been. But a letter had arrived from him for Alice, which Eliza felt entirely entitled to intercept at the docks and read first, and then bring to Alice at Larson's shop. It was a six-month-belated birthday note, the tone light and breezy. *How is it possible that I have a child of twenty when I am only a young man myself?*— that sort of thing, with no hint of trouble, only a confident recounting of an adventurous three days spent hunting one particularly elusive and stubborn whale. *We've killed 40 whales, my dear daughter,* he wrote, *which means we'll be coming home soon, and victorious. I'll buy you and your mother and sisters all the dresses on Petticoat Row, and fabric from the mercantile to make more! I'd tell you to share this news with your mother, only I know she's reading it herself right now!* Her husband did know her well, even if they only saw each other for a few months every few years. Eliza had stood in the street and read it twice, relieved to hear that the voyage was indeed so profitable, but also wondering anew what had occurred since then to delay the trip.

Eliza had then been flustered, running into James like that and totally unprepared. He was with a young woman who at first made Eliza ripe with jealousy—she felt for certain that James would desire a woman younger than she. But it turned out to be his cousin Betsy, the bride-to-be for the upcoming wedding at Hadwen House.

The second time is more deliberate, as James comes by Larson's shop on Thursday asking for her. Larson calls to Eliza from where she is perched precariously on a ladder in the stockroom, looking for pairs of Oxonian leather shoes from England to sell at above-market price. People are always willing to pay more for something imported, and these are quite nice, but Eliza can't find them anywhere. When she hears Larson call out, "Mother! You have a visitor!" she wonders who it can possibly be.

She sees the quizzical looks on Alice's and Larson's faces, and guesses correctly. Eliza and James stand awkwardly in front of the shop for a few minutes and chat at the top of Straight Wharf, where they stare out at the small sailboats and schooners coming to and from in the calm harbor.

James—being no half-wit—senses Eliza's hesitation to stand alone in conversation with him for too long outside of the shop, so he asks what time she might be free that evening to go for a stroll.

She suggests ten o'clock. After the girls are asleep.

But now that he has arrived on her back porch, Eliza again feels skittish. What if someone sees them?

"We're two old friends out for a walk," James says.

"At this late hour? Who would believe it?" Eliza counters.

"Don't you?" James asks. Eliza is suddenly foolish and misguided and tossed about, as she had been with him as a lovesick girl. No, she doesn't really believe it. Is this really just a friendship? Does he not feel something stirring within him as she does? But what could ever come of it?

Thus, Eliza does not go for a walk with James, but instead suggests something more private and, she knows, much more perilous. She invites him inside once again. The last visit had been such fun for her, and—apart from her fantasies— rather chaste in actuality. After a few minutes of polite and witty banter in the living room, James asks if her home has a roof walk attached.

"Why yes," Eliza says. It is a necessity in a house of this size, to put out any chimney fires quickly should they occur. But the wooden hatch to the outside is rotting and she can't get the metal latch to open properly.

"That sounds rather dangerous," James says and Eliza agrees. But she has a long list of home repairs to pay for, and this one is at the bottom of it. If Henry were home, he could fix the issue at no cost, and probably in no time at all. He had years of experience making repairs both big and small on his ships while at sea, becoming quite a handyman.

James shakes his head. He stands and looks toward the stairs. "If you have a tool kit I'm happy to assist."

And so, tools in hand, Eliza leads James up the staircase, past the girls sound asleep in their bedrooms, and past her own bedroom door—with the thought of the he's-at-home in the tall bureau making her blush—to a small closet that hid a steep spiral staircase to the attic. By pulling open a hatch with a retractable ladder, one should be able to get to the roof walk.

"You see, here?" Eliza says, showing James the issue. The metal latch rattles back and forth, but won't fully release to open the door.

"Hand me that wrench," James says, pointing as Eliza touches the jumble of metal and wooden tools one by one. "Yes, that one. Do you have some candle grease?"

Eliza finds some collected in a jar in the kitchen and returns with it.

"There," James says, using the lubricant and pliers and a bit of force to unstick the rusty hinge. He pushes the wooden door up and open, his face framed now by stars that twinkle overhead. "Shall we?" he asks, gesturing outside.

And so she extends her hand and he helps her to the walk. "Thank you for repairing that," Eliza says.

"I like knowing you and your children will be safe," James says, looking out over Nantucket town.

There isn't much to view; once daylight fades and the town grows dark, the harbor is more a direction to imagine by inhaling the salty air than see with one's eyes. But the weather is mild and pleasant, with a hint of a warm summer breeze. The pointed, shingled rooflines of homes are cast in silhouette against the moonlight, each road below the next as Main Street slopes gently down to the harbor. From Eliza's roof walk, one can see the homes on Fair, then Orange, then Union, each perched lower than those on the street above, a line of schoolchildren in order of descending height.

"I hardly ever come up here at night," Eliza says, gazing across the sleeping town.

"How lovely it is," James had said. "As are you."

A rush of emotions swells in her all at once, from desire to shame. With a canopy of silver

191

stars winking above and no onlookers able to spot them from below, Eliza and James have their own private balcony in the sky.

James leans against the wooden rail around the raised platform, and Eliza prays that the carpentry is secure.

"You lean a lot, I've noticed."

"I what?"

Eliza heads over to the other side of the railing and slouches against it, demonstrating his favored stance. "At the town meeting, too."

James laughs and nods in recognition. "I often aim for a casual, relaxed attitude," he said. "Especially when I'm anything but."

Eliza has a tendency to do the exact opposite, her body growing increasingly tense and straight-backed the more anxious she feels.

"Can I ask you a personal question?" James says, pushing off from the railing and walking toward her.

"Well—" Eliza says, looking anywhere but at his chest as he approaches. She fears he will finally ask why she had refused him all those years ago. For she had. And there was no easy answer to that, for either of them.

"Have you and Maria spoken since the town hall meeting the other night? I thought you were good friends, but you each expressed opposite opinions, and I wondered—"

"If she hates me now? For my comments?"

Eliza bristles. "She and I have been close for years. I hope it would take more than a mere opposing viewpoint to alter that."

James nods. "Well, then. I'm glad to hear it."

"Why? Did she say anything about me afterward?" Eliza asks, worried.

"Nothing much," James says. "I'm sorry to have mentioned it."

"Because if anyone needs to apologize for their behavior at the meeting, it's her." Eliza recognizes the edge to her voice, but can't help control it.

"Women! That sounds like the type of complicated situation that I would like to avoid. Forget I ever asked."

"What do you mean, *women?* Surely men have disagreements? And much more violent ones at that."

"And they handle them head-on."

Eliza shakes her head at James. The hypocrite! He comes to visit her, and talk, yes, but he never deals with Eliza head-on, choosing instead to circumnavigate around their central issue—their past—like it is an island blocking the mainland. Writing to Charlotte to find out more about Eliza's life, pressing Maria about their differing opinions. Coming here at night to visit her. Confusing her so.

"I apologize. Men are much worse creatures than their female counterparts, myself included.

Women are better at close companionship with one another, which must be difficult when those ties become knotted."

"I thought she was a true friend, but now I'm not certain," Eliza admits. Plus, Maria is so busy with work at the Atheneum and astrological pursuits that Eliza wonders if Maria even has time for her anymore.

"I'm here if you'd like to confide in me," James says.

Eliza wants to. She wants to tell him about her longing, how every time she looks at him she feels waves of desire. But she settles instead for what is being offered: kinship, friendship. A place to bare at least some of her aching soul. And so she tells James all about Larson's failing shop, her daughters' somewhat spoiled natures, and, finally, chagrined, Eliza's own impending bankruptcy.

While sharing these concerns, including the embarrassment of her finances, Eliza feels unburdened. But, in a tiny corner of her mind, she also understands what a betrayal this is to Henry to admit these difficulties to another man, especially to another man who happens to be perched on Henry's own roof walk.

But lately, Eliza has felt particularly distant from Henry. Why would he not tell her his whereabouts at sea? Perhaps her so-called betrayal of Henry is only a natural response to him being the first one in the marriage to show distrust. And anyway, with James it was too late to take the words back. They talk more about Eliza's worries and James's hopes for his own future. They share old stories from their childhood remembrances. They talk on the roof until daybreak, when a burnt orange-yellow light comes breaking through the deep blue, rising first over the easternmost point of 'Sconset before pulling high enough to illuminate the gray edges of Nantucket town.

Realizing the late—early—hour, James, his clothing somewhat rumpled, his blue eyes tired, makes haste to leave before Eliza's twin daughters awake. And when they do, dear Mattie and Rachel, Eliza is in the kitchen, preparing eggs for breakfast, wearing her nightgown.

She can hardly wait for the wedding at Hadwen House tomorrow, where she'll see James Crosby again.

THREE DAYS BEFORE THE FIRE
Friday, July 10, 1846

16

MEG

This Friday afternoon, as Benjamin puts the finishing touches on their new storefront on Main Street with Lucy by his side, Meg visits Jane the midwife at her small, rose-covered cottage a few blocks from her own home and convinces her that her previous orders for continued bed rest are uncalled-for. Jane makes a we'll-see-about-that kind of expression, but agrees to accompany Meg to the African Meeting House for a pre-arranged meeting with Absalom Boston and other prominent Black leaders in the New Guinea community. Since yesterday, when Lucy and Jenny were forcibly removed from the school-house, Meg and Benjamin have been working on a plan with these men's input.

"But I thought you said you've been staying in bed," Jane says, as they walk up busy Atlantic Avenue. "Not changing the course of history." She's well into her fifties but still moves quickly and has a childlike light in her hazel eyes. Jane has three children of her own, all sons now grown and moved off island for more opportunities. No daughters to pass down her craft to.

"I've been changing the course of history while also listening to you, my midwife,"

Meg tells Jane, rolling her eyes. It's been only slightly embarrassing to have the greatest and wealthiest men she knows visit her briefly in her bedchamber to begin brainstorming their plans, but what choice does she have? Slowly over this past decade and yet suddenly, too, Meg—doting mother and wife turned sharp businesswoman—has added a new title to her name: social and political activist.

Meg spent her waking hours propped up in bed reading law books and newspaper articles and taking notes. Meg has read so much about the law since yesterday that she should be granted status as an attorney.

The key to their success? How to win against the school committee this time, when all the other times have failed? That's what Meg is about to finalize today.

The wooden doors to the African Meeting House are open when she and Jane arrive at the corner of York and Pleasant Streets, undoubtedly to let in any air on this hot Friday afternoon. Absalom is there, along with Edward Pompey. They welcome her inside and Jane makes her goodbyes. "I have to visit three other expecting mothers today, so I better get a move on," she says, and waves, as Meg sits in the front pew, her heart beating fast from the walk and the heat. She takes a minute to catch her breath and says hello to a group of women on the left side of the hall, who seem to be organizing some sort of clothing drive.

"For slaves coming North," Edward Pompey says, noticing Meg's curious look. "If Benjamin has any spare shoes from the cobbler shop, we'd love to add them to the donations. We'll be sending these on to New Bedford next week."

As the center of life here in New Guinea, the meeting house serves as a place of worship as well as a general place to gather. Meg attended school here as a child, before the York Street School opened, and the hall still smells as she remembers, of warm wood, which makes her suddenly nostalgic. Meg misses her parents, who used to walk with her between them on the way to Sunday church services, all dressed in their best clothes, a worn family bible tucked under her father's arm.

"Well?" Absalom says, sitting beside her on the first pew. Not one to mince words, he's ready to discuss their plans.

"The way I see it," Meg says, her eyes steady on Boston, "we cannot sue on behalf of my daughter Lucy and Jenny Cole and the others expelled from the grammar school."

"But why not?" Pompey wonders aloud, clutching a cane in one gnarled hand and standing beside them. "I thought you said we were going to sue." Pompey is growing old, but his impact on Nantucket's fight for equality is still young. As part of his work for school integration, he filed a petition a year and a half earlier with 104 signatures of Black neighbors for an amendment of the common school law to the State of Massachusetts. That was followed by a second petition of support from over two hundred white community members. Six petitions in total were sent to the Massachusetts House of Representatives. All of that was followed with a compelling personal letter from Eunice Ross detailing her own experience being denied entry to the Nantucket High School, and then, victory: chapter 214 of the Acts of 1845 was passed, guaranteeing equal education for all throughout Massachusetts.

Absalom understands both points of view and nods. "Because there is a public grammar school on York Street for the Black children of Nantucket, it's hard to sue the town for that; after all, the school committee members can—and continuously do—argue that they are providing an 'equal' education for our younger Black children, just not together under one roof with the white students. Nantucket has three elementary schools, so they can segregate but still say they are meeting the law's requirements for a public education for all."

"But not so at the upper level," Meg adds.

"Nantucket has only one high school, Meggie, to which you were denied access," Absalom says.

"And Eunice Ross and my own daughter Phebe Ann besides. And yet you and I pay the town taxes to support that public high school, do we not?"

"That we do," Pompey adds. *Wealthy men are always especially aware of just where their money goes,* Meg thinks, almost smiling. "And yet, here we still are, battling prejudice. Because Nantucket is blatantly disregarding the law."

But Meg and Absalom know that this law contains a second directive: the right for a parent or guardian to sue on behalf of their child, should their rights not be met. "Which is why I want to sue the town for denying Phebe Ann and Eunice Ross access to the high school."

"And I'd like to sue as well, on behalf of myself," Meg adds.

"Why, I knew you were ambitious as a girl, Meggie," Absalom says, shaking his head back and forth. "All that math and reading. I knew that you had a passion for knowledge, for learning. That you wanted to attend the high school, that was always clear. But I had no notion that you cared about the politics of such things."

Meg sits back against the church pew and thinks about that for a moment before answering, gathering her thoughts in a way that reminds her of solving a complex mathematical problem. She studies Absalom's criticism and praise from several vantage points before putting her mind's pencil to paper, working through the complicated steps to come to a simple answer.

"I was learning before. But now I understand."

A slow smile spreads across Absalom's face. Pompey's, too. He sits down on the other side of Meg and leans toward her, listening.

"What's that you understand, Meg?" Pompey asks.

"That education *is* political."

Pompey nods. He takes his cane and knocks it twice against the hard polished wood floor. It sounds to Meg like a "Yes, indeed," or "Hear, hear," a clear gesture of agreement. And Absalom? Why, he stands and pulls Meg right up and out of her seat, belly and all, hugging her like a bear might do to a cub.

"What do we do next?" Meg asks, gently dropping back down to earth, at least physically. While her feet are planted on the ground, her mind soars.

"Next?" Absalom echoes. "We tell everyone our plans. Black, white, rich and poor: let's share our objective throughout town this weekend. Meggie, you and Ben can tell everyone who visits the cobbler shop on its opening day tomorrow!"

"We should divide and conquer to spread the news," Pompey says. As it's hard for Pompey to walk, it's decided he will share the news more locally in New Guinea. Absalom wants to head to the docks, to tell the mariners and get word out on ships, to let the whole Eastern seaboard know. "Meg, maybe you can walk part of town tomorrow after work," Pompey adds.

Thinking about who supported her and Benjamin at the town council meeting on Monday night, Meg agrees, mentioning possible visits to her former teacher, abolitionist Anna Gardner, Maria Mitchell, and several others. "And—I think I'd like to tell William and Eunice Hadwen," she says.

"Ah! Is that because they are prominent abolitionists and supporters of our causes, or because you've heard they finally moved into that grand new home—and you want to have a peek inside?" Pompey laughs.

Meg shrugs and makes it seem like she isn't interested in being nosy, but is it wrong to be just a little bit curious about the home that everyone has been talking so much about? And when will she ever have this opportunity to come knocking on their particular door again?

"Yes. Tell everyone, those on our side and those not. For when the prejudiced members of the town council get word of our plans to sue, they'll get worried. Legal action is expensive, and they know I have the means to fight them with lawyers and time in court. Let's light a fire under them and watch as they simmer and boil. Then you and I will meet at town hall early Monday morning and file suit."

They shake on it.

Being a force for change was not what Meg ever thought to be, but, clearly, it is who she needs to be. She has never felt closer to understanding her father and grandfather than she does today.

TWO DAYS BEFORE THE FIRE
Saturday, July 11, 1846

17

ELIZA

The wedding day for Betsy—the Mitchell cousin—has arrived, and what a beautiful day it is: the sun is shining, hydrangeas and roses are in full bloom, and the whole of Nantucket Island seems gilded in golden summer light. What with the daily stressors of life, Eliza sometimes forgets that she lives in such a charming and special place. She vows today to put her troubles aside and enjoy everything her island community has to offer. She will be social, she will smile and chat with her neighbors and friends, and she will not think at all about her monetary worries, nor about why Henry isn't returning home as planned.

For today was supposed to be the day his ship the *Ithaca* pulled into the harbor. Today was supposed to be their reunion after forty months apart.

Only instead of turning right at her doorstep and walking down Main Street and to the docks, Eliza turns left and ambles up the beautiful extension of town known as Upper Main Street, where the wealthiest of Nantucketers call home.

It is not lost on Eliza that quite literally, instead of turning toward where her husband is not, she turns toward where her old flame is.

It's a glorious day indeed for a wedding. If only the heat would let up a little bit. It's five o'clock in the afternoon and the sun is still burning bright.

Eliza's first thought, upon entering Eunice and William Hadwen's stately new mansion on Upper Main Street for the wedding of two practical strangers, is *how phenomenal.* A servant welcomes Eliza into the large foyer, past the great winding staircase, and into the even larger double sitting room with double chandeliers dripping cut glass like ice, she also thinks, *how garish.* Next, she is ushered by yet another female servant through the perfectly decorated rooms, with Oriental rugs and overstuffed horsehair settees done in jewel tones, with floor-to-ceiling damask silk curtains framing light-filled windows, and she thinks, *how utterly ostentatious!*

But of course she loves—and covets—absolutely everything, from the extravagant decor to the classical architectural details. Eliza wishes she had a companion to turn to and whisper with, perhaps one of her daughters: *Look, the fireplace is bedecked in green marble, and dentil moldings trim the ceilings in the cavernous rooms, and that dining room table could seat thirty!* Her girls Rachel and Mattie were not invited, but Alice and Larson were. She doesn't see them here yet, though, which is a bit of a relief. She feels a bit awkward and petty about how she reacted to Alice's helping Meg the other night.

On the whole the newly constructed Hadwen House does not disappoint. What makes the home especially grand is that it is one of a matching set, two identical homes built side by side with complementing colonnaded porticos, connected by a shared garden in the back. 96 Main Street, with its Corinthian columns, is where the Hadwens themselves reside, and 94 Main Street—with matching exterior but for the Ionic columns— is where their business partners and extended family, the Barneys, now live.

"To the garden, please," another servant says, which means Eliza is going to see this fabled backyard more quickly than she anticipated. Eliza pauses by a side table with an ornate floral arrangement on it, pretending to study the flowers. Like everything else in this home, they are massive and imported from elsewhere. Before exiting outside, Eliza had wished to sneak away and find the kitchen, for rumor has it that the kitchen is actually quite large and located in *the basement,* like the mansions of Newport! Oh, how she hopes Eunice Hadwen might lead them on a guided tour during the reception hour.

Eliza cranes her neck sideways to look into the room on the left, but all she catches is a glimpse of another emerald Oriental carpet laid upon more gleaming hardwood floors. This servant is too efficient at her job, ushering Eliza through the home and toward giant glass French doors that open onto a back porch and, a few steps below, a vast lawn of perfect green grass.

How is it that Hadwen and Barney can have such a verdant lawn when Nantucket hasn't seen rain for weeks, her own backyard dry as tinder? Can supreme wealth buy a reservoir against droughts? Seemingly so. Eliza scolds Henry in her mind for not continuing on as a captain for these businessmen. In the late 1830s, Henry had done well as captain for Hadwen and Barney's ship the *Alpha*. Then Henry had taken off on that dreadful and cursed voyage under a ship owner from New Bedford, and what happened? Fortune gone. Meanwhile, observe the continued success of Hadwen and Barney! These homes stand as a testament to their business acumen; there is simply no partnership as fruitful and prolific as theirs, no homes to match their elegance and wealth. But instead of dwelling on her own misfortune, Eliza reminds herself that today she is here to celebrate the beautiful and hopefully blessed union of two young souls, and chastises herself for making this—as she has been doing with much else these days—about herself. She steps down from the stone patio to the lawn below and smiles, thankful that she has been included in such an elegant affair.

The first person Eliza sees amid the partygoers on the grass is of course James Crosby. He's with the Mitchell clan, including Maria and all of her siblings. James's eyes lock on Eliza and a jolt of excitement fills her. This sensation is quickly followed by guilt and shame.

She doesn't know what she expects—or even wants—to happen with James, if anything. She only knows that, of the twenty years she's been wedded to Henry, she has only spent a total of nine months living on dry land with him, that time spread out in bits and pieces that never quite add up to a whole life. She has spent more time in her life with James Crosby than with Henry Macy, which is why she has made sure to look her finest for the nuptials at Hadwen House, even going so far as asking her daughters for help. Rachel made alterations to Eliza's favorite dress, a pale ice-blue silk frock, lowering the neckline slightly and squaring it off, and adding elaborate embroidered detail to the bodice and ornate lace to the sleeves. Mattie has helped Eliza style her hair like Queen Victoria's, with a middle part and two thin braids that loop around the ears before joining a coiled bun in the back. It's only an updated hairstyle and freshened-up dress, but Eliza feels quite empowered, like a soldier donning armor. But also, when she peers down to see the very top of her own decolletage, which she has powdered a bit with rose-scented talcum from France, she feels somewhat scandalous.

Certainly Maria seems stunned by Eliza's appearance, her dark eyes wide and eyebrows arched high. Good. That's the impression Eliza was hoping to achieve.

"It's nice to see you, Maria," Eliza says.

"You as well, Eliza," Maria says. Maria cocks her head to the side questioningly, as if Eliza were a bat from Madagascar.

"Mrs. Macy, what a pleasant surprise. How nice it is to see you here," James says, his eyes sparkling with mischief.

Ah, then: she is to pretend her invitation arrived from elsewhere.

"The pleasure is all mine, Mr. Crosby," Eliza says, trying not to smile too widely.

As James tips his hat to her, Eliza walks on past the group to find and thank the hosts. Every step further away from him is tense with satisfaction, like stretching soft taffy between one's fingers.

This wedding is certainly going to be a pleasurable affair.

18

MARIA

Something is definitely amiss with Eliza Macy. Only, *what,* exactly? Her dress is too revealing, her manner too forward, her whole demeanor stiff and unpleasant. She is acting very much unlike herself—or, like the worst parts of herself—as if cast in a play and given a complicated role she didn't have time to study for. Is Eliza upset in general, or does it seem like her displeasure is focused on Maria?

Maybe James will know. He and Eliza said hello just now as if they hadn't known or cared if the other would be at the party, but Maria knows for certain that James invited Eliza himself. Her cousin Betsy the bride mentioned it to Maria when she stopped by the library the other day to return a book of poetry. Betsy thought it odd, but Maria said they were old friends and dismissed it as that. But now she wonders if there's more to it. The way they greeted each other, smiling coyly with Eliza practically batting her eyes at James, was certainly strange.

Maria spools her mind back in time, trying to put together any missing pieces. James and Eliza were close as youths. Although Maria is much younger than they are, she recalls her family talking about the possibility of James asking Eliza Macy for her hand in marriage. In fact, now that she thinks back on it, she remembers Eliza's sister Charlotte bragging about it at the town's annual Fourth of July fireworks festivities, telling Maria that her big sister Eliza was planning on marrying the most handsome and nicest man. And then, *Oh,* Charlotte said, *he's your cousin, Maria! James Crosby is his name!*

Even then, Maria was not interested in marriage, but she did get swept up by the romance of it. Rumor was James might be proposing to Eliza Cowan that very night, just as the first fireworks lit the inky harbor. The entire wharf was buzzing with anticipation, as all the Mitchells and Crosbys thought it would be a perfect match.

But the only sparks that flew that Fourth of July were the ones created by the ancient Chinese art of fireworks, the science of gunpowder and fire and pressure combined, then manipulated by human ingenuity. No proposal, no wedding. Had the Cowans not agreed that their next-door neighbor, James Crosby, was right for their daughter?

The next thing Maria knew, she and her family were saying farewell to James at the same pier the following morning. James was headed to college in Boston and, as it turns out, beyond. He had not returned again to Nantucket since, until last week. Maria and her family had corresponded with James through letters. James apparently had a fascinating, entrepreneurial life off island, and whenever a letter arrived from him, William Mitchell would read it aloud to his wife and children after dinner, sometimes two or three times, so that they felt like they were memorizing his fabulous tales of life out West. And then Eliza Cowan had quickly gone and married Henry Macy, and that had been that. End of story. Or was it?

Maria is about to ask James if he knows what's upsetting Eliza when Linley enters the garden. She is accompanied by her parents, devout Quakers dressed in plain garb like Maria's own parents. Linley, however, wears a lovely lavender frock, like a beacon in the darkness. It is modest in design with a high lace collar and long sleeves, but the cut of it suits Linley's long torso. It may not be showy or in fashion like Eliza Macy's dress, but it's far superior for it is tasteful in its simplicity. Maria feels a sense of territorial pride, knowing Linley is hers.

And, in the past week, Maria can surely attest to that fact: they are a couple. Maria is smitten. Their relationship is a secret, but that does not diminish its power. In fact, it is like a candle under a hurricane lamp, growing brighter and stronger by the protection of glass casing around it. No gust of wind can blow it out.

The two have visited every night this week.

Since that night on the rooftop last Monday, Linley has joined Maria in stargazing. And holding hands. And kissing. And touching.

Since Maria's father is so busy rating chronometers for sailors, Maria suggested that Linley stand in for him, giving William a few weeks' reprieve from work on the rooftop observatory. He looked both relieved and perplexed by this proposal, for hadn't they always worked so well together, side by side night after night for years and years?

Yes, of course, I'm only trying to help you, Maria had responded, hoping she hadn't hurt his feelings. *You do so much for the family, and I want to repay you the only way I know how to, with extra time.*

Her father smiled tentatively with his kind, tired eyes and acquiesced.

Maria feels slightly guilty for lying, but concedes that it is a rather small, white lie at most. Who is it harming? No one, as far as Maria can tell. Doesn't Maria deserve to be happy? And doesn't her father deserve his sleep? Or more time with his many children?

Only Maria's mother, Lydia, seemed curious about the relationship. The first few nights of Linley's visitations, Lydia showed no interest in Maria's friend. But, by Thursday and Friday, she was peppering Maria with questions at breakfast.

Tell me more about this friend of yours. I know

she's from a good Quaker family, but where does she work? What are her life goals?

She works at the milliner's. She hopes to own her own hat shop someday.

Then why is she so interested in astronomy, I wonder?

A childhood passion that followed her into adulthood, Mother.

This had seemed to satisfy Lydia. After all, education was paramount to her. Curiosity was always rewarded.

No one else in the Mitchell family or in town seems to notice Maria and Linley or care about the nature of their relationship. During the day, Maria and Linley have both been too busy with work to meet, thereby circumnavigating any prying eyes by not even being in each other's company. Instead they pay pennies to Joseph Allen as courier and tell him only that Linley is helping Maria to try and win the prize from the King of Denmark by writing out complicated mathematical calculations that will help Maria locate a comet. Each note from Linley is better than the last, filled not with mathematical calculations at all, but poetry and sketches and, in the last letter, a lock of Linley's white-blond hair.

That gesture in particular feels like a promise.

Maria watches Linley from across the lawn and touches a silver oval locket at her neck, where the coiled hair now lives attached to a silk ribbon.

Lydia Mitchell gives Maria a questioning look, no doubt wondering where that piece of jewelry came from. Maria smiles and turns her back on her mother. She bought it yesterday at Kelly's jewelry store. All by herself. For herself. With her own money. So there, Mother.

Maria excuses herself and meanders through the beautiful, manicured garden, lost in thought as she waits for a good moment to approach Linley.

The letters have been wonderful, extending the time they have together and deepening their connection. Letter-writing is an art form every-where in the world, but particularly on Nantucket, where sons and mothers, fathers and daughters, husbands and wives, separated by oceans, rely on pen and paper to keep their bonds alive.

Maria sees the perfect opportunity to approach Linley. She's standing with her family when Maria surprises her from behind, pulling at one of Linley's curls. Linley turns her head, sees Maria, and moves gently away. "My parents," she whispers. "And the Warrens."

Maria follows Linley's gaze to Charlie Warren and his parents, who are in conversation with the party's host, William Hadwen.

"Why do they matter?" Maria asks.

Like Maria and Liney, Charlie has left the Friends and is no longer a practicing Quaker, although he dresses simply still. He is handsome in the way of an overgrown boy, with floppy brown hair that he keeps pushing off his forehead. His face is sweet more than manly, round more than chiseled, and his cheeks have a mottled pinkish hue, as if he's shy or slightly embarrassed.

Since everyone is so engrossed in conversation, Maria pulls Linley away from the tight cluster. She suggests they amble through the lush garden before the ceremony begins.

Once they are lost amid the blooming hydrangea, Maria feels comfortable enough to speak of their private matters. "I placed your hair inside this," Maria says, fingering the locket at her neck.

"That's clever. I was hoping you'd find a way to keep it with you," Linley says, her eyes very big. They are the most beautiful eyes Maria's ever seen.

"Today your blue eyes look violet," Maria says.

"They change depending on what I'm wearing," Linley says, shrugging off the comment and running her hands over the pleats in her purple dress, as if having chameleon eyes is a nuisance more than a gift.

"Mine are chocolate brown every day of my life," Maria says.

"I'm willing to wager this is untrue," Linley says. "But to be sure, I'll have to look at you every day."

Another promise. Maria loops her arm through

Linley's, and Linley looks around, concerned. Maria holds on tighter. "It is perfectly respectable for two ladies to meander arm-in-arm through a beautiful garden."

"True," Linley says, her shoulders relaxing. "I'm just being overly sensitive. Of course women can touch one another in public. In that way we are fortunate. Men cannot do the same."

"Imagine! Two grown men taking in the scenery with their arms linked through one another's!"

"That *would* be scandalous," Linley admits. "Much preferable to be a woman."

"Quite right. However. We cannot attend college like men of our same station can. Or stay unmarried without being labeled a *spinster.*"

"Much preferable to be a man, then," Linley surmises. "Or a *bachelor.*"

"Much preferable to be a woman always!" Maria says, as the pair continue to amble, making one more loop around the garden before finding seats for the wedding ceremony. "Now all we need is the right to vote." She shares news with Linley of the latest town council meeting, where she spoke about the acquisitions for the Atheneum, and mentions the contentious deliberation between Eliza Macy and Meg Wright over the dueling cobblers' shops in town. Maria understood that Eliza was trying to help her son-in-law, but she wasn't certain the woman understood how negative and small-minded her words made her sound. Was she really that way? How long could one live side by side with neighbors—friends!—and not even really know the contents of their heart?

And she supposed the opposite holds true as well, for what would a person like Eliza Macy have to say about a person like Maria Mitchell? As if hearing her thoughts, Maria spots Eliza in the garden, laughing with James. So they are friends again. She really would like to get to the bottom of that.

"Are the schools segregating—again?" Linley asks, bringing Maria back to the real issues in her town, not the hidden undercurrent of secret wonderings and rumors.

Maria shakes her head sadly. "Forcing children from the schoolhouse. Completely inhumane. I don't know how these men can call themselves Christians."

But Maria does not want to discuss politics and the island's future in this moment. Instead, she wants to discuss her own future. Move from being courted to becoming the courter, a unique option for two women who believe that one's roles in life must not stay fixed as the points in the heavens. Perhaps their separate, distinct futures might truly join together and become one. Like particles from the ether pulled together by outer space to form a star, a mass of friction and heat.

Should Maria make a formal declaration of her feelings? Tell Linley her hopes for their future?

Maria looks up and sees Charlie Warren stationed right between them and the bubbling fountain, a wide and inviting smile.

"Hello, Charlie," Maria says as he joins them.

"Hello, hello!" Charlie says, putting a hand on Linley's arm but directing his words at Maria. "I see you've run off with my wedding date."

"Your—?" Maria asks. What could Charlie mean? Maria looks at Linley with confusion. Charlie doesn't notice, as he turns to greet some other guests, including Maria's parents.

"My father," Linley whispers. "It doesn't matter. It won't matter. I was going to tell you, but I was enjoying our conversation too much. My father surprised me today with this arrangement. He ultimately wants to see me settled, he says."

"Settled?" Maria echoes. "You are not land out West!"

"Shhh," Linley says, her eyes wet. She's clearly upset. Maria knows she's only adding fuel to the fire, but she's upset, too. Women have come so far, especially on this little island, but not far enough. Not yet. For as much as a woman here can speak publicly and own her own shop and handle financial matters while her husband is away at sea, she cannot be fully independent. Not really. Not unless she can choose who to love. A young woman should not be thought of as property for her father to trade in.

Incensed, Maria shakes her head and looks away.

That's when she sees Martin Graves looking directly at her, nervous but determined. He gives her a toothy smile and tips his hat to her. His hair is parted severely to one side and greased back with pomade.

Martin is a childhood friend of Maria's and—of course!—distant cousin to the Mitchells. When they were mere babes, family lore states, Lydia and Martin's mother Norah once bathed the two together after a visit to the beach. The details of this story horrify Maria, while Martin thinks it is laced with metaphorical and allegorical meaning that the pair are meant to be together. Preordained by the stars. Which is why, every few months, Martin comes calling on her at home. Maria is always able to sidestep an actual visit, but to do so without causing offense takes more work than her calculus studies.

What she thinks is *ugh*. What she does is wave.

Maria is not normally a jealous or cruel person, but seeing Linley with Charlie stirs something deep inside her. Hurt by Linley and in need of a diversion, Maria fakes a smile and walks toward Martin Graves.

19

MEG

Wright's Cobbler Shop at 21 Main Street is officially open for business!

At just past five o'clock Saturday evening, after a full and exciting day of greeting shoppers in the new storefront, Meg says goodbye to Benjamin and Lucy and makes her way to the Hadwens'. She's decided to begin her news-sharing tour there and then work her way home before supper.

Seeing Lucy shining shoes and making change for customers, several patrons in the shop today expressed their anger over renewed school segregation, asking if Lucy—and Meg—were all right after such an assault. "Oh, we're just fine now," Meg had said with a smile. "Now that we're going to sue the town, that is." The customers, Black and white alike, applauded. One man even bought a new pair of boots just to celebrate. He called them his "stomping on injustice" shoes.

Meg reaches her destination winded from the walk. It's getting harder each day to move comfortably. But she doesn't dwell on her pregnancy long, for she can hardly believe the scope and scale of this architectural wonder as she climbs the steps from the street up to Hadwen House. Much like the Methodist Church at the top of town, Hadwen House is built in the Greek Revival style, with a white colonnaded front and a deep portico, reminiscent of the images she's seen drawn of the White House in several of the national publications at the Atheneum. She feels simultaneously overwhelmed and underdressed.

Only upon arrival at the imposing, side-by-side mansions of these two men does she realize this is perhaps not the right time to come calling. This Saturday evening, Hadwen House is buzzing with activity.

But, already at the front door, Meg is quickly ushered inside by a servant. A Black girl. As she gapes openmouthed in awe at the glamour around her, Meg is ushered by yet another Black servant through the house's many formal sitting areas and into the back garden. "You don't want to be late for the ceremony, Mrs. Wright!" the girl says, introducing herself as Amity, the daughter of the barber, William Harris. "My father was most proud of another Black man opening a store on Main. And owning the building outright!"

A Black man *and* woman, Meg wants to say as a correction, but instead she accepts the praise and sends her regards to the Harris family.

Meg stands on the patio above the garden, where she takes in the decorative surroundings and realizes that the ceremony the Harris girl was referring to is a wedding. Oh my. Scanning the crowd swiftly, she sees that she is the only Black

227

person at the event who is not hired help. She is entirely out of place here. In public, Black and white Nantucketers walk side by side through the streets of town, but their worlds are largely separate, with different grocery stores, separate churches, and their own respective firemen corps. Benjamin is a fireman with the New Guinea brigade, which is as real as the white corps but, unlike their white counterparts, the Black firemen do not get paid a yearly stipend of two dollars by the town for their services. Most ironic of all in a place that prides itself on progressive notions—the Anti-Slavery Societies are segregated, although the Black and white Nantucket chapters work together. Certainly in the privacy of back gardens—and now apparently again in the schoolhouses—segregation grows as natural as those climbing roses.

Meg clutches the basket on her arm, trying not to feel angry. But how can she feel anything but? Standing in the Hadwens' garden, she is getting a rare glimpse of a parallel world. In New Guinea, everyone she knows is riled up with purpose, with concern, with politics. All the fighting and planning, trying to end segregation and abate the fearmongering. Constantly thinking about the color of one's skin as compared to that of her neighbors. Meanwhile, on Upper Main Street, everyone is attending a party! The only thing people have to care about is showing off their wealth to one another and celebrating the normality of keeping the beautiful status quo.

And so Meg, with all eyes upon her, steps down into the garden and pretends to belong.

20

ELIZA

Eliza is able to enjoy one more brief moment with James—in which he pretends he hasn't seen her in years—before he is swept off with the bride's family. Not comfortable standing alone at parties, and not seeing Alice or Larson anywhere, Eliza decides now is a good time to greet and thank Eunice and William Hadwen.

The hostess is a pretty woman with porcelain skin, brown eyes, and black hair swept off her neck into a soft bun. A proud and devout Friend, Eunice Hadwen somehow makes Quakerism seem chic instead of quaint. Today she wears a beautiful but simple gold necklace, perhaps made by her husband's own jewelry company, though William left that business once he saw how much more prosperous one could be by turning whale oil into candles. Her black dress is set off by an intricate, handmade lace collar. Irish, no doubt. A rose-colored shawl is draped casually around her arms, bringing out the natural pink in her cheeks.

Eunice makes small talk with her guests as she circles the grounds and politely ushers them into seats on the lawn. Having no children of her own, Eunice Hadwen often takes a niece or cousin or other young Nantucket lady under her wing, and Eliza assumes that Betsy, the bride today, attended one of Eunice's informal but quite educational finishing schools. Eliza hears snippets of her conversation as she passes by. "Why, thank you so much, Mary. Yes, William and I are indeed enjoying our new home . . ." and "Absolutely, we must!" and "Yes, you heard correctly; it's in the basement!"

Wanting to make a good impression on the hostess, Eliza thanks Eunice Hadwen for including her as a guest. "But, of course, Eliza dear; having you is our pleasure," Eunice says, speaking in the plural for herself and her husband, walking just behind her. Eliza greets and thanks William as well.

"Will we see you at the next abolitionist meeting, Eliza?" William Hadwen asks, also invoking the plural. He is a tall man with handsome features and short salt-and-pepper hair. "I've just gotten word from the national chapter of the Anti-Slavery Society, where there is much talk about Henry!"

"My Henry?" Eliza asks.

William nods, leans in close and whispers conspiratorially. "Of course it's a secret mission, but surely he must have confided in you about the great work he is doing for the cause." Seeing other guests approach, he steps back from Eliza and changes the topic, raising his voice to its regular level. "And, anyway, there is much we wish to discuss about slavery in the new territories, now that Polk has declared war with Mexico."

"Oh, yes. War with Mexico. I am looking forward to it," Eliza says, still trying to make sense of William Hadwen's first comment. Realizing from the look on the man's face that this might have been a flippant response to what will surely be a fraught conversation, Eliza tries a different tack. Several more people have gathered around them now, wanting to speak to the host and hostess, and so Eliza must perform well in front of not just the Hadwens but her fellow neighbors, too. She shakes her head to show what a pity this terrible political situation is and delivers her next words with more gravity. "What I mean, Mr. Hadwen, is that I—Henry and I together—we—would very much like to pledge a sum of a hundred dollars to the cause."

A hundred dollars! That's what she spent last year at the greengrocers! She instantly wishes she had offered ten dollars, or even twenty-five, but didn't want to come off seeming stingy. There's a war with Mexico to think of, and Eliza's reputation too.

"Well," Willian Hadwen says, and clasps Eliza's hands in his own. "We will gladly accept that most generous offer," he says, ushering her toward a seat. "Which we can further discuss at another time."

There. Eliza exhales. She'll not have to procure

the funds for at least a few weeks. Maybe she can sell off another piece of furniture. Something small. Or perhaps, by the end of the month, when the meeting is to occur, William Hadwen will have forgotten her pledge, delivered as it was in the midst of such a busy event as this.

Someone bumps into Eliza and does not apologize. It is Maria Mitchell. Maria had been walking and whispering with Linley Blake before, Eliza noticed, but now she stands with Martin Graves, looking uncomfortable.

"Maria? Are you quite all right?" Eliza asks. Things have been strained between the two women ever since the town hall meeting on Monday night, but Eliza doesn't wish Maria any ill-will.

Maria nods her head. "I'm quite all right. Terrific, really!" she says, louder than necessary. "Martin and I are having a really lovely time!"

"Why, that's—" Eliza begins.

"Wonderful!" Maria adds, peering over her shoulder as if looking for someone.

"We're just wonderful!" Martin echoes, although he looks perplexed. The toothy grin doesn't help.

Although distracted, Maria steadies her gaze for a moment. "Eliza, I must ask—did I just hear you offer money to William Hadwen? The host? Today of all days? And to dress so immodestly— *at a Quaker wedding?*"

"Why, I—" Eliza begins.

"I feel like I don't recognize anyone anymore!" Maria exclaims, marching off in the opposite direction, Martin following quickly behind her.

Eliza opens her mouth, shocked, but no words emerge. She tries to keep her embarrassment and rage from escaping. There is no one to speak to anyway.

Eliza's dress is beautiful, and quite *à la mode*, as they would say on the Continent, not that she's ever been. And, by donating money, Eliza was only trying to be generous! And, if she's being perfectly honest, to look charitable in front of such important people. Is that a crime? No, Eliza decides. It is not. Yet, as she slinks off to find a seat for the ceremony about to begin, she decides that it is probably best to stay silent for the rest of the party. Looking down at herself, she suddenly wishes she had brought a shawl, despite the heat.

There must be chairs for a hundred or so people, Eliza surmises, trying to pick a seat for herself as she regains some composure. If she sits at the end of a row, anyone trying to join her will have to awkwardly step over her feet to get to their chair. She will find herself standing and moving every time another person enters her row. So, no, perhaps instead she should claim a middle seat. But, isn't that awfully lonely, to take a middle spot in an otherwise empty row of chairs, hoping someone joins to fill in the row on both sides?

At the last wedding she attended, two summers ago, she sat with Alice and the twins. But Alice still isn't here yet today. She's always running late these days, her eldest daughter. Probably because Larson made them move to the edge of town, out by the Madaket Road, where land is cheaper. How Eliza wished Alice and Larson had taken her up on her offer to let them live with her. Alice is so social and fun, bringing friends by for tea and knitting circles. Eliza misses the closeness they used to have.

At that wedding, Alice had invited Maria and her siblings and a few others to join them, so Eliza didn't feel excluded or lonely, even with Henry off at sea. Alice had still lived with Eliza, Mattie, and Rachel in the Macy house, and before the ceremony, Eliza had lent Alice a pair of sapphire earrings that matched her dress and her emerald eyes—and Alice had done Eliza's hair. The family of women had walked to the Unitarian church together. After the party, they had invited Maria back to their house and all had stayed up late into the night discussing the details of the ceremony and party. Maria had even fallen asleep on Eliza's couch. When Alice lived at home, there were so many spirited nights like that which Eliza now misses like a phantom limb.

Five thirty now and still no sign of Alice and Larson. Eliza ends up taking an end seat in a row near the back where she can try to enjoy the spectacle without being seen, seated well behind the bride's and groom's close family and friends. The wedding was called for six o'clock at night so as to make the most of a long summer's evening, after the heat of the day has passed. The roses in the garden are reminiscent of her carefree summers from childhood, and tears rise unbidden to Eliza's eyes. Oh, drat. Weddings always make her emotional, and the recent coolness between her and Maria still has her a bit rattled, but Eliza had hoped to keep her composure today of all days.

"Here," a male voice says, and a handkerchief is waved before her. The sinking afternoon sun is in her eyes, so she shades her face with a hand and looks up as James Crosby takes the seat beside her and places his monogrammed cotton handkerchief in her lap. He looks so handsome, clean-shaven and freshly pressed, his blond hair neatly tucked behind his ear. His leg touches hers, just like it did that first time he visited her in her parlor, and a jolt of sensation moves through her.

"Thank you," she says, pressing the cotton square to the corner of each eye. For a man who keeps showing up when least expected, this time James picked the perfect moment. He settles in next to her and she feels less alone.

"There is something quite moving about a wedding, I agree," he says.

Eliza nods, dabs her eyes, then lets a calm

contentment settle over her. The handkerchief is warm from James's body, and thinking of this only makes Eliza feel even more aware of his physical presence beside her.

"Although this one seems to be about the Hadwens' opulence, showing off one's wealth, more than the sacred connection of two mortal souls, if you want my opinion," James says, smirking slightly.

"You're exactly right, James," Eliza says, seeing the garden with a new clarity. Those bountiful roses, the plentiful food and refreshments to be served later, all the staff hired to cook, serve, and clean for the guests. William Hadwen sits with his back perfectly straight, and Maria and the other Mitchells are seated across the aisle. "Throwing one's money about at a wedding . . . it is positively garish."

"You look lovely, by the way," James says. "That dress," he adds.

She presses her leg closer into his but makes no mention of their proximity. She doesn't know what's wrong with her suddenly, but she believes she would climb into his lap if she could. The nuptials before them stir something inside her. She is overcome with a sense of desire. It has been a long time since she has felt drawn to a man.

"Shouldn't you, as her first cousin, sit up front with the rest of Betsy's family?" Eliza says, aiming for breeziness. James's parents are in the first row, seated next to Eunice and William Hadwen on one side and Nathaniel and Eliza Barney on the other, Nantucket royalty. Not that she wants him to go! Why suggest such a thing? Eliza chides herself.

"I'm the black sheep, remember?" James says.

"Because you didn't join the family candlery?" Eliza asks, passing the handkerchief back to James, who tells Eliza to keep it. Although she'd like to place the cotton square inside the bosom of her dress, she pushes the handkerchief up her right sleeve. "I find it hard to believe that they would take such a drastic stance against you, considering how successful you've become," Eliza adds, trying hard not to think of just how successful James Crosby has become.

"Nantucketers have stodgy notions about what's right and wrong, Eliza. You must sense that pressure constantly, living here your whole life, with prying eyes and gossipmongers listening in on every street corner. I don't know how you can stand it."

Eliza shrugs, pretending that his comment doesn't cut directly to the core of how she lives her entire life, including today, and how close she is to cracking under the weight of it all. She also pretends not to notice how singularly attractive James looks, distinguishing himself from the crowd of Nantucket men in their identical black wool suits, by wearing a perfectly tailored gray suit and matching gray silk tie knotted at his neck. He looks like he comes from somewhere else, another place and time entirely, which, Eliza realizes, he does. He is at once achingly familiar and exotically foreign to her.

People settle into the seats around them and the ceremony begins, and, by the grace of God, Eliza manages to make it through without any other public blubbering. Perhaps this is due to the fact that she's hardly paying any attention to the wedding, consumed instead by the way the back of her hand rests next to James's, knuckles brushing between the two seats.

After the young couple declare themselves married before God and adorable Archie kisses his fetching bride Betsy, James moves his hand away from hers and prepares to rise. Eliza quickly tries to think of what else they can talk about to keep this moment from ending. But something is intense in the way James looks at her, his blue eyes the color of the indigo light in the sky, and whispers, "That should have been us."

It is uttered so quickly and so quietly that Eliza isn't sure she heard James correctly.

"What did you—?" she begins, but James is fully standing now, and waving to someone near the front of the garden. "James!" Eliza whisper-calls, standing quickly beside him. "James?"

But he won't address it. "Now, if you'll excuse

me, I must congratulate the happy couple. And then . . ." His eyes scan the property and fix on the house. Eliza is too flustered to speak, lest she miss James saying something else of consequence. "And then I think I'll go find that kitchen everyone is abuzz about. I hear it's in the basement, of all things."

And, with a delightful smile, he walks off.

Well.

For the next several minutes, Eliza sips sherbet punch, nodding along with the other women from her knitting circle as they talk about how wonderful the ceremony was, her hands shaking and her mind racing. Did James truly suggest that she and he should have married? And, if so, why make such a bold statement only to walk away? And why switch the conversation so quickly away from matrimony to . . . what? The kitchen?

Was he suggesting she should meet him there, in the basement?

Perhaps not. But Eliza can't very well ask him right out here in the open, in the Hadwens' garden. She may be thirty-eight years old, and true, sometimes her vision isn't what it used to be when reading late at night by candlelight, but she's not hard of hearing by any stretch of the imagination. She can detect mice skittering through the walls in wintertime and the whistle of her next-door neighbor's teakettle every morning, if her windows are ajar. So she can certainly decipher five whispered words.

Eliza scans the crowded garden, looking for Alice once again. No sign of her. Eliza feels completely alone.

She swallows the remainder of her too-sweet punch, finding a new resolve. Then she deposits her cut-glass cup by the giant punch bowl and heads into the house, winding her way between revelers as the sun begins to set, in search of the fabled kitchen.

21

MEG

Sitting off to the side, trying to look comfortable, Meg survives the ceremony, the first wedding she's ever attended for a white couple, and her first Quaker wedding as well.

The service is quiet. Contemplative. Interesting. No jumping the broom, the custom she's learned from her formerly enslaved grandparents, and no communal singing like the Baptists. No music at all. The parents of the bride and groom make speeches, along with several guests who feel moved to speak.

Witnessing someone else's customs up close like this is fascinating.

Now she stands and stretches, her baby kicking once for good measure. If she can just get ahold of either one of the Hadwens, she'll quickly share her plans to sue the town and be on her way. In fact, perhaps she should just sneak out a side exit here in the garden and return at another time.

Since Meg hasn't been invited as a guest, she isn't sure whether she should congratulate the couple. But as they pass by on their way up the aisle, she quietly offers a blessing. The couple thank her and continue on up toward the house.

"Meg Wright, is that you?" a voice to Meg's

left says. She turns and sees Alice Handler, Eliza Macy's daughter, coming down the back steps and into the garden.

A friendly face, thank goodness. "Hello," Meg says. "Yes, believe it or not, it's me."

Alice seems flustered and out of breath. Her blond hair is coming out of its bun and her cheeks are flushed. "I cannot believe I missed the entire ceremony! Tell me, how was it? Boring like all the rest?"

Meg blinks, unsure what to say.

"I'm joking, of course. These Quaker services are lovely. Especially if you need a nap." Her green eyes are wide and merry.

Meg laughs good-naturedly. "I suppose it was rather . . . staid."

"I did mean to be punctual," Alice says, "but I was helping Larson unpack new merchandise in the store and then I lost track of time. I'll just pretend I was witness to it. You won't tell on me, will you?"

"Your secret is safe with me, Mrs. Handler."

"Alice, please. Mrs. Handler is my mother-in-law. And I don't want to be compared to her at all if I can help it. And not just because she's deceased."

Alice takes a moment to fix her hair, removing and then replacing a lovely silver comb. She motions with her chin to Meg's torso. "You're still carrying high, I see."

Meg laughs again. "Yes. And do call me Meg."

"Why is that humorous?" Alice asks.

"That you chose to comment on my pregnancy instead of the more obvious fact that I am the only Black woman who is not a servant at this wedding."

"Well, Meg, seems like a waste of a perfectly good conversation to focus on our skin color."

Meg can't argue with that kind of logic. Unsure of what else to say, Meg asks, "Do you have children?"

"Very soon, I hope. We've been married two years now and I'm itching for a child of my own. I've been drawn to the practice of midwifery because I am so drawn to babies. The way they scream, the way they suck, the way they are so clear about what they want and need in life."

"The way they exhaust a new mother, mostly," Meg says, aiming for humor but landing more on the truth of it.

"Maybe I'm drawn to infants because of that bond. My mother died when I was two, and although I've had a wonderful life with a wonderful family, I do feel her absence. Eliza married my father and raised me as her own."

"I wasn't aware of that," Meg says. Although it explains why the two don't look anything alike . . . although they both speak boldly about how they feel. Meg could share the loss of her infant son with Alice, but some things are too hard to talk about, even with an attentive listener.

"Speaking of, have you seen my mother anywhere?"

"No, I haven't," Meg says, thanking her lucky stars.

"I suppose you'd want to avoid her, even if you had," Alice says, quite pointedly. "And I wouldn't say I'd blame you. So do I. She's been quite awful lately."

"It's all right," Meg says, feeling suddenly uncomfortable.

"No, it isn't all right at all." Alice's face darkens. It feels like she has more to say, but she pulls her lips into a tight line instead.

"Why hello, Mrs. Wright and Mrs. Handler," William Hadwen says, coming up the now-empty aisle a moment later, tipping his hat to Meg and Alice.

Although William Hadwen must think it odd for Meg to be a guest at this event in his back-yard, he is polite enough not to mention it. Meg immediately explains her purpose for showing up so that she doesn't have to feel like an interloper even one second longer than necessary. Both Alice Handler and William Hadwen nod their heads in tacit understanding.

"Well done, Meg," Alice says.

"Suing the town! That is going to be something to see!" Hadwen says. "What a fine idea, indeed.

I look forward to talking to Absalom and you more about it."

"That sounds fine, Mr. Hadwen," Meg says, "another time. And I sincerely apologize for interrupting your party."

"Everyone is welcome at a wedding!" William Hadwen says. He suggests she get some punch. "Or sit in one of the parlors, if that suits your condition better," he adds, noting her obvious belly with a smile.

She thanks him and watches him walk away.

Then Meg and Alice wish each other well and part ways. "Actually . . . while we were talking, I think I might have seen your mother by the punch bowl," Meg says, and Alice thanks her. "Although, now I'm not sure if she's still there anymore."

As Alice goes in search of her mother, Meg heads into the house without stopping for a refreshment. For while she is parched, she would rather die of thirst than have to be anywhere near that woman.

Even if Eliza did happen to raise a wonderful daughter.

22

MARIA

Maria makes a terrible mistake by encouraging Martin Graves's advances. She means only to pretend flirtation as a way to fluster Linley, but Linley doesn't even notice. And instead, Martin has indeed noticed quite a lot.

Maria manages to avoid Martin during the wedding service by sitting with her family. The solitude of the ceremony helps calm her frantic mind. But afterward, as the attendees celebrate in the garden, the questions and worry and doubt comes bubbling right back, circling Maria's brain in a constant, incessant orbit. *Whatever does Linley mean by the word settled? Is her father planning something for his daughter? Does Linley know more than she lets on? Am I about to have my heart broken again?*

And the whole time, Martin stands by Maria's side like a broken appendage, utterly useless and completely annoying. Maria drifts toward some friends from the women's auxiliary, suggesting Martin enjoy some lemonade at the refreshments table so that he no longer just trails behind her like a lost puppy. "I'll meet you there in a moment," she adds, and he smiles with his huge horse teeth before walking away.

"You make a lovely couple," Peggy MacGowan says, noticing Martin. Peggy hails from Scotland, with the creamy skin and bright red curls to prove it. Although Peggy appears delicate, her voice is low and rich, with the most wonderful cadence of accented English. So even though Maria doesn't like the implication of Peggy's words, she can't help but love the sound of the brogue in her speech. "Lovely" comes out in a singsong *louv-leh*.

"Oh, Martin and I, we're not really—" Maria begins, but Peggy waves her off.

"How I wish I could find a suitable match for my niece Ainsley," Peggy sighs, gesturing to the young woman beside her and introducing her to Maria. Ainsley is as pale as Peggy, but her hair is mousy brown instead of rich red, and the combination makes her look rather wan. "Visiting me this summer. Just turned twenty-two. Her parents have combed the entire highlands for a husband with no luck. We are all hoping she can locate a mate here in New England."

Ainsley shrugs—all hope is lost!—and Peggy pats her pale hand, limp at the girl's side. A wedding must be difficult to watch if you are at all pressured to be the one standing in a gown in front of the community. Maria touches the locket again at her neck, the silver cool to the touch, tracing the delicate filigree etching. Does Linley feel such pressure today?

"Well. Best of luck to you," Maria says. Ainsley smiles and her long angular face seems to grow even longer. *Poor thing,* Maria thinks. What a blow to one's confidence to be told that an entire country does not find you eligible.

"Maria!" Martin calls, waving a very long arm. "May I tempt you with something sweet?"

Maria will not be tempted by anything Martin has to offer, but her stomach grumbles and her hunger betrays her. So she walks over to the refreshment table at the edge of the garden without complaint. Elaborate puff pastries with whipped cream and cherries have been laid out on the table with the punch, each one looking like a petite gift.

How fun—and somewhat naughty—to have dessert before one's dinner meal. Maria picks up a delicate confection and pops it into her mouth, chewing with satisfaction. She doesn't notice that Martin is extending his cake out to her, waiting for her to do the same.

He raises the pastry to Maria in a gesture of solidarity and toasts, "To us."

"To us." Maria chews, although to what *us* she's cheering, she isn't sure. Like a pact of some sort, sealing her fate: doomed to live a dull life with a perfectly respectable man. But no. Maria's parents have made it clear that, while they prefer Maria marries—she will be twenty-eight next month—they appear perfectly happy with her living her life in pursuit of science. The Mitchells have many other children and therefore many other opportunities for grandchildren, for their lineage to continue. So Maria shakes off the cloak of catastrophe and turns toward the groups standing nearby. They seem merry, and Maria hopes their mood is catching.

The Warrens and Blakes stand there, laughing. Charlie Warren is standing very close to Linley Blake, his smile wide, her smile placid. Linley is the Blakes' only child. What do they wish for her? And then Maria's stomach does a flip, for isn't it obvious?

Suddenly Maria isn't hungry. She excuses herself from the group and walks away. She plucks a pink rose from a vine wrapped around the gazebo and peels its petals one by one, watching them fall at her feet to the grass. *She loves me, she loves me not. She loves—*

A moment later, there is a rustling of petticoats by Maria's side. "Ah, you've escaped! You must see the way Martin looks at you," Linley whispers.

Maria shakes her head. "Like I'm a strawberry shortcake," she says, and Linley practically spits with laughter. But Maria doesn't laugh, for it is probably exactly the way she herself gazes at Linley. With that kind of hunger.

Charlie and Martin look over, and Maria is sure they know the women are talking about them.

Her face grows hot under the scrutiny, angry that she is so misunderstood by these men. She shouldn't have to explain herself at all to anyone.

"Your father and I are going to find our seats inside for supper," Maria's mother says, passing by on her father's arm. "It's so nice to see you spending time with Martin Graves!" Lydia adds.

Maria fakes a smile and then rolls her eyes at Linley. "You see what I said about life being complicated by romance," Maria says. "This wasn't at all how I wanted tonight to be."

"Nor how I wanted it to be, either," Linley says. "But maybe—"

"Maybe what?" Maria asks, a nervous tingle dancing up her spine.

"Maybe a complicated romance is the best we can hope for?" Linley says, picking one of the last petals off the rose in Maria's hand.

"Linley," Charlie calls, "shall Martin and I go inside and get seats at a table?" The two men stand together by the giant cut glass punch bowl looking lost.

"Yes, please!" Linley says, a little bit too brightly.

"No—wait!" Maria says. She cannot spend the entire meal seated next to Martin Graves, pretending. She spots Peggy MacGowan and her niece Ainsley climbing the steps to enter the party and races up to the French doors to catch up with them. Then she calls across the garden to Martin, signaling him to join them, which of course he does, obedient servant that he is.

"Martin! I'm so sorry that I won't be able to dine with you tonight. But I think you'll find even better company with Mrs. MacGowan and her niece. May I present Ainsley, who hails from Scotland." Ainsley and Peggy perk up with interest while Martin looks confused.

Maria continues on, undeterred. "I hope you don't mind my matchmaking, but Ainsley is hoping to meet a wonderful American man, and I thought instantly of you."

Understanding dawns on Martin's long face, and his countenance changes from one of disappointment to one of renewed hope. The pair speak shyly but with definite interest, and Maria thinks them a match made in heaven. Look at them, Martin with his horse teeth and Ainsley with her long, horsey face. Martin tips his hat to her, which she takes to mean he's thankful to her, and pleased. Perfect. She can picture their equine children already.

He extends his arm out to Ainsley. "May I escort you inside?"

"Why, Martin, that would be just *louv-leh,*" Peggy says.

"Yes, so very *louv-leh,*" Ainsley says, smiling wide.

A triumph. Now, there's only one more match to solidify, the one between her and Linley.

Maria encourages Charlie to follow the rest of the wedding guests inside, leaving Linley and Maria alone in the darkening garden. The living room looks festive from where they stand apart, people's muted voices carrying across the lawn, and candelabras and chandeliers make the mansion glow with dancing light.

"Hear me out. If we both marry in the traditional sense, and then stay the best of friends—and more—in private . . . We can have everything, Maria," Linley says.

"Everything? That sounds like nothing," Maria says. "Nothing that I want, anyway."

"Maria," Linley says, her lilac eyes filled with tenderness as she takes both of Maria's hands into hers. A glass shatters inside, and gasps of surprise from the guests echo around them in the night. "My parents have arranged my marriage to Charlie Warren. They just told us. We are to be married at the end of the month."

Maria wants to say something. She is an adroit and accomplished speaker of several languages, but in this moment, she cannot find any words.

23

ELIZA

About twenty minutes after the ceremony, Eliza goes in search of James Crosby. Only once inside the house, she gets waylaid by guests wishing her well and asking after the girls, and by host William Hadwen, who thanks Eliza again for her generous pledge of funds. Eunice Hadwen pulls Eliza aside to inquire about Henry's latest journey.

"I hear he's on quite a mission!" Eunice says, leaning toward her conspiratorially.

"Yes, quite!" Eliza says, having—again—absolutely no idea what this is about. Does the whole world know more about Henry than she does as his wife? Well, she has no patience currently to figure it out or ask. She is too busy wondering if James is really waiting for her in the kitchen. She tries not to be rude, instead changing course by asking to see the kitchen. "I hear it's an absolute marvel!" Eunice nods proudly and points her toward a staircase leading down.

She's been dillydallying. Will James still be there? And, if so, will she summon the courage to confront him, question his intentions, and, for her own sake, break off further contact between them?

The basement level smells like roast chicken and starchy potatoes. A supper feast is being prepared for the hundred or so guests, and the kitchen space reflects that, with a cook and several assistants at the massive stove and giant ovens. To think that the earth had been moved for this kitchen to be built! Excavation of dirt and land for a subterranean wonderland.

The space has high ceilings and cream tiled walls and—most unbelievable of all—windows, placed high into the ceiling near the street level, capable of letting in natural light. But no sign of James Crosby.

The banging of pots and pans and shouting of orders from cook to server makes this a most chaotic place to be on a day like this one, and so, although Eliza would love to admire the room some more and sit a spell at the large, marble table in the center of it, she crosses through the maze of people and trays of food, exiting into a dark and quiet corridor.

"James?" Eliza whisper-calls, the tight hallway cooler than upstairs.

Eliza enters a large pantry, where she can just make out food storage in the dimness: sacks of grain and flour and jars of canned fruit line the open, wooden shelving, while barrels of what must be cured meats and pickled vegetables stand in the center of the room. So much sugar and flour! To think of what terrible concoctions

Mattie could make of all that! She considered smuggling some out and then quickly despises herself for entertaining such debased thoughts. To debate theft! What has become of her?

Eliza exits the pantry and peeks behind more closed doors, finding a chilled room with meat and fish packed in hay and resting on blocks of ice, a laundry room smelling of lye, and a small office with a desk and chair, before turning back and locating a small wooden door she had passed on her right. What could be in here?

The door creaks open, and there is James, leaning his back against a wooden barrel and holding a bottle aloft, inspecting its label. In his other hand, a small silver candle holder is hooked through his fingers, its light glowing softly and illuminating shadows on the wall.

"James?" Eliza asks. "What are you doing?"

"Snooping," he says, placing the bottle back on a shelf next to others like it and smiling at her in greeting. "As I see you are as well." He seems nonplussed that she has found him.

Eliza lets herself smile. "It is *quite* a kitchen."

"And pantry," James says, motioning her closer. "Look at what I discovered here."

"What's this room used for? Not a wine cellar?" she asks, stepping a few paces in the dark.

"I thought so, too, when I first entered, seeing these casks and bottles. But the Hadwens are Quakers, so no, not wine." James brings the candlestick close to the label on the replaced bottle. "Vinegar."

"Vinegar!" Eliza says. "This whole room?" She looks around with amazement. It isn't a large space, but it is filled to the brim with barrels on their sides and shelves of squat amber bottles.

"Italian. From a town called Modena."

"He must be importing it to sell," Eliza says.

"And it should be worth a great deal, knowing William Hadwen. He has a keen sense for investing," James says, not that Eliza needs to be reminded.

Eliza wrinkles her nose. "I don't particularly care for vinegar. Burns my throat." Instinctively, she touches her neck, and James's eyes travel with her gesture, to the bare skin there. He looks away, clears his throat, suggests they go back to the party, where dinner is being served.

The crashing sound of a large pot being dropped is followed by crude cursing and hearty apologies. The sounds remind Eliza that a world exists outside of this room. Time will march on no matter what she says or does, or doesn't say or doesn't do in this moment. A cook will or won't burn her hand on a hot pot handle, a servant will or won't trip on the corner of an Oriental rug upstairs, and lemonade will or won't go flying across the room, splashing onto someone's taffeta skirt. One guest will remark that the chicken is dry, while another will compliment the peppered potatoes.

Life will go on, and Eliza will pretend to fit in, and strive for acceptance, and do the best she can under the ever-changing circumstances of her wave-tossed existence.

But if she can stay in this dark room with James Crosby for one moment more, perhaps she can make sense of the life she chose, and the life he escaped into. She wants to be forthright suddenly, after so much time spent pretending.

"Did you mean what you said in the garden? About how that should have been us getting married?"

James places the candleholder down on a barrel between them and rubs the stubble on his chin. His eyes are suddenly sad, his expression tired. World-weary. "Yes."

"You say that like I should have known," Eliza says. "How could I possibly know?"

"How could you possibly *not* know?" James asks, crossing his arms. "After I asked your father for permission that day—"

"What day?" Eliza says, startled. "When?" A flood of questions fills her mind. "Permission to marry me?"

"Yes, Eliza! Don't act like you don't already know all of this," James says. "His response was hurtful enough to hear when it occurred, but now—to pretend you never knew—is, well, just cruel of you."

"But, James," Eliza says, stepping toward him

in the flickering light, "I did not know. My father never told me."

His face changes, his expression turning from anguish and anger to something softer, as the lines on his forehead uncrease and his eyes open wide. Understanding. "But then, why did you think I left so quickly the next day? Without saying goodbye?"

Eliza shakes her head, tries not to cry. But her tears sting as she talks. "I never knew—until this very moment. I just assumed you didn't care for me, that I had misread your signs. I assumed you wanted adventures, bigger and better things, and that you feared I would hold you back. Keep you from your dreams."

"But my dreams always included you, Eliza." James sighs. "I had a plan. The one I outlined in detail for your father, that day in July, just before the town fireworks. I thought we would marry and go to Boston. That you would join me and work in a milliner's shop while I was in college—I do know how much you like hats." He smiles here, for the first time since beginning this difficult conversation, and Eliza smiles, too, shakes her head.

"That I do," she acknowledges. Especially overly adorned felt hats with flower details, that can hide one's expression in a crowd, and that fly off one's head in a swift breeze.

"And, once I graduated, we'd be free to pursue

a full life together, with our children, I hoped, and go where opportunity knocked."

"But my father said no?" Eliza says, completing the tale.

"In so many words, yes," James adds. "His language was quite . . . colorful, if I recall."

"Oh, James," Eliza says, stepping close to him. "I'm so sorry. More sorry than you can imagine."

James looks as forlorn as she feels. "No, it is I who needs to apologize. I should have tried to contact you myself, explain in my own words. To gain some sort of understanding for both of us. All these years, my feelings for you felt unresolved."

"I would like very much to murder my father," Eliza says, her tone sardonic.

"And then I'll help you bury him," James says, also with irony. For what can be done of this situation twenty years past its time? Eliza laughs until she cries, gasping for breath in her dress's tight bodice.

"I would offer you my handkerchief, only I gave it to a beautiful woman at the ceremony," James says.

The handkerchief! Eliza pulls it free from her sleeve and pats her eyes dry. "Well," she says. "I hope this . . . conversation . . . helps you resolve your feelings for me once and for all."

"It does not," James stays, stepping so close to Eliza that she feels his breath in her ear. "It has stirred up old feelings, brought them to the surface."

Eliza is reminded of a shipwreck from when she was a girl. The winter of 1814, maybe, caught in a squall off the Cape and never heard from again. Until Eliza and her parents, picnicking at Smith Point the following summer, found the ship's debris lining the beach, including the wooden plaque with the name, *Anna*. It had become achingly real, proof that the ship had once lived.

"But we must keep them buried, these feelings of the past," she says, not believing one word, her heart thumping in her ears.

"I believed my fate is to always long for you, Eliza Cowan. To love you in the past, from afar. But now I think it's possible for us to have this moment—"

The words warm her body. Hearing him utter them after so long fills her like a fever, and her bones ache. She looks up at James in the darkness. "No games, remember," Eliza warns.

"No games," James says, touching her face. His eyes are filled with honesty and desire.

After twenty years of longing, Eliza leans in and kisses James Crosby.

His lips are tender and soft, his craving for her absolute. He wraps his arms around her and she clutches him, her mind everywhere and nowhere simultaneously.

The kiss is extraordinary. Deep and passionate

and *right,* as if they were meant to be doing this very thing together. It is one kiss, one moment, and yet also contains Eliza's entire life.

The only clear thought Eliza has? *This was well worth the wait.*

24

MEG

Up on the porch at Hadwen House, Meg feels self-conscious all over again. It's time to leave. The light outside is fading now and she wants to walk home while she can still see the path in front of her. Looking out over the backyard, she can just barely make out two figures in the dusk, leaning in close to one another. Lovers, perhaps. No, they are two women. One is Maria Mitchell, perhaps consoling the other? Or being consoled by the other? She can hear sobbing, and thinks the sound is one of heartbreak. Meg looks away.

Moving inside, Meg tries to navigate her way to the front door. She finds herself in the large living room, crowded with tables and chairs set up for the reception. She has to walk between many people, some standing and talking with fellow guests, others already seated for dinner. She spends several moments sandwiched between an ornate fireplace mantel and a tall potted plant with fanlike leaves while servers and diners move through the room. A path clears, and she can see the front door now. Meg frees herself and her belly from the tight corner.

"Excuse me," a guest says. "Can you please

clear this extra place setting? My husband won't be joining tonight after all."

After a moment, Meg realizes the woman is speaking directly to her, with a china plate, cup, and matching saucer extended out toward Meg's middle.

"Oh, um—" Meg begins, looking around for help from an actual servant before finally accepting the items.

"Thank you so very much," the woman says, turning back toward the others seated at her table and commenting to them. "Can you imagine! What kind of husband would let his wife work in that condition?"

Mistaken for a servant simply because of her skin color, and then shamed for being employed while pregnant? Cheeks aflame from the dual humiliation of those remarks, Meg ducks away from that table and bumps right into Amity Harris, the barber's daughter who is working at the wedding. Amity steadies a tray of glasses which shift slightly but don't fall. "Oh, thank goodness! Amity, can you take this for me?" Meg sighs. She must get out of here at once.

But Amity shakes her head and motions to the glassware in her hand. "Sorry, I can't presently. But if you head toward the back stairs there—" she says, pointing over her shoulder with her chin, "someone can take it down to the basement for you."

"The basement?" Meg wonders.

Amity raises her eyebrows dramatically and speaks with a fake upper-crust Boston accent. "Of course, dear! Because that's where the kitchen is located in this place!"

Amity passes by and leaves Meg laughing, albeit with bitter bile in her throat. She composes herself and tries to leave her anger behind. Fine, then: to the basement.

And there it is, a staircase going down into the cellar. How thoughtfully rich of them. Servants pass by on their way up, some Black and some white, all with arms laden with trays of food. Meg heads carefully down the stairs and into the incredible-looking and hectic kitchen. It is high-ceilinged and bright, a modern masterpiece underground.

Men and women bustle around her, some in aprons, some in crisp serving uniforms, and others, like her, in simple dress. She steps toward the giant center table, made of a slab of what looks like marble, and motions to put the plate down on the honed surface. "Don't crowd my workspace," a red-haired, red-faced woman says in a clipped tone. She shakes a wooden spoon at her. "Extra dishes go back there. And while you're at it, get me some more pepper!"

Meg doesn't like to be bossed around, particularly not by strangers who have misunderstood who she is and why she's there. She could explain, but what exactly would she say to this busy woman whose kitchen she has stumbled into? And when she looks around, Meg sees a mixture of people, reminiscent of what her own father experienced on a whaleship, representative of a different kind of equality, where everyone is hard at work and what matters most is how well you pull your weight.

Also, she is curious about Hadwen House; Edward Pompey wasn't wrong about that. Mistaken for a servant, she can explore rather freely. She may even return with pepper for that cook.

Meg walks through the kitchen and into a barrel-ceilinged, white-plastered hallway that is fantastically cool for July. To think about keeping a root vegetable cellar in a place like this! Meg pictures glass jars lined up, to can and can and can all of one's summer and fall harvests and store them like secret treasures.

Looking for a room housing china, she tries one door and then another. No such luck. Then she hears laughter coming from a room down the hall. Definitely a male's timbre, low and deep. Some servants, then, replenishing supplies for the party. Thinking this must be the right place, she opens the door and comes upon two people pressed against each other, locked in an embrace, kissing.

Meg drops the china, which splinters to pieces at her feet. She gasps and mutters an apology.

The startled couple separate, jumping apart at the sound of Meg's voice. In the flickering candlelight, the man's face is unfamiliar to her. But the woman—with a look of complete horror in her wide, brown eyes as she stares directly at Meg—is Mrs. Eliza Macy.

PART II

FLAMES

THE DAY OF THE FIRE
July 13, 1846

25

ELIZA

Two days have passed since she and James kissed, and still Eliza's mind and heart races with the memory of that feeling. That *whoosh*.

For the past forty-eight hours, Eliza has been trying to convince herself that she can forget the moment and let James go. After all, she let him go once before. But she didn't know then what she knows now: that he has always loved her. Another *whoosh*.

True, that run-in with nosy Meg Wright, who seems to appear wherever Eliza goes these days, even in the cellar of a mansion, may have changed things. After Meg discovered them in the pantry, Eliza felt the air shift between her and James. The passionate buzz in Eliza's mind was replaced by a realistic fear of getting caught with James in public, and worse, of a more sober understanding that what they were doing in the cellar was wrong.

Meg is a threat, yes, but who can she possibly tell about what she has seen? And would anyone believe her if she spoke such hateful gossip? Eliza tries to talk herself out of a growing panic. True, Meg is not at all in Eliza's social circle, but hasn't the woman shown at the town council meeting that she holds some power over this tight-knit island community? And she even heard a rumor that Meg was joining forces with Absalom Boston to sue the town!

Eliza is rattled. But then she thinks about what James whispered to her at the end of the wedding.

I am staying over my father's candle shop by the wharf before I depart from Nantucket on Tuesday. Come to me, he said.

Come to me. A clear declaration. James was pursuing Eliza, desiring her. She imagines more. She wants more of him, more time together. But, concerned about being discovered, she makes no future promises to visit.

And despite Eliza's worst fears, Meg has not shown up at her door, not sent a letter or made any move to reveal what she knows or blackmail Eliza in some way. Perhaps the danger has passed.

James's ship leaves tomorrow for New York and beyond. It is now or never for them.

What is it that she wants? To be loved, even briefly, by the only man who truly fills her mind and heart with desire. To give up control, stop second-guessing and worrying, stop looking over her shoulder to see who might be laughing behind her back. To not have to indulge in constant worry: how anyone and everyone on this tiny island might view her actions or judge her choices. She wants something perfectly selfish and self-serving, the will to drown herself completely.

As fate would have it, Alice sends Eliza an invitation to dine with her and Larson that evening. Eliza feigns illness and takes to her bed, urging her daughters to go along without her. In fact, since there is no school they should leave soon and pick some flowers at the edge of town to bring as a gift. Take the long way, it's a nice long walk, amble, get some air. They should arrive early to Alice's, and help their dear sister with meal preparations. And they should stay as late as they want, play cards into the night after they dine.

Eliza coughs. Walks slowly up the stairs. Rachel and Mattie, with concerned eyes, wish her well as they gather their bonnets and depart. (Truth is, after days of personal deliberations, now that Eliza has crossed this bridge of decisions, she certainly is a bit nauseous! Another cup of tea with laudanum helps. Only a few drops this time. Eliza sees that, like everything else, she is running low on medicinal supplies, too.)

She waits until almost sunset.

Eliza dons the same pale-blue dress she wore to the wedding and dabs the same rosehip perfume behind her ears. Everything must be as it was when she and James last kissed. She pauses in the front hall and gives herself a long look in the gilded mirror, assessing, testing to see if her reflection will talk her out of any action. But the two women are aligned—she and herself—and they go out into the still, dark night.

The harbor, which by day is a hive of activity, is cloaked in mystery by dusk. The water is a sheet of ink; no wind ruffles it, no boats disrupt the calm facade. The air is heavy with silence instead of voices calling orders to and fro. Gossip thrives on the streets of downtown, but secrets can drown in this harbor.

A slight mist blankets the docks, and Eliza disappears right into it.

At the top of Commercial Wharf, the large wooden door to M. Crosby and Sons candle factory is unlocked. Eliza enters and calls out a tentative hello. The smell of wax and oil hangs in the air pleasantly, like warm milk. A sliver of sinking sun through a large glass window outlines shapes within the manufactory, from barrels of oil yet to be processed to several long wooden workstations. Her eye is drawn to the impressive, two-story lever-press in the center of the space.

"Hello?" Eliza calls again, her voice echoing around the cavernous room as she wanders through. There is a staircase in the back right corner, thin boards cobbled together somewhat precariously. Eliza takes hold of the rickety banister and climbs.

On the landing high above, there is more light. The flickering of a candle under the sloped eaves of the roofline shows exposed beams, like the underbelly of a ship. A chair sits in the corner with a jacket slung over it, and a makeshift bed lies on the floor.

What Eliza thought was the glow of one candle is actually many. They circle the room and flicker softly. *So much waste,* she thinks, as a mother who must conserve every candle her family has left. *So much danger,* she thinks, as a woman who has survived two Great Fires on this little island. *So much beauty,* she thinks, as a woman enchanted by an alluring man.

James lifts his head from a small desk, sees her, smiles. The smile is slow, spreading from his lips to his eyes in delight and knowing. That smile is confident, and, while James acts surprised, Eliza wonders if he really is. He puts down a fountain pen and runs a hand through his soft blond hair, which curls at the nape of his neck, brushing above his shoulders.

"You came," he says.

"I did," she replies.

James leans back in his chair and studies her. Like at the wedding reception, as if gazing has its own nuanced language of words. His legs stretch out straight and cross at the ankles, his hands rest upon his chest. Eliza tries not to fidget and allows herself to be seen. She stares back.

James's sea-blue eyes are merry with a hint of mischief.

She steps toward him as he rises from his seat.

They meet in the center of the room, their bodies touching, their lips connecting. They kiss. The room spins. Time drops away, and the only thing real to her is James and this moment. Only the now matters.

And yet, time is elastic as they kiss, time stretches and bends.

Eliza is the girl who fell in love with James twenty years ago without ever touching him, the innocent girl filled with hope and promise. She is also wife to a man she never sees, a mother who knows that life is comprised of disappointments, disillusionments, and struggle. This Eliza knows loneliness. She knows want and desire.

And she understands now what she did not at eighteen: that it isn't a sin to want. It is, in fact, wonderfully human to have those yearnings, to desire things and people. To go after something with a fierce hunger. Money, loyalty, friendship, love. Touch.

They break apart. James steps toward the pallet on the floor and reaches out his hand. Eliza takes it.

26

MEG

Monday night is a true celebration in the Wright house, for earlier in the day, Meg and Absalom Boston successfully filed their lawsuits at town hall.

Meg and Benjamin's home is filled with people and food. Their neighbors have come to revel in the joy and strength of the simple act of signing one's name on a line next to a declaration that states you have been wronged and intend to hold the town responsible. And, like those reparations hopefully piling up next to one another, the bounty of edible treats has piled up on Meg's kitchen table, and the crowd of people is just as dense. Meg notices that Faithful hasn't come by, and hopes that her friend's arthritis isn't acting up.

"I would excuse myself to the porch," Meg says to Benjamin, balancing a plate of summer squash and roasted chicken on his arm, "but there are so many people out there right now, I'm afraid it would collapse under my added weight." Candles and lanterns flicker through the window. Absalom is out there with Pompey, Harris the barber, and several men and women from the Baptist church choir.

Benjamin laughs good-naturedly and then asks a friend to vacate his seat for his very pregnant wife. Her bed-rest orders have all but been forgotten with the excitement of the past few days. Meg decides to celebrate with her favorite dessert, a mixed berry pie made by her midwife, Jane.

As dusk settles in, people are starting to head for home. Absalom invites a few people to his tavern for a nightcap and Meg can hear their voices carry through the sleepy streets. Benjamin locates some matches and lights a few more candles around the room, including one on a wall sconce by Meg. He helps light the lanterns people have brought to travel home with. Then he hands a lit candle to Lucy and tells her to light the hurricane lamp in the parlor and the lanterns on the front and back porches.

"Tell me about it again," Benjamin says, leaning against the butcher-block counter in the kitchen. Benjamin had to work in the shop, so Absalom accompanied her to town hall. He picked her up in his horse-drawn calash and off they went.

"I've already told you three times," Meg says, and smiles. "You're worse than Lucy with a bed-time story."

"One more will do just fine, then," Benjamin says. "I can't get enough of good news."

And so Meg retells the story of the day one

more time. Several stragglers hear Meg speaking and gather around.

Meg looks from her husband's face to Lucy's and to some of the others', loving the way their eyes glow in the candlelight with emotion. When she gets to the part where the town clerk stood and shook her hand, people whoop and cheer.

At around ten o'clock, after most of the revelers have gone and she's cleaning up the kitchen, Meg thinks about Saturday at the wedding, where she shared plans of the lawsuit, but also saw a glimpse of the underbelly of Nantucket's wealthiest at their worst, from being treated as a servant to witnessing Eliza Macy's embrace with another man. Candle nubs flicker around her as she uses the dull edge of a knife to clean off the melted wax from the wooden table and the brass candlesticks. Benjamin hums softly to himself. He has put Lucy to sleep, and fetched clean water at the pump at the end of the street. It sits in a bucket at their feet. The room is still and peaceful, content.

Meg told Benjamin on Saturday about the prejudice she experienced at Hadwen House, and as she relayed and relived it, he listened with hurt and anger in his eyes. But ultimately they agreed that it helped fuel their action, their need for change. Each and every act of bigotry—no matter how small it might seem—adds up to more proof that they must seek justice for their daughter.

But now Meg wonders about the other bit of news from that night. Should she tell her husband about what she accidentally witnessed in the basement?

For the past two days, she's been carrying that secret around along with the plan to file suit with the town, wondering what to make of it. The legal action has been handled today, filed through the proper political channel. But Eliza Macy's secret? That's something else entirely. It's something Meg knows she could use, should she ever need to. That story—should it get out— is political, too, albeit in a different, but equally powerful way.

But is she that kind of person? To fashion a weapon from a person's secret transgressions and use it against them? Has Eliza Macy turned Meg into the sort of person who thinks this way, with venomous strategy?

"Ouch!" Meg says, pulling her hand from some hot wax that dripped on her thumb.

"Here," Benjamin says, reaching for a salve they keep in the kitchen for burns, and applying it to her finger. "Better?"

"Yes." And what would Meg say to Benjamin? That she saw Eliza Macy kissing another man? Although she and Benjamin have an intimate relationship, she's never actually spoken to him about such things.

To think that Eliza Macy of all people would commit adultery. She acts so high-and-mighty with her bold opinions. Quite wrong, and quite bold. Eliza Macy's tryst at the wedding actually falls right in line with the rest of her misdeeds. She's a terrible neighbor, a bigoted human being, and now also a cuckolding wife.

Has Eliza done this before? Does she know this man intimately? The idea is both shocking and exciting to Meg, who would never dream of behaving that way. That's only something a person with nothing to lose would do.

Meg reflects back on what Faithful told her about Henry Macy and is doubly angry at Eliza Macy. Eliza is rich thanks to Henry Macy, and taken care of. Certainly, it must be difficult to keep one's marriage afloat when one partner is most always away at sea. Meg sees this with Faithful and Big Daniel. But they make it work, don't they? You don't see Faithful running around consorting with other men, do you? The thought almost makes Meg laugh out loud. Faithful: that's who Meg wishes were here right now. That's who she could tell this secret to.

"Meg? Is something bothering you?" Benjamin asks. "You seem miles away." The final candle in the room goes out, and Benjamin finds a match, strikes it, and relights it.

Meg turns to her husband, the words on the tip of her tongue.

Maybe all it takes is to say it, to light that match and let the words glow, to spark it like a flame and shine it into the world. But for now, she takes him by the hand and leads him to bed.

27

ELIZA

Eliza cannot believe the moment is here, that she is here with James, kissing him, embracing him. She feels the muscles in his arms as he takes off his shirt, runs her hands over the smooth expanse of his back. He bends his head and kisses the soft flesh at the base of her low neckline, in the dip between her breasts. She's never been kissed there before, and her body thuds with desire.

James lowers her to the bed, soft with down feathers. Unbuckles his belt as she snakes off her undergarments and raises her skirts. She pulls him on top of her and he is inside her quickly. Eliza is filled by him, wraps her legs around his torso and pulls him closer. Her whole body is lit with sensation, and her blood pumps from her toes to her throat. That wave fills her mind and replaces thought. She holds on tighter. The sensation settles, focusing on a spot deep inside her, and she calls out sounds that are not words, exactly, although they convey every feeling she has. Desire, regret, and humility that an energy so big and great exists in this world.

And then loss.

For what Eliza had imagined for so long is actually here.

And soon it will be over.

But not yet, not quite now. First they hold each other, and James whispers into her hair. They undress fully, touching each other's bodies while the candles burn down around them and the moon rises, and make love again. Slowly and deliberately this time. Eliza cries.

"Stay the night," James says. His eyes have turned from Caribbean Sea turquoise to Nantucket harbor blue.

Oh, how she wants to. It has been almost four years since she has slept in a bed with a man beside her, years since the warmth of another human being has kept her company. And the last time Henry was home, in the spring of 1842, he had been on Nantucket only for one month, and distracted by planning his next trip out.

When Alice, Rachel, and Mattie were small, they used to pile into her bed and nestle around Eliza like a litter of pups, and their little breathing noises and heartbeats kept some of the loneliness at bay. But that, she now sees, is no replacement for a man. Nothing is, especially not the ivory phallus that Henry gifted Eliza all those years ago.

Henry was hoping that Eliza would not stray, hoping that by giving her a piece of a man she would not miss the whole of him. But he underestimated the aliveness of his wife. And he did not know her secret: that part of her heart has always been chasing another man.

Eliza has broken every vow she ever made to Henry and their children. As she lies beside James, she waits to feel remorse.

"Stay the night," James repeats. "And see me off in the morning."

"I can't stay," Eliza says. From town, they hear the distant chimes of the church bells ringing the hour: ten o'clock at night.

"Because of the children?" James asks.

Of course she must be home to greet them when they return from Alice's. But it is not that, or not solely that. Eliza is always being left behind, first by James all those years ago, next by Henry—time and again by Henry!—and then by Alice. Over the next year or so, both Rachel and Mattie will find suitable matches, and they, too, shall leave Eliza behind. So when James's schooner pulls out from the harbor at dawn, Eliza cannot be there, waving from the shoreline, waiting on the pier.

She must be the one to leave him behind.

And so she kisses him and kisses him and kisses him farewell.

Then she rises, dresses, and walks home.

It is the same route she takes home whenever she brings a letter to the docks for Henry. Most recently, a week ago. One week and a lifetime ago, and still no further word from him. Anger rises in her—how dare he leave her and the children for so long without reasonable explanation and under such financial stress? Especially knowing their precarious financial situation! And then, to feel as if the whole town is talking about her husband behind Eliza's back. He left Eliza lonely and vulnerable, which is precisely why she ran into the warm protection of another man's arms.

Eliza wonders, not for the first time, whether Henry has been unfaithful, and what form that dalliance might have taken: a cosmopolitan woman in a faraway port, the mirror image of herself? An exotic beauty, the inverse of Eliza, from somewhere in the Pacific? Or—Lord help her for thinking it, but she knows some sailors do this very thing out of desperation or desire—lying with another man?

She used to think those were silly fears, unfounded and imaginary, like a child believing in monsters or ghosts. But now, after what she herself has done tonight, she acknowledges that it is possible—probable, even—that Henry has taken a lover.

But what good does it do to think of such a betrayal? She must live within the boundaries of the known world, or she will go mad. She is only inviting these terrible thoughts in order to even the score between them.

Henry's hastily penned letter comes back to her now: *My love, I am sorry to say that I am not yet able to return home to Nantucket this summer. There is still something I must do. Send love to the children and be strong for me.*

Be strong! These words from a week ago are almost comical, for Eliza has been weak—*weak in the knees,* as her mother used to say about what love felt like—weakened by the strength of passion between her and James.

Eliza glances at the harbor on her right, where the full moon casts silver reflections on the water, and wonders, *Henry, where are you and what are you doing there? When will you return to me? And, when you do, will you sense the distance created between us by this summer's deceit?*

Eliza reaches the heart of town, where the Straight Wharf ends and Main Street begins. It is getting close to eleven at night; she should pick up her pace, as the girls said they'd be home before midnight. The whale oil from two weeks ago must have been shipped out by now, and yet here lie thousands of tons more. Wooden casks made by local coopers line the docks.

Round-bellied and jolly, Eliza has always thought of those barrels. They are repositories for her hopes and dreams, the continued sale of them ensuring her content life. She taps one in a friendly hello as she passes, careful not to disturb these rows of sleeping liquid gold.

The rope walks and sail lofts, haylofts and taverns are shuttered for the night. Eliza heads up Main Street and toward home.

The charred scent is faint at first, a hint of smoke tickling her nostrils, as if from a remembered bonfire. A memory of a smell more than the thing itself.

But as she passes the corner of Union Street, the smell gains weight. It takes shape and dimension. Yes. It is real. *Fire.* Her brain dares to name it. But where? From someone's potbellied stove, or an open-fire pit with a chicken on a spit? No. It is too dangerous to cook over flames in such a hot, dry landscape. Illegal. A town of tinder! Until it rains, Nantucketers have been told in no uncertain terms to keep their fire usage to a minimum. They do not want a repeat performance of the Great Fire of 1836, or, worse, the catastrophic one from '38.

"Hey! Missus!" a voice calls from the dark. A man is standing in front of Kelly's jewelry store, waving his arms. A sailor in striped linen pants and a short, navy jacket with tarnished brass buttons. His voice has an unfamiliar lilt to it— Irish? English? Somewhere overseas. Eliza looks around for others, but finds only him.

She quickens her steps and joins him, peering in the window. The jewels and watches that usually sit on plush velvet displays are removed at night for safekeeping; the window is bare. No signs of distress; there is only darkness inside the shop.

"Smell that?" he asks, his eyes black marbles. Whiskey lingers on his stale breath, and she thinks, *yes,* for it would be hard to miss such a fetid odor. And then she realizes that he means the scent of smoke.

"I do," she says. "But the shop looks unharmed?"

"There!" he says, pointing toward white mist escaping under the door frame and around the cracks in the storefront windows.

Before Eliza can think of what to do next, the sailor turns himself sideways and uses the force of his body to knock down the door. "Get water!" he calls before disappearing inside the shop.

Eliza dashes to the nearest cistern on Main Street—there's one half a block away—fills two tin pails left for the public's use, and runs back to Kelly's store, sloshing liquid as she goes. Once inside, Eliza sees no flames, feels no heat. The white mist has exited onto the street, although a sulfurous odor lingers. She worries that this is some sort of ruse to rob the jewelry store, and that she's been fooled into assisting a vagabond. Indeed, the sailor is acting strangely; he has his hand pressed against the wall between the jewelry store and Geary's hat shop.

"Warm to the touch," he says. He presses his cheek and ear to the wall, listening as well as sensing by touch.

Eliza reaches out a hand and tentatively places her palm flat against the plaster. Heat radiates out and she pulls her hand away. "It's on the other side."

"We can douse the wall here with water," the sailor says. "Cool it down."

Eliza isn't certain that this strategy will work, but also isn't able to articulate any kind of counterargument. She has but a second to think. She nods her head in agreement.

Eliza hands a pail of water to the stranger and takes hold of the other. "And a one, and a two, and a three!" the man calls.

They throw the water, which hits the surface, and the wall of horsehair plaster in front of them melts away. Just disappears. Revealing another wall.

And this wall is made of flames.

28

ELIZA

Can fire scream? Eliza wonders, an empty pail hanging limply from her hand as she stares at a wall that is not there any longer, as she stares into the dancing, lapping beast of flames before her.

Can fire cry?

Something is creating noise, a primal sound. But where is it coming from? Is it from inside her, or the sailor beside her, or is it emanating directly from the wall of flames?

The sailor drops his metal pail—a clanging echo—and pushes Eliza out onto the street. "Fire!" he calls, head raised skyward as if invoking the gods. "Fire on Main!"

He grabs Eliza's elbow and runs with her past the brick sidewalk, until they are standing on the cobblestones in the middle of deserted Main Street. Glass windows explode outward from the heat and pressure of flames, the shards loud and tinny, like cymbals.

Eliza crouches into a ball, protecting her face with her hands, her body turned away from the storefronts. Her eyes are shut tight, but she can sense the sailor beside her, breathing raggedly, also low to the ground. The blast is followed by silence, and then an ominous sound, of fire catching and spreading. Ferocious heat radiates out into the street.

"Fire!" Eliza says, her voice brittle and unsure. "Fire!" she says again, standing and backing away. She repeats the word a few more times with purpose and volume, chin raised to sky. The sailor echoes her pleas.

This part of Main Street is made up almost entirely of commercial space, the businesses closed at night, and so at first, no one hears them. Eliza runs up a block to Orange Street and instructs the sailor to head down Union Street, to alert people on these side streets directly off Main, where clapboard-and-shingled homes with cedar-shake roofs line up side by side by side.

The sailor waves as he goes. It is the last time Eliza ever sees him.

Sweet relief: the night watchman sounds the alarm from his perch over the town, ringing the church bell as he calls out, "Fire! Fire on Main Street!"

The engine corps will arrive in minutes, which means this disaster is no longer Eliza's responsibility. She needs to get home to check on her children. But something nags at Eliza, a knot in a neat row of embroidery, like a mistake caused by her own hand.

She didn't start the fire, no. But did she and the sailor accelerate the force of it by bringing down that wall?

Or worse: Did her lovemaking with James somehow bring disaster to her beloved town, in some sort of cataclysmic, divine fate?

No. Sheer craziness, fire and brimstone the likes of which Eliza never believed. Sexual relations with a man who is not your husband does not automatically bring doom to your doorstep! She's not thinking straight.

Speaking of bringing doom to your doorstep, Eliza glances across Main Street and sees the new cobbler shop in her periphery. All that fighting and wasted breath over this storefront, which, because of its prominent spot in the middle of town, faces critical danger.

29

MARIA

"Fire!" A voice calls to Maria in her dreams. She tosses and turns in her bed, pushing away the handmade quilt with her feet. After work at the Atheneum, during which she sulked and tried not to cry about Linley's arrangement of marriage to Charlie Warren, Maria found herself needing a few hours of sleep after dinner. She planned on waking at midnight to head to the roof for her nightly stargazing and calculations. Without Linley.

But it can't yet be the midnight hour, can it? And why would Father wake her by calling *Fire*, of all things? No—it must be a ferocious nightmare. Maria sinks back into slumber: just one more moment. A second more. Her limbs grow heavy against the mattress.

Maria's inner eye pictures a comet sailing through the night sky, a falling star, an explosion of meteors in an astronomical shower, louder and more dynamic than the fireworks from the Fourth of July. Linley's blue eyes reflect the dancing light as sparks rain down on Nantucket town.

"Fire!" There it is again. This sound is not from Father, nor from her unconscious. It is coming from outside. She bolts upright in bed, steps toward the window. A single, eerie voice echoes through the darkness and sounds the alarm: "Fire! Fire on Main Street!" The call is close; it must be coming from the lookout post on Orange Street, from the tower atop the Unitarian church, one block from her home. Her bedroom faces south, so while she can peek down Fair Street and see the shops and homes that line the top of Main Street, she cannot see any further. Nothing from her limited line of vision in the black of night seems abnormal at all. George Riddell's Dry Goods Shop on the corner of Orange and Main is undisturbed, the windows of Eliza Macy's house dark.

Perhaps it is a false alarm.

Nonetheless, Maria walks the short hallway of her home, knocking on doors, making sure that everyone is awake.

"What in the world?" Harry calls out from behind his door.

"Get up, Harry! Now!" Maria says.

At once he is at the door, his brown eyes round and excited, hair on end. "Did you do it? Did you discover a comet?"

"Maria discovered a comet!" Phebe shouts, opening the door next to Harry's. She jumps up and down on the bed to wake her younger sister. "Kate! She's famous! Famous famous famous! She won the prize!" The bedsprings creak and squeak as Kate is tossed to and fro, finally gaining enough purchase to yank Phebe by the hair. "Ow! The King of Denmark will come to visit!"

"Girls! Enough!" Lydia says, coming up behind Maria and adjusting a robe around her night-dress for modesty. Kate and Phebe go instantly quiet.

Maria sighs, taking in the heap of her sisters, hating to share this most un-celebratory news with them. "I did not discover any such thing! There's a fire in town. The alarm was sounded a minute ago."

An electric charge fills the air the moment she utters the words. Silently, the Mitchells form a single line and scoot to the front hall. Their father is there, already waiting, already watching.

He turns to look at them, his expression grave.

He makes no sound, but gestures with a wave of his hand for them to join him. Kate tucks under one of their father's arms, and Phebe takes the other side. Their mother places her hand atop Kate's shoulders from behind. Harry takes Maria's hand.

And together, they look down and toward the right and watch as several buildings along the south side of Main Street burn bright, the flames orange against the black sky.

"Just up from Union Street. Kelly's jewelry store, looks like," Maria's father says. "And the hat shop, too."

There are two figures on the street below, buckets in their hands.

Maria wonders what to do; should she run into the street to try and help those two? Douse the flames with water? Or sand, like they do for a chimney fire?

"May we protect one another this night, and every night after," Lydia says, addressing her family. "And may the inner light of our people help heal any damage done."

"Amen," William says, and the others echo their amen, including nonreligious Maria.

"Here come the firemen!" Phebe declares.

Although the Mitchells cannot make out the names on each fire cart, they see two distinct companies arrive simultaneously from two different directions, bells clanging atop their carts. One neat line of firemen marches down Main Street from the west, and another turns from Union Street in the south, each parade punctuated by the hand-pulled fire carts at the rear of the procession. The entire Mitchell clan breathes a sigh of relief.

"We are safe here," Lydia says, mostly to Kate, the youngest. "The brick should not catch fire." She glances meaningfully at William and Maria, conveying with her dark stare her greatest fears to them without uttering a word.

For while the Pacific Bank is not in imminent danger, the Atheneum most certainly is.

Maria excuses herself from the front hall and changes quickly into her brown summer dress, her fingers fumbling with the buttons at the back, her hands shaking. "Oh, drat!" she curses. In the end, she asks her mother to fasten them for her, as she buttons up her shoes.

"Don't forget your bonnet!" Lydia yells as Maria dashes down the stairs to the first floor of the home, past the sleeping kitchen and out into the narrow hallway, where she grabs her black silk-and-lace bonnet from the coatrack, pulls it down over her dark pin curls, and flies down the final set of stairs.

The humid air is singed with scent. Maria covers her mouth and nose with the crook of her arm as she pauses for a moment to watch the scene unfolding on lower Main. The firemen have arrived and voices are raised as men shout orders, their tone edged with panic. Do they need help? But there is no time to investigate: her priority is the Atheneum and the contents inside. She worries quickly about Linley, but the Blake home in town is well to the north of this fire, beyond the reach of these flames. Besides, Linley is Charlie's worry now, not Maria's— an acknowledgment that singes her heart, but she must stay focused on the Atheneum. Maria hastily ties her bonnet strings and crosses in front of the Pacific Bank.

To think that her mother still manages to be

ever-mindful about modesty at a time like this! *Well,* Maria thinks, walking briskly past the Methodist church, *at least she is always true to who she is, my mother.* Maria wouldn't put it past Lydia to try to introduce Maria to a handsome young bachelor fireman, should one show up at their door tonight.

Several people are gathered on the steps of the Methodist church, men and women both, their eyes fixed on the spot where Geary's hat store used to stand. As Maria crosses on to Center Street, she shakes her head at them. *Don't just stand there, do something!* she thinks. Are they just going to watch their beloved town burn down?

Maria turns toward a commotion. The bright blaze of fire highlights the crowd of firemen and the two fire engines on site.

And is that—no, it can't possibly be—Eliza Macy. Wearing the same dress from Saturday's wedding night? On this Monday eve, just before midnight? And is she . . . yelling at a fireman?

Maria squints. Makes out the light blue shimmering silk fabric. The brown hair, loose and manic. Yes, it most certainly is Eliza Macy.

She calls out Eliza's name. Several onlookers turn toward Maria, but Eliza cannot hear her over the distance and shouting, the sizzle and roar of the flames. Eliza seems to get swallowed up by the growing crowd, and Maria gives up. Why is this woman out on Main Street in the heart of the town's fire?

Nantucket's women are independent and self-sufficient creatures. Maria isn't sure there is a way to reach her, either physically in this moment, or metaphorically ever. Instead, she heads toward the Atheneum, standing several blocks behind the north side of Main Street, its white columned facade blessedly undisturbed. She pulls the key from her dress pocket and opens the door.

A familiar smell welcomes her in the darkness: books. Newspapers. Maps. The warm odor of old wooden pews, from when this building was a church, those seats now used for the educational lectures that have made this space holy in a powerful new way.

Tonight it smells exactly like kindling.

Thousands of volumes, many of them rare. Collectibles of curiosities gathered from two hundred years spent spanning the globe in ships, archived and displayed here in a way not seen elsewhere in the world. Instead of filling her with her usual sense of pride, the vulnerability of these items floods her with fear as she glances around the first-floor museum and thinks about the library upstairs. So many *things*. So many items and objects to get to safety. How can she possibly move them all? And how to prioritize which to handle first?

Monday's newspaper sits where she left it at

the end of the day, still waiting to be filed away.

"Miss Mitchell!" a voice calls out. And another, "Miss Maria Mitchell!"

Two men remove their stovepipe hats as they enter, bowing slightly at her in greeting. Both are out of breath, their brows slick with perspiration. One is a young man she recognizes from town; he works as a postmaster. Daniel Hayes. The other is David Joy, co-founder of the Atheneum.

"Maria," David Joy says, stopping for air. He must have run all the way from his home at the edge of town. "We must remove everything from the interior that we can, furniture and museum objects included."

He shares what news he has of the trajectory of the fire, of wind direction and containment efforts on Main. Since the flames are south, they decide to head north.

"Should we start with this?" Daniel asks, pointing to the wooden bureau by the door.

"Yes," Maria says, and the men nod in agreement, positioning their hats back on their heads and moving on either side to lift the piece of furniture.

"Careful down the steps," Maria says, an understatement if ever there was one. But there's no time for her usual history lesson as David Joy and Daniel Hayes carry the oldest surviving piece of furniture from one of Nantucket's original twenty settlers bouncing out into the night.

30

ELIZA

Engine 6, the Cataract, and Engine 8, the Fountain, arrive on Main Street at the same moment. Before going home to check on her daughters, Eliza decides to quickly tell these men about the origins of the flames. Eliza follows the brigade to the middle of Main Street.

"Sir!" she calls to the man before her who appears to be in charge of the Cataract, shouting directions as he unwinds the hose from the side of the cart.

"Hook this up to the cistern in front of the Customs House!" the man yells, and off a fireman goes with the hose. "The rest of you, ready the cart, position it just so and prepare to pump!"

"Sir!" Eliza tries again, but the night is loud as the fire crackles and booms.

The flames have now spread from their original position and engulfed Washington Hall. The crowd roars around her. So many firemen, suddenly. So much heat.

"This is no place for you, ma'am!" the captain of the Cataract engine yells, the fire reflected in his eyes as he stares at her. "You're getting in danger's way here and you're hindering my men from their work!"

The fireman charged with hooking up the hose is back, and Eliza steps aside to let him pass.

"Captain," he pants, the hose limp in his hands. "It won't reach."

"Try the other cistern then, up by the Pacific Bank," the captain orders.

"We're positioned too far from that one, too," the young man says. "We'll have to join with the Fountain. Connect the hoses."

"Not a chance," the captain says.

The Fountain! Perhaps Eliza can get a word in with the captain of that engine corps. She wants to let him know that she was on site when the flames began, that it spread from the hat shop to the jewelry store when she and the sailor accidentally took down the wall with water. She waves to get his attention. "Sir, I was here when the fire begun and I "

But he lightly pushes her hand away and continues walking on toward the other captain. "Let me get this fire under control!" he demands.

"You?" the Cataract captain says. "It's *our* blaze."

"I beg to differ, because we have hooked our hose up to a cistern and you've got nothing. Have your men connect your pipe to ours and we're ready to go."

"And what? Let you take all the glory?" the fireman with the hose says, dropping the tube at his feet and raising his fists.

"Hey!" a fireman from the Fountain engine corps calls, sensing the rising anger, smelling a fight. He's tall, well over six feet, and he walks right up to the other fireman. "Cataract, connect the hose to ours already! You want this town to burn?"

"No, but it seems like you do," the Cataract says. "You vain men from the district by Upper Main Street, I've heard you talk at meetings, bossing the other companies around. You think you own the whole town because your jurisdiction includes the Hadwens and Starbucks and all the fancy rest of 'em? Well, tonight we were here first, which is the rule: first on scene gets the fire. So move aside and let—"

The end of that sentence is knocked right out of him by a blow to the nose. The fireman's head snaps back, eyes bulging in surprise. But the man bounces back quickly and manages to land a solid punch in the gut of the Fountain fireman in front of him.

A heap of men pile on one another as Eliza removes herself from the fray. More men attack each other, raw anger and bloodlust and base animal instincts fueling punch after blow as the fire gains strength around them.

What is she doing out here, among these violent men? She tries to move up the street, but a tide of onlookers pushes her further down Main Street toward Union Street and the harbor, where she

306

watches, incensed, from the eastern side of town.

Idiots! Like little boys fighting over the last molasses cookie.

She will never understand men.

"Sirs! We must attack the flames, not one another!" the captain of the Fountain says, as another building ignites. Within a minute or two, the firemen exhaust themselves, settle down, and get to work. The hoses are connected, and an unenthusiastic stream of water attempts to douse the ever-growing flames. A weak cheer goes up from the surrounding crowd.

Applause! For finally the men have stopped being fools! Hooray!

Precious time has been lost. Although, if the fire can stay contained where it is, the men—and the town—still stand a fighting chance. More engine companies arrive and pack themselves onto an already crowded Main Street. Nantucketers are scrappy and fierce; if they can slay a 100,000-pound sea mammal, Eliza believes they can slay this beast, too.

A new shout comes from her left, past Union and over toward Washington Street. "Fire!"

The crowd on lower Main reacts around her: *Did you hear that? Is it what I think? An ember must've jumped!* And then, a verification, the call from the east: "Fire! Hamblin's hayloft is on fire!"

Hamblin's hayloft? But Hamblin's hayloft is on

307

Washington Street, not far from M. Crosby and Sons' candle factory. Not far from James.

The hayloft will go up in seconds: it almost doesn't make sense to send firemen in that direction, but go they do, Engine number 5 heading toward what can only be pure destruction.

A growing sense of dread pulses through Eliza's body. She must get home at once, up Main Street. No! She must check on James, down Main. And then what? Bring him to her home? She couldn't possibly. And what if, during the time she dashes to the harbor, the fire spreads westward and toward her precious children, her precious home?

Eliza must do something, anything. Make a decision and go. Control the panic building inside her. She pushes herself through the onslaught of bodies and frees herself from the pack. Glancing toward the harbor, Eliza says a prayer, makes a wish. For that is all she can offer him right now: she has left James, and that is a decision she will stand by. Her children are her priority.

The fire wardens from each engine company form a small circle in front of the cobbler's new shop, clustered together away from their men. Heads bent, deriving a plan. A plan! Eliza has a plan: put out the fires! Stop talking and get to work, men!

As Eliza passes the fire brigade at the corner of Federal Street, she's reminded now of the way Main Street is always the place for such dramas to play out, the central stage of Nantucketers' lives. *Only this is not a farce, gentlemen,* she feels like yelling. *And your costumes this evening are not merely for show.*

"Gunpowder," one warden says. And another voice, "Yes. Like we did in '38. Explosives are the only way through this." The captain of the Cataract looks up and meets Eliza's eye as she passes. She feels a jolt of worry, as if someone was just talking about her.

31

MEG

Their argument is quick and awful.

Word travels through New Guinea that Main Street is on fire. One man on horseback delivers the news, and another comes by a few minutes later with a horse-drawn calash to collect volunteers and ferry them to the town center.

Benjamin locates the long black coat he uses as a fireman's jacket in the cedar chest, shakes out the years of wrinkles, and puts it on. Although the Black fire brigade overseeing New Guinea is as organized and official as the white corps in theory, in practice they are not given matching uniforms, nor paid monthly by the town for their services like the white men are. They look like a ragtag crew when assembled, which is why, after the Great Fire of 1838, Benjamin had Meg fashion him a coat resembling the ones worn by the white men, as well as a matching helmet. The jacket won't offer much in the way of fire protection, but it will provide Benjamin with an important emotional armor nonetheless.

Of course Benjamin should head to town tonight, Meg argues, but not as a fireman. As an owner of a new shop on Main Street, as a businessman. He should do everything he can to protect their livelihood, their property.

"But Nantucket town is our livelihood," Benjamin counterargues. "Without a Main Street, without a bustling town center, we are nothing." Meg is being selfish, he says. This fire is about things bigger than themselves.

"I understand very well this notion about things bigger than myself," Meg counters. "Do you think I went to town hall today and filed paperwork for legal action to stop segregation of the schools *just for myself?*"

But Benjamin seems not to hear Meg's protests as he stomps around the house, moving from kitchen to bedroom to parlor, readying himself for action. So she tries another tactic, then, a more emotional plea. *It's too dangerous. We need you here. I need you here. Our coming baby needs you here.* But her words are puffs of smoke.

"Mama, what's wrong?" Lucy says, rubbing her eyes and peering in from her bedroom. Lucy is a deep sleeper and has been since birth. Nothing ever stirs that child before dawn, but now here she is, awake and curious just before midnight.

Seeing her father dressed as he is, Lucy pulls her mouth into a tight line. "Another fire?" she whispers. She wasn't yet born for the last fire, but she's heard the tale so many times.

Eight summers ago, Benjamin raced off into the night—a hot one, just like this—and didn't return. Meg had been pregnant then, too. The difference was that Meg's father was alive and well, living with them in this house. After many hours without word of Benjamin's whereabouts, Wendell Lewis had gone searching in town at dawn, searching through shelled-out, still-smoldering buildings for any sign of life, eventually finding Benjamin in a makeshift infirmary in the back of Doc Ruggles's home office on Orange Street. And then he had fetched Meg.

The doctor shared what he knew with Meg, while standing over Benjamin's sleeping form, unconscious from morphine. While battling the blaze in Joseph James's rope walk, a beam had come crashing down, pinning Benjamin underneath. Other firemen quickly freed him, but he had sustained second-degree burns along his torso, and his leg had been broken in three places.

"It was weeks before you could work again, and months before you could walk!" Meg yells. Now that Lucy is awake, there is no sense in Meg keeping her voice down, and raising it feels good besides.

Benjamin sinks down into his particular dining chair, the one that faces the kitchen, and thus, Meg. His warm hazel eyes look sorrowful but resolute as he takes in Lucy, who leans into her mother. Benjamin's gold buttons are done up wrong; he missed the topmost one, causing the rest to be fastened in a crooked line. Meg decides out of spite not to tell him this.

"We're an island community, and we've got no one to help us but one another. Your father taught me that, Meg. And this is not going to be like '38. I've had more training, for one. I know what I'm doing now. The whole fire corps does. We learned so much from the last one that I bet by the time I get to Main Street, this fire will be extinguished. I'll just have to hitch a ride straight home." His smile is a tight line of false cheer.

Meg should acquiesce. And the mention of her father brings her pause, pulls at her heart, as Benjamin undoubtedly knew it would. But she resents how sure Benjamin sounds, how downright *excited*. And although Benjamin's burn scars have mostly smoothed over, barely visible unless you know where to look, Meg's own scars from eight years ago have never fully healed. She worried of being a widow with a baby to care for—a concern newly true again—and she finds a fresh wound: her husband fighting for a cause she doesn't know if she believes in anymore.

"You're going to risk your life for them? For men who pull innocent children from school-houses because of the color of their skin? For men—and women!—who don't ever want us to have a shop in town?"

"Yes! No! Those are two separate issues," Benjamin sighs. "You've seen yourself that we

313

have allies within the white community. Many! They support your lawsuit. They agree with us."

Meg knows her husband is right. The Hadwens and Barneys, Mitchells, and Warrens, so many good people have happily joined her cause. They discuss politics and social change, as a generosity of spirit, a cause to take up and help the other. But what if the other is you?

"Eight years ago, you encouraged me to join the volunteer fire corps—"

"Eight years ago I believed different things about the people of this island." Meg pauses, lets that sink in. Back when Meg herself was hoping to attend the high school, before men like Jenks and West ejected her daughter from a school-house, before six petitions and a lawsuit, before Eliza Macy. Before Meg became exhausted by being a Black member of her community. "If your house was on fire, Benjamin Wright, I do believe they'd let it burn."

"Mama," Lucy says, her eyes huge and wet. "I don't care where I go to school. I liked the York Street School, from before. All my friends go there and it's right down the street—"

"Lucy, not now!" Meg barks, frightening her daughter. Blinking back tears, Lucy retreats to her bedroom and closes the door softly behind her.

A bell rings from the street. "Anyone wanting a ride into town, come now!" a voice calls from out on Prospect Street. "Got room for one or two more this trip!"

As a savvy businesswoman, Meg understands that her business partner must go. But, as a wife and mother, all she wants is for her husband to stay. So she says nothing; there is nothing more to say.

Benjamin moves toward the front door, his hand on the handle. She thinks he will leave without saying goodbye, but then he turns and shakes his head sadly. "Do you remember when we met? At about Lucy's age. No, younger. I was in short pants and just starting to read. You approached me in the schoolyard and declared, *My father's a whaling captain. He left port yesterday. He is braver than anyone I know.* Five years old and as pleased as punch about who you were and where you came from."

"I understand! You're brave! I believe you."

"That's not my point."

Meg crosses her arms. "I've got no time for puzzles."

"Nor do I!" Benjamin barks back. He sighs, composes himself. "You've always been hot-headed, Meg. That I can understand. But I've never known you to be hard-hearted," he says.

And before she can respond, Benjamin is out the door.

"Your buttons are crooked!" she calls, but a horse whinnies loudly in the street and the door

315

slams shut on her words. She forgets to tell her husband that she loves him.

Their argument is quick and awful, and it replays in her mind throughout that long and terrible night. How could she forget to tell her husband that she loves him?

Meg does not want to be alone, so she enters Lucy's bedroom instead of her own. She lies down on the bed next to Lucy, hoping that the girl's steady breathing will lull her to sleep. Her mind is growing fuzzy when, an hour later, around one in the morning, Meg bolts upright against searing pain. She steadies herself on Lucy's warm arm, extended on top of the bedcovers. There is a pull in her abdomen, a fizz in her groin, and then Meg's water breaks.

32

MARIA

I'm the Pied Piper of Hamelin. This almost-humorous thought occurs unbidden as Maria makes a fifth trip to clear items from the Atheneum, and then a sixth, with the institution's proprietors, several US naval lieutenants, and regular civilians alike following her path to and fro. They have found a temporary home for the books and objects in the large parlor of Tobias and Mercy Gardner on the corner of Center and Broad Streets.

Navigating the streets is getting increasingly difficult as more people empty the entire contents of their homes onto the sidewalks away from town, choosing Federal, Broad, Center, and North Water Streets as their main thoroughfares north.

Panic comes and goes in waves. Now that many of the most precious items from the library and museum have been transported to safety in the north end of town, Maria stops for a moment to catch her breath before entering the Atheneum one final time. Her face is damp with sweat, her muscles ache, and, at some point unbeknownst to her, she has lost her bonnet.

Little Joseph Allen runs toward Maria from the direction of Main Street, his linen shirt smeared with grime, his pug nose caked with dried blood. "Miss Mitchell! I've been ordered to tell you that the fire has jumped!"

"Joseph! What happened to your face?"

"A firemen accidentally bashed it with his elbow in the fight!" he says, punching his arms out in dramatic re-creation of the event. "Do you hear me? The fire has jumped!"

"Yes, thank you, I'm aware. I heard that the flames lit Hamblin's hayloft. I know that the wharf is in danger." It is a horror to think about, but being in the opposite direction of the Atheneum, it's not of immediate concern.

"Yes! But no! Not what I meant. It jumped again!"

"Miss Mitchell, excuse us, please," a male voice says from behind her, on the steps of the Atheneum.

She and Joseph Allen stop talking.

"Pardon," another man says. He is flanked by several others, who carry between them a giant jagged-lined jawbone of a sperm whale.

"A whale moving through the streets of town, chomp-chomp!" little Joseph Allen says. "You taught me that their bones are hollow and light, like bird bones!"

"Joseph, what are you saying about the fire?"

"Oh! It's crossed over Main. Now some of the buildings on the *north* side are going up!"

Dear Lord. The north side is the Atheneum

side of Main. Maria counts streets in her head, a prayer to keep the fire away. First it would have to hit Madison, then Cambridge, then Pearl. *Madison, Cambridge, Pearl.*

"Lucky thing we have just about removed everything from inside," Maria says. "Is your family safe, Joseph? You should tend to them."

"We're on the Madaket Road, Miss Mitchell. We're fine. I came to town to help people. For a nickel, I helped move furniture out of some old captain's house on Orange Street!"

"A nickel! Joseph, you should be helping your neighbors for free, this night especially!"

"All the boys are doin' it," Joseph says, somewhat sheepishly. "They're taking the silver and people's china and . . ."

"If *all the boys* were to jump off the dock in January, would you—" She's interrupted from sounding like her mother by the presence of several firemen.

"Miss Mitchell!" It's Obed Swain, a veteran fireman who also serves as a town selectman. "We are creating a firebreak on Federal Street to keep the flames from spreading, so please do take heed."

"Create a firebreak, with gunpowder? But where?" Maria says, glancing quickly up and down Federal. She remembers that this strategy worked well in the last great fire, eight summers ago.

"We're doing everything we can to save the Atheneum. That place is important to us all, Nantucket's greatest treasure. And the Mansion House, as the only hotel on the island. We figure, if we eliminate a structure between here and Main Street, perhaps the fire will die out, the flames having nothing to catch onto."

"On behalf of the proprietors, we appreciate that so much. All your efforts," Maria says.

"What he means is, he's blowing up Mr. Hussey's house on the corner of Cambridge!" Joseph explains, hopping from foot to foot. Always one step ahead of her tonight, little Joseph Allen.

"It's the only way," Obed Swain says. The regret in his voice tells Maria that the decision was not made lightly. Still, she is shocked by the sudden sadness of it, with no time to prepare or mourn, as if a friend was just diagnosed with a terminal illness.

"The fire is gaining power on this side o' Main," Swain adds. "We've got to stop it in its tracks. We're about to set the keg in place inside the Hussey home." He gives the two firemen beside him the order to light the gunpowder, once the Husseys have removed some of their most beloved possessions.

Mrs. Hussey sobs loudly and calls frantically for her husband. "David! David, where have you gone off to! They say we need to empty out the house!"

"I should go help the Husseys with their belongings," Joseph Allen says, and he's off before Maria can stop him. *Help* is a generous term for it. A Nantucketer to his core, Joseph's got commerce and entrepreneurship in his blood. The boy—already excited by the prospect of watching a full-size house get blown sky-high—is now enraptured by the notion that he might make a profit before watching the show.

Maria can't bear such a sight. A house being destroyed to save the other structures around it; a choice between Hell and the devil. Not to mention that the Husseys lost their only child, an infant son, just last year. So much loss to one small family, one home. Is one of those rooms an empty nursery? With a tiny crib in a corner, gathering dust? Now even those memories will be taken from them.

This maudlin thought hurts Maria's already aching heart, and reminds her of her own deceased sibling, little Eliza. Gone years and years now. Maria decides to race home for a moment and check on her family.

But moving is difficult, for all about her is continued chaos. Nantucketers close to Main Street are trying every which way to save their homes; Maria watches with mounting trepidation as one woman on Pearl Street drags wet rugs out a second-story window and onto the roof, hoping to keep flames from igniting. She steps back as

321

she tries to cross Federal, as a spooked, riderless horse pulls a cart with people's valuables willy-nilly south, directly toward the heart of fire. A silver platter falls off the heaping pile and clangs in the street, where a young child dashes out to claim it.

An all clear is followed by a count from the firemen. Maria covers her ears as the cobbles shake beneath her shoes, but, may God himself forgive her, she turns around and watches the house explode. She blames her scientific mind for this lack of decorum, for she needs to know how things work, even the most destructive of forces.

The Hussey home bursts up and outward, taking a deep inhalation followed by a ghastly exhale. First, a skyward trajectory: the roof flies off, the windows shatter. And then the house sinks down on itself, wooden boards collapsing into smoke and dust. After a moment, the air clears and all that is left of the home—where the silversmith-turned-dentist David Hussey and his wife lived and cooked and gathered and slept—is debris, a pile of sticks. Obliterated.

Paper rains down on the street like fat flakes of snow, with pages of books and scraps of newspaper the last bits to settle from the blast. Joseph jumps up to catch a page on the breeze. One corner is charred but the rest remains legible. "A recipe for Indian pudding!" he tells

Maria, pressing it flat in his hand. "I'm sure Mrs. Hussey will want it."

Maria isn't certain that is true; of all the written documents from that home, Mrs. Hussey is probably least likely to become sentimental over a recipe memorized by every woman on Nantucket Island. What about the unique love letters written during courtship, or the sketches made of a baby's handprints, the stacks and stacks of envelopes tied together in ribbon, years of correspondence from one's beloved grandmother or sister who is long passed? Those missives released from homes around town now fly through the night air. Maria senses that, for days after this fire, Nantucketers will find scraps of someone else's handwritten notes in their backyards, as they pick their way through their own rubble. They will pause for a moment and try to decipher its meaning without context, a husband at sea, an old woman on her deathbed, the word *love*.

She thinks of her own journals, thankful that atop the brick home they are safe.

"Don't charge Mrs. Hussey for her own recipe!" Maria calls, watching Joseph approach the forlorn couple.

Maria feels a twinge of guilt upon seeing the Husseys huddled in the street, because this act of destruction was done to protect her beloved Atheneum. She hopes to high heavens that such a grand sacrifice is worthwhile for the greater good.

Shaken, she wends her way through pedestrian traffic up Pearl Street and down Center toward the Pacific Bank, toward home. Maria must see her family, even if only for a moment, to help her connect to something good, something created by tenderness instead of destruction.

33

MEG

This cannot be happening, Meg thinks. *I can't possibly be going into labor on a night like this.* She's not due for two weeks yet. She thinks of Benjamin's parting words, that maybe tonight's fire is a false alarm, and prays that it is true for both her town and her body. Not real, just a false alarm.

Meg slips out of bed next to a sleeping Lucy, the sheets beneath her wet, her nightgown sticky with fluid.

So this is real.

Benjamin. She never told him she loved him.

Hard-hearted indeed.

Meg crosses into her bedroom, strips off the cotton gown and changes into dry underclothes and the first dress she sees. Then she goes back to Lucy.

"Wake up!" Meg says, nudging her daughter, who rolls away from her and continues to snore. "Dear God, Lucy!" Meg yells.

Lucy startles and sits upright, her eyes wide and frightened. "The fire?" she asks.

"The baby," Meg says.

Afraid to let Lucy run off alone to fetch the midwife, Meg walks with her daughter through the dark night to Jane's house, a block from their own. Lucy carries a small lantern, the soft glow bounce, bounce, bouncing against her leg like an oversize firefly. Although the lamp is really not needed tonight; people are out and about as if it's Monday morning at the market.

The pair pass several wheelbarrows piled with personal belongings followed by people on horseback. Entire families weep while dragging rolled-up rugs and arms filled with knickknacks. A scorched scent fills the air. It's true then: Nantucket town is burning.

Another contraction. Meg stops walking as the cramp overtakes her. She folds herself in half over her belly, trying to control the searing band inside her. This child is a force to be reckoned with, all right. Meg imagines she'll spend the rest of her days trying in vain to temper the impassioned little rascal. *(You can't go off to sea! But I must and I will! The sea is no place for a girl!)* Yes: raising this one will be a battle of wills.

They reach Silver Street. Lucy runs ahead to Jeffersons Lane, knocking furiously on Jane's rose-covered cottage door. "Help!" Lucy pounds. "Baby coming!" When there's no answer, Lucy opens the latch and lets herself into the dark home.

But Meg spies something Lucy does not: a small note pinned to the wooden front door, partially hidden by ivy and climbing pink roses. With a sinking feeling, she reads it. Three words, scratched out quickly in Jane's neat script: *Birthing in Sconset.*

Now what? Meg thinks, sinking her huge body onto the small wooden porch. *Now the hell what?*

Her first thought is to take Lucy home and then go in search of medical care, but Lucy shakes her head no: too scary. Meg feels instantly terrible. What kind of mother leaves her seven-year-old home alone during a raging fire? *Stupid woman. Why would any God let her have the gift of another child, when she can't properly protect this one? Think. Who's close by?*

"Let's head to Jenny Cole's," Meg says. Faithful has been present at many a birth, including the two for her own children. Faithful's no midwife, but she's got more knowledge than most. The plan is certainly better than trying to deliver alone with her daughter at home.

"But she lives closer to the town center," Lucy points out.

"Not by much," Meg says.

"I don't want to go that way," Lucy adds, although she walks obediently alongside her mother, back to Silver Street and onto Orange. The smoke is thicker the closer they get to town and the harbor, and the crowds, too; Lucy and Meg are the only ones heading north, swimming against the tide like the striped bass at Great

Point. Meg shakes out a handkerchief from her dress pocket and tells Lucy to cover her mouth and nose.

Lucy's eyes are pinched in worry as they climb the steps to the Cole home, until they spy Jenny, opening the door. "Lucy!" Jenny says, embracing her friend in a glorious hug, as Lucy drops the cloth mask from her face. "Why are you out in this fire? Are you here about Daniel?" But before Lucy or Meg can answer, Jenny has run off to fetch her mother. "Ma! The Wrights are here about Daniel!"

Daniel? Meg wonders. Jenny's three-year-old brother?

Faithful comes to the doorway, hands on hips, her large shape taking up the full space. Faithful's skin appears so dark tonight that she almost melts into the night, but her bloodshot eyes glow. "What in the devil?" she asks. Another wave of pain tightens across Meg's abdomen and she buckles under the strain. "Meg!" Faithful says.

"My mama's in labor," Lucy explains. "And the midwife went to another birth, all the way in 'Sconset. Daddy's at the fire. Can you help us?"

Not that Benjamin would be any help to us tonight, Meg thinks, breathing in and out, in and out, staring at her shoes, the pain finally dulling at the edges. She straightens and holds onto the frame of the Cole home for support. "Just let us in, Faith!" she barks.

"Daniel's got the croup. Coughing all day and night, with a fever, and I've not slept for two straight nights now." Faithful shakes her head. "That's why I missed the celebration at your house earlier tonight. I can't take you in, Meg. I've got nowhere for you to rest and it wouldn't be safe for you besides. I'm very sorry."

"But—" Meg starts.

Faithful wipes her brow. "How about I take Lucy off your hands. She can stay in the other room with Jenny."

Lucy looks frightened still, but her shoulders drop considerably at Faithful's offer and Meg knows she's relieved to be staying put. "But, Mama, what about you?"

Faithful answers. "Dr. Ruggles lives at the end of the street, just up ahead. He doesn't usually help us Black folks, but do you think he would . . . ?" she wonders, glancing off in that direction, and then answers her own question. "No, I suppose not. So you should head to Delilah Johnson's. You've got no choice. God bless you and that unborn child. Now, I've got to close this door on you because the smoke is bad for Daniel's breathing." There is sorrow in her voice, but also decisiveness. "If anyone is strong enough to handle this tonight, Meg, Lord knows it's you."

Faithful gently pushes Lucy inside the house. "Mama," Lucy calls, "please come back to me soon!"

And before Meg knows what's happening, she's completely on her own. In labor, during a town fire, alone amid the chaos.

34

MARIA

"Father!" Maria spots him out on the street, directly in front of their home. His back is to Main Street. William Mitchell stands with arms crossed and gaze skyward, the fixed pose of an astronomer. It is how Maria usually thinks of her father, only tonight the behavior looks odd. William is a dedicated scientist, but certainly now is not the time, not with fire at his back. Besides, what celestial orbs could he possibly see through the cover of smoke? And the view is always much better from the roof.

The roof—an excellent place to gather data. Yes. Maria will check on her family's well-being and suggest that they together head up to the observation platform on the roof, not to look at the heavens per usual, but to better ascertain what's happening on the ground below them. Tonight the Mitchells will study wind direction and airflow and call out new areas of concern to alert the firemen.

Maria greets her father and assures him—a Proprietor and Trustee of the Atheneum—that everything of value has been safely removed from the building and moved north with the aid of so many volunteers. In fact, two of the naval officers who helped her reposition the items are here now, in some sort of heated debate by the Methodist church. Maria points them out to her father, who nods. "Lieutenant Goldsborough and Charles Henry Davis, both from the Coast Survey. They have come ashore with their men to help us battle the flames," William adds. "We had just been speaking about what course of action to take next when you arrived."

"I have been thinking about that as well, Father, and I believe our best course of action now is to head to the roof," Maria says.

"The roof!" William says, his sharp features glowing against the darkness: prominent nose, soft chin, receding hairline making pointed peaks on his forehead. His eyes are lined with age and worry. She knows him so well, and knows that he will think this a good idea. Instead he shakes his head, as if confused. "But my dear daughter, I'm afraid our roof has caught fire."

And to Maria's horror, the flames peek out now several stories up, small but burning bright. The Pacific Bank is made of bricks, but the observation platform built atop is constructed of wooden beams. A spark from Main must have carried itself here on the breeze.

"Our home!"

"Your mother is coming out with your brother and sisters as a precaution, although we still believe the building itself is safe."

"The Dollond!" Maria exclaims.

"We'll pray that your telescope survives," William says, "although of course you care more about human life?"

"Of course!" Maria says. He's teasing—and yet not. The bright fear in his eyes lets her know that he, too, cares greatly about the telescope and all of his precious chronometers.

Your telescope. It is the first time her father has given ownership of the brass telescope directly to Maria, and she is moved by the gesture. If it survives, she will treasure it her entire life.

And another, terrible realization: What of her journal? All those secrets stashed under a wooden plank on the roof. Maria cannot possibly race up there right now and grab ahold of it, can she? A new wave of sickness comes as she considers the alternative: Maria Mitchell's innermost complaints and desires set free upon Nantucket. Individual pages from her diary floating out from the rooftop and descending upon the town. Her own distinctive script! She is such a prominent figure among this largely Quaker community; it would be scandalous. And her father, such a proud Nantucketer, a man much admired. What would people say about him? The Friends would cast him out. Him and Mother both. Would her mother ever forgive her?

Her father speaks. "If caught with the right gust of wind, that pyre threatens to ignite the entire

333

Methodist church next door. The naval officers are discussing the predicament right now."

Maria's father remains relatively calm—stoic even—as he tells Maria this. It is the Quaker in him.

The Quaker, the Nantucketer, the scientist: William Mitchell is, like many of his neighbors, built for calamity and self-sufficiency, exactly the demeanor necessary for people living on a sandpile thirty miles offshore. Measured almost to a fault. If Maria were to scream right now, howl at the moon like a crazed wolf, what would William do?

Probably shake his head disapprovingly before shrugging his shoulders and moving on to the task at hand: making another levelheaded decision for the town and its people.

And so she does not howl. Instead, Maria crosses her arms in front of her to keep that scream tightly fixed beneath her breastbone. She studies the Methodist church as if seeing it for the first time, although she passes it every day. What to do?

The church is a classically designed house of worship in the ancient Greek style. With a triangular pediment and six-columned Ionic portico, it is a marvelous bit of architecture. Together with the Pacific Bank, the top of Main Street makes a grand statement about the people of Nantucket, where commerce and prayer live side by side.

It cannot be destroyed, by fire natural or man-made. Maria will not stand for it! She tells her father as much, begs for him to do something—anything—to protect this holy and beautiful place.

Losing patience, her father holds up his hand to silence her and then quickly speaks over her. "Maria! Shush now all of your *talk!* This begging and pleading will not save the neighborhood beyond the church!"

Maria swallows the rest of her thoughts. It means something terrible for Father to reach his boiling point.

A fire raging out of control from the Methodist church would cause Center Street to the north to be lost, as would an entire community of homes behind the church, the carnage stopping only when it reached the open meadows and cemeteries past town. "Father?" Maria asks.

"If the church goes," William Mitchell says to his daughter, "we all go."

35

MEG

Meg must get herself to a midwife immediately. Delilah Johnson's house is down by the harbor, on Candle Street. Delilah's husband, Jonathan, is a cooper; they live over his shop. Delilah and Jonathan never had children of their own. Delilah used to be the best midwife for the Black and Wampanoag women of Nantucket, but over the past forty years, she has gone from wise middle age to somewhat diminished, ripe old age. Rumor has it she can't see so well and that she now walks with a cane. Most of her clientele have moved on to Jane's care.

Except that Jane is in 'Sconset, on the other side of the island, which might as well be on the other side of the world.

With any luck, Delilah will be home and capable of helping. Meg will have the baby, and walk home with her newborn—hopefully alive—in the light of morning. But it is a risk to get down to Candle Street right now, and, as Faithful pointed out, Dr. Ruggles's home office is closer, down at the end of Orange. He helped Benjamin during the last fire, seemingly not caring about Benjamin's race. Would such a man now birth Meg's baby?

It doesn't matter if he would or would not: Meg won't ask. Not after what happened to Lucy at school, not after all she's come to question. No. She wouldn't step foot in a white person's house tonight if it were the last one standing.

She turns away from the Coles'. Orange Street is even more chaotic than it was before. Amid the aimless horses and homeless people, boys carry furniture to and fro, shouting out directions to one another as they maneuver wingback chairs and chifforobes. Lord on high, is that a grandfather clock, marching on its own through the night? No—a man stands behind it, for Meg can see feet and hands animating the heavy and cumbersome object, its chimes jangling and discordant. And someone's pig got loose and is squealing its head off.

"Gotcha!" a woman shouts, capturing the swine in her arms and cradling it.

The pig makes a ruckus of protestations. "If we can find some place to sleep, we've got ham for breakfast!" the woman says, and her delighted offspring cheer at her heels. "Go find your father and tell him!"

Candle Street. How in the world is Meg going to get there?

And where in the world is Benjamin? Has their shop caught fire?

Meg starts to walk north toward town when an explosion rocks the street. The event is far

337

enough away from her that she can't see which home it was, but close enough to have heard the deafening blow caused by gunpowder. Everyone on Orange Street has the same reaction as Meg: they duck their heads and cover their ears, freezing in place for the moment. After a few seconds, they straighten up, grab their dropped belongings, and return to what they were doing.

A few minutes later, the boom happens again. People freeze. Then people breathe again.

It is not unlike experiencing a contraction, Meg thinks. The immediate agony has passed; carry on.

Where is Benjamin?

"Ma'am, outta the way, please!" a white man on horseback calls. He's heading south on Orange Street, away from the direction of the blast. He is a disheveled mess, brown hair windswept, white shirt torn from shoulder to elbow. But his soft blue eyes are kind, and his horse is a beautiful thing: a dappled white mare with black eyes fringed with long lashes. As they come close, that horse turns her full gaze on Meg. She flags the man down, and he whistles to the horse, who slows.

"What happened back there?" she asks.

"They blew up Doc Ruggles's house." He shrugs, as if the explosions of doctors' homes are a regular occurrence. "Created a firebreak. Took two kegs. The first one didn't quite do the trick.

But the second one cleared the lot flat, so there's nothing there anymore to catch fire. It was on the corner of Orange and Main, see. Now they can keep the fire from spreading thisaway."

"Oh," Meg says, feeling instantly bad for the doctor . . . and instantly lucky that she hadn't gone to call on his services.

"Those firemen are trying just about everything! Gunpowder, firebreaks, hooking up hoses, climbing ladders against homes half-gone and dousing 'em with buckets of water, and runnin' around doing all they can for the town," he nods. *Those firemen* are husbands and fathers, she wants to correct. *Stop thinking of them as one nameless mass.* "They're trying, all right, but Main Street won't be saved tonight."

"All of it?" Meg wonders. "Even the north side?"

"*Especially* the north side!" the man says. "Ka-boom!"

Their shoe shop. Gone. Everything they worked for, destroyed. And to think, how they fought at the town meeting the other night to buy the building right on Main Street. How important that felt, how right and just. And how fulfilling it was to see the look on Eliza Macy's face as they took control of their destinies.

Meg and Benjamin were smug enough to believe they had control over anything at all.

How many buildings—homes and businesses—

will perish this night? And how many souls? Meg closes her eyes against the tears that threaten to well up. No: she will only allow herself to cry once this is all over, after her baby is born and both mother and child are alive and well. *Not yet, Meg. You must stay hardheaded and hardhearted.* She puts her hand on her belly. The dappled horse neighs in the street.

"Ma'am, are you . . . with child?" the man asks. She nods.

"What in heaven's sake are you doing out? Let me give you a ride home." He motions to the calash hitched to his horse.

"I need to get to Candle Street."

"Candle? Well, that's not going to be easy, see, down by the harbor there's been a . . ."

Another contraction takes hold of Meg, and it must look fierce, because it robs even this fellow of his powers of speech.

Meg steadies herself on the horse's warm flank. "Can you get me there or not?"

His eyebrows raise in doubt, but he holds his tongue. "Climb in," he says, which she does, quite indelicately. He whips the horse's neck and off they gallop, in the opposite direction of Candle Street.

36

ELIZA

The fire is approaching her home. Eliza can hear the blaze now. *Hear it.* This, she understands, is even more frightening than smelling the char on the wind. More powerful than the echoes of shouting back and forth, calls between firemen and shopkeepers and neighbors in the pitch-black as they try to control the flames and keep the town and its inhabitants safe. The fire is a crackling, insidious beast, and it is on the move.

They have no choice now: the Macys must pack up and leave. *Rachel, Mattie! This instant!* The twins arrived home safely from Alice's just after Eliza did, both girls so panicked that they hardly took one look at Eliza or what she was wearing. What would happen to their jewelry and favorite silver combs if the house caught fire? And what of Papa's letters? They are upstairs now, clearing out some old sea chests of Henry's to fill with belongings. She can hear them worrying and pacing in tandem. Eliza must call to them, but she can't.

Eliza is frantic, her body frozen in the front hall, her eyes scanning left into the dining room, and then right into the sitting room. So many beautiful things. That portrait of the children above the fireplace, done by a well-respected Boston artist. Marshall? Martins? She can picture his face but can't summon the name. Her mind is a sieve, a blur, awhirl.

Now her eyes flitter to the tall porcelain urn Henry brought back from his last trip to the Orient, hand-painted with flowers and butterflies in deep pinks and imperial reds. And the over-stuffed, velvet horsehair settee with matching chaise. The mahogany grandfather clock from England. All of it, every last object, bought with money earned from whaling. From her husband's profession of hunting down a living, breathing, giant sea mammal and rendering it into oil. *Oil,* Eliza thinks with some irony, that fuels fire.

Insistent and sudden knocking at the door pulls Eliza from her paralysis. "Hello!" a voice calls, followed by more banging of the brass knocker in the shape of a whale's tail that Eliza had commissioned as a first anniversary gift for Henry. "I'm from the Nantucket fire department! Is anyone home?"

Instead of answering, Eliza moves into the dining room and positions herself by the curtains flanking the large front windows, where she can see a man in uniform on her front steps. He cannot be here simply out of courtesy; the fire must be headed further up Main. He's calling on her the way death eventually will, and she wants him to go away; she's not ready. She will never be ready.

Eliza turns away from the window and examines the wooden sideboard and the tall glass-fronted cabinets angled into each corner of the room. Which objects to grab first? Her mother-in-law's china is the obvious choice, but it's quite delicate and, with service for twenty-four, there are so very many pieces. She can't possibly take it all with her. She grabs the large soup tureen from the center of the table—the one she uses for Christmas and Easter and Thanksgiving and christenings—and cradles it to her breast. It has handles; Rachel and Mattie can carry it between them when they depart.

"Please answer the door!" More knocking, an intruder.

Eliza needs time, but as with her finances, or her fleeting moments with James, there is no time left. Still clutching the bowl, she walks slowly to the large, high-gloss black door and opens it onto the night.

The scent of Nantucket burning fills Eliza's nostrils and stings her eyes.

She blinks back tears and studies the man before her: dark-skinned, tall and slim, with the top of his jacket buttoned askew, in haste no doubt, to get to work. He removes his hat and nods before speaking. It's Benjamin Wright. He raises his eyebrows in surprise, and quickly shakes his head. He looks at her with a changed expression, like he's apologizing.

"Ma'am, it appears—"

"I know, certainly, I know!" Eliza says. "I can see that the fire is approaching Upper Main Street. I was beginning to clear out some objects from my home when you knocked."

Benjamin rubs the back of his head with his fingers. "Let me explain. I heard the fire ward's plans for your home and, although I'm not working with them directly, I thought I should warn you—"

"I appreciate your warning. Now please, I must collect my children and—"

"Excuse me, sir!" a gruff male voice calls from the street. "This home is under my jurisdiction, not yours."

He's one of the fire wards. White-haired, broad, and ice-blue-eyed, dressed in a uniform decorated with medals and shouldered by gold-fringed epaulets. She knows him from church but has never seen him in full regalia: Josiah Pine. "You," he says, looking directly at Benjamin, "are to return to your engine company at once. You are not under my command, and I won't have you confusing townspeople by going door to door unauthorized. If you men from New Guinea want to help, find a fire and put it out!"

Benjamin Wright lowers his gaze and turns, walks down Eliza's steps. A sudden flash of fear springs up Eliza's spine. Does Benjamin know anything about Eliza's dalliance? Would a wife share such a thing with her husband?

The commander clears his throat and says, "Mrs. Macy, the roof of the Pacific Bank has caught fire. We have reason to be concerned now about the Methodist church to the north side as well. Your house lies due south of those buildings, and marks the beginning of Upper Main. It is in a precarious position. In order to slow the progress of the flames, we need to use gunpowder to create a firebreak."

A firebreak, yes. A gap between buildings, so the fire has space to die out. Eliza thinks this wise. Nantucket firemen did that years earlier, for the Great Fire of 1838. It may have slowed the progress of the fire, although it also unnecessarily destroyed homes. "But what does that have to do with me?" she asks Josiah Pine.

Josiah Pine places his top hat back on his head as if readying himself for battle. "Mrs. Macy, if you please: I am here to blow up your house."

37

MARIA

Maria and her father watch as the flames from their rooftop observation deck dance their way across the sky and alight the left-hand corner of the Methodist church. The flames lap against the church's cedar shingles. Firemen call out to one another and aim their hoses high. The spray of water falls just short of the roofline, hitting it in spots but not dousing it completely. Maria's heart dances in her throat.

William Mitchell approaches the naval officers. Although he's not dressed in any sort of uniform, his calm, approachable demeanor commands respect. They converse with a fire warden. These naval men have taken control of this situation, and William asks about their strategy as Maria listens in. They stand by a wooden keg, reminiscent of the one brought into David Hussey's home.

"What's that for?" Maria asks, completely forgetting her manners as she interrupts the men.

The lieutenant considers the question—and the source—before answering. "Gunpowder, Miss Mitchell. For the church."

"You cannot fell this structure! It's blasphemous to do so."

"I don't think God wants your entire community destroyed, miss. I believe he'd see it as a worthy sacrifice. And I would think you'd understand that, seeing as how we are trying to save your Atheneum by doing the same to a structure on Federal."

Maria's logical mind very much dislikes when sound logic is used against it. She stops to think. Use science, try a new tactic. "One keg of powder is not nearly enough for so large a building," she says.

"We'll get more," Lieutenant Goldsborough says.

Maria would not like to play chess against this man.

"Actually, the town is running low on supplies," the fire warden adds. "We've blasted over a dozen structures thus far."

"This location may be worth putting all our efforts behind," the lieutenant says. "Stop the fire right here, at the top of town, with one great explosion."

"Or take the Pacific Bank with it!" Maria cries. "Who's to say what will happen if you load the church with explosives and set a fuse? A blast that large could demolish the entire block!"

"We know what we're doing," the other naval officer says, although he looks troubled and, Maria senses, doubtful. He must wish he had stayed on his ship, docked at a safe distance in the harbor, watching the spectacle through a telescope.

"Maria," her father says to her in a softer tone, like she is eleven again and first learning to chart the stars, "these men follow orders through a chain of command, and, much as you think you're on the top of that chain, my outspoken daughter, I doubt they'll give your comments priority."

This stings. Why wouldn't they listen to her, a well-respected scientist? Is it because she's female? Unmarried? As a person who has spent much of this night giving commands that people have listened to—if not much of her life doing the same—Maria is outraged.

She studies her father, who is studying his shoes. Then she has an idea. "They'll certainly give your comments priority, though, Father." Male, mature, and a venerated town member besides. There is practically no one more well respected on the whole of Nantucket Island. "Tell them not to do it."

As she waits for her father's reply, Maria overhears the naval officers urgently discussing plans with the fire wards, volleying shouts back and forth over the noise of the chaotic night. It is a litany of questions, with no one providing sound answers. "Should we place the kegs here, or farther inside? How many do you think? And how to light the fuse? Where has Micah Palmer gone off to? Has anyone seen the other hose? It looks like the steps of the Methodist church have caught flame!"

A line of women helpers suddenly mobilizes, creating a chain from the cistern near the bank to the base of the church steps. They call out as they pass a filled bucket forward, their legs strong and steady as their torsos pivot from the woman behind them to the next in front of them in line. *Go, go, go, go, go!* they chant, handing off the buckets. *Next, next, next!* they call, their voices spirited and strong.

My people! Maria thinks with a surge of pride. She will join them in line and show her father what taking positive action can do, what women in particular can do. Put men in charge and watch them strut and show off like peacocks, making grand gestures with gunpowder and power. Put the women in charge and watch how small, organized acts of collaboration can have just as large of an impact.

"Using gunpowder this way is not a precise science, Maria, and I know how that might frustrate you," William Mitchell says.

Not a precise science! He's using the discipline she loves against her. Exasperated, Maria paces back and forth. She looks behind her, down Main Street, where fire rages on both sides of the street. Firemen on the corner of Federal and Main are still holding the flames steady; the firebreak created by razing David Hussey's home might actually work.

Maria turns back to the beautiful church.

The fire warden snakes a long fuse up the steps and through the bright red doors. Several men from the naval ships have rounded up kegs and now return with them, panting and soot-stained. "Well done. You found three, at least!" Lieutenant Goldsborough sends them into the church.

As the men prepare, Maria does what she always does when vexed: gaze skyward.

The sky is an ashy white of smoke, creating the effect of low-hanging clouds blocking the stars. The waning gibbous moon gives off a weak gray light. The domed shape hangs over the church's pointed roof like a prop in one of her sister Kate's silly plays. Maria expects to see flames, only there aren't any.

There aren't any more flames.

The fire on the roof has died out.

Maria calls out to the men, but the officers and firemen are too busy shouting orders back and forth and making sure the building is all clear. They don't hear her. A mangy black dog runs into the middle of the street and barks frantically, as if joining her cause, only the noise adds to the chaos and drowns Maria out further.

Lieutenant Goldsborough is about to light the fuse. "Wait!" Maria yells as she runs toward him.

The officers stand too close to the building to see what she did from farther away.

The lieutenant turns his head sideways. "Miss Mitchell, stand back."

"*You* stand back! Step out this way and see for yourself," Maria says, pointing past the triangular pediment to the wood-shingled roof beyond. Maria's father joins them.

Lieutenant Goldsborough drops the coiled rope fuse and follows Maria several paces into the street. He gazes up. His eyebrows raise in question. "Luck or divine intervention? A shift in the weather?"

"I cannot explain it," Maria says, perhaps for the first and only time in her adult life. She shrugs at her father, and he shakes his head at her: they have no answer. Tears spring to her eyes. Whether a force beyond science, or merely science itself, shifted the wind, they'll never know.

But the church has been saved, and for tonight, that is enough.

Somewhat dumbstruck, William Mitchell excuses himself to go check on his family; Maria says she will be there shortly. She wants to embrace her mother, and kiss Phebe on the temple. She would like to pray with her mother for the second time tonight.

And then remove her diary from its precarious position on the roof.

"Miss Mitchell!" Little Joseph Allen waves to her from the corner of Center Street. His pockets sag, weighted down with coins as he walks.

"You're not here to ask for some sort of ransom, are you, Joseph?" Maria smiles. "For keeping the books at the Atheneum safe for me?"

"Nay, miss," Joseph says, somewhat sheepishly. "I wanted to let you know that I gave that recipe back to Mrs. Hussey for free—and a whole load of others I gathered too. Federal Street was littered with 'em!"

"Good for you, Joseph," Maria says, ruffling his already mussed mop of hair.

A commotion behind them on the corner of Main and Federal startles them both. The concentration of heat there has suddenly become quite fierce, and the pair watch as firemen stand back and scream out, overwhelmed by the blaze. The wind shifts, causing a wave of current above Main Street. The flames are quickly engulfed by a suction of air, creating a circular vortex.

That cone of fire swirls together and lifts, creating a fireball.

Maria—and all of Nantucket town, it feels like—watches with awe as a hellion ball of fire shoots across the sky, a planet of flames arcing in a northeastern direction. Past Madison, Cambridge, and Pearl Streets it flies, spit from the mouth of a demon. Shot cannonlike over town, the ball of fire is an apocalyptic wonder, until it falls from the sky and lands somewhere out of Maria's line of sight.

But even without seeing she knows: the fire has flown north, which means the contents of the Atheneum are in imminent and renewed danger.

And so is Linley Blake's home.

"Let's go!" Joseph Allen says, his former zeal for the drama transformed to fright. He takes off up Center Street, weaving in and out of traffic and bedlam, Maria fast on his heels.

38

ELIZA

The fire ward leaves, saying that he and some of his men will return with gunpowder in fifteen minutes. Fifteen.

What can Eliza possibly salvage from her life in fifteen minutes? What would Henry want her to save? She should have told the children immediately. Now she's lost precious time. Only, what to tell them, exactly? That their home and all of their earthly belongings are about to evaporate like morning fog burned off by the sun?

Instead she stood at the door stunned, frozen.

There is a buzzing inside her head, a lightness behind her eyes. Eliza gets to the living room couch in time to sink into the velvet cushion underneath her and breathe through the spell. She will not faint dead away.

Breathe.

Now, where is her tea?

Her teapot from earlier in the night has gone cold, the cup that she drank from before visiting James still upstairs in her bedchamber where she left it. At what, seven in the evening? And now it's what—she glances at the grandfather clock— quarter to two in the morning. Only hours earlier, she was locked in a loving embrace, her heart beating fast for an entirely different reason. And now her heart beats in anger. *Rage!* Who are these firemen to tell her she has minutes to vacate her home, which she's lived in for nearly twenty years? That her precise location is more or less important to the trajectory of the fire than that of her neighbors?

Time passes quickly and she's wasted precious minutes of it being shocked. Perhaps because she does not want to leave this house. Will not leave it. But how can she stay? What could she possibly say to the firemen to remain on the premises?

In the kitchen, Eliza pours cold, over-steeped tea into a new cup, adds a dash more of the dwindling laudanum to the amber brew and slurps it down in one gulp. She prays that James and his father's candlery business will survive. And she will go to the harbor tomorrow morning to see his ship off. Yes, she's just decided. She will stand on the shoreline and wave and wave and wave.

"Mother." Rachel stands in the shadows, her long honey hair half hiding her face. She leans against the door frame between the kitchen and hall.

"My darling," Eliza says, stepping toward her daughter and stroking her hair. Rachel looks at her with pale gray-blue eyes, her father's eyes. Something in her melts when she sees Rachel like this, her heart breaking for the girl whose home has been blown to pieces before it has even been touched by gunpowder. *I did this to her,* Eliza thinks. *I singlehandedly destroyed Rachel's and Mattie's lives without them being aware. Lied to get the girls out of the house. Put my desires before my family.*

When Eliza first saw that wall of flames in Geary's hat shop, she thought she had brought destruction to her town. Now she knows it is much more personal than that; she has brought Lucifer to her very doorstep.

The medicine numbs her brain, which dulls the edges of guilt and calms her hysteria slightly. But not enough, not quite enough. She mustn't distress the child, but at the same time, Eliza must compel her to act quickly. "Rachel, please tell me you've packed up some belongings, including clothing for the next few days. Not just the precious things, but some staples as well. We are going to need to take more items than I originally anticipated." She tries to keep her voice measured.

"You don't need to pretend with me. I heard your exchange with the fire warden."

Little pitchers, big ears. Eliza nods. "So you know what we need to do."

"I know what he *said.* I know what he *told* you to do." She crosses her arms defiantly.

"Rachel, they are one and the same." The twin who is older by ten minutes can be strong-willed.

"Does that mean you have to do it?" And now Mattie joins her sister's side, with a matching countenance, her matching blue-gray eyes hard with defiance. "Mother, don't let them do it." The twin who is younger by ten minutes can also be strong-willed, after her sister shows her the way. "Remember when they blew up Lizzie Chase's house eight years ago and the fire came anyway, trampling right across the lawn and moving on to the house next door?"

Rachel picks up the rest of the story, like a ball being tossed back and forth between them. "Lizzie and her family were homeless for months! They had to live in the Mansion House Hotel until they could rebuild! And their parakeets died in the blast."

"Well, good thing we don't have any pets," Eliza sighs. "You make fine points, and you're not really children anymore, are you? But this fire is at our doorstep. Truly and sincerely! What am I to do? Fight it back with my words?" She knows she looks and sounds irrational, but why not? Hasn't the whole night been like this, charged with tinder and ready to explode since sunset?

"Perhaps!" Rachel says, her tone raising to match her mother's. "Why not? Words are powerful tools. Weapons sometimes."

Oh, to have raised daughters who feel compelled to speak! To share their opinion freely!

357

She blames and lauds their Nantucket education in equal measure for this, where Quaker ideals of equality make girls bold freethinkers (and speakers!). Although. Hadn't Eliza just done the very same last Monday night at the town council meeting?

But she has no time for dissention now, toying with verbiage, parsing words and their meanings. The minutes are ticking by.

"What would Father do if he were here? How would he speak to those men?" Rachel asks. She holds a worn piece of parchment in her hand and she lifts it to Eliza, who can see the slanted black script across the page. It is one of Henry's many letters, a well-read and much-loved one, given the state of it.

"*If* he were here." Eliza says it as a dare. "Which he's not."

"We're not trying to disrespect your opinion, but—" Mattie adds.

"Then don't!" Eliza says, shaking. Oh, how she wants to scream. How she wants to tell Mattie, *Your dear, perfect father should be back by now, only he abandoned us and wouldn't say why, so what he would or wouldn't or might or mightn't do is of no consequence! Everyone on the island seems to know more about your so-called wonderful father than we do. Since he has failed to entrust us with his whereabouts, my distrust of him grows greater each passing day! All we have are his letters, months of delayed—and incomplete—correspondence!*

The hurt look on the twins' pretty faces softens Eliza, who tries another tactic. "Fine. Educate me. How would your father handle such a request? Captain to captain, I would think," Eliza says. "But this is purely theoretical. And—" Eliza cuts herself off from saying more, afraid she might say something unkind about Henry, or admit to something terrible about herself. Spill her most recent and most unscrupulous secret onto the bare wooden beams of the kitchen floor, like blood or oil: *Your father left me lonely and vulnerable, and I had no choice but to take up with another man.* How Henry has never really been there for her in her greatest times of need. How men will love you with empty promises and then leave, disappointing you over and over.

"Because of that, *you* have had to be in charge. For years at a time." Rachel finishes the thought, waves the letter once more, as if a nautical flag. "And you do it well, Mother. Father would be so proud."

Eliza blushes, not from the compliment, as her daughter probably thinks, but from shame. "I don't know that to be so, Rachel. But I do know that I am not him, and I cannot ever be a man, no matter how much I try to be in charge." Just tonight, out on Main Street, the firemen refused to listen to her, to view her as anything more than a nuisance.

Perhaps they know nothing. Perhaps all anyone ever does on this island is guess about what's best for themselves and use that force to decide for their neighbors.

"Mother, what should we do?" Rachel asks for the pair.

Eliza isn't sure. But she can't stand here idle with a house to empty, so she passes Rachel a huge copper pot, the one for stews. "Put down your father's old letter. Here. Take this. We'll want to save it."

She realizes the pot itself is so large that it can be a vessel for other items. The silver-handled ladle goes in. Her favorite teacup, and the saucer and pitcher that match. She rolls those in newsprint and places them deep into the pot. And the little glass bottle, of course. In, with the pretty lace-edged hand towels from Belgium.

Mattie collects other treasures, somewhat randomly, gathers them in her arms, and dumps them into another pot.

Eliza grabs more items of the right shape and size to fill the pot in Rachel's arms. A teaspoon with decorative scalloped edging, and a book of Mattie's borrowed from the Atheneum, the one with the red leather cover. Mattie read it straight through in one day and three more times since. She refused to let Eliza return it! *The Three*

360

Musketeers goes into a pot. They will move in with Alice and Larson if they must. In that sad little dark house on the edge of town.

Only for a while, though. Only until they can rebuild.

Rachel's long, thin arms strain beneath the weight, but she holds steady.

"You see this blue silk dress and these brown curls? That is what the firemen see, a woman! That is what the whole town sees. Women who are good at making decisions . . . precisely until the men return. When your father comes back, he'll—"

"But he's not here tonight. You have to *be him* tonight," Mattie says. She bangs the teakettle on the wooden table for emphasis.

"But that's simply impossible! When you marry you will discover—" Eliza says, only she can't think of how to end the sentence. Too many things her girls will discover, many of which are less than positive, and almost none of them would be believed if she were to share them now.

"We took a vote upstairs and decided we don't want them to do it," Mattie says, with finality.

A knock at the front door interrupts them. "Captain Macy, are you in there? By order of the Nantucket Fire Department, I am here to order you to vacate this home."

Of course they want to speak directly to the captain. Eliza pushes past the children and into the front hall. The girls follow her like ducklings in a row, Rachel setting the large pot down on the floor.

"Captain Macy isn't here," she calls out to the men on the other side of the door.

"Yes she is," Mattie says, squeezing Eliza's hand and looking into her eyes. "You are our Captain Macy, Mother." In the other hand, she holds the letter that Rachel had let go of in the kitchen. She passes it to Eliza. With one glance, Eliza recognizes the correspondence: the one detailing when Henry's ship was attacked by pirates, in '41.

"You are our Captain Macy. And Captain Macy would never give up the ship," Mattie says softly, echoing her father's words from this most infamous letter. Eliza looks back and forth between her two daughters, who say nothing else, but cheer her on with their matching eyes.

Children! What fools. Eliza shakes her head in disagreement, but opens the door.

Josiah Pine is back, with a partner. The man is introduced as Phineas Johnson. Hats removed, hands over hearts, the two men look as if they are attending a funeral, wishing condolences on the death of a house still standing.

Eliza takes a deep breath, inhaling and exhaling her beloved community's ashes. The red-bricked Pacific Bank diagonally across the street still stands unharmed, unfazed, impenetrable like a fortress, although a crowd of people stand in front of it, looking skyward.

Not give up the ship, hmmm? Is that to be their psalm tonight?

Something in Eliza's brain—vacant and mindlessly acting under duress until this moment—snaps into place. By staring down her fear of the firemen, suddenly Eliza is capable of decision-making again, of clear thinking. They are humans, like herself: no more, no less. And, having witnessed the chaos that ultimately led to the fire raging out of control, Eliza is fully aware that these firemen do not know what they are doing.

"What is the current wind direction?" she asks the men.

"The fire is spreading of its own accord at this point, ma'am. But if I had to reckon a guess, I'd say north. North and east," Josiah Pine says.

"So why are you forcing me into this decision right now, when my house is to the west?"

". . . precaution?" Johnson, the second fireman, says.

Josiah Pine echoes the word without the questioning tone at the end. "Yes, precaution."

"Can that precaution wait until we have further information about the exact movement of the fire?" The men's eyes dart away from hers, they shift from foot to foot. Eliza continues.

"Certainly, if it was your wife alone in your

home, Captain Pine, you wouldn't want her to surrender before the battle had really begun?"

"I don't like you to bring my family into this—it isn't personal," Josiah Pine says.

"My home may not be personal to you, sir, but to me, it's the entire world. And, as such, it deserves a moment's pause before a decision can be made to destroy it."

"Maybe we shouldn't be so hasty, sir," Phineas Johnson says, glancing quickly at Pine.

What does Eliza have to lose, but her house and all of her dignity?

"Gentlemen," she says as she clears her throat. She straightens her shoulders and tries to think herself taller than her five foot two inches. "My children and I have discussed it, and we've decided that, at this moment at least, we are not leaving the premises. Not budging one inch. So, if you insist on blowing up this home, you are going to have to do it with us inside."

"What did you just say?" Josiah Pine asks Eliza, in response to her proclamation from the front door of her home.

And so she repeats her words, and in doing so, gains confidence. "That I am not leaving this house. Not yet, anyway. So, if you must use gunpowder, you'll have to blow it up with myself and my family inside."

"Not leaving? But—" Phineas Johnson, the fireman standing with Josiah Pine says.

"It's true." Eliza, for the third time, repeats her declaration. She is getting rather good at it. She is also beginning to enjoy the stunned look on men's faces when she says such a thing. Imagine: to defy men's orders! She should make more of a habit of it!

What are they going to do? Pick her up and haul her off to jail with her children looking on? (Actually, they might. Best not to suggest it. Keep her words short and sweet and let the men decide what to do in the face of them.)

The two men step down into the street to discuss. The fire marshall gesticulates wildly, his hands moving this way and that, leading an imaginary orchestra in a crazed symphony.

Eventually, Pine shrugs. Eliza steels herself for his response as he climbs the steps. "I shall not force you at this moment," he says. "But if your selfish act leads to further destruction, it's on your conscience, not mine. May the Lord forgive you this night."

May the Lord forgive her indeed.

39

MEG

Meg bounces along in the back of the stranger's buggy as the dappled mare continues to head away from town. If the contractions don't cause the baby's birth, then this frantic jostling just might.

The carriage seems to be moving more vertically than horizontally, as they haven't covered much ground in the past fifteen minutes. People and horses and pigs and—is that a chicken?—keep weaving in front of them, making it hard to pass. Finally, they begin moving quickly again.

"You do know where Candle Street is, right?" she shouts over the clackety-clacking of the vehicle's wheels, her hand on her belly as if trying to keep the child intact.

"I do indeedy, ma'am," he says, tossing the words out behind him. "I'm trying to sneak up on Candle Street, you see, from thisaway. We'd be blocked heading through town. Now hold on tight, I'm going to turn."

"Hold on to what?" Meg asks, her body pushed to the other side of the carriage by the combination of speed and force as the horse and buggy bank left. They straighten out for a moment and turn left again. Once Meg's upright again, she asks where they are.

"We're out on Washington," he says. "I'm gonna have to let you off at Commercial Wharf; you can walk from there." The harbor on their right is black ink.

"Slow, Nancy," he says to the horse, who moves from a canter to a trot to a walk as they approach this crowded section of the wharf. Nancy. A fitting name for this pretty dappled horse. Meg's not familiar with this area—populated with cooper shops, flour and grain stores, and a steam mill—because it's where the inner workings of male-dominated industry resides, which Meg's life hardly ever overlaps with.

Meg thanks the kind man and dismounts from his small carriage. "Stay safe and have faith, is what my dear wife Nancy always said," the man says, tipping his hat before heading off into the night.

But this Nancy must have died, so Meg wonders: Is this good advice or a curse?

Either way, Meg regrets her decision to disembark almost instantly, watching the man head back in the direction of New Guinea. Toward her home. Her community. A place without fire! Why didn't she just make her way back to the comfort of her own bed and ask a neighbor to help in the birth? Any neighbor is better than this.

Hotheaded indeed, as Benjamin said. Too quick to judge, too quick to act.

Getting her bearings and trying to see through the smoke, Meg watches a cluster of boys roll barrels down the street. She is reminded of the games children play at the sheep-shearing festival in May, rolling hoops from barrels like that blindfolded, to see who can cross the finish line first. Of course, those barrels are not yet built, and these, Meg suspects, are filled with precious oil. Are these boys helping or are they stealing? Tonight, both might be true simultaneously.

More people pass, hauling sails and rope, bolts of fabric, and armloads of candles with them, scurrying past her into the dark night like rats on a sinking ship. As before, Meg seems to be the only person moving toward the blaze, and as if in warning, she's seized by another sharp pain across her abdomen. This one came on faster than the last. The contractions are speeding up, then, and she must find help soon.

Meg stops under a sign that reads M. Crosby and Sons at the top of Commercial Wharf. She can see Candle Street from here.

She can see that Candle Street is on fire.

Meg leans against a barrel set out in front of the store, feeling that all hope is lost. She has no idea where Benjamin is. For all she knows, he's injured like the last time or worse—already gone from this earth—and she would have no way of knowing.

Meg brought her daughter, Lucy, closer to town and, therefore danger, and knowingly left Lucy in the safekeeping of a woman whose home is filled with disease. And Meg's midwife, Jane, the only woman Meg would ever truly trust to help her deliver a child into this world, is on the other side of this godforsaken island. 'Sconset is eight miles east of town, on the edge of the world. The next land mass after 'Sconset is Portugal.

Can 'Sconset smell Nantucket town burning? Can Portugal?

Oh, Jane, come help me. Say something sharp and witty to bring me back to myself. But all she hears is desperation, both from within her mind and all around her.

Meg's never been one to wallow in pity or wonder *why me.* But she fears now that she is going to have this baby alone, in the middle of the street, in a town that is engulfed in flames, and then this baby, just like the last one, will die, and these simple, sad facts are making her feel quite sorry for herself indeed.

A blast from the north rattles the ground and shakes the barrel that Meg is leaning against. The vibrations travel up her legs, even pulse in her teeth. Can it be another building leveled by gunpowder? Possibly. But this is more menacing, more sinister and grand. Another blast comes, and then another—*pop, pop, pop,* like fireworks over the harbor, one after another after another. Boom and boom and boom.

"The casks have gone up! The oil's exploding!" someone shouts nearby. "Straight Wharf's already gone and burned, and now look at South Wharf!"

Meg looks north, past where she stands on Commercial Wharf to South Wharf, the next one in line along the harbor, and to the obvious: barrel after barrel igniting, flames shooting into the dark sky. Trancelike, Meg walks further out onto Commercial Wharf, following the man who called the alert.

The harbor is on fire. Meg didn't know water could burn.

Baby, my child: Are you seeing this with me?

Several passengers on a nearby dinghy watch transfixed in the night, bobbing on a light current in Nantucket Sound. If they don't row back to shore soon, they might be cut off from the mainland, encircled by fire. Someone picks up the oars and rows back to safety.

Witnessing this destructive force in all of its terrible glory, Meg feels lit, too, by an opposite life force. There is no time for pity, or to wallow, or to wonder *why me.* There is only time to act. If water can burn this night, anything is possible.

She knows where she has to go. Now it's only a question of bypassing danger to get there. Meg turns and, fighting against more labor pains, walks as briskly as she can, circling the perimeter and winding her way back up through the edges of a town of ash.

40

MARIA

A cataclysmic fireball shoots across the sky. To imagine that the natural world is capable of such destruction. Maria will never look at the universe the same way again.

When she and Joseph Allen arrive at the corner of Broad and Center Streets, several dwellings are already engulfed by flames and the New North Wharf itself is in danger. A completely separate, distinct conflagration has arrived to this corner of Nantucket town, which means the contents of the Atheneum face renewed danger.

The tide has turned, and people who an hour earlier were moving themselves and their belongings north are now scrambling to find a safe position: not much room east, for there's only water; not south, for there's only fire; not north nor west, for new flames block their path. But they can move one block east.

Yes, east it is. Maria calls out directions and, in moments, assembles a capable and willing team. Her neck still aches and now her feet hurt as well, but there will be time later to rest, after she carries the twelve books of John Milton's *Paradise Lost* to safety. *This horror will grow mild, this darkness light.* How she wishes she believed in

God's power to vanquish Satan as vehemently as Milton did. Maria works and walks and runs and scoops and hurries and hustles. She passes others doing the same, frantic and bleary-eyed, arms loaded down with poetry and religion and civics and science, weighty knowledge a burden.

Around her, people are fleeing their homes with whatever they can carry and emptying the remainder of their belongings onto the street, hoping that, if the home burns, at least the contents will not. Others are taking advantage of their neighbors' absences by stealing from these abandoned lots. Looters. Calamity brings out people's best and worst. *Love thy neighbor as thyself, but first, take their silverware.* Some books will not make it from place to place in such a disorderly fashion; there will be some natural attrition due to oversight or theft. But she will do everything she can to save anything she can, which is all she can do as a mere mortal on this earth.

Once all items have been relocated, there is suddenly nothing left to do but collapse. Maria's arm throbs. Her elbow is bleeding.

"Maria!" a voice calls out from nearby. Linley Blake waves from her family's front steps. Her long towheaded hair glows bright like a beacon in the darkness. "Can you come to me? My parents asked me to guard the house! I swore I wouldn't step foot off the porch unless flames attacked."

Maria cradles her injured left arm in her right and walks toward Linley. Maria hasn't seen her since the night of the wedding, the night Linley became engaged to Charlie Warren. When Linley told Maria the news, she was struck dumb. She could say nothing as Linley sobbed and sobbed. And then Maria found herself in the awkward position of consoling the very person who had just broken her heart. She felt so shocked by the news that she knew she couldn't stay for the reception. She fled the party, rushing out the back garden gate and not stopping to hear Linley's frantic calls, things like *wait, Maria, let's talk this through.*

Dumb, yes, that was the right word for it indeed. Maria had fallen for Linley just as she was to be taken away from her. It was like Helen Albright all over again.

Thinking about what she penned in her journal that night, about how she wanted to kiss Linley and touch her everywhere and ask her to live with her, Maria feels her cheeks color. She has to remind herself that her journal is, for the moment anyway, completely safe, and so, too, are her thoughts, for no one can actually read Maria's mind. Not even Linley Blake.

Maria composes herself as best she can to greet her friend.

"How is the Atheneum?" Linley asks.

"A roving exhibition," Maria says, climbing

the few steps onto the Blakes' porch and trying to keep her voice light. "After the initial clearing out, we had to move the contents twice more. The books and objects now have a temporary home here in your neighborhood. We hope to move them back into place in the morning."

"I'll help you later, and in the morning, too," Linley says, her violet eyes big with tears as she takes Maria's arm and gives it a squeeze. Maria winces from the pain. Linley's face falls in concern. "You're injured! Come inside for a moment. Sit in the kitchen and let me take a look at you."

"I cannot, I'm afraid. I must check on my family." This is true and also an excuse.

"Of course. As long as you aren't trying to avoid me," Linley says. "We never finished talking about Charlie and the engagement. And I know now is not the time. But there's so much I want to say, and . . . if you could hear me out—"

Blood is now dripping from the wound onto Maria's hand. She can be stubborn and prideful another time. Right now, she needs some help. "I'll come in. To bandage my arm, not my heart," Maria says, revealing more than she should.

Maria follows Linley through the darkness into the house, leaving the charred scent of her beloved town behind. Three minutes, she tells herself. Or five at the most.

Physically spent from dashing around town for

hours, Maria blinks away the smoke from her eyes as the noise outside muffles, her arm sharply painful.

Linley lights a small lantern in the kitchen and pulls out a chair which Maria sinks into.

"Let me have a look," Linley says, pulling out another chair and the table and sitting very close to Maria, who pushes up her sleeve and extends her arm. Linley cradles Maria's elbow gently and gingerly pushes on the wound, on the soft flesh just above. Maria winces. "Sorry. It looks like a fairly deep gash. But the wound is not that wide across. Like a nick from a knife, almost. A tight bandage should do the trick."

Maria scans her memory while Linley moves around the kitchen, collecting supplies. "I cannot imagine. Is it possible I got cut by the corner of a sharp book?"

"That would have to be quite a tale!" Linley jokes, hands on hips.

"A Polynesian shell, maybe? An elephant's tusk?"

"The possibilities are endless with you, Maria," Linley says, smiling fondly and shaking her head. "An Inuit spear, a swordfish's sword! Only *you* would not know how—or from where—in the world you were injured."

Linley applies a damp cloth to the dried blood, cleaning around the affected area before putting a salve on it. She takes a worn bedsheet from a cabinet in the hall and holds the white fabric between her teeth, deftly tearing it into two. She repeats the movement on the smaller piece, tearing it again and again, ripping it into long bands. "There," Linley says, winding a long soft cloth around the spot above Maria's elbow. "As good as new!"

"Thank you," Maria says, wanting to linger but knowing she must return to the fire, to the books and artifacts that make up her public life. She stands and pulls the sleeve down over the bandage.

"Wait!" Linley says. "One more thing." She touches Maria gently on the back and nudges her to sit. Linley's brow furrows and she scans a high shelf in the kitchen, bringing the lantern with her as she reads labels on different jars. "My mother has an herbal remedy from France for my father's arthritis . . . Here!" she says, plucking a small glass jar off the shelf.

"Arthritis! Although certainly I have aged threefold in these past hours, I'm not quite elderly yet, Lin," Maria jokes.

Her friend rolls her eyes. There is a pitcher of blue hydrangea on the table, the flowers the color of Linley's eyes exactly. Linley moves closer, standing directly behind Maria seated in the chair. She lifts the back of Maria's hair, which has come loose in the night, sweeping it off to one shoulder and exposing the back of her neck.

"Can you point your chin down?" she asks softly. "I don't want to hurt you further."

Maria nods. Closes her eyes.

"Now this might feel chilly," Linley warns, touching Maria lightly. "But it warms when massaged into the skin."

The contact of cold cream on Maria's over-heated body gives her a tiny shock, and her shoulders hitch in surprise. Linley laughs. "My father always does the same. Even when your mind is told something is going to feel a certain way, it cannot really prepare your body for the coming sensation."

"You sound quite scientific," Maria says. "Or perhaps philosophical."

"Goethe's *Sturm und Drang*," Linley says. "You taught me about that: shocking one's audience with extremes of emotion."

Yes, Maria thinks. *And you taught me the same in return.*

Maria does not speak, as all of her concentration is now focused on the movement of Linley's thin delicate fingers up her neck to her hairline. Next they dip down below the neckline on Maria's dress to touch the skin and muscle of her shoulder blades and upper back.

"Better?" Linley asks.

Maria nods again. Swallows.

Linley seals the top back on the jar and places it on the table.

Maria stands and turns, facing Linley. She leans forward and kisses Linley on the lips. Linley makes a noise of such complete joy, almost like a note of a song, and then leans into Maria and kisses her back. The kiss deepens. They step close to one another, bodies touching, embracing. The kiss contains everything Maria needs to sustain her through the rest of this night, for the rest of her life.

Linley may become Charlie's wife soon, but for now, in this suspended time, she is still Maria's. Linley is now another person on this earth that Maria loves, which means she's another person to worry about losing. She has to let her know.

Maria pulls away. Linley's eyes are still closed. "I love you," Maria says.

"I love you, too," Linley says back, blinking into the darkness, looking as if she has just awoken from a spell. Maria mumbles an incoherent goodbye and makes haste to the front door, where she flees the cocoon of safety at Linley Blake's home and strides into the all-too-real fire and brimstone of the night.

She exits the lofty heavens and ventures back into battle with the very core of Hell. The pain in her arm has lessened and her shoulders do feel better, although a strong mint scent lingers in her hair and radiates from her skin. She turns her head and breathes her right shoulder: yes, it's from the herbal remedy. The odor is not entirely unpleasant, especially when she considers the method by which it arrived.

From that night forward, mint will forever make Maria pine for Linley Blake.

And pine as well for her beloved Atheneum, which, five blocks to the south, unbeknownst to Maria, has just gone up in flames.

41

ELIZA

Ten minutes. Twenty. Twenty-five. The tick, tick, ticking of the grandfather clock will drive her mad. She will sell it after this night, if it makes it through, never again wanting to be reminded of how quickly and slowly time passes.

After cheering in victory for sending the firemen away, Rachel and Mattie went upstairs to continue packing their belongings, for there was still the chance of destruction coming to their doorstep in a more natural fashion, should the fire spread up Main Street and consume their house along its way. Eliza thanked her children for their love and loyalty, and for their faith. For their collective power to believe in her. She had them pile their packed sacks and the two sea chests by the landing on the second floor, to grab in a hurry should they need. "We won! Now you should also try to rest." Rachel kissed Eliza on the cheek and followed Mattie upstairs.

Yes, the Macy women had won, technically. But what exactly was their prize? Uncertainty? Luck? Time? Might they only have forestalled the inevitable?

Two thirty in the morning. That first call she gave with the sailor was at about 11:00 p.m. How much longer can this blaze last? Eliza has taken a gamble that it will not reach their doorstep. Much as Henry gambles about which way to set sail and where to search for whales in the Pacific, there is no guarantee that her strategy will work. But she trusts her intuition, as Henry would tell her to—as any good captain of any Nantucket ship would.

Eliza tries to not think about James at all. Tries not to feel her heart pull toward him to protect him from danger. He is a grown man with clear-headed instincts—except, it seems, when it comes to her. She decides that James will be fine; she will search for him in the morning.

Eliza scans the living room and sees a parchment and quill on the small desk in the corner. The ink in a pot that has dried out. It was yet another letter that Eliza was about to write to Henry, another complaint, another worried rant writ large and sent off to sea, but she had stopped herself from composing it the other night. All she had written was *Dear Henry* and a comma.

Sometimes, Eliza writes letters she does not send. Letters in which she shares her innermost fears and greatest failings. Composing these letters feels cathartic, her soul laid bare. She scribbles furiously, reads them over and rips them to shreds, tosses them in the fireplace. Tonight she could write one and add it to the pyre that has become Main Street. Just open her door and say to the wind, *here, take this with you!* She scolds herself the moment after having the terrible, ironic thought.

Tick, tick, tick goes the clock.

In the kitchen, Eliza adds a few drops of tepid water from her teakettle into the glass jar of dried black ink. She returns to the living room, stirs the loosening ink with the quill, and sits.

She composes a confessional letter addressed to Henry, perhaps, but for God's eyes only, in which she admits to her adultery, and worse, how she has always loved James. Eliza writes about her feelings of shame over not having enough money to live on, much less to keep up the pretenses demanded by Nantucket society as a captain's wife. She tells him about the pledge of funds she made to William Hadwen in a fit of pique, when she wanted to look both wealthy and charitable, and how she fears that pledge had an immediate adverse effect on both her reputation and her purse strings. She writes of her anger toward him, for his failed journey the trip before this one, and for leaving her without answers now as to his whereabouts. And, as her hand begins to cramp, she tells him that she only married him for his money, for his stability, and for the love she felt for his child, Alice. And now, Alice seems angry with her!

And although she is to blame for all of this trouble, she has worked herself up to such an emotional froth that Eliza concludes the letter by blaming Henry entirely for all of her missteps, misdeeds, and miscalculations, and ultimately, for her family's undoing.

She folds the letter and seals it with candle wax that burns her thumb. She truly and sincerely thinks about walking out into the night with it, tossing it into a burning house. And, as much as she wants to stay safe inside her home, she is curious to see what the world looks like outside her door. Just a quick peek. To the top of Main Street, by the Pacific Bank. A few hundred feet or so from her home.

Eliza goes to the front door with the letter in her hand, but a rattling at the back door surprises her, and she thinks the firemen have returned to try again. From the clock she sees that an hour has passed. Three thirty in the morning.

"Hello! Hello?!" a woman calls, her voice tinged with a frantic edge. More rattling. "Hello? Is anyone home?" And then, "Rachel? Mattie? Mother!"

Alice.

Eliza drops the letter on a small table in the front hall and goes back through the living room and around to the side door kitchen entrance.

Alice is here! They can make amends. Eliza is hardly upset with her eldest daughter any more. She opens the door and Alice barges through.

Eliza longs to pull her into a hug, but Alice

shrugs her shoulder away. "Where are my sisters? Are they safe?"

"As safe as I am, yes." *Not that you seem to care about me, the woman who raised you like her own,* she wants to add. "They are upstairs packing trunks in case we must evacuate."

Alice nods curtly, stands stiffly. Eliza invites her to sit, but Alice refuses. She inquires after Larson, and asks if their home is unharmed.

"That's why we are coming to collect you. It's safer if you stay with us tonight."

"We?" Eliza asks. "Larson isn't here."

"Well, Larson journeyed with me into town, and then—despite my protests—kept on walking, to try and salvage items from the store."

"Oh no," Eliza says. "Just a block from here is in a terrible state. He shouldn't have gone." No wonder Alice is so upset. It's aimed at Eliza, but that emotion is displaced; she's worried about and angry at Larson. Eliza feels better.

"I was out earlier and I saw—"

"You were out? Tonight, in the blaze? What-ever for?" Alice asks, her gaze suddenly sharp. She looks at Eliza as if seeing her for the first time. "And why are you wearing that dress, of all things?"

Eliza backtracks. "I only stepped out onto the landing, to try and see what was happening. The firemen came to the house and I—"

"And so you put on your finest gown?"

Alice, Eliza notices, is wearing a simple linen shift and two different shoes. Her fine blond hair is braided for sleep.

"No, no, I—" But then she stops herself. What could she possibly say about her outfit choice that could explain it rationally? She worries about Larson but doesn't want to push the subject. What if Eliza says something to make Alice chase after him down Main Street? She must keep the conversation flowing. "As I was saying, the firemen came knocking on our door."

She then shares the story of the fire warden's plan with Alice: that, an hour ago, her house was to fall victim as a firebreak. "But I said no."

"You said no?" Alice says, the hint of a smile forming on her lips. "To the fire warden?"

"Yes!" Eliza says, smiling, too. How bold she was. How completely mad.

"Well, good for you," Alice says, standing up from the table, feet now bare of shoes.

"They ordered us to leave . . . and the girls and I said no!" Eliza says, incredulous about her own pluck.

"Indeed you did!" Alice says, genuinely pleased.

"Sent the fire warden away!"

"And good riddance to him!" Alice adds.

The women lock eyes. The familiar banter, the comfortable patois of a mother and her grown daughter. It almost feels normal. Almost.

"They made it seem like I didn't have a choice," Eliza says.

"But you did. We always have choices, Mother."

Yes, Eliza thinks. She reflects back on the day she first met this spunky, stubborn baby who would become her daughter. *We always have choices, Mother.* Like whether to try and help the widower with the screaming toddler in a candy store or just turn and go. Like choosing honey sticks or black licorice as a favorite sweet. Like choosing who to love, and who to marry.

Eliza then ponders the many choices she made this week alone. Perhaps some of them were incorrect. Eliza obviously upset Alice the night of the town hall meeting. And although Alice didn't come here for an apology, this is the perfect moment to mend the relationship.

"I hate to think that you are still angry with me about last Monday night," Eliza says, sitting hesitantly in the kitchen chair next to Alice.

Alice raises her eyebrows at her mother. Drums her fingers on the table. "Yes? And?"

"And so I want to apologize. Sincerely."

"Apologize for what, exactly?" Alice asks, her green eyes narrowing.

"You know what, Alice! Must you make this so hard?" Eliza says. "Just let me say I'm sorry!"

"I understand, Mother! Just tell me the content of your apology, and I will gladly accept it."

"I'm sorry that I interfered in your business and spoke at the town meeting on your behalf last week. I thought I was helping, but I can now see how, as a grown woman, that must have been embarrassing for you. And for Larson, too."

Alice is staring at Eliza with a confused expression, so Eliza continues on. "Perhaps I haven't yet made my point clear. In the future, I will stay out of your business choices and not share my opinions so publicly."

"Huh," Alice says, looking amazed, but not in what Eliza would call a good way. "You certainly are a strong-willed person, Mother. And sometimes, you're even right. Like when you spoke up to the fire warden."

"Well, thank you, dear Alice," Eliza says, shoulders relaxing. She did it. She said the correct thing.

"But not last Monday. Do you really have no idea as to what you did wrong? About what you said and how you behaved?"

Eliza tries to hold Alice's gaze, but her emerald eyes are fierce, and Eliza looks away.

A knock on the door breaks their cold silence. "Oh, for heaven's sake!" Eliza yells, whether at Alice's confusing statements or the knocking or both she's not even certain. If the fire warden appears again, she'll give up and give in. Nothing is worth fighting for anymore if her daughter hates her, for then her life has already gone up in flames. She opens the door. "You win! Blow up my house if you must!"

But it is not a man in uniform. Standing on Eliza's doorstep is Meg Wright, her face contorted in pain. "I'm so sorry to bother you, Mrs. Macy," Meg says, clutching her middle. "But I'm looking for your daughter. I saw her storefront downtown and was reminded that she has some rudimentary training as a midwife. I don't know where she lives, so I came here. You mentioned your address at the town meeting, and I—"

Eliza turns toward Alice, who joins her by the front door. "Meg!" Alice says, startled by the form of this tall woman, stooped over and clutching her midsection in pain. "Are you in labor?"

"Alice, please," Meg pants. "Help me deliver this baby."

42

MEG

The contractions are coming fast and quick now, Meg's body readying for labor. Meg's brow is slick and her mind is white-hot and blank. Every rational thought has been pushed aside. She cannot think about who is right and who is wrong, who is proud and who is stubborn, who is Black and who is white. Who took action and who stood silent, watching injustices take place. Who kissed a man who is not her husband, and who witnessed the infidelity. If she is to survive this night, then Meg can only think of Eliza Macy as another woman, another human being on this earth who knows this journey as she does, as another woman who can help her contend with the chaos inside her own body and make it stop. And hope that Eliza Macy can do the same.

There is only the baby to think of.

As Meg turned away from the harbor, she thought, *What kind of imbecile goes out in a fire?*, before realizing the irony: she'd done exactly the same. Gone out in a fire! What a mistake that was, in retrospect. Leaving her home, abandoning her child, thinking that she might bump into Benjamin, perhaps, like in some sort of fairy tale where the embattled prince saves the doomed princess from a cursed existence. Slaying the fire-breathing dragon.

Now at the door of the Macy home, Meg explains to the two stunned white women how there's no one left to help: about Jane's trip to attend a birth in 'Sconset, about the Candle Street fire and Doc Ruggles' home. How Benjamin doesn't even know she's in labor, out somewhere battling the flames. She asks Alice Handler if she'd help with the delivery. But Eliza Macy speaks first.

"Candle Street? Down by Commercial Wharf?" Eliza asks, her face pale.

"Yes," Meg says, confused by the question but polite enough to answer it. Anything to get Alice to help her. She turns her attention toward the daughter. "If we could go back to your house, I'd be ever so grateful," Meg says.

"My house? It's so far away."

A glance is exchanged between Eliza Macy and her step-daughter Alice Handler. Eliza ever so slightly shakes her head no, and Alice puts her hands on her hips in response. A conversation without words. And then Alice speaks. "Mother, *this* is what I was talking about."

This? Meg wonders. *Is this . . . me?*

Meg waits as a decision gets made by two well-off white women, two supposedly liberal abolitionists. Related by marriage and family if not by blood. They raise funds for the fight against slavery and speak fervently at meetings. Meg once even witnessed Eliza Macy with tears in her eyes, so overcome was she with the pain and suffering of slaves in the South, so moved by the words of Frederick Douglass in the Atheneum! And yet now—what is it—five or six years later? At the Nantucket town council meeting? Contentiousness bordering on hostility. And on her own doorstep? Hesitation.

"Oh, for heaven's sake," Meg says. This baby is pushing on her patience as well as her bladder.

"I want to help you, really I do . . ." Eliza Macy begins, a sentence that seems to require a "but" next.

"Of course, you must come inside," Alice says.

"I don't think that's a good—" Eliza begins, her eyes frantic.

"My water broke about two hours ago. I need to lie down. Can't we go to your house, Alice?" Meg prompts again, having no idea where Alice lives.

"No, there's no more walking for you tonight! It's not safe. You've journeyed enough on foot and in active labor!"

Alice, small but strong, pulls Meg up the step and into the house. Meg has no time to wonder why Eliza is dressed so formally, nor what she would like to say to her daughter if she could get her alone.

But Meg needs not guess at Eliza Macy's

feelings, she just has to look at the woman's face! Is it shock, annoyance, disbelief . . . or fear? And, if so, fear of what, exactly? That Meg is a Black woman in her home, or that Meg is the keeper of her deep secret? That look from Eliza Macy is all of those feelings and more. That look might just give Meg the strength she needs to get through this night.

Meg steps across the threshold. The door shuts behind her. The three women stand together, like points on a triangle on the plush Oriental rug in an overly decorated space. There is shouting outside, the cacophony of disaster. It is frightening, and no place to be. Inside the Macy home, only loud silence and the ticking of a clock, which somehow terrifies Meg even more.

"I saw your husband," Eliza Macy says. At first, Meg thinks she is talking to Alice, about Larson Handler. Meg thinks she saw him, too, trying to check on his store just now, no doubt. But Eliza Macy is looking directly at her.

"Mine? Benjamin?"

"Yes, he was trying to warn me that the fire department wanted to blow up my home."

"And he was . . . unharmed?"

"Yes." Eliza shrugs. "Although he received quite a dressing-down from the fire ward."

"When was that? Do you know where he might be now?" Meg cares little for whether Benjamin was yelled at as long as he's alive. Perhaps he is just up the street and Meg can stand on the stoop and call out to him.

"This was about an hour and a half ago. Maybe more," Eliza says.

A clamor on the stairs makes the women turn their heads. "Mother! Did you say firemen?" one girl asks, rushing down the stairs, her long honey-colored hair trailing behind her. An identical voice is followed by another girl with identical hair. "Have the firemen returned?"

The two perch on the landing, pale eyes wide, waiting for their mother's response.

"Alice!" one says, noticing her older sister. The two enter the parlor and hug Alice identically. She puts one arm around each of them.

"Hello, hello," Alice says, "I am so glad to see you both!"

"No firemen, girls," Eliza says to her daughters. "Just Alice who has come to check on us. The house is fine. And Meg Wright is here."

Meg tries to force a smile, but as a new contraction comes on, it turns into a grimace.

"She's in labor," Rachel says.

"Mother, where can we bring Miss Meg?" Alice prods.

"I could give birth right here on this rug," Meg says. Her labor from this point on could take hours—or minutes.

It feels incredibly freeing not to care what someone else thinks of her in a moment like this.

"Yes, there is always that option," Alice says. "Shall we prepare the center hall rug for birthing, Mother?"

"She'll be more comfortable in the borning room," Eliza says.

So Alice puts an arm around Meg and guides her through the living room past the kitchen, and the girls follow at the rear of the procession.

43

MARIA

The roads are blocked heading south toward the Atheneum. Maria circumnavigates the ring of fire and heads west on Chester Street and then back toward town on Center Street.

The smoke is so thick she can hardly breathe. Maria pulls the collar of her dress up and tucks her nose inside its neckline, keeping her shoulders raised and her body stooped over slightly so her mouth and nose stay covered.

A commotion by Joseph Coffin's brick mansion on the corner of Broad stops Maria in her tracks. The fire has consumed all of Center and Broad, but this brick structure, much like her own home at the Pacific Bank, eludes the flames. People have gathered by the back side of the enormous home, a safe position on the edge of disaster.

Except they are not just gathered there to avoid the blaze, they are gathered around someone. Someone on the ground. Hurt. A large group surrounds the person, though, and it is so dark that Maria cannot see who it is, or how many there are. The sounds of moaning from the injured party blend in with the cries from onlookers and the sizzle and hiss of her town.

"Miss—" Joseph Allen says, seeing Maria and

coming around toward her. He's always where the action is, this boy. She knows in large part his curiosity is due to the macabre excitement of disaster, but there's something else to it. She trusts him, little Joseph Allen, and would want him by her side in good times and bad. Maria will have to promote him to Head Atheneum Boy once they are back to work in the library, a position she invents for him on the spot.

"Joseph, what's the matter? Can you tell who has been hurt? Or how bad the injuries are?"

"Nay, miss, I just arrived when you did, but from the other side of town and over there I saw—"

How is it possible that Joseph still has so much energy? Maria is too concerned about what's happening in front of her right this minute to hear some grand and exaggerated story about what's happening elsewhere. She's tired. Her eyes are burning. Her throat is so very dry.

There's an opening in the tight circle and Maria squeezes through. Joseph, being lithe and small, elbows his way in, too. "Miss Mitchell, I just think there's something you need to hear, and I feel like I'm the person to tell ya—" he says.

"I appreciate that, but can it wait?" Maria asks, loudly, because the noise of the fire is quite deafening. This sets her off on a coughing fit. Someone offers her water from a tin cup and she swallows it down and thanks them.

Someone bends down in front of Maria, giving her a clear view of the scene at her feet. Several men sit on the street corner, breathing heavily. Three men in total. Two are in firemen uniforms and the other is not.

"I'm here, I'm here!" a man says, from behind Maria. He is out of breath, his words coming slow as he reaches the group. It's Dr. Ruggles.

The crowd parts to let him in, and he crouches by the men and asks about their injuries.

"He musta run around the whole outside of town to get here!" Joseph says. Maria only nods. "You know, they blew up his house, too! Only it didn't work the first time so they had to—"

"Shhhh, Joseph," Maria says. She's trying to hear the men in conversation. Dr. Ruggles nods and opens his leather medical bag, digging through. One man has burns on his arm, the sleeve melted to his skin. He must be in shock, for he doesn't even cry out in pain when the doctor applies an ointment of some kind and a bandage.

Onlookers ask what they can do to help. *Does he need some water? Should I fetch a loved one? I'd offer they stay in my house, only I don't have one anymore.*

The other two seem exhausted, although Maria cannot see any physical injury. Perhaps they are hurt under their clothing. "We have to transport these men somewhere," the doctor says to the crowd. "Somewhere close, and quickly, and away from the smoke."

Everyone looks around them as if trying to conjure a hospital from thin air. Maria has an idea.

"What about the Coffin house, right here?" she says. Joseph Coffin built the beautiful structure for his new wife, only she didn't like it very much. They moved off island a few months ago, with no plans to return. "It's furnished and abandoned."

Doc Ruggles stands, puts his hands on his hips, and considers the building. "Anyone want to break down the side door?"

Joseph Allen is the first to volunteer.

He needs a few larger helpers, but they manage to enter in short order. Two of the men can stand and walk in by themselves, but the third loses consciousness and must be carried inside.

As the man is lifted by several others, Maria sees his face. "Oh no," she says.

"Do you know him, miss?" Joseph asks, back by her side.

"Yes, Joseph, I do." She watches as he is carried up a few stairs and inside the home. Should she follow? Should she ask the doctor for details of his condition? She dashes up behind the others and takes the man's limp hand in hers. *Please,* she thinks. *Please.*

He opens his eyes for just a moment. Blinks. "Tell my wife," he says.

The wooden handrail keeps Maria steady as she steps back down into the street. Joseph is still there.

"Miss, I know you don't want to hear it, but I'm going to say it anyway," Joseph says, feet firmly planted. He removes his cap and looks her straight in the eye. Maria could silence him again, but he clearly has something he wants to say. And if Maria admires his dogged nature, then she also must at times indulge it.

"Yes, sir," she says.

"Some news is hard to accept, but my mother always tells me it's best to hear it from a person who cares the same way you do. Like a relative instead of a stranger."

The sadness in his eyes, the sense that much has been lost. She lets him declare it. "Miss, the Atheneum is gone."

It feels like a punch to the stomach. As if understanding where the pain is, Joseph hugs her middle, awkwardly but with deep feeling and sincerity.

"What can we do now?" Joseph asks, moving away. He likes being needed, useful.

Maria thinks about sending Joseph on a new mission, to tell a family about their beloved husband and son-in-law who might be dying inside the Coffin home right now. But she doesn't want to put him in any more danger by having him run around town again.

And, like Joseph just said, it's best to hear difficult news from someone who knows you well.

"Will you do this one last thing for me?" Maria asks.

"Anything, miss."

"Go home, now," she orders.

"But—yes, miss," he says.

"I'll walk with you part of the way, Joseph," she says, and the two head west out of town.

And then Maria turns onto Main Street.

44

MEG

In order to avoid a full-on wave of panic, Meg imagines that she's talking to her friends and family, imagines that they are the ones surrounding her as she prepares to bring forth life. Imagines that she's still alive in the morning, though who can predict that?

As she gets settled on the bed, another contraction hits. All the time, Eliza Macy talks. Talks, talks.

"Rachel, can you get another pillow from upstairs?

"Mattie, can you fetch the laudanum? I think I threw it into the copper pot earlier. Meg can have whatever's left of it. And please light another candlestick, this one here on the bedside table. Meg, breathe through it.

"Alice, are you certain you know what you're doing? Because I most certainly do not know myself.

"Rachel, stop jotting notes in your journal! This is not the time for scientific observation or artistic expression! Go fetch the pillow as I asked!"

So much talking. Meg prefers Jane's way of birthing, by humming and singing and telling old stories, by bringing calm to the room instead of chaos.

That being said, the laudanum is a marvel. It dulls Meg's nerves and makes her fingers tingly. She wiggles her toes, brown against the crisp white sheets. Where did her shoes go? Meg doesn't remember removing them. Ah, well. The voices around Meg recede. Her mind clouds with the sound of her own breath, an oceanic fog.

"That's good, Meg." The younger woman with the green eyes is at the end of the bed. She's telling Meg things to do and complimenting her. The other woman in the room is in a fancy dress. Is she going to a ball? Meg's knees are bent, her skirt raised. This woman is peering between Meg's legs. She should say something, but then she feels another contraction and pain shoots instantly back into her body, and she is reminded of why she's there and who she is.

"Alice, is she getting close?" the other woman asks. She's standing in the doorway, at the edge of the darkness, wringing her hands. "Alice?" Something must be wrong.

Alice. The woman's name is Alice! "What time did your water break?" Alice asks Meg.

Meg pulls herself out of the fog to answer. "Just about one o'clock in the morning."

"It's four thirty now. Three plus hours ago," Alice says. "And your pains are close together. Are you ready to push, Meg?"

"No," Meg says. "Not yet." Not until Jane gets here, not until the fire dies down to embers and Benjamin finds her. Not until Lucy gets home in the light of morning, home to her own bed.

"We'll wait a little bit, then," Alice says, and Meg is grateful to be heard. "You rest for now, Meg."

But I must never rest, Meg thinks. *Didn't my papa once tell me that? Or, no; rest for a moment to fight again. Yes, that was it. I'll do that.*

One tall, thin girl with honey-colored hair stands on the other side of the bed, on the windowed side. She fixes her pale blue eyes on Meg and smiles. Touches Meg's brow with a damp towel. "That's cold," Meg says. "Nice."

The girl is pleased with this answer. She leaves the cloth on Meg's forehead and turns away. Meg can hear water; something being wrung out. Another wet cloth appears. The girl places it on the back of Meg's neck.

Meg wants to stay alert, stay wary. Make sure that no harm comes to herself or her child. But the pull of the drug is powerful, and she closes her eyes and dozes. The girl leaves, says she'll be back in a little while. When Meg wakes, she hears voices new and old, current and echoed from another day, another time.

In her dream, two women talk. They talk in a way that sounds both friendly and irritated at the same time, both real and imagined, beyond Meg's grasp and yet completely understandable to her. She feels like she's in between sleep and alertness, like when Lucy's eyes grow heavy during a bedtime story. Meg is fighting to stay awake and to sleep simultaneously. She wants to hear every word. Some of the sentences are sharp as tacks, others as dull as pencil nubs.

"I'm so very glad you're here tonight. I couldn't handle this birth without you. She's finally resting," a voice says. It is the not-Alice woman. The mother. The one who owns this house. This bed.

"Mother. You couldn't have handled it? Or, more likely, it wouldn't have happened. You wouldn't have agreed to let her in this house to give birth if I wasn't here."

There is a pause.

"She was afraid to step foot in your house. Admit it."

"I'll admit no such— She must've had quite a— Out there in the fire," Eliza says. "That would make anyone—"

Of course, Larson's shop caters to men of all professions, not just the more menial ones.

"Fearful of the fire, yes. But Meg looked like she was afraid of *you,*" the woman clarifies. "She came looking for me, and clearly didn't want to see—"

And their shoes are lacking true craftsmanship

besides. Only people without discerning taste would buy from the Wrights.

"And yet you forced her into my—!" The other woman's voice is suddenly fierce, even in a whisper. Why do they whisper? "Did you do this to—some sort of point?"

"Based on your reaction to Meg and this situation, I can see that I have more than proven my—"

"Alice, you seem to have a lot of points to make tonight—of which are against me."

"I have one point to make, Mother. And that is you are a bigot."

"I am no such thing!" the other woman says. "She's here, isn't she? In my house, giving birth. What else must I say or do to please you, Alice? And, what is that noise? Is that someone knocking on the door again?"

"Don't try to change the subject."

"I'm not trying to change the subject. I fear that the firemen are back, and then what are we going to do? How are we going to help Meg then?"

This sounds terrible. Drastic, chaotic. Meg knows she should be very worried about who is knocking on the Macys' front door and what this might mean for her, but she cannot summon the energy to care.

45

ELIZA

"Mother!" one of the twins calls out from the front parlor. "Someone is here to see you!"

"Is it the fire department?" Eliza calls back. She tries to keep the worry from her voice for Meg's sake, but isn't sure she's able to.

"No!" her daughter says.

"Then send them away, Mattie! Or Rachel!" Really! No one ever visits her and now her house is busier than the docks when the ferry from New Bedford pulls in. For modesty, she makes sure Meg's body is tucked under the quilt. Meg's breathing is steady and her eyes are closed. She seems peaceful, at least for now. She's not going to be giving birth for a while yet.

"Miss Mitchell says it's urgent," her daughter says, now closer, quieter, in the room with them. It's Mattie. "She's looking for Alice."

"Miss Mitchell?" Eliza asks. And then she turns to see it's true; Maria is standing in the borning room doorway.

"Hello, Alice, Eliza," Maria says. She has soot on her face and dress, and her dark eyes are bloodshot from smoke. She makes the room reek of char.

"Hello," Eliza says, trying to be polite. "Is every-

407

thing all right, Maria? What are you doing here?"

But Maria is too focused on the scene in the room to answer Eliza. "Is Meg Wright—?"

"Giving birth here in my house? Yes, she is," Eliza says. "During a fire. Which I see you've been out in."

"Well, I—" Maria stammers. Blinks. Looks from Meg to Alice to Eliza and Mattie. The room is suddenly very crowded.

Sensing that something is wrong, Eliza sends Mattie away. "Why don't you and Rachel knit something for the baby?" she suggests. They nod and leave happily. When in doubt, give your children a project to keep them busy.

"Meg arrived in labor, and my mother did not want to let her into the house," Alice says.

"Well, now everyone in the room is filled in on the ways in which I am a terrible person," Eliza says. She goes to the basin on the nightstand and wets a clean towel. Hands it to Maria. "For your face," she explains.

"Just apologize, Mother. Maria was there on Monday night at the town hall meeting. She knows. She agrees with me."

Maria walks over to the nightstand and peers at her face in the mirror. "I'm a fright!" she says, cleaning away the grime and wetting her eyes.

After drying her face, Maria turns to the Macy women. "I do feel that an apology is in order, Eliza."

"Believe me, I'm sorry!" Eliza says, "I should never have opened my big mouth."

"That's not a great apology," Alice says.

"And you don't owe it to us," Maria adds. "If you could be honest about your bigoted ways to Meg, well then—"

Meg stirs in the bed, repositioning herself, but does not wake.

"But I'm the secretary of the Anti-Slavery Society!" Eliza declares.

"You take down minutes, which means what, exactly, when you won't let a Black woman into your home?" Maria fires back, also in a loud hush.

"Of course I let Black people into my home. Mrs. Jacobs worked here for years when the girls were little."

Maria crosses her arms on her chest. Sighs. "There is an important distinction to be made between someone working in your home and one invited in as a guest. But I can see that this is going to take some time, and now is not it."

"But, Maria, this is actually a perfect time to address my mother's small-mindedness . . ." Alice says.

Traitor! To think Eliza tried to help Alice and Larson, and this is the thanks she gets.

But Alice continues talking, and places her hand on her midsection as she does. "Because, there's a new life coming, and it's important for me to know that the world I am bringing her into is a fair and just one."

New life? And not Meg's baby? "Are you—?" Eliza begins.

Alice's green eyes are bright with the truth of it. And now she accepts Eliza's hug. "That's why Larson and I invited you to dinner tonight. Only you sent the twins along and didn't join. I was so upset."

Yet another failing, another reason to feel such guilt and shame. "I promise to love your daughter with every fiber in my being," Eliza says. "More even than I love you." She smiles. "Which is quite a great deal."

Maria congratulates the two women, but she looks sheepish, and her demeanor is reserved. "My timing could not have been worse, I'm afraid."

"Tell us, Maria," Eliza says.

"Larson is with Doc Ruggles. He inhaled quite a bit of smoke."

Eliza feels Alice's knees start to give way but she catches her before she falls. She looks up at Eliza again with those eyes.

Those green eyes. Augustine's eyes. Eliza never met Alice's mother—the first Mrs. Macy— but she misses her now. Maybe Augustine would know what to say in this moment, how to both comfort Alice and be strong for her. Maybe Augustine wouldn't have said things at a town hall meeting to upset Alice. Maybe that pair of mother and daughter would never have argued, would always have been like-minded. It's clear that Augustine gave Alice her eyes. She must have passed on other traits, too, about social and political action, about ways of seeing her neighbors, her community. For the first time in her life, Eliza tries to be Augustine.

"We will bring Larson here, to us," Eliza says. "We'll take care of him, and he will recover and be fine. Better than fine!"

Alice presses her hands against the wooden floor and pulls herself upright. Leans her head against the wall, covered in a burgundy wallpaper with climbing vines of blue and yellow flowers. Her legs are outstretched, her feet bare.

"I'm not certain that's possible," Maria says softly. "I was thinking, rather, that Alice could go to him."

"But, if the two of you leave, who will help Meg?" Eliza asks, afraid that she already knows the answer to this.

"You," Maria says.

How can she possibly do this enormous thing alone, without support? Even if she enlisted help from Rachel and Mattie . . . if Meg were to die! Eliza couldn't have that on her conscience, on her hands. A Black woman and her baby, dead in her house.

But then Eliza looks into Alice's pleading,

411

troubled eyes and makes the difficult but wise decision to keep quiet. "Go to Larson," Eliza says. She reminds her eldest daughter that her mismatched shoes are under the kitchen table. She tells her that she loves her more than is possible, more than the love of two mothers combined. Maria leads Alice out with a gentle hand on her back.

The room gets so very quiet and still.

And then, only ten minutes later, Maria returns.

"Oh! You scared me," Eliza says, hand on her heart. "Why are you back so quickly? Did Larson . . . ?"

"No, no. I gave Alice a well-lit lantern and directions to skirt the edge of town safely," Maria says. "And then, as I began to walk with her, I turned around. The Atheneum is gone, my family is safe inside the Pacific Bank. Alice is on her way to Larson, and well . . . there's no one else for me to care about. I thought you and Meg needed me more than anyone else did." Maria looks at the figure in the bed.

Eliza feels grateful, and then only slightly upset when she realizes her longtime friend is here for Meg much more than she is for her.

46

MEG

Someone is calling her name, stroking her hair. Meg opens her eyes. Sees a face looming over her. Miss Mitchell! She's here. Meg likes Maria Mitchell. Yes, very much. She waves to her from the bed. "Lo," she says, hitting most of the word *hello*.

"Lo to you, too, Meg," Maria says. "May I sit next to you?" she asks.

Meg nods and feels the mattress sink. Maria takes Meg's hand in hers.

"How about this night, hmmm?"

"Hmm," Meg agrees. It is quite a night, after all.

"Are you . . . comfortable here?"

Meg nods.

"You're going to have a beautiful baby soon, Meg," she says. "And I'm going to help ensure that."

Then the other woman speaks. "Do you really distrust me that much, Maria? That I wouldn't do everything in my power to keep this woman and her baby healthy and alive?"

"I do know that, Eliza. But, at the same time, I know you feel differently about . . . certain people . . . and I just don't understand why you won't admit to any—"

"I have nothing to admit to."

But Meg is awake now, alert. And she thinks the woman does have something to admit to. Didn't she see two people in the Hadwens' cellar, leaning against each other, locked in an embrace, kissing? Wasn't one of them this Eliza at the end of the bed?

Someone with the strong scent of a fireplace is standing over Meg, talking right above her now. "Alice told me that it seemed like Meg was ready before to push, but that now the baby isn't—" Maria says.

Meg shouldn't have seen that at the wedding, those two locked in an embrace. Not the bride and groom. Someone's bride with someone else's groom. She's paying the price for it now. Lying in the cold, sweat-soaked sheets, Meg gasps as another contraction comes on, this one more fierce than any of the others combined. She cries out. "I'm sorry. I'm so sorry! I didn't see you kissing that man! I was looking for something else, Mrs. Macy!"

"Eliza, what is Meg talking about?" Maria asks.

"She must be hallucinating," the other woman says. "Calling out like that. Is—stuck? Turned?" the woman asks.

There is a pause.

"Eliza, did you kiss James? And . . . did Meg see you with him?"

"Now you must be delusional, too! Out of your mind, everyone, the fire—everyone crazy."

The baby, the pain, the pain, the baby. Meg cries out. Shrinks her body into a tight ball around her center. "I'm sorry. Make the pain go away. I promise I'll never tell about what I saw at the wedding."

"It's all right, Meg," the librarian says, coming close and staring right into her eyes. "Stay here with us."

Maria. She knows her. Meg locks eyes with her as the contraction passes, her body lengthening out on the bed.

"I can explain about James," Eliza says.

"I'm sure you think you can," Maria says. "Although I'm not sure I want to hear it. The less I know the better. Let's attend to Meg. Feel here," she says, and the two women press hard on Meg's abdomen, one on each side. "I have read about births, and I attended those of my younger siblings, but I was never in charge of one. I think this is the head. Does that seem right to you?"

Meg doesn't like that these women aren't sure. If the baby dies inside her and they cannot remove it then she will die, too, here, in this stranger's home, alone. And no one will go out in the fire to tell Benjamin. And no one will know to tell Lucy.

Meg sleeps. Then a younger girl comes back and says that it is close to five in the morning.

That the fire seems to have moved on to other parts of town.

It is quiet outside. It is quiet inside. Meg is so tired. She has been laboring for only four hours, and yet it feels already like a lifetime.

Maria asks if this is what it was like when Meg gave birth before, to Lucy. "Lucy was easy," Meg says, wanting to drift off to sleep. "It was Elias that was hard."

"Who is Elias?" Maria asks.

Meg doesn't answer.

More time passes. The two women begin to talk again, in that same hushed-but-charged way, like a storm brewing in the distance. Meg listens but only hears parts.

"Maria, let me explain about James. Meg revealed—of it, but—"

"I think you'd better not, Eliza. Although I do want you to trust and confide in—as a friend, some secrets are just better left— The less I know about this, the better."

"So, we're friends, but we don't actually share our thoughts and concerns with—? We only talk about one another behind—backs? How very Nantucket of you."

"Eliza, this island is lonely for many— It must be incredibly lonely for you. Without Henry for years—"

"How could you possibly understand, Maria?

416

You are—constantly by family, and by—at the library. You are so busy and your life is so full that you don't even have interest in or time for a husband."

"I get lonely, too. There's a lot you don't know about—"

"And with your work, Maria, you don't have to worry about financial— about how to put—on the table."

"Are you bankrupt, Eliza?"

"Of course! How could you not have known that? Henry's last voyage was not profitable and this one's been delayed—for no apparent reason that I can see!—and Larson's store is failing and the girls *eat* so much . . ."

"So . . . Is that why you protested the Wrights' cobbler shop?"

"Meg and her—were trying to undermine Larson's shop!"

"They were trying to get ahead, not undermine anyone else."

Silence.

"Not that it matters now, all the—I did for Larson."

"Oh, Eliza. He'll survive. You'll see."

"But his store will not— Both shops are certainly burned to ashes by now. All of Main Street is. None—matters. If it's true that Candle Street burned, that maybe James was injured or killed—"

"Eliza! Are you crying?" Meg hears a rustle of sorts, as if from skirts, a chair scraping against the hard wooden floor. "There, there. You and James have always loved one another, haven't you? How so very—that must be."

"We made love last night," the woman whispers. "Just before the fire."

"Oh, Eliza. What have you done?"

Silence. Meg sleeps.

Hours pass. Years. Moments.

A burning agony wakes Meg and rocks her forward, until she is sitting up in bed and crying out for help. Animalistic moans, demonic chords. The two women are instantly out of their seats in the corners of the room, instantly by Meg's feet at the end of the bed.

"Girls! Come now!" one of the women calls. The two identically pale girls rush in and position themselves by the top of the bed, each one taking a hand. Meg looks into the gray-blue eyes of the one on her right, and sees past her to the window and the matching light outside. It is the light of dawn.

The house that was next door is a shell of ash.

The woman stares at Meg. Meg remembers her name now, remembers everything about this terrible woman: Eliza Macy. Eliza Macy guides Meg to place her feet on the wrought iron railing at the foot of the bed. Then she pushes her arms against Meg's shins and cradles Meg's knees in her hands.

Eliza's brown eyes are bloodshot and fierce. "Now, push, Meg. Push as if your life depends on it. You hear me? Push!"

PART III

ASH

THE MORNING AFTER THE FIRE
Tuesday, July 14, 1846

47

ELIZA

A newborn baby is cradled in Eliza's hands, wailing, crying. Whole. The child is furious, her bloody fists raised up and out, her motions jerky and small and the most powerful ones Eliza has ever seen. Here's a foot with five curled toes, and another, and here is a bottom solid and slick in her palm.

"That will do," Maria says, sighing out her own labors. She just helped deliver the afterbirth. "Let me take the baby, clean her up," Maria says, extending her arms and scooping the infant into a white bedsheet, wiping the baby's eyes, which are coated in a waxy white substance. Her lips are puffy and pink, her nose a tiny nub, her hair silken black fuzz.

A dull morning haze tinges everything in the room with misty-gray light. They have made it through the night. Although Eliza isn't quite sure of the time, she'd say it's just after six in the morning. She notices the empty glass vial on the bedside table and feels a tug of worry in her gut: she's out of medicine. As if by the power of suggestion alone, Eliza's body and mind crave it, just a few drops in her tea. Especially when she thinks of what she confessed to Maria about James.

"There, there," Maria says, rocking the little body up and down as the baby soothes, swaddled tightly now. "Time to meet your mama, sweet girl."

"A girl?" Meg says, her voice otherworldly. Exhausted, elated. She hikes herself up on her elbows, scoots her torso upright on the bed.

Eliza remembers that transcendent moment from after Rachel and Mattie were born, when she took in the meaning of what she had accomplished successfully: *You mean to say, I created them, and I'm alive and they are alive, and we're all in one piece?*

Rachel quickly moves to the head of the bed and fluffs some pillows behind Meg's back. Meg thanks her and extends her arms out to take her baby daughter from Maria.

"All this time, we thought you were a boy," she says, speaking to the child. "You sure fooled us."

After hours of tension and suffering and pain, a post-battle calm has settled over the borning room. Like a field of warriors, bruised and bloodied after a night's skirmish, they are stunned into companionable silence and buoyed by the shared realization that they collectively beat back death. Eliza is bonded to these women now, Maria and Meg both, in a way that would have seemed impossible to her yesterday. And, oh: her perfectly capable, mature daughters!

"She's a beautiful baby," Mattie says to Meg,

standing next to her twin sister and blinking back tears.

"And strong. Like her mother," Eliza says.

Meg looks up from her baby and focuses all her attention on Eliza. "I owe you a debt of gratitude."

"You owe me no such thing," Eliza says. She feels embarrassed suddenly, exposed. Her eyes sting.

"It's what any decent human being would do," Maria adds pointedly.

Maria turns to the twins. "I've got clean linens at home; will one of you come with me to fetch them? Then I can prepare breakfast for everyone and bring it by."

"Yes, ma'am," Rachel says.

Maria looks exhausted.

Eliza thinks of Alice. Of poor Larson.

"Mattie, can you get to the Coffins' house on Broad Street, do you think? I'd like to check on Larson, if it's safe," Eliza says.

"I would very much like to go. May I change into a clean dress first, Mama?" Mattie says.

"Yes, of course, both of you should do so," Eliza says, thinking of a hundred more things to say just as the girls turn away from her. "Be very careful. We don't know whether the fires have completely been extinguished. I recall pockets of town still burning in the morning light in the last great fire. And try to gather as much information as you can about what was destroyed and what remains." She lowers her voice and whispers to her daughters, hopefully in a way that Meg cannot hear. "And inquire about the cost of human life. In particular, as to the firemen. Ask anyone and everyone you see if they know anything about Benjamin Wright, the cobbler."

"Yes, Mama," the twins mumble in unison, keeping their eyes averted from the mother singing to her newborn child on the other side of the room.

In the hallway, past the kitchen. By light of day, the piles of items look haphazardly thrown together in preparation for a quick departure in the middle of the night: the filled copper pot, a cast-iron frying pan, a half-used candle. This is what she thought would be useful out in the world? Should her home have burned to the ground or been exploded by gunpowder, Eliza anticipated needing to have a cup of tea for one afterward? Perhaps frying up an egg out on Main Street? Really! What had she been thinking?

On a small table sits the letter Eliza penned to Henry while in a frantic, crazed state, sealing it with wax at two in the morning. How desperate she had felt, desperate enough to confess her sin of infidelity and beg for his forgiveness. Desperate enough to think writing it down could erase the truth of it from her worries. And proud that she had stood up to the fire marshal and fought for their home. She will light a fire for their morning tea and destroy the letter over the open flames.

On the floor in the front hall rests the large soup tureen that she had clutched so tightly when the firemen first arrived on her doorstep. An elegant, useless object. All of it: the urns on the mantel in the living room to her right, the china service in the dining room, the blue silk damask curtains and the Oriental rug—all of it elegant and useless. Entirely unhelpful in case of emergency.

Perhaps if she had lost it all, she would have mourned and longed for it, thing after thing after thing. But having it all remaining in pristine condition feels—well, sinful. Laughable and wrong. It feels like guilt and excess and gluttony.

Now all she cares about is to know Larson is all right.

And James.

Eliza hikes up her long skirt with one hand, clutches the banister with the other and slowly climbs the stairs. She, too, must change out of her soiled dress. In her bedroom, all she wants to do is sleep, just strip down to her naked body, crawl underneath the coverlet, and doze for hours. She pushes past this—a few more hours, and slumber will be her gift—and opens her wardrobe, searching for and locating a simple olive frock.

Eliza accidentally catches her reflection in the long mirror. Once she's seen it, she must walk toward it. She had forgotten herself over the night, forgotten her physical self as she tended to the matters of the mind: decisions, choices, doubts, fears, actions—that's what she had been clothed in all evening. But, in actuality, she had been dressed in the blue ball gown from the wedding at Hadwen House. A ball gown! With the low, square-cut lace neckline now shredded, the bodice bloodied, the full skirt streaked with ash.

And her face. Eliza's face is pale, her large brown eyes rimmed with red. Her chestnut hair is half piled on her head and half loose around her, wild and untamed like in the Pre-Raphaelite paintings she saw once in a book of Italian art. Almost ravishing, somewhat ravaged.

Which is exactly how she feels.

"Mother." Mattie is at the door to her bed-chamber, wearing a clean dress, with something folded over her arm. "Do you think it's suitable for me to give Miss Meg a fresh nightgown of mine? Her dress from last night is unwearable, torn in places and covered in blood. I left it folded in the corner of the room. Miss Meg is wearing only her chemise."

Yesterday, Eliza might have balked at the idea. It would have felt uncomfortable and strange. And a nightgown such an intimate article of clothing. Not to mention the financial threat the Wrights posed to them. But today?

Today Eliza is not who she was yesterday, in ways both noble and humbled.

What difference does it make whose nightgown is whose after a night like the one they have experienced? All she knows is that she is still standing, and that, in and of itself, is a triumph. "By all means, give her a nightgown." As the girl turns to go, Eliza stops her. "Oh, and Mattie?"

"Yes, Mama?" Mattie says, Henry's blue eyes staring back at her, filled with honesty and naivete. She would never believe what her mother is capable of. She hopes the twins never find out.

"I am so proud of you and Rachel." Eliza swallows.

"Thank you, Mama," Mattie says. "But you're misguided."

"In what way?" Eliza asks, fear creeping up her neck. Is it possible the girls already know of any one of her many shortcomings?

"To think that we gave you strength, when really, it is the other way around. We were brave—*are* brave—because of you."

Eliza is about to thank Mattie, but her daughter continues speaking over her mother's gratitude.

"And we know—" Mattie begins.

"Know what?" Eliza asks.

"Rachel and I know about your financial troubles," Mattie says, blue eyes steady. "We've only known recently, though. After Father's last letter arrived, you seemed so agitated, and not like your *regular* agitated self. So, Rachel and I decided to read the letter."

"You did what?" Eliza says, her voice rising.

Hearing the raised voices, Rachel comes out of the twins' bedroom, also in a clean dress, brushing her hair. Mattie tells her sister what she and Eliza are discussing. "It's true, Mama," Rachel says, coming closer to her sister, the hair-brush limp now in her hand. "Why didn't you tell us? We would have gone to work immediately. And been more responsible with the pantry staples. To think that I made so many stupid, awful cakes—!"

And now both girls are blubbering, and Eliza breaks down into tears as well.

"Hush, Rachel, Mattie," she says, hugging them close to her, one arm around each, the girls' heads bent toward one another's. She used to feed them this way when they were babes at her breast, cradled head-to-head, one on each side of her. They sob and sob and sob. "Let it all out, that's right," Eliza says. A rush of emotions wells up in her own heart until, like syrup in a pot, it bubbles over and spills out, making a mess everywhere. She, too, is a blubbering fool, and the trio hugs until their jangled crying turns to a jostle of laughter.

"We will manage it," Eliza says, grabbing a handkerchief from the nightstand inside her bedroom and wiping her eyes. The girls nod and pass around the handkerchief to dry their faces. James's monogram is on it. Eliza snatches the cloth back quickly, crumpling it in her hand.

"But how will we?" Rachel asks.

"I have no idea," Eliza says, smiling sadly at her daughters. The girls lean in again for another kiss before heading downstairs. They call out that they are leaving with Maria, and Eliza begs them—again—to be careful, and to bring back news.

Last night, when the girls were packing up one of Henry's old sea trunks, they found a few discarded jackets of their father's, which they left on Eliza's bed. The clothes were moth-eaten and too tight for Henry now. Probably from his first or second voyage as a young mate, before he developed that solid musculature and slight paunch of age. Although damaged, the wool was still fine in places; perhaps someone could make something of the scraps. They are still on her bed now. She shakes them out: yes, someone who lost much could use these. She will donate them. As she's refolding them, Eliza feels a bulge in one of the jacket pockets, and discovers a tightly rolled wad of dollar bills.

Fifty dollar bills, to be exact.

Eliza shoves the entirety into her dress pocket. She knows just what to do with it.

Eliza hears someone knock quietly and then

enter through the front door. She remembers that wealthy houses were targets for robbers after the last great fire and wonders if looters are so bold as to knock before stealing. But it's not a thief; it's James Crosby. In the flesh. Alive.

"Oh!" Eliza says, rushing down the stairs and into his outstretched arms. She cannot help herself.

"Liza," he says, his lips against her hair. "What a night. What a thing that was."

Whether he's referring to the great fire or their hours leading up to it, Eliza can't be certain, nor does it matter: his statements are true, and he's warm, and his heart is beating against her ear.

They are standing in the front doorway where her daughters could walk back in at any minute. Eliza closes the door and pulls James into the dining room, to the corner where she hid last night from the firemen. The curtains are drawn. She knows she shouldn't, but she kisses James. It is a different type of kiss than before; less bright heat, more soft glow.

Crying, she pulls away. "I'm sorry," she says, wiping away tears. Her emotions are being tossed every which way. Elation, yes, and waves of grief, too.

"That's not quite the greeting I was expecting," James says. He smiles, but his eyes are concerned.

"I wasn't expecting any greeting at all."

"What? You thought I'd leave on the first ship out this morning as planned? And not come check on your well-being?"

"I thought—" Eliza halts, because how can she form the words, say aloud that which now seems overly dramatic: *I thought you may have died.*

James pulls her into a comforting, protective embrace. "I would never leave you like that. And I'm not merely saying that because I'm stuck on this island for the time being. One ship set out early, but word is, there are no more ships leaving the harbor today."

She laughs despite herself. It is a consoling notion that James Crosby will forever be charming and disarming.

She asks about his parents, who, thank goodness, are fine. When the fire first spread through town, James rescued them, walking them safely the few blocks to the Crosby and Sons candle factory. "But they lost their house on Union Street," he says. "In fact—the entire first block of Union Street is gone, Eliza. Including your childhood home."

That brings a dull ache. If her childhood home is gone, then metaphorically, so, too, is her childhood. "Thank you for letting me know."

James looks suddenly anxious, which isn't an expression she's used to from him. "I didn't come to tell you that, though. I came to ask you—" he stops here, his mouth set in a line, the dimple on his left cheek poised like a question mark.

"Yes?" Eliza asks.

"To leave with me."

"To—?"

James takes her by both hands and pulls her further into the dining room, and closer to him. "Last night wasn't the end of something for us. It was just the start. The fire showed me that. The whole night, I kept praying that you were safe. And then I realized, you, Eliza Cowan, can never be safe here on Nantucket. How can you be, when Henry leaves you alone for years on end! He is never here to provide love and support. You told me that you don't trust him anymore, that you feel he's lying to you about his actions and whereabouts. He's left you penniless and scared, and—"

"While that may be all true, but—" Eliza says, feeling oddly protective of Henry. It's one thing for Eliza to complain about him, and quite another for her lover to do so.

He speaks in a rush. "Henry doesn't take care of you, Eliza. Not the way I would. Not the way I can. With me, you would have a companion every day for the rest of your life. And money at your disposal, to give you the fine things you deserve. And look at this island! Nantucket is a ghost of her former self. She will never be the same after last night."

James leans in and kisses her softly on the lips.

Eliza's heart hammers in her throat, but the feeling is one of panic, not passion. Last night was a fantasy, Eliza sees. Not life. "Are you suggesting that I divorce my husband? Abandon my daughters? Leave Nantucket?"

"Your daughters are all almost grown, you said. They are going to abandon *you,* you said."

"I was complaining! Unburdening myself. In fits of frustration, I tend to say a lot of things that I don't actually mean." Eliza glances toward the hall and the living room, wondering whether her voice can be heard all the way to the borning room on the far side of the house. If so, Meg Wright is certainly getting an earful.

Eliza moves away from James and back into the entry hall, and silence grows in the space between them.

James steps behind her and presses himself against her back. "And I know he doesn't satisfy you like I do." His words tickle her neck and the delicate spot right behind her ear.

Well. He does make a good point about that. Eliza thinks about last night and feels herself pulled toward James's body once again.

If she could go back to those stolen moments with James, she would. To savor the time with him, to savor her life of blissful ignorance from before the fire. If she could go back to those moments afterward, walking through town, and somehow save it from destruction, she would do that as well. But how could she have known? And what would she have done differently?

Last night, she was lit from within, consumed. On fire. Today, she is changed, rising from the ashes along with her beloved town.

Eliza faces James. She looks into his deep blue eyes for what she knows with complete certainty will be the very last time. "I am sorry. Nantucket is my home, my everything. I love this whole place—this place and these people."

James's face falls. He looks at his shoes and shakes his head. Blinking, he meets her gaze. "Well, then, it's time for me to leave once and for all. Because Nantucket keeps breaking my heart."

And before Eliza can say anything in return, James Crosby leaves.

Eliza sinks into the living room sofa, too stunned and exhausted to cry. He offered her so much. Love, companionship, passion, and even money.

Was she a fool to turn it down?

No.

But it would be so very nice to have money.

And then she remembers the cash in her pocket, and heads toward the borning room.

48

MEG

Meg considers the little face staring up at her, a little heart-shaped face peering out from her swaddling. Serious dark eyes. *What to call you, little thing?* She had only thought of boy names. In all fairness, having a baby two weeks early and in the middle of a town fire can do that to a person—catch one off guard.

Meg starts at the beginning of the alphabet. Abigail, Beatrice, Constance. Deborah, Effie, Francis. Grace—her thinking here is interrupted by the sound of a man and a woman talking, their voices getting louder and then quieting. Eliza, no doubt, giving someone else in this world a piece of her mind.

How Meg wishes Eliza had left the house with Maria and the twins, just to give her a little bit of solitude and privacy. Before the Macy girls departed, one of them brought Meg a dressing gown, which she accepted but hasn't yet changed into. She wants instead to don the dressing gown her mother-in-law gave her as a gift before she died. It was passed down from Benjamin's grandmother, one of the last Wampanoag on Nantucket. The garment—made of soft hide with tiny beading around the neckline—was acquired through a trade with an Algonquin chief from Cape Cod. The dressing robe is probably much too warm to wear in summer, although it kept her comfortable after her first pregnancy with Lucy, who was born on a frigid day in February. Meg wore it after her last birth, too, for Elias was born in December—the same December that he died.

Meg pushes the thought away. Why think of death at the moment of birth? But she cannot help herself: the darkness is present, a shadow in the corner of a bright room, a whisper in her ear: *your newborn baby might die. Your husband might already be dead. Your daughter Lucy, too.* The wonders of life are inextricably linked to the marvels of death. Perhaps it would be more foolish of Meg not to allow that duality into her thinking.

Duality. Two ways of seeing a thing. If Meg never leaves this room, she will never know. Answers don't yet exist. She and her baby can stay suspended between times, between before and after, between knowing and disbelief. Meg heard Eliza whisper to the twins, telling them to ask about Benjamin when they go out in town, as if Meg was too fragile to be told directly. As if she wouldn't have thought it herself without being reminded, when really, the weight of their breath was all around Meg. She wanted to shout it from her place of convalescence into the hall-way and beyond, to the entire Macy family and then Nantucket town: *Someone tell me the fate of my husband and child!*

Hoping Eliza doesn't barge in, Meg relieves herself in the chamber pot and cleans up herself as best as she can with some clean bedding. She pulls the starched nightgown over her head and breathes in the scent of rosewater. Settled together back in the bed, the baby is now suckling, and Meg cannot move again until after the feeding is done. Her baby daughter has latched on easily, this one. She knows exactly what she wants and how to get it.

Meg knows, too, what she wants. And after the baby feeds she will go get it. But first: new motherhood. Rest. Gain back some strength from what the night and the birthing depleted.

On the bedside table sit a water pitcher and glass, a slice of bread and a peeled hard-boiled egg. Meg is ravenous. She eats with one hand, popping the whole egg into her mouth, finishing the bread in three bites and leaving crumbs on the sheets, downing water right from the pitcher until it dribbles out the side of her mouth. She can hear Eliza still talking to someone in the front hall.

Ah: Mrs. Eliza Macy. Meg doesn't quite know what to make of that woman. Eliza is greedy and rude, entitled and spoiled, strong-willed and short-tempered, and—let's not forget!—a bigot and an adulteress to boot.

But, in the end, Eliza has also shown herself to

be capable of more: a woman who, when under duress, kept her wits about her and did something right, something good. A person who stepped outside of her small-mindedness and risked herself for Meg.

The front door slams shut, and there is silence.

Before long, Eliza's steps echo in the hall, and then the woman's newly cleaned face and neatened hair peek around the door frame of the borning room. "All's well in here?"

Meg nods, then notices that Eliza seems to have tears in her eyes. She waves them away. "It's nothing. Don't mind me. A friend just stopped by and well—never mind. I'm just quite worried about my son-in-law."

Meg can do many things, but showing support for Larson's shop isn't one of them.

"He was injured last night in the fire. You probably didn't know. That's why Alice left in the middle of the night."

"Oh, that's terrible."

"They say he inhaled too much smoke. His lungs were weakened and he collapsed."

"I'll wish for the best for him. And . . . any news about—?"

"No, nothing. But my daughters will find out for you."

Meg nods. She realizes that they are the only ones in the house now. The room grows quiet.

The baby suckles and occasionally squeaks like a piglet. Her little legs kick out and settle, kick and settle.

Eliza steps into the room, but only to its edges, an invisible wall between them. She has changed into a drab olive day dress and presses out invisible wrinkles in the skirt with her palm.

"She seems quite healthy," Eliza says.

"Yes," Meg agrees.

"Do you have a name for her yet?"

"No," Meg says, although she has.

An awkward silence hangs between them.

Eliza begins. "The night of the wedding at Hadwen House, I—"

"I'm sorry that I saw that," Meg says. "And I shouldn't have mentioned it last night." She repositions the baby slightly, pushing an extra pillow under her elbow for support. She tries to imagine that Eliza Macy is truly a friend, someone with whom there is ease and honesty, like with Faithful Cole. Doing so requires quite a stretch of the mind. In the end, Meg simply cannot manage it.

"Women say the most outlandish things while giving birth. Why don't we think of the whole thing as merely that: a fantasy of a pregnant woman who wasn't quite in her right mind."

"I'll try." The baby unlatches from Meg's breast. Meg covers herself with her dress and positions the baby's tiny torso over the roundest, highest part of her shoulder bone, cradling the infant's wobbly head and patting her warm back. The baby burps. "Good girl," Meg coos, wiping spittle from her baby's perfect bow lips. Deftly, as if she has been doing this all her life, she positions her onto her other breast, where the baby begins to suckle anew.

Eliza paces. "Have you shared the story with anyone? Your husband? A friend?"

"As I said, I don't like to lie."

"So, you did tell someone?"

"Because I was so shocked, yes, I did. But that person can be trusted," Meg says.

"Trusted by you, but not by me!" Eliza says, clearly agitated now.

Meg wishes to recant it all, shove the words loose in this room back in her mouth and swallow them like that egg. "You'll have to take my word."

"But you don't understand. There is more to the story than what you witnessed, Meg." Eliza pulls a rocking chair from the corner and positions it by Meg's bedside.

"There always is," Meg says, hoping against hope that Eliza Macy will not unburden herself right now. The last thing Meg needs is more of this particular woman's intimacy.

"The man—James—he was my first love. My one true love."

Meg doubts this fact would matter very much to Mr. Macy, nor to any gossipmonger on the streets of town. Certainly not to the Lord above. It would be an interesting tidbit to add to the tale if she ever gets to share more of it with Benjamin. But Eliza's confession moves Meg just the smallest bit, perhaps because, cradling her newborn daughter in her arms, she is at the moment taken by the power of love. And perhaps, too, Meg is intrigued by the notion that Eliza is a woman capable of such deep, true feeling for another soul. Eliza's abundance of negative qualities makes her unlikable; the admittance of love and desire makes her human.

"I've got no interest in other people's business," Meg says. "And I've already been too much in yours." The baby is full and tired. Her eyelids close heavily and her mouth opens the slightest bit, releasing from Meg's breast. Sated, she has fallen asleep.

"Here," Eliza says, standing from the rocking chair and handing over a stack of rolled paper. Money. Not paper. "Quite a good sum," Eliza says.

"What is this?" Meg asks, worry creeping up her spine. She nestles the baby between her torso and the extra pillow on her lap, but even with free hands, she does not want to touch the money.

". . . I thought that I could—"

"You could what?" Meg asks. "Bribe me?" She says it all in an exaggerated whisper, trying not to wake the baby.

Eliza's large brown eyes go wide. "This is a gift—for the baby—and you and your husband. And you have another daughter, who may need—"

"Need what? A school to go to? Would you like to buy me one of those?"

"If I could, I would," Eliza says. "I will help you any way I can."

"It's a little late for that, don't you think?" Meg says, squirming in the bed. The borning room is suddenly hot. Although the windows are open, the smoky air smells poisonous.

"I found the cash in one of my husband's old sailor jackets. I thought money would make it right between us. You can help me by keeping your word of silence—and maybe sharing some of this money with whomever it is you told—and I can help you rebuild, in any way you need. I don't understand the problem," Eliza says, sounding frustrated.

No, Eliza Macy doesn't understand the problem. Which is, of course, exactly the problem. Meg could lecture her, point out all the ways this woman is completely misguided in her thinking, but will it matter? Will a woman like Eliza ever understand? Anger fills Meg's chest, for why should she even have to explain at all?

"Your husband," Meg says.

"Yes?" Eliza asks, her tone defensive. "What about him? I thought you said you weren't going to tattle."

"That's not what I mean. He's a captain, and people say—"

"Don't drag him into this. I know people talk about that last failed voyage, but he's a good man, you know."

"Oh, I know. That's what I'm trying to tell you. That Captain Macy is a better person than you'll ever be."

"Excuse me?"

"I assumed you knew," Meg said, suddenly the one who is uncomfortable. "Although Faithful did say it was a secret."

"Meg," Eliza says, "Everyone in Nantucket seems to know something about Henry that I do not. You must tell me. Please."

"I didn't think the captain would keep something so important from . . . you know."

"From his wife? Ha. You know more than most about the failings of my marriage," Eliza says. "Is it something . . . serious?"

Meg considers this question, for yes, it is something serious indeed. She takes a deep breath and then dives in. "Your husband is using his whaling ship to ferry slaves to freedom. At great risk to himself and to his crew. According to Faithful Cole's husband, Daniel, who is serving as first mate on the *Ithaca*, Henry was in prison for trying to free a Black man from a stockade. Daniel only left the ship once, fearing capture—a freeborn man can be enslaved just by stepping on

447

Southern soil!—and sent Faithful the letter. The plan was to bribe the guards to let Captain Macy out and then take off from the port of Orleans in the night, with seven slaves—four men, one woman and two children—hidden onboard."

"Henry—in prison? And freeing slaves?" Eliza says, looking completely shocked, and hurt, too, for her husband not telling her. "But how do you know if it worked? And where are they now?"

"I don't know. I only know from Faithful that they've done it before. Several times. That last ship—the one everyone said was unlucky?—came back from the Pacific filled with oil. Only Captain Macy—Henry—and his men agreed to barter it all for human life."

"They came back with practically nothing," Eliza recalls.

"Nothing but seventeen souls. Slaves delivered safely to New Bedford, according to Faithful," Meg says, feeling a lump of emotion in her throat. She cradles her baby even more closely to her heart.

"Well. I am overwhelmed," Eliza says, pulling a monogrammed handkerchief from her sleeve and dabbing her eyes. "I feel like I don't know my husband at all."

Eliza wants to know more, but Meg has already said too much. She tells Eliza she is tired. She says she wants to sleep while her baby sleeps.

"Of course. Thank you for your honesty. I'll go

tidy the house more from last night. Here's a bell to ring in case you need me. And let me know if you'd like to look through our family bible for possible names for your baby."

Eliza picks up the money and tidies it into a neat stack, which she leaves next to the bell.

Say nothing. Do nothing. Wait for this woman to leave.

It takes all of Meg's control to not laugh in Eliza's face, or yell at her for being so obtuse. As if Meg would use a name from the Macy lineage for her own offspring! Oh, certainly, offer to bribe me and then suggest I name my precious child after your forebears, people who probably—no, certainly—had slaves.

But the presence of the bell is something. There is power in that. It means that, for a moment in time at least, Eliza Macy is willing to be Meg Wright's servant.

Meg considers ringing the bell and sending Eliza away, ringing and dismissing her all morning, but she has real things to do, and time's a-wasting.

She shuts her eyes and pretends to sleep, willing Eliza Macy from the room, finally hearing footsteps retreat.

49

MARIA

Maria helped a woman give birth. She said her goodbyes to Linley, lost her beloved Atheneum, watched a man almost die, and *then* helped a woman give birth. She can hardly believe that any of it is real.

And Eliza Macy! Talk about a conflagration! Eliza Macy and James Crosby, intimate. Who would believe it? That Eliza was capable of such passion and such deception, both. But, Maria supposes, one never really knows what's going on inside someone else's mind, body or soul. And as much as she is flabbergasted, Maria cannot judge what one person does when she herself has secrets that can never be shared or revealed. So. Maria will take the secret with her to the grave.

But she may never look at Eliza Macy quite the same way, either.

Maria, Rachel, and Mattie leave the Macy house and cross the street to the Mitchell home above the Pacific Bank. Once inside, Maria greets her parents and siblings with hugs and tears, everyone talking over the next Mitchell, each just so glad that they have all survived. Rachel and Mattie Macy join in the bittersweet greeting while Maria quickly explains about

Meg's birth and asks her mother for clean linens.

Leaving the girls in Lydia's capable hands, Maria races to the roof. She pushes open the wooden hatch and climbs the ladder. Her journals, her instruments: she must see them all, know that they are in one piece. On the platform now, Maria looks out over Main Street and gasps, for what she sees is an impossibility.

She can see the harbor clear as day.

Her view is unobstructed, with no sail lofts or taverns or structures of any kind to block it. Save for the other brick building, the Customs House, anchoring the bottom of Main Street, there are no buildings left standing whatsoever. Every storefront and every pub and every home between the Pacific Bank and the very tip of the Straight Wharf is gone. And the pier, too, is gone. The fire obliterated it all.

Maria squints and focuses her sights on what used to be Pearl Street in front of the Atheneum. Now it's only a heap of smoldering embers. She can make out the borders of the building, see the plot of land on which it once stood. But even the name of the structure has gone up in smoke as well. Planks of charred wood collapsed into nothingness.

This square plot of land can no longer be called a library or a lecture hall or a former-church-turned-museum. Gone are the arched glass windows, gone the pews, gone the white Doric columns and the large wooden door. There is no longer a cabinet of curiosities from around the globe to visit here, no bat from Madagascar to study, no hand-painted Audubon guide about which to ooh and ahh.

The Atheneum was a holy place for the natural and the man-made to come together and be celebrated, from science to literature and art. This version of the building Maria sees today also causes one to pause, take stock, and look with awe, only now at the way that man-made worlds can so quickly come to ruin at the hands of nature's fearsome gifts.

Maria weeps. It is a messy, mournful keening, and she's glad no one is witness to it. When she blows into one of her father's handkerchiefs, ash comes out her nose.

Once she's collected herself a bit, Maria assesses the damage done to the roof. The wooden planks on which their small observatory is built were burned partially, the raised platform charred along the edges. Maria tests the sturdiness of the structure. She steps up and onto it, pushing her foot down heavier here and there as she walks slowly across it.

The shed has sustained some damage as well. Maria slides open the bolt on the small door and examines the contents. The Dollond is there, although damaged. The base melted slightly, perhaps from heat more than any actual flames hitting its surface, but the brass telescope atop still appears to be in perfect condition. She removes it from the shed and clutches it, sending a little prayer of thanks to the heavens for keeping this tremendously important object safe. She sets it aside and extracts the other telescopes and instruments, finding that much of the equipment is either damaged only slightly by heat or—in the case of one or two chronometers—completely unscathed.

But Maria's heartbeat still thrums in her ears, her nerves not quite calm. Maria kneels in front of the shed, loosening the floorboard and dislodging the one just to the right. Reaching in, her fingers connect with the leather-bound journal. Yes. She extracts it. It is unharmed. Maria grabs the box and a fountain pen. She views them all, the survivors of the great fire: Maria's own personal cabinet of curiosities.

Maria replaces the board, but not the objects. Those must be moved to another, less dangerous spot. Maria doesn't know where she will store them in the long term, but for now, she must bring them down to her bedroom for safekeeping. She piles them by the roof hatch.

But first, she returns her full and complete attention to the Dollond.

Now, let's see if you still work, she thinks, setting up the small telescope in a way she hardly ever does, by clear light of day.

And work it does. The lens is a bit cloudy, but the glass is not cracked, so Maria wipes it clean with a rag from the shed. She is used to pointing the telescope heavenward, but, as poor Icarus discovered, one must not fly too close to the sun, and so Maria gazes out instead of up.

She focuses the telescope on the harbor. There she sees mostly ruin, for all boats docked close to shore last night have burned, their carcasses floating arcs dotting the water. Further out, some of the more sizable boats have escaped harm, except for one ghostly sloop, now only the shell of a ship.

Commercial Wharf avoided damage, but all of the other piers and docks have disappeared. One small rowboat heads out to a large ship. Maria recognizes the red-and-blue uniforms of the lieutenants from the Coast Guard, who must have spent the entire night on land, unable to get back to their naval ship. But here they go now. Although Maria disagreed with the officers about how to handle the sparking fire at the Methodist church, these men—non-Nantucketers—risked their lives to help her small community, and so she whispers a thank-you that she hopes gets carried to them on the soft summer breeze, still scented with ash.

Maria wonders if the smell will ever truly leave her.

"Miss Mitchell!" a voice calls from the street

below. "Look!" Maria peers over the edge, where Joseph Allen is jumping up and down on Main Street, likely trying to propel himself on to the top of the building with sheer force of enthusiasm. He clutches something brown and boxy in his hands, which are extended overhead. "Look at what I found!"

"Stop moving, Joseph!" she orders, which he does on command. Maria squints and focuses on the object. Gasps and claps her hands together. "Chaucer?"

"*The Canterbury Tales* by Joffrey—"

"One pronounces it *Jeffrey*—" she yells.

"By Jeffrey Chaucer!"

"Wonderful!" she tells her trusty assistant.

"I found it all by its lonesome up on Ash Lane!"

"Well done. I need to finish up some work I'm doing here, so can you leave it on the steps at the side entrance for me?"

"Yes, miss," Joseph yells back up to her. "And then I'll find some more!"

Maria remembers: *The Three Musketeers* at Eliza Macy's home. She will retrieve it later. "Did you follow my instructions and go home last night, Joseph?" Maria yells back. "Be honest, please."

"I was about to, miss. But then there was a commotion up at the jail, and I—"

Just couldn't help myself, Maria thinks, filling in the rest of the sentence herself. "Joseph Allen!

I'm sure your mother is worried sick about you."

"No, miss, she says she never worries about me because I've got a good head on my shoulders. To which I say, *that doesn't make me special; everyone has a head on their shoulders, otherwise they'd be dead!*" He smiles wide at this, proud of his own clever joke.

Maria laughs, shakes her head. "Remind me to take you along with me to my next knitting circle gathering, Joseph. We could use a little more pluck."

"Whatever you say, miss!" he says, waving and running off toward Orange Street.

Maria sighs. *One book found and only two hundred more to go,* she thinks, based on how many books were taken out from the collection at the time of the fire. Two hundred of two thousand, and how many of those were in homes that burned to the ground?

Maria returns to her scouting. Joseph can be her eyes on the ground while she's looking out toward sea. She positions the telescope further north, to the protected harbor and the jetties beyond, and on toward Cape Cod.

And then, movement! One ship is heading out, raising her sails just past the Brant Point Light and turning into the Nantucket Sound. Maria wonders where it is headed, and hopes that the ship carries news of their devastation to others up and down the coast.

Because, as Maria follows the horizon line past that ship and out into the harbor, all she can see is blue and more blue. Which is when one new, chilling fact asserts itself in this scientist's mind—a fact she's always known, but has never had to think of in this way: Nantucket is an island thirty miles out to sea. Should the people of Nantucket need food and shelter—as they now do—they have no neighboring town to rely on. Nowhere to go. They are completely cut off from the mainland, and completely on their own.

Maria angles the telescope down, closer to town. No, she realizes, the best way to view her town is with the naked eye, and she steps away from the instrument.

Down on her right: where Cole's granary was, now nothing. And behind that, the mill: nothing. Up Main Street, to where Adams & Parker, the grocer's, stood: nothing. No medicines at the pharmacy, for there is no pharmacy. No bread at the baker's for there is no baker's. No dry goods from the dry goods store, for there is no storefront anymore.

On this Tuesday morning, the harbor is a still and silent wasteland. No one is coming today to help them rebuild, because no one yet knows what has happened here.

50

ELIZA

Henry—ferrying slaves to freedom on some sort of maritime Underground Railroad? Eliza didn't even know such a thing was possible, much less that her husband played so prominent a role in the operation. But it makes sense. It's like she's been looking at one of her daughter's jigsaw puzzles—a map of the world—where one critical piece of geography has been missing. She's finally found the last piece, snapped it into place, and the whole landscape comes into clear view.

It is satisfying, knowing the truth, seeing the whole. This news hasn't changed anything, and yet it changes everything. It gives Eliza renewed hope in her marriage, a sense that she's staying on Nantucket for the right reasons. It is wonderful, knowing Henry is indeed such a good man. And, as Meg pointed out, a much better person than Eliza will ever be.

But, really. All she did was offer this woman money. Is that so terrible? Money *solves* problems, her parents always told Eliza, not *causes* them! It is a belief held by Henry, and by every whaling captain living on this land over the last two hundred years. Indeed, financial stability is a core belief held by each and every last Nantucketer! That and Quaker pacifism: may we be rich and peaceful.

But Meg had looked upon Eliza with such ugliness. Ugliness and pity. Eliza immediately wanted to leave the room, although she had to stay longer once Meg made that bold declaration about Henry's dangerous and brave work in the south. Has Henry truly been imprisoned?

Despite feeling anything but, Eliza remained calm as Meg spoke.

And, to prove—to both herself and Meg—that there was nothing untoward about her gift, she had left the money right out in the open on the nightstand.

Eliza doubts that Meg will ring the small service bell, but she has left it there anyway as a sign of goodwill. To show just how progressive her thinking is, that not only could a Black woman give birth in her home, but that Eliza would wait on the woman, should she need.

Eliza paces the living room. She is not a terrible person!

Then why in God's name does she feel like one?

Several minutes later, a knock at the door pulls Eliza from her trance. She is hoping it's Alice with Larson, but it's only Maria, with fresh milk and a basket of supplies, looking sheepish. "Early this morning, I thought I'd make tea for everyone—and then I noticed you hadn't any sugar left. Or any other provisions, really."

Eliza feels every defense drop. Every excuse, every bit of armor protecting her against hurt or injury, falls away. Much like the wall between Kelly's jewelry store and Geary's hat shop last night, a barrier melts, leaving her completely exposed. "That's because I have nothing. And no one," she says, before the first bitter, pathetic tear falls.

"Well," Maria says, concern mixed with a hint of something else in her eyes. "At least now you have a bit of sugar?"

"And laudanum?" Eliza asks. "I've developed a bit of a headache."

"Probably from the lack of laudanum," Maria says, not unkindly. "I'll see what I can find in town and return with it later."

Over breakfast and tea with sugar—thank the Lord! Sweet sugar!—Eliza tells Maria about the visit from James, which in the retelling feels almost like a dream. A man who you have always loved comes to rescue you from your difficult life, promising to whisk you away and make all your problems magically disappear? Who would believe it? And who would deny themselves such a real-life fantasy?

And then she must tell her about Henry! Wonderful, strong Henry.

"What a morning you've had, Eliza, and

you've not yet even left the house to see the town in ashes!" Maria laughs, for what else is there to do in the face of so much extreme chaos? "I knew men—and women, too—were using their merchant and whaling ships for this purpose, but I had no idea that Henry was part of the scheme."

"No idea!" Eliza echoes.

"You love Henry more than you think you do," Maria says, shaking a half-eaten roll at her and chewing. "And, quite frankly, being a pioneer woman must be quite hard. Riding a horse? Living in log cabins and tents and moving from dusty prairie town to town? Eliza! You may think it romantic, but that life just wouldn't suit you. Besides, if you left Nantucket, who would I beat each week at whist?"

Eliza smiles despite herself. "How can you be so kind and jovial when all I've done is be awful?"

Maria puts her breakfast down and crosses her arms, studying Eliza. She is still wearing her dress from last night, covered in soot and grime. "You're not awful all the time, so there's that to consider in your favor."

Eliza winces. Then, in hushed tones, she tells Maria about what she did, offering money to Meg.

Maria shakes her head, in a how-could-you sort of gesture reserved for toddlers who act rotten and should know better. "And to think I'd hoped you might have learned something from what we all experienced last night."

"Skin color has nothing to do with it!"

"So you're telling me that, if the woman in that bed right now were white, you'd still have offered cash in exchange for her silence?"

Eliza says nothing.

"You'd have hesitated allowing her into your home—and into your borning room—during the greatest fire this town has ever seen?"

Eliza looks away.

"You'd have questioned her right to open a shop on Main Street, if Meg were white?" Maria's voice is as fierce as it can be in a whisper.

Eliza whispers back, the two sitting side-by-side at the Macys' kitchen table. "I was protecting my family. I was keeping my defenses up against any enemy, especially if—"

Hearing her own words, Eliza halts. If . . . what? If that person is easier to pick on, or belittle, because society has already ganged up against her? If she's different than you, or an outsider in some way? If she doesn't look like you?

In hindsight, even Eliza can see the faults in this logic. But would she go as far as to call it bigotry? "I suppose I did treat her differently than I might have. Than I should have."

"Well." Maria nods. "That's something."

"It's water under the bridge now. I'll aim for a better attitude—more openness—in the future."

Maria shrugs, in a let's-wait-and-see sort of noncommittal gesture. Then she excuses herself; she must rest.

Eliza follows her to the front door and is left looking at her reflection in the hall mirror. What does a bigot look like? She isn't certain, only she's having trouble looking herself in the eye. Maybe that is the telltale sign of one. And an adulteress and a liar. She may have to stay away from mirrors for the rest of her life.

Eliza peers down, to the small table for mail by the front door.

Only something is wrong. Something is missing.

Eliza looks around. Scans the room. Where is the letter? Penned in a fit of guilt and angst, and folded and sealed with Henry's name written across the front.

Eliza had left it on the mantel in the living room.

And then moved it.

To the table in the front hall, yes?

Only it isn't here.

Eliza's heart pulses in her temples as she glances about, moving from one spot to the next, touching every surface, round and round and doubling back. Her hands flit across bare surfaces and air. She had meant to burn the letter in the morning, over breakfast, only she hadn't set a fire yet for tea.

Where is the letter?

Her hands rest on the table. There is only one answer that makes sense, which she will have to wait to confirm to be certain. One of the twins must have taken it with them this morning to send while out in town.

The full consequence of this lands like a punch to her gut.

Eliza must intercept the post before her letter finds its way to a departing ship. It must never leave Nantucket Sound.

"Meg, I'll be right back!" Eliza calls, fixing a bonnet on her head. "In ten minutes or so!" She slams the door behind her.

Out on the street, the full reality of the fire's devastation becomes clear to Eliza, and she wishes she had forbade her daughters from going out. She hopes Larson is healing well, but sending Mattie there was too dangerous.

Debris lies everywhere on Main Street. Eliza hikes up her long skirts and steps over planks of felled, charred timber. Everything is gone, reduced to something unrecognizable.

Except: the bank. Citizens Bank. She retraces her steps to study it, or more precisely, the lack of it, while she tries to let her beating heart settle. The thick, wrought-iron door to the bank remains standing, but it has melted and warped into a stooped, grotesque mangle of metal. A door that now acts as merely ornamental, a portal to nothing. Eliza wonders what this means for her financial future, and for the future of anyone who placed their fortunes in a bank that has gone up in smoke. It can't be good. She's certain the bank manager will not forget about her debt, even if he no longer has official stationery on which to write out his statements. In fact, he'll probably demand payment immediately, to use to assist others who lost so much during the fire.

Good thing Meg didn't accept Eliza's money. They are going to need every dollar of it now to get them through these rough few months ahead, as the town gets back on its feet. To buy bread and salt with, grain and flour.

Eliza scans the decimated town, for where can one procure such items now? Dread and anticipation course through her veins.

The air is still so rank and noxious that men who have come to help clear away debris around Eliza have fastened handkerchiefs around their faces, to cover their noses and mouths from the fumes. William Geary is among them, noticeable for wearing his stovepipe hat no matter the situation, even one in which such an item might remind those around you that your hat store was the origin of the fire that devastated the entire town.

"That wall," Eliza hears Geary say, pointing toward the air where his shop used to stand, across the street from Citizens Bank. The wall

465

he is alluding to only exists in the town's collective memory. "I turned off all the stoves before leaving at 9:00 p.m. Same as always. But a stovepipe in the wall kept burning. So the firemen tell me, anyway."

"I heard that two strangers saw the fire and tried to put it out in the jewelry store," a man in the crowd says. Eliza pauses.

"Yes, men with buckets of water," another adds.

Eliza studies her shoes, her ears straining toward the group. She decides that this is perhaps another of her secrets to keep, away from the annals of history. Already a story is woven—*two men with buckets*—and that is close enough to the truth of it.

At the corner of Federal Street, the roof of Meg and Benjamin Wright's shop has collapsed in on itself, with one large beam still holding up a bit of the building's frame. Eliza spots something bright in the midst of all the blackened wood and uses her shoe to kick aside debris.

Wright's Shoe Repair, the sign says in blue-and-white paint, the letters grimy but legible.

Amazing that it remained intact, considering the rest of the street. The rest of the town! Eliza uses James's handkerchief to clean soot off the board as best she can. She props the sign by what used to be the store's front door.

She steps back, then adjusts it a little. Tilts her

head to study the scene. Then she continues on.

When the Wrights come to see what became of their shop, their first vision of it might give them hope.

51

MEG

Her baby's name is Hope.

The name came to Meg as she moved through the alphabet, guiding her to the letter *H* and the "huh" sound of first breath. It is the sound of exhalation, of sending one's prayers out from the body and into the heavens. Hope is Meg's wish that her husband and daughter are alive and well. It is knowing that, while their cobbler shop is certainly decimated this morning, they are resilient and capable enough to rebuild even better tomorrow. Hope is the only way to explain the premonition she has that this baby will live past Elias's ten days, that this daughter will thrive, that Meg will not have to bury another child in her lifetime.

Hope is all Meg has left.

And Meg would rather be damned to Hell than have Eliza Macy be the first person to hear her precious daughter's name said aloud in the world.

Meg waits several minutes. She hears Eliza moving through the house, pots being put away, the quiet mutterings of a woman talking to herself. Then sounds of conversation, with a man, or maybe a woman, or possibly both. Next, Eliza calls out, saying she'll be gone for ten minutes or so. Perfect. Meg eases herself off the bed and cradles sleeping Hope in a blanket around her swaddling. She finds her shoes tucked under the bed, fastens them closed as she quietly leaves the borning room, and slips silently down the dark hallway, leaving her soiled dress behind. Meg exits the Macy house through the kitchen's back door, hoping against hope for good news of her family, and squinting against the sharp gray morning light.

She pauses in the side yard to fashion a sling. Around her waist, over her shoulder, under her baby's bottom and then knot. She gives the strap a pull to test its strength and finds that the contraption holds.

The next-door neighbor's house is no more. The ten feet between that home and the Macys was all that separated one fate from another's. Meg is glad she didn't know just quite how close they were to complete destruction last night. As she passes the family, a mother, father and two small sons standing around the ruins in mismatched clothing from the night before, a shiver shoots up Meg's spine and physically shakes itself out at her hands. *Like stepping on a grave,* her mother used to say about that sensation.

Meg gives the family a conciliatory smile and continues down Main Street. Ordinarily, a Black woman in a long nightgown and leather shoes cradling a newborn in the heart of downtown

Nantucket would cause people to stop what they were doing and stare. But today, amidst so much devastation, she goes unnoticed.

"We're going to fetch your sister first," Meg whispers into the sling where Hope sleeps. "Then we're going to find your daddy."

Main Street is too much to take in all at once; Meg cannot face it yet. Their cobbler shop is probably gone, but for the moment at least, the shop still exists as in her memory, which is how she'd like to keep it for now. So instead, she turns onto Fair Street. The corner homes have fallen victim to the blaze, but, beyond that, the rest are standing. Rows and rows of homes! Hope flutters in her heart.

She passes a man pulling a cart filled with furnishings. His face is smeared with grime and his cap is pulled low on his forehead. He chews the tiny nub of an unlit cigar and nods in passing, but says nothing. After the crackle and boom of last night, the town has gone mute.

Meg walks slowly further out on Fair, where there are suddenly children's voices. Laughter. In the middle of the street, a game of hopscotch. One girl with long, tangled auburn curls draws the lines on the ground dirt path—no easy feat—and the other tosses a pebble to mark the box she will skip over.

"Good morning!" they say when Meg passes, as if nothing at all is amiss. Life must carry on, for children especially, and this may be the most heart-wrenching sight of all.

She hurries her steps as she passes, her urgency to see Lucy growing by the second.

This end of Orange Street looks as it did last night when Meg brought Lucy to Faithful Cole's home. The door is slightly ajar. Meg knocks anyway before entering.

"Faithful? Jenny? Lucy!" she calls out. The front room is quiet. "Daniel? Is anyone here?" A ray of sunlight slants from the window across the bare kitchen table. Breakfast dishes are out.

"Where could they be, Hope?" Meg asks. In response the baby opens her eyes.

A shadow crosses in front of them, and then a small sob. "Mama?"

"Lucy!" Meg says as her daughter hurtles across the room and clutches Meg's waist. Lucy buries her head, nuzzling and grabbing tight, the pair—the trio—rocking back and forth. "Oh, my baby girl! You're all right!"

Lucy is crying, sobbing now, and Meg joins in, the tears falling freely. "But I'm not—Mama, I'm not," she says.

"You're not?" Meg asks, pushing her daughter to arm's length to get a better look at her. Eyes: clear. Arms and legs: attached. Able to communicate and move, to walk and talk—what else is there? Maybe something not visible to the eye, like damage to her lungs from smoke? Lucy appears to be breathing well. "What do you mean, you're not all right?"

Lucy shakes her head in frustration. "I'm fine, Mama. But you called me your baby girl. I'm not your baby any longer," Lucy says. She extends her pointer finger and delicately traces the slope of the baby's nose. "See?"

"I do see, Lucyloo," Meg says, smiling. She lowers herself into a kitchen chair and unties the sling from around her neck. "Come and meet your sister, Hope."

They'll be all right, Meg thinks, watching her one daughter inspect the other. Meg and her girls. They'll be known as the female cobblers of Nantucket Island, and they'll run a business together. She'll teach her daughters how to balance the books, how to ply leather into shape, how to be courteous but firm with the customers. How to haggle a bit with the tanners, a penny here, a nickel there. They can survive with the strength of one another, and with Faithful's help. Which reminds her: "Where is Faithful?" Meg asks Lucy. "And where are her children?"

"Jenny and Daniel and I were sleeping. Mrs. Cole said she needed to go out by morning light and look for something. I can't think of what, but I didn't argue because she's a grown-up and one must be respectful, you taught me. Before she went out she said to *sleep, child.*

"Only I wasn't sleeping because how could I

sleep when I didn't know where you and Daddy were?" Lucy stops to yawn. "I listened for your voice all night and all morning, because I knew you'd be back and I didn't want to miss you. Besides, Daniel was coughing all night and keeping me up. He was in Mrs. Cole's room, though, so's not to 'fect me and Jenny. Now he's snoring like a hog."

"Infect," Meg corrects. Lucy's story is circuitous, and as she speaks, her eyelids grow heavy. Cradling Hope, Meg guides Lucy to the bedroom with Jenny and tucks her daughter in next to her friend. "You can rest now, baby."

"I'm not your—"

"You'll always be my baby, Lucy. There's room for more than one in this family," she whispers, stroking her daughter's back as Lucy turns away and snuggles into the pillow next to her friend. A bassinet stores extra blankets in the corner. Meg removes all but one and places Hope inside. The baby startles slightly, her tiny hands jumping out and away from her body, and then she breathes deeply, turns her head to the side, and relaxes back into heavy sleep.

The sound of uneven footfalls on the wood planks—Faithful's limping gait—let her know that her own dear friend has returned safely.

"Faithful," Meg says in an exaggerated whisper. "Thank you for all you've done." She closes the door to the bedroom and rounds the corner into the main room, now modulating her voice. "Have I got some stories for you!"

Faithful is there, breathing heavy from walking, hands on her substantial hips. And behind her, framed in the entranceway, tall and beautiful as the sun shining overhead behind him, is Benjamin.

"And have I got some stories for you, my love," he says, and smiles.

52

ELIZA

When Eliza reaches the harbor, she is doubly glad for that earlier gesture on Main Street at the Wright's shop, since there is no hope to be found at all down here. Larson's men's shop, at the intersection of South Water and Main Street, is gone, as are all of the businesses along the Straight Wharf, Long Wharf and North Wharf. Gone also are the wharfs themselves, now only a few scorched pilings and then, well, water. Perhaps tomorrow this will upset her. Perhaps tomorrow she will speak to Alice about starting over, once Larson recovers. But to this news today, Eliza is numb. Many from town are milling about, and she inquires with each person as to whether or not they have seen a ship depart this morning. Some shrug, others shake their heads no. Eliza's fears are momentarily quelled.

Commercial Wharf is the only one of the four main piers that is still standing by morning light, and is, therefore, where all the local fishermen and sailors and merchants have gathered. Amazingly, M. Crosby and Sons Candlery, at the base of Commercial Wharf, is intact, just as James said, just as it stood last night.

Eliza walks to the end of the pier, lost in thought. Nantucket keeps breaking James's heart. Well, it breaks Eliza's, too. The destruction, the despair. Her island may never come back from this, although she doesn't wish to believe those words from James could be true. And, now that Eliza has made the decision to stay here and wait for Henry's return? What will their future look like? How can they move past all that space and time, all the lies of omission and worse. But then, Eliza places all of that history side by side with her new insights about Henry's years at sea, and feels inspired to try. If only she hadn't penned that damned letter. James said that one ship left this morning . . . so perhaps a correspondence did as well. What that may mean for the fate of Eliza's marriage is too difficult to contemplate. After keeping her home safe all night, it is entirely possible that Eliza just imploded it.

Half-burnt casks float on blue-black water, the color of a bruise. Slats of wood and pages of newsprint. A once-pink bootie, a tin can, some-one's bible. The harbor is calm now, but inky with oily residue and the flotsam and jetsam of Nantucket.

Out on Commercial Wharf, many men mill about, aimless after a night of so much purpose. Tired firemen, their uniforms askew, their feet bare, lean their backs against a few lone barrels of alcohol that they are simultaneously drinking from. One man is smoking a pipe, another fishing off what's left of the pier. Gossip about how the fire began is the talk of Main Street, and hearsay about the aftermath is the talk down by Nantucket's harbor.

And here is Josiah Pine, the fire marshal who led last night's charge on her home. He recognizes Eliza and waves her over. It is from him, seated with the others and drunk on ale at eight o'clock in the morning, his speech slow and slurred, that she learns the town's grim statistics.

"Josiah! Tell me everything that happened."

He looks up at her but cannot seem to focus on her face. "What 'appened, Miz Macy, is that we lost three hundred buildings and eight hundred people."

"Eight hundred people dead?" Eliza gasps. Her knees give way.

"No, no. You didn't leh me finish. Eight hundred people lost *their homes.*"

"Homeless," Eliza says. "Where will they go? Where are they now?"

"Wanderin' about, I guess," he says, gesturing with his hands and sloshing beer all over himself. He drinks from the one tin cup they all share between them and passes it to the man on his right. "Did you not see them everywhere?"

Eliza did see people milling about the ruins, but she hadn't put together that they were all doing so because there was nowhere else to go.

"And no food left on the island," Josiah Pine adds.

"But there is a bit of drink to be had," another drunk fireman weighs in.

"And it coulda been much worse, if nah for us," Josiah says, and the dozen or so men around him nod in agreement and raise the one glass.

Men. She's tired of them. All of them: the good ones, the faithful, the loyal, the kind. The rich ones and poor ones, the ones who break your heart and the ones who are a mystery. The greedy and the hungry, the soft-skinned boys and bearded men. The ones who leave, the ones who stay.

Eliza Macy is exhausted to the bone, wrung out and powerless.

All of her rage comes to the surface. Look at these careless, useless men who now cannot stay sober enough to help the town's many helpless and homeless!

"I saw your men fighting in the street over who got to claim the pump, Mr. Pine. This grand display of manliness delayed the rescue efforts and probably caused the fire to spread even more. So, I ask you, sir, how is it possible for you to think—no, actually *say!*—that it could have been any worse?"

"Because," Josiah Pine says, looking up at Eliza through a haze of inebriation and exhaustion, his light blue eyes watery with emotion and drink. "Because, Miz Macy, *nobody died.* Three hundred buildings gone and eight hundred people homeless, yes. Including me and my family. But not a single Nantucket soul was lost in our great fire." His watery stare moves toward the horizon line of the harbor. "And now we just gotta keep it that way without food or shelter until help comes. But Lord only knows when that will be."

53

MARIA

Maria wakes, not aware that she had even fallen asleep. The light is dim, fading into dull gray outside her window. She's still wearing her dress from the night before. She's not sure any amount of soaking in lye will get the scent out of it.

Her head is heavy, her stomach empty. It must be early evening.

Maria's father knocks on her door, calling her name gently, softly. She stretches her arms, yawns. Invites him in.

Concern creases the corners of William Mitchell's eyes. He still has not slept. Maria feels guilty for taking such an indulgence when there is much to be done.

She says so to her father, who shakes his head. "You needed a few hours to regain your strength. The whole town did. People must mourn their losses and rest. But now, we must organize and act, for many people are in need of shelter. We've invited a family here. Come meet them. And, if you think you are up to it, I want to show you what's happening at the Methodist church." He leaves her to get dressed.

Maria changes into a clean dress quickly, brushes out her hair and pins it back.

In the hall, William Mitchell introduces Maria to a small Quaker family, the father and mother standing uncomfortably while their child sits quietly on the couch, back straight, looking afraid. Maria recognizes the towheaded boy and his mother from the library. "Hello, David Hallett," she says.

David's shoulders relax and he gasps, pointing. "Mama, look! The bird book lady!"

"David, don't be rude," Mrs. Hallett admonishes, stepping up to him and lowering his finger. "Apologize to Miss Mitchell."

"No, it's quite all right," Maria says, bending down to be eye to eye with David. His mossy green eyes look very serious in such a round face. "Did you have a house in town that was lost in the fire?"

"Yes," David whispers.

"Well, then you must share ours," Maria says.

"You lived in the library," David says. It is not a question, and so Maria doesn't answer it. "But now you have to live here, too. Because the library got burned up."

"Something like that, yes," Maria concedes.

He glances up to the high ceiling of the hall, as if measuring whether or not he can fit inside, or deciding if he likes it. "What is that?" he asks, pointing to the piano in the corner, and dropping his hand when he remembers not to point. Simultaneously, Maria and her father speak.

"That belongs to me," Maria says. "Not my family."

"It's a musical instrument, David," William says. "But it's not part of the Quaker faith."

"That is nothing of importance," Mrs. Hallett says, looking uncomfortable just by being in the same room as an object so objectionable. Mr. Hallett sniffs and turns his head away from it.

Maria pulls David's attention from the temptations of the devilish piano—for how much fun would the little boy have by banging on the keys, making a cacophonous racket?—by motioning to the shelves lining the room's walls. "We have lots of books here, as you can see. Like we did at the library."

He nods again. "Do you have a bird book here?"

The Audubon guide. Oh, how she and David Hallett will miss it. "No, I'm afraid we don't. But—we have coloring pencils. And paper. So we can try and draw the birds from memory. After you rest. Would you like that?"

David puts one finger up his nose, which Maria takes as a yes.

Maria's mother, Lydia, appears with a tray of food, and Maria wishes the family well. She gives them some privacy and goes downstairs to the kitchen, where she grabs a mealy crabapple from the dwindling stack in the bowl on the table. Harry is bent over a ledger, scribbling furiously.

She chews and considers his work. "Have you moved at all these last few hours?"

Harry shakes his head. "Father and the other Proprietors wanted to get started on a list of goods lost from the Atheneum, in addition to your compendium of books."

"Let me see," Maria says. *One snail shell from Polynesia, one shark's tooth from Cape Cod, one shark's tooth from Cape Verde. Three coins from China, one sea pearl from Japan, two carved natural wood canes from Africa, one grass skirt of unknown origin, two woven shawls from Thailand* . . . the list goes on and on. Harry has, from memory, done a fairly good job of cataloging the artifacts from the museum. "Oh, Harry." She's too overwhelmed to say more.

He shrugs at the monumental task he has begun, the boy who likes to compete with her and his other sisters for attention—in the form of general praise and good marks in school—trying once in his life to be humble. And doing it when it matters most. "I pictured myself in that space, with the whale's jaw on my right and the window on my left, and imagined what you had curated over the years and placed in each position throughout the room."

Maria stands and kisses the top of Harry's head. "You've done so well. Thank you."

The Methodist church next to the Pacific Bank looks a bit like a day at the market, crowded with townspeople, only the backdrop is grim and there's no one selling or buying. People mill about on the steps of the church looking bedraggled and hopeless.

While Maria slept, the large building that she helped save from extinction has become a make-shift shelter, thanks to the women's auxiliary. Phebe and Kate help hand out blankets and make families comfortable. People sleep on pews, on the floor, even on the raised platform near the altar.

"They are everywhere," William says. "In every church on the island, and in people's homes as well. The town selectmen are meeting tomorrow to make a more formalized plan, but right now, we need to ensure that Nantucketers are sheltered and fed."

"Thank goodness no one blew up the church," Maria says, trying to keep the edge of anger and irony from her voice. She shouldn't have had to argue so passionately for the building's safekeeping.

"What's obvious by light of day is not always so in the midst of a dark night," William replied.

Maria can tell this is as close as she will get to an apology and says no more.

Her father recognizes a sea merchant and his wife and begins to converse with them. Clearly, they have been displaced; the children are clutching the mother's skirts, now their only semblance of home. Their house on Cambridge Street was partially destroyed, so William invites the family of five to stay in the Mitchells' parlor for as long as necessary. They thank Maria's father profusely and step away to gather their meager belongings.

"But Father, isn't the Hallett family sleeping in the hall? How will we fit them all?" Maria asks.

"I thought your mother told you. The Halletts will be sleeping in your room. You will join Kate and Phebe for the meanwhile. We wanted to leave the hall free for another family. As you can see, many need shelter."

"But—" Maria instantly thinks of her journals, her secret notes from Linley. Private, personal thoughts that she placed in the back of her wardrobe, behind an old pair of winter boots. Her rants, her unkind notions, her desires— now existing in the same space with a devout Quaker family. Oh no, this cannot be. Maria removed her papers from the rooftop, falsely thinking they would be safer inside the privacy of her room. But "safer" is only a qualifier, a way to show something by degrees. Perhaps there is no place truly safe for them to exist.

"But what, my dear?" William asks his daughter. They glance around to see who might unintentionally overhear them and step closer to one another. "Maria, I know that you are a private person, and that you need your solitude to work. However, I also know that you are not selfish. Would you deny these people comfort, a warm meal, a place to lay their heads at night and remember that God watches over and protects them?"

Maria stops her father's sermon, gently placing her hand on his arm. It is impossible to argue with such goodness, even if it borders on heavy-handed guilt and righteousness—a Quaker specialty. "I apologize. Of course I want to help any way I can."

Her father smiles benevolently at his daughter, his grace and love supplanting the tortured fervor there a moment before. Maria smiles in what she hopes to be an authentic display of comfort. She picks up two nearby buckets and goes to the pump for water, although what she really needs is air.

"Need help?" a voice says from behind.

Maria turns. Linley looks fresh-faced and beautiful.

"Hello," Maria says, self-conscious. When was the last time she brushed her teeth?

Linley smiles. "I can take a bucket," she says, her hand brushing Maria's wrist. Maria's heart swells and, just as quickly, deflates. There's Charlie Warren in the space between them now.

"No, thank you," Maria says. She moves around Linley and heads to the pump. "But I'm sure they could use a hand inside," she adds, pretending she doesn't notice the way Linley's face falls as she follows behind Maria.

"I wanted a moment alone with you. To discuss last night," Linley says, her eyes glancing furtively at Maria and then away.

Maria pumps water into the first bucket and then the second, enjoying the physical exertion. There is much to discuss and yet nothing Maria wants to say. Feelings! Who has time for those? People are living in stables and churches, in others' homes, transient like soldiers of war. A family of three is moving into Maria's own bedroom, probably already sleeping together under her own blankets.

Maria can conjure astronomical phenomena, can imagine planets and stars and meteor showers, but right now, her vision is not expansive as through a telescope. It has become limited, close, concrete. Only what she can see right in front of her. Maria Mitchell sees survival, not wants and desires.

She holds tight to the metal handles and hoists the buckets from the ground. "I am most lucky to have your friendship," Maria says, wanting to grab Linley around the waist and hold on tight. But thanks to the heft of the buckets—and her own conscience—her arms remain at her sides. "We need one another's strength right now, one another's support. Let us get through this terrible time. And, when and if we do get to see

487

Nantucket's future, well—beyond that, I cannot say."

Linley blinks those fantastical purple eyes. "But we said that we loved one another."

"And I meant it. But you're marrying Charlie." Maria stops here. It's the end of the story, after all. She steps away from the pump when she sees others approach, and Linley follows.

"Does marriage have to change us, and what we want? I've been thinking about it for days, and . . . I thought we could still love one another."

Maria balks. She tries to keep her voice down while her emotions run high. "You would become a married woman—a perfect couple in the eyes of all of Nantucket—and I would become, what? Your lover? An adulteress?" The word makes her think of Eliza Macy, and no, Maria does not wish at all to be like her.

"Well, when you state it boldly like that . . . no. It sounds quite terrible."

"Linley: you must choose. This is life we are speaking of, not a poem by Tennyson, and not one of Grimm's fables. Life is dangerous and— as we have just witnessed—it can change in an instant. An existence in which a true, real person simply cannot have it all. And a woman perhaps least of all."

Linley's face crumbles. They climb the church steps together, but each walks through a separate set of doors.

THREE DAYS AFTER THE FIRE
July 16, 1846

54

MEG

Absalom Boston stands on a table in his tavern in New Guinea and reads aloud from the parchment in his hands. A crowd of Black and white, men and women, sailors from the Azores and Cape Verde and merchants from Europe, pack into the dark room, sitting at tables and standing in corners, leaning in from outside, where the windows are open onto the street. The neighborhood listens to his steady voice read the pronouncement drafted by the seven town leaders and sent yesterday to mainland America.

"Friends: the undersigned, Selectmen of the Town of Nantucket, have been constituted by a vote of the town a committee to ask at your hands such aid as you may feel able to render to our unfortunate and distressed people." Boston pauses to clear his throat.

Meg and Benjamin arrived early and are seated up front, where they have a side view of Boston's highly polished black buckle boots. Lucy watches with awe as the larger-than-life figure reads their fate back to them while baby Hope sleeps in her sling on Meg's bosom.

"Seven-eighths of our mechanics are without shops, stock, or tools: they have lost all, even the means of earning bread. Hundreds of families are without a change of raiment. Widows and old men have been stripped of their all; they have no hopes for the future, except such as are founded upon the humanity of others."

Meg is witness to the misery. She cooks what she can for the needy. Gives away their clothing, an extra dress, a pair of boots. Their chickens cannot produce eggs fast enough. She *knows*. But hearing this litany, this list of their losses delivered in this straightforward way, does something to shake Meg's soul.

"We are in deep trouble. We do not ask you to make up our loss, to replace the property which the conflagration has destroyed, but to aid us, so far as you feel called upon by duty and humanity, in keeping direct physical suffering from among us, until we can look round and see what it is to be done. We need help—liberal and immediate."

The long-standing island nation of Nantucket, she who has never needed help from anyone, is begging for outside aid.

Nantucketers—and Nantucket—will not survive without it.

The Wrights walk home in a blur. Meg thinks she might fall, were her hands not intertwined with her husband's, keeping her connected to her own physical being and placing one foot in front of the other. Waking up with her baby Hope breathing warm sweetness between herself and her husband, Meg felt certain that the worst was behind them. And then this pronouncement: a reminder that the worst may yet be to come.

Her emotions keep cresting like a breaking wave, *up up up* and crashing *down.*

The emotional ramifications of new motherhood are enough, with moods swinging this way and that, from elation to exhaustion, from tears to laughter. Must Meg ensure the survival of her baby and bear the weight of the entire town's survival as well? As much as she cares deeply about town events, she probably shouldn't have gone to this gathering. The couple says nothing to one another, but the deep crease between Benjamin's brows tells her that he feels this weight, too.

Seesawing, up and down. Their business is gone, but their home is intact. Baby Elias is gone, but Meg's two daughters are alive and well. Downtown was ravaged by fire, but New Guinea was completely untouched, with its shops open for business and its homes a refuge for refugees. They will run out of food soon, though. The entire island will.

They can fish, yes. There are some cows, certainly. And chickens. But theirs is not an agrarian society, the land too coarse and grainy like sand. Unfertile soil. Small family gardens abound, but three days after the fire they have already been stripped of most of their fruit and vegetables. Nantucket's one corn mill stands here, in Newtown, but there isn't enough corn to feed into it to create enough meal. There is just not enough of anything for everyone.

All in all, however, the predominantly Black community on Nantucket fared better than the predominantly white one. The irony of this is not lost on Benjamin, who still is bruised by the hateful rhetoric tossed out at him during the fire and the hateful actions aimed at the Black schoolchildren—including Lucy—in the days leading up to it.

"I wonder if anyone came by our house with our missing goods this morning while we were out," Benjamin says.

The night of the fire, Benjamin headed to town to join the brigade. But the other firemen—the white ones—wouldn't let him join, and so, as he awaited his own company's men, Benjamin cleared the cobbler shop of its most valuable assets, including the lush leather hides hanging over the beams, a few pairs of new shoes, the ledger of accounts, and his best tools. He waved down a boy with a cart, flung the goods into it, and paid a nickel to transport it all safely to New Guinea. *A saltbox house with a blue door, on Prospect. Large chicken coop in the side yard. Can't miss it!*

But the items never made it.

"It was quick thinking," Meg says.

Benjamin laughs. "Terrific! Yes: *here, why don't I empty my shop and give you the valuables?* Really smart."

"I didn't say it was *smart* thinking. I said it was quick."

"A lot of good it did," Benjamin adds. He glances over at Meg and his daughters, and his face takes on a tortured countenance. He feels guilty. He wasn't there for Meg or Lucy or the new baby the night of the fire—a fact for which he might not ever forgive himself. To deal with the sting of it, Benjamin acts out anger at himself by second-guessing every choice he made that night.

Meg shakes her head. "Many people have similar stories of theft, Benjamin. Their family's silver: gone. The heirloom teapot: missing." Advertisements for stolen goods are the entirety of news making up the one remaining newspaper. "Some even come listed with rewards! Everyone is looking for their belongings, which they gave to some passerby for safekeeping or misplaced during the commotion."

"Further proving that our small island town is bankrupt in more ways than one," Benjamin says. "And, look at that: white people buying right from Johnson's Grocery," Benjamin says as they pass the corner of Atlantic Avenue, where a line of tired-looking people snakes out the door and around the block. "They wouldn't shop here before, but now that they've got nothing and we've got something, they'll buy from Black folks."

Although Meg doesn't like Benjamin's tone about the matter, she can't fault his logic. The wealthy white population—including some of those seven town selectmen who penned that document—have lost their homes and businesses. Their pride must be put aside in order to ensure their survival. Meg feels sympathy for them, as well as anger from all that came before, up and down like a seesaw.

Eliza Macy stands in line outside the grocer's. Her long, wavy brown hair is neatly tucked under a bonnet and she wears a simple peach-colored cotton dress. She's out of place here, but Meg recognizes her immediately and feels her presence viscerally.

After Eliza left that money on the side table in the borning room, Meg ran out with the baby without explanation or goodbye. She doesn't want to have to explain now, and so she begins to pull Benjamin down a side street. But it's too late; she's been spotted.

"Meg!" Eliza calls, waving the Wright family over. She motions to show that she cannot step out of her place in line.

Are we really going to do this? Benjamin asks merely by raising one eyebrow at Meg.

I'll make it quick, Meg answers in a tight smile.

"Sorry to call out like a student in a schoolyard, but I didn't want to sacrifice my spot! I've been standing here for close to two hours, and I'd rather die than lose my place now and let someone else get ahead of me."

I bet you would, Meg thinks.

"What a beautiful baby daughter you have, Mr. Wright," Eliza adds.

"About that we agree, Mrs. Macy," Benjamin says.

There is an awkward pause; no doubt Eliza Macy is expecting to get a thank-you for helping Meg with her labor and delivery. Benjamin may feel that sentiment, but Meg knows it's not something he will ever utter to Eliza Macy.

The weather hasn't altered all month, never once letting up its relentless reminders of summer, and the day is already stiflingly hot. The sun burns through Meg's bonnet and sears her scalp. Eliza looks wan; she must be thirsty.

"And, who is this lovely little girl?" Eliza asks Lucy.

"I'm the big sister," Lucy says, with much pride. Eliza laughs.

"And how is your family?" Meg asks.

Eliza sighs. "Alice's husband Larson is still rather ill. He has terrible coughing fits and is still having trouble breathing. He's in a makeshift infirmary at the Methodist church, but we're bringing him home within the next day or so.

Doctor Ruggles thinks that his lungs will heal with time and rest."

"Well," Meg says, "I do hope so. Please send Alice my regards. We are needed at home, so we'll get on our way and leave you to your—"

"I'm sorry I didn't get a chance to say good-bye," Eliza stammers. "You know, that morning. I thought you would stay longer, but of course you needed to see your family. Mattie cleaned your dress from that night. Ever since, I have wanted to find you and visit you here in New Guinea, only I've been so busy with the boarders, and cooking and cleaning for everyone—"

"Boarders?" Benjamin asks. Meg wonders the same.

"Yes," Eliza explains, her gaze moving excitedly between Meg and Benjamin. "I took in several families after you left. One of them is even colored, like you," she says. "They live in the borning room."

"Well, isn't that something, Meg?" Benjamin says, his hand pushing gently against Meg's spine. "Like us. Now, if you'll excuse us, Mrs. Macy, we really must be going."

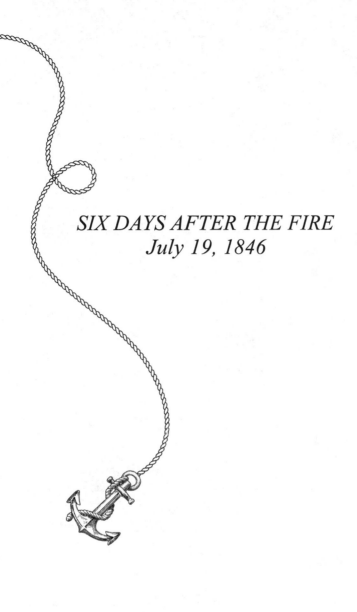

SIX DAYS AFTER THE FIRE
July 19, 1846

55

ELIZA

Eliza wakes hungry. Her stomach grumbles, gnawing every day a little more as she takes a little less sustenance. She's been married to Henry for twenty years now, but for the first time, she truly empathizes with what it physically and emotionally feels like to be a sailor far from shore, who must ration food and share it with everyone else onboard. She almost wishes they had hardtack to chew on like those sailors, something shelf-stable and crunchy and filling.

She opens the curtains to the deep, predawn light and says hello to the bluebird who showed up just after the fire, peck, peck, pecking, pulling Eliza from her leaden dreams the first morning she awoke in her own bed. Ah, that morning, that day: the stark light of reality against still-smoldering embers: Meg was gone, and her baby, and the letter to Henry, and James Crosby.

Trees downtown were gone as well, with their sturdy branches and downy nests. The shingled roofs of lumberyards, the chimney cornices and sail loft perches were also noticeably absent, and so the bird—like many other island residents—found himself homeless and came calling on Eliza Macy.

"Good morning, Charity," she says, for that's what Eliza has named the bird. Charity is a beautiful thing, with her round, tawny belly and blue-cloaked head and matching cape of long, cerulean tail feathers. It's too bad that she is slowly poisoning herself by eating the chipped paint on the outside window sashes instead of digging for something fortifying like grubs.

But Eliza supposes Charity, like the rest of Nantucket's population, must eat what's put in front of her. As the saying goes, beggars cannot be choosers.

Before the house stirs, Eliza dresses and goes up to the roof walk with a pair of Henry's binoculars, searching each morning for a sign of a ship entering the harbor laden with supplies. In the past few days, there have been several small boats, but nothing substantial, nothing commanding that announces to the harbor that help is here. Letters of support, yes, and even monetary contributions have come to the islanders. But what good is money when there is no food to buy? Should they begin stuffing their mouths with dollar bills, much as Charity the bird dines on whitewash? *Here, Mattie and Rachel,* Eliza imagines herself saying to her daughters in the days to come, *suck on these nickels.*

And, although she knows it's not probable, Eliza looks for signs of the *Ithaca,* with its flag waving proudly, unmistakably: a horizontal, red-striped border on a white background, with a giant *I* in black in the center.

No ships coming or going yet today.

Eliza thinks of those most unfortunate ships from history, the wrecks floating adrift with only a few survivors, the vagabonds washed up on deserted islands. Stories of men eventually resorting to cannibalism to stay alive one more day, like their own Captain George Pollard, and crewmen Thomas Nickerson and Owen Chase. Of course these men only did what they had to do, but every time Eliza sees one of them downtown, she crosses to the other side of the street. She supposes that isn't very charitable of her.

The harbor is still, the sky brushed with light clouds, the air hot and dry as it has been for the last few weeks. From her rooftop lookout, Eliza feels her stomach churn thinking of her careless, callous letter to Henry. Would it ever find him, or would it be lost at sea? For despite Eliza's best efforts to track the letter down that morning after the fire, she was unable to do so.

Eliza went home that morning and waited for Rachel and Mattie to return, and, when they did, she confirmed her worst fears about the matter. Yes, Rachel had handed the letter off to a naval officer. The one addressed to Father. Rachel had thought her mother would have wanted Father to get the news of the fire as quickly as possible, so that he could hurry home. Isn't that right?

Hadn't she done the right thing? So why was Eliza looking at her as if someone had died? Had someone died and Eliza not told them? *Mother,* Rachel asked with growing worry, *what is the matter?*

Nothing, my dear, Eliza had said. *Nothing at all.*

The home that Eliza fought so hard for the night before now felt empty and devoid of meaning.

And then she heard someone crying. Outside her house, Eliza found a young girl with gold ringlets weeping while her father tried to console her. He looked apologetically at Eliza when she met them on the sidewalk and asked what the matter was. "I'm sorry, miss, to be making such a scene in front of your house. But Tess lost her dolly in the fire. We've searched all day but I'm afraid—" but he couldn't complete the sentence, as emotion started to get the best of him, too.

"I have three grown daughters who have lots of dolls. I'm sure we can spare one for you."

The father—a Mr. Ezekiel Jones—hemmed and hawed, no we can't, that's awfully kind but—and so Eliza did what she did best and insisted. "Rest out of the heat a moment while I fetch that doll? And maybe have a biscuit, if I can find one?"

Once Eliza learned that the Joneses not only had lost the doll, but the entire house around it, and that little Tess's mother had died in childbirth just a year earlier, well, Eliza invited them to stay as long as they needed. Rachel and Mattie, returning a little while later, were delighted to have the houseguests and prepared the spare room next to theirs for the small family.

The girls were helpful, as they had been during the fire and the birth. Perhaps Eliza had underestimated them. Perhaps she had let her own indulgences and needs keep them from being the kind, giving souls they actually were.

The next morning, Charity, the little bluebird, came knocking. For the first time in weeks, Eliza had slept heavily, without dreams, true, but also without worries. And without laudanum to help aid her sleep.

Meg was gone. Had snuck out, afraid of Eliza or ashamed of her or plain fed up. And yet Eliza had been so proud of what she had done, of what they had accomplished together, her and Maria and Meg! It felt like Eliza had set something right after doing so much wrong. But then Eliza had gone and derailed things yet again. She saw almost instantly—yes, right in the moment it was happening—how terribly she mishandled the relationship with Meg. Who bribes a friend, if the woman is truly a friend? And seeing the Wrights in New Guinea, well, Eliza had been taken by surprise. She had the perfect opportunity right then to apologize, to recognize something and name it, and yet she had failed once again.

Charity peck, peck, pecks, making such a

racket at the window. Eliza takes it as a sign. She can't change the past, but she can do something right in the present. She has started to do so by making room in her home which, in its own way, helps to fill the emptiness in her heart.

And next she'll find a way to make amends with Meg Wright.

Eliza comes down from the roof walk, tiptoes to the kitchen so as not to wake any of the boarders—some now sleeping in the living room—and puts on a pot of weak tea. Yesterday, Alice was able to have Larson brought here on a stretcher, which added two more "guests" to her roster. He was awake, but not very strong, and he seemed to have shrunk in the week since the fire. Alice hardly left his side, except when waves of nausea from her new pregnancy caused her to run out of the room and vomit into a small bucket. The couple moved into Rachel and Mattie's room, forcing Eliza's twin daughters to sleep in her giant bed with her. With all the calamity around her, she doesn't let the small delight about this new sleeping arrangement show.

Scanning the kitchen now, Eliza sighs. She stood in a long line at Johnson's Market in New Guinea the other day to get provisions, but already most of that is gone. Feeding eighteen people requires more creativity and luck than one sack of flour and rice can provide. Hoping to make the most profit from the great demand for

506

small supply, shopkeepers have raised the prices of goods since the fire. A five-pound bag of rice, which cost two cents on July 13, commands double today. While she loathes the fact that merchants have done this to their fellow citizens, she cannot begrudge them their commercial rights. Being opportunistic is a Nantucketer's birthright, she supposes. Good for them for continuing to prosper.

Eliza has used most of the cash Meg rejected to feed her guests. She should save the rest, but it feels so good to use the money in this way, helping others. Without question, she will use all fifty dollars if she has to. She only hopes there are still staples left to buy. Last she heard, the market had a lot of spices—cinnamon, cloves, and sage—but nothing of substance to flavor with it.

Maria enters the kitchen just as Eliza is preparing plates of breakfast, her arms clutching a heavy basket.

"I bought butter, blackberries, and a little bit of flour this morning from a woman in Madaket," Maria says in greeting.

"Wonderful," Eliza says, relieving her friend of the basket. She places it on the table and extracts the items, handling each blackberry like a precious jewel. With a bit of cornmeal she has left over, she can make some johnnycakes and mash the blackberries into a basic jam to go on top. After Eliza admitted her financial woes to Maria, Maria has shown up every day with more and more, from wheat to rice and sugar. There is something to be said for admitting you need help.

"And, oh! I kept forgetting to bring it over," Maria says, extending a small glass vial in Eliza's direction.

Eliza tingles from the thought of spiking her tea again, of dulling the edges of experience just a bit. It's been almost a week since she last had some. But her headaches have dissipated, and she needs to stay sharp and alert to run this house. Eliza waves the bottle away. "That's all right. I don't need it anymore."

"You're certain?" Maria asks.

Eliza shakes her head yes. "Now let's get started on breakfast."

Between trips to Johnson's, plus Maria's contributions, Eliza has been able to supply two meals a day for everyone. People wake hungry, with much to do physically throughout the day, clearing their land to rebuild, digging through debris for any remnants of their former civilized life, so she tries to start everyone off with a hearty breakfast. They come back in the late afternoon glassy-eyed and bone-tired, so she gives them an early supper and listens to the ones who want to reminisce—like Betsy Conway, whose house on Pearl Street went back three generations—and lets the others be.

For the past six days, the town has existed in a state of in-between, suspended like souls floating on the River Styx, somewhere between life and death. They are waiting. Without supplies from off island, they cannot move forward, and they don't wish to look back. They can clear debris, but then what? There is no lumber on Nantucket with which to build. No forests here, no brickyards. No natural well of materials except that which comes directly from the sea. And so the boarders go out in the morning, do what they can to feel useful—which isn't much—and return defeated to the Macy house.

Eliza knows what it's like to wait for a ship to come in. She knows better than most.

The women talk and share what else they have learned about any aid being sent to the island, including the letter from the selectmen that was printed and shared among community members. Rachel and Mattie join them in getting breakfast ready. Although she is exhausted, Eliza enjoys all of this company and being so consumed with work. There is always something real to do, unlike before the fire, when all Eliza seemed to do was worry and get into everyone's business.

Since the night of the fire and the morning following, Maria and Eliza have made peace with one another, their friendship back on solid ground. During labor, when Meg blurted Eliza's secret about James, Maria had been consoling and kind instead of harshly judgmental. She had been a good friend, just when Eliza needed her to be, even knowing about her affair with James, and even while calling her out for her misguided prejudices. And, ever since, Maria has proven herself to be a loyal and true friend once again. Sometimes, you need tragedy to remind you of one of life's most important questions: *What would you take from your home in a fire?*

The next time, and every time after that, Eliza knows she would grab flesh instead of porcelain. She would flee from the conflagration with her children and her friend, hearts beating, souls alive. They were not perfect like a work of art from France, or a grandfather clock from England, these people, herself most of all. But she needs nothing else to survive.

Eliza's guests are starting to stir. She can feel the morning shift in the air from a sleepy home to one charged with people's chatter and movements as they dress for the day, their worries making more noise than their physical presence. It's become Eliza's favorite time of day, being able to greet them and get their hard day started right.

"Hello!" a male voice says from out in the front hall. The voice isn't familiar, not like Stephen Cary's deep baritone. He's the young bachelor who has been sleeping on the Oriental carpet in the living room, who Mattie keeps looking at with too much interest.

"Yes, hello, how can I help you?" Stephen says. "Are you looking for Mrs. Macy?"

Eliza should set out breakfast in the dining room; she usually puts out dishes and cutlery on the dining table with platters of whatever food she has available that day, and people help themselves. Setting out dishes makes the meal special, even if there are only bits and pieces to eat. Eliza asks Rachel to bring the food inside for serving and goes to see who Stephen is speaking to.

"Mrs. Macy," the man says, tipping his hat to her. Tall, thin, gray-haired: the man of Eliza's waking nightmares. The bank manager.

"Mr. Edmunds," Eliza says, swallowing bile at the back of her throat. "As you can see, I'm quite busy at the moment. I'm about to feed a good many people their breakfast. Can your visit wait?"

"I'm afraid not," Edmunds says.

Of course not, Eliza thinks.

"Why don't we talk somewhere more private," he suggests.

"Yes," Eliza says, leading him through the house, out the back door, and into the garden. She makes him stand next to the oft-used outhouse. "Now, Mr. Edmunds, what is this about?"

"I sent word of the bank's fire to the owners of Citizens in Boston. All the cash lost, all of the bank notes and promissory letters and records of debts gone," he begins. Eliza is familiar with the

511

tale and urges him to hurry up and get to the part of the story that includes her. "Well, Mrs. Macy, I asked them how to proceed. I received word back this morning of what they intend to do."

"Yes?" Eliza asks, her heart hammering now in her throat, replacing the burning bile.

"Citizens Bank has decided that they will not be reopening on the island. They are taking their losses and moving on."

"What does that mean for me?"

"It means, Mrs. Macy, that, because of this accident of fire, your debts have been forgiven. That what you owed the bank has, quite literally, gone up in smoke."

"Oh!" She hugs him, nearly knocking him to the ground, and invites him in for tea. "The weakest tea you've ever had!"

Mr. Edmunds smiles, although his face is still a bit ashen, and declines. "Looks like I'm out of work now. I have a wife and three children to care for, so although our house was spared, there's nothing left for us. We'll leave Nantucket in a few days, as soon as the boats start running again. My wife's got a sister in New Paltz, New York, so we may move there."

Eliza wishes him well as he departs through the back garden gate. Though the house next door was destroyed, the garden is thriving, with gorgeous long-necked violets, periwinkle hydrangea and full, pink roses. Mary Foster had tried for years to get flowers to grow with little success, and now look.

As she heads back into the house, Alice is there, perched on the back porch waiting for her. Maria, Rachel, and Mattie stand beside her.

And Eliza knows before knowing: Larson is gone.

She rushes up the back porch step and catches her daughter before Alice crumples completely to the ground. Together they howl and scream into the summer sky.

ONE WEEK AFTER THE FIRE
July 20, 1846

56

MARIA

An alarm rings out while Maria sleeps, bells from the top of the Unitarian church followed by a call of *Fire!*

This isn't real, Maria tells herself, half-awake. She's still sharing the lumpy, small bed with Phebe and Kate. Kate steals the covers and Phebe snores. Sleep is impossible. Not to mention, when Maria does slip under, terrible dreams plague her mind, making her wake with a gasp. The second night of sharing the bed, she spent the entirety staring at the ceiling, picturing constellations and wishing the plaster whorls were galaxies. Ever since, she's chosen to stay awake on the roof, stargazing and trying to re-create the calculations lost.

Maria is close to tracking that comet, which makes her close to regaining control over her life. She has tried not to think of Linley. And, without access to her journals, which are stuck in Maria's bedroom with the Halletts, she hasn't had a single opportunity to compose her thoughts.

What's more, Maria hasn't been able to reread Linley's lovely notes. Without the notes, and without Linley, she feels very lonely and sorry for herself indeed.

So, she has stayed on the roof each night and focused all of her energies on scientific pursuits. Discover a comet, win the prize from the King of Denmark. But, at around three this morning, Maria's eyes burned and her vision blurred. Her head pounded. So she crept down the roof ladder and got into bed with her sisters, her body heavy, her mind blank.

Fire! Again the call. Her sisters stir beside her. Kate takes the last of Maria's coverlet and rolls to her side with it tucked beneath her. Phebe opens one brown eye and looks at Maria.

"Did you hear that? Or am I dreaming?"

"I heard it," Maria says, suddenly alert. She sits up and places her feet on the floor as the call comes again. *Fire!*

"Girls," Lydia says, knocking on the door and entering simultaneously. She looks both panicked and weary, aged tenfold in this past week. "Get dressed. The Halletts are already up and out. They went to file a claim for their losses with the town councilmen."

Maria ties a robe over her nightgown and wipes the sleep from her eyes. It's morning outside. Dim light comes in through the small window.

"Kate, get up," Phebe says, prodding her sister's bottom with her foot.

"Nuh," Kate says in return.

"Let her sleep for now," Maria says. "We'll come get her if we have to evacuate."

What is left to burn? Perhaps a fire has sprouted in another part of town. Perhaps it is only something small, like a kitchen fire already under control. Maria hopes so, for most of the fire pumps and hoses were damaged or destroyed on July 13, which means there are now limited resources left to battle another fierce blaze. Her heart beats fast as her mind jumps three steps ahead: a new fire, limited capacity to extinguish it, an isolated community already hungry and fatigued and living with their neighbors . . . and if other people's homes are lost, then what?

William Mitchell, already in the hall, greets them.

"What in the world is going on?" Harry asks, coming up behind Maria.

William shrugs. "I'm not sure. Nothing looks out of the ordinary. Well—except for the obvious, that is."

The bell again, three clear rings from the church tower post. Everyone waits, completely still. And then the call. *False alarm! False alarm!*

William's shoulders relax, Harry breathes out audibly, and Phebe claps, slowly and with sarcasm. "Well done, lookouts! Scare us to death yet again!"

Maria is annoyed as well. "This is . . . how many? The third time the town has called a false alarm since the night of the real fire. Can they not tell the difference? Do they think alerting us before having proof of anything is wise?"

"They're nervous. Anxious. As we all are," William says. "They are only trying to help. We must be charitable with not only food and shelter, but with our patience as well, Maria."

Patience! Virtues! Being a good neighbor! Maria knows all of this. But these continued false calls of fire are unsettling, and today she is angry about it, tired of feeling on edge. But Lydia gives Maria a piercing look and Maria says nothing but "Yes, Father," in response.

With another crisis averted, Maria realizes that the Halletts are not home, which means her room is vacant. Good. She excuses herself from the family and quickly walks toward the bedrooms, opening the door to hers. Ignoring the Halletts' belongings, which make her room feel not at all like her room—it even smells different—Maria crosses to the large wooden wardrobe in the corner. Kneeling on the floor, she extracts her journals, some loose papers, and the box of Linley's notes.

"What are you doing?" Maria turns at the sharp sound of her mother's voice.

Like a naughty little girl instead of the woman she is, she clutches the journals to her breast. "Nothing."

"That looks very much like something," Lydia says, entering the room. Her arms are crossed and her eyebrows are raised.

Lydia Mitchell has raised nine children. If there's one thing she knows how to do at the highest level of expertise, it's mother Maria with only a look.

Maria sits back on her heels and drops the journals on the bare wooden floor. "I keep some personal papers. Correspondences. A journal. Notes. You wouldn't understand."

"Personal papers?" Lydia asks, her eyes growing wide. Lydia crosses the room and sits on the edge of the bed, facing Maria. "All of this? And you keep them here?"

"No! I mean, yes. But only temporarily. I kept them hidden on the roof, under the boards of the observation platform, but when the roof caught fire last week, and I saw other people's words flying through the night sky, I imagined—"

Lydia nods. "I do understand." She looks like she's seen a ghost. "That night during the blaze, I caught a piece of flying paper and I read it. A death notice for infant Laban Hussey, David and Elizabeth's baby, dated a year ago. *Beloved son,* it read in Elizabeth's hand, with details about the funeral, and was stamped with his footprints dipped in ink. *Your father and I shall never forget you.* Poor soul only lived one day."

"I recall it well," Maria says. The Mitchells had attended the small internment at the Quaker cemetery and then walked with the Husseys back home, a solemn procession of black-cloaked grief.

521

"And then I read another, although I knew I shouldn't have," Lydia says. "It was a piece of a love letter—no names—but there was enough information to make me wonder whether the affair was a secret one. Young lovers, without their parents' permission. Or, perhaps a more mature couple joining together out of wedlock."

"Mother, I—"

Lydia shakes her head. "I don't want to know, Maria. Whatever you have to confess or tell me. Whatever is in those correspondences and diaries of yours is private and shall remain so."

"But I cannot leave them here. If the Halletts were to come across this during their stay . . ."

Lydia considers this, her mouth a tight line. "As our houseguests, I do not believe they will snoop. Although that little boy might pry accidentally, looking to play hide-and-seek or some such."

The answer is not satisfactory, and both women know it. Maria presses on.

"And what if there is another fire? What if the bank combusts, and my papers get released upon the town?"

"*Our* papers," Lydia says.

"Pardon?" Maria asks.

"Our papers, Maria. In such a case, all of our papers would be in a similar predicament. Not merely yours."

Maria pauses. "You have—"

"Personal correspondences, yes! Items that are

not meant for anyone's eyes but my own. Just as you have, and your sisters, too, I would imagine."

"But, you—" Maria begins, not knowing quite what else to say. "The Friends would say—"

"The Friends," Lydia sighs. "A Quaker life is particular and wonderful . . . and difficult. Especially of late, with the Hicksites and all of the factions and strife within the religion. There are many restrictions and no one to confide in. I share much with your father, of course. He is the main vessel for all of my doubts and worries. But sometimes I—" Lydia pauses, looking torn.

"You what, Mother?" Maria asks, craving more of this openness from her mother and hoping Lydia will not clam up now, on the brink of true, meaningful connection.

Something shifts and settles in Lydia's expression. "Sometimes I write to my friend Polly Campden, the suffragist in New York, who is quite *worldly* as well as vocal about her views on women's rights. Although the elders might agree with her political and social point of views, they would certainly find her word choice and way of living in the world . . . upsetting. She likes to drink red wine when she visits France, for example. So. It would be best not to have any personal documents of ours getting into the wrong hands."

Maria stands from her spot on the floor and hugs her mother tight, practically exploding with delight. She feels Lydia's heartbeat against her own, the scent of talcum powder mixed with breakfast grease on the collar of her dress. Her perfect mother is human after all. Maria would like to pen this new and wonderful fact in her journal, ironically enough.

Lydia looks at Maria with a twinkle in her eye. "I would imagine that Harry also writes down his thoughts and feelings every once in a while."

"Harry has feelings?"

"One or two," Lydia says, standing and placing her hand on the door handle.

"But we still haven't solved the problem of how to keep our papers safe."

"I've been thinking about this very issue for a week, Maria. And I'm afraid I have the answer."

Maria looks at her mother in puzzlement. Why should her mother be afraid of the answer?

"There's only one thing to do. If you truly want them safe forever more, gather your writings and follow me," Lydia says. "Quickly, before the Halletts return."

Maria scoops up her journal, the papers, the box. It has just this moment dawned on her what Lydia intends to do.

Maria scrambles to catch up with her mother, who is calling Maria's father and siblings to meet by the fireplace in the hall. Once everyone is assembled, Lydia explains her conversation with Maria and their shared concerns for a breach to the Mitchells' privacy, in case of another disaster. "With every church bell that chimes, my worry grows."

"It is of great concern, of course," William concurs. Her father, too? This is truly astounding news. Maria wonders what William might be hiding amid the papers in his office and is glad she doesn't know. William Mitchell, respected Proprietor of the Atheneum, maritime astronomer and expert rater of chronometers, proud Quaker, bank manager. The public and private personas of her father are aligned, but the smallest infraction, particularly something documented in writing, could be calamitous for his reputation.

"I have some letters that I keep somewhere safe," Phebe says, somewhat shyly. "Notes passed during classes. I'd die if anyone saw them."

"Safe where?" William asks his daughter.

Phebe swallows. "Between the pages in my bible?"

Harry pretends his voice is an octave higher when he says, "Corinthians 12:1. Dear Tilly, don't you think Paul has the nicest blue eyes?" Phebe punches him in the arm.

"I keep a small diary," Kate says. "But I don't want to give it up. I do love her so."

"You can confide in me, Kate," Maria says. "Anything. Always."

In the end, everyone has some detrimental evidence against them, missives they wish to have kept away from the curious eyes of their Nantucket neighbors. It is agreed that there is only one way to ensure that no one ever reads those innermost thoughts.

Lydia lights a match over the kindling in the hearth, which Harry helps stoke with some crumpled pages of yesterday's copy of the daily *Warder*.

Her siblings come forth and present their papers in an almost ceremonial way, heads bowed, mood serious. Lydia steps away at one point and comes back to her place kneeling by the hearth with a package of browned letters tied together with string. "These were my mother's correspondences," she says. "On her deathbed, she made me swear that I'd never read them but always protect them."

"No, Mother, you cannot destroy those," Maria says.

"And letters from my dear sister, may she rest in peace," Lydia adds, holding out a few other notes. "I like to read them every Christmas morning. That was Claudine's favorite day of the year. I hear her voice and picture her with us still. But the letters contain some secrets and—"

"Mother, please," Phebe says. "Some things can be kept, surely."

But they cannot keep any of it. Fire made them aware of this problem, and fire is the only solution.

As Lydia tosses her family's letters into the flames, Maria excuses herself to her room once again and lifts the hinged top off the smooth wooden box. She unfolds Linley's letters and reads through each one quickly. Maria laughs at Linley's silly jokes and funny drawings, cries over the beautiful poetry, and shakes her head in recognition of Linley's longing and hopes for their relationship. What a smart, wondrous creature.

She returns a few minutes later and joins her family, keeping her eyes fixed on the box. Maria senses someone settling on the couch beside her and raises her gaze.

"I hope whoever it is feels the same way about you, Maria," Phebe whispers.

"Pardon?" Maria asks.

"Clearly, you are in love." Phebe shrugs, gesturing to the pile of notes.

"Maria, it's your turn. Everyone else has gone," Lydia says.

Maria considers her sister's words, stated in such an offhand way, as if completely obvious. Love. So simple. But love has never been simple for Maria.

"Maria?" William prods. "I know this is difficult, but please. Before the Halletts return."

Maria's mother wipes a tear from her eye and sits back from the fireplace.

The letters she destroyed were the only

remaining memories of her deceased mother and sister. She will never get those words back. And, moreover, she will never get those people back. She has lost them permanently.

Just as Maria will now permanently lose Linley.

And so Maria hands over the stacks of letters— love letters, she sees now—and her journal to her mother's open arms. Maria has no need for them anymore.

"Oh, wait—there's one more," Phebe says, quickly running down to the kitchen and back up, breathless. She passes Maria a folded piece of paper tied with red string. Maria's heart hops into her throat. "But it's nothing you'll have to burn," Phebe continues, nonplussed. "It's just something from Linley. She dropped it off last night, while you were in that meeting with Father and the other Proprietors. I didn't want to bother you. And then I forgot," she says, shrugging.

Last night! That was hours and hours ago now, practically ages ago. Maria had spent most of the day at the Macy home, reeling with the news of Larson Handler's death, trying to console Alice and Eliza and the Macy girls as best she could. And commingled with that devastation, was the wonderful news of Alice's pregnancy. It had been a blur of emotions at the Macy home, and then Maria had tried to stay awake on the roof.

Maria feels that there is really only one reason Linley would write to Maria now. How could

Phebe shrug about it? Doesn't she know that Linley's are the only words that matter?

No, of course not. Which is entirely the point of burning them.

Maria opens the letter slowly, as if she has not a care in the world, as if her entire fate doesn't rely on whatever might be inside. Every pair of Mitchell eyes watches her read it, so she tries not to betray any emotion whatsoever.

If the words are a confirmation of what she already knows—that Linley is indeed marrying Charlie—then she will not cry. And if the words are a different sort of proclamation altogether, why then—she will also try not to cry.

Maria scans the note quickly, memorizes its contents—four simple words—and tosses it into the fireplace.

"There," Lydia says. "We have burned it all."

But while her family gazes forlornly at what was lost to them, Maria looks into the licking flames and sees that she's finally been found. She gets dressed quickly and hurries to Ash Lane. Most of the street has been consumed by the fire, leaving only the Blake house standing. The contrast is startling, breathtaking. Here, amid all this ruin, is a house still standing. And here is Linley in the side garden, tending to her roses, a long strand of white-blond hair in her eyes.

Maria calls out Linley's name. She cannot wait a moment longer.

Linley looks up and smiles, picks a red rose, and opens the side gate for Maria. They embrace, Maria holding on tight, clutching her friend and confidante, her love, her North Star.

Four little words is all it took for Linley to convey everything.

They pull apart and Linley hands the rose to Maria, who is careful to watch for the thorns. "Do you mean it? What you said in the note?" Maria asks, blinking back tears.

Linley nods and smiles. "There is only you."

Hearing Linley utter those four words aloud fills Maria with complete joy. For the first time in her life, she thinks it is actually possible to have everything. Linley has forfeited marriage and children for a less predictable life beside Maria, which means that Maria now believes in the infinite possibilities of the cosmos. And she knows without a doubt that she will find her comet.

"But how—?" Maria asks, one of about a thousand questions.

Linley takes Maria by her free hand and leads her through the small back garden, amid a tangle of overgrown hedges, to where they cannot be seen from the street or the house. "I told my parents that I did not love Charlie, and that I wished to stay unmarried. I said that the fire helped me see more clearly what I wanted from my one life here on earth."

"And how did you explain the rest?"

"I said that many modern women on Nantucket—citing you as one example—have full, rich lives without a husband. When they asked how I will support myself, I told them that I planned to open a store on Petticoat Row. I have no idea what I'll sell—besides the hats I've been trained to make at the milliner's—but they agreed that there will be much need for goods now as the town rebuilds. We will use the front room in our house as a makeshift store until then, my father said, and he agreed to help me import items. And my mother asked if she could be my first employee. They still hope someday I will change my mind, but for the meantime, they have agreed to the Quaker doctrine that women are as equal as men, and as such, they are letting me make my own decisions."

"They sound like excellent Quakers indeed!" Maria says, delighted and still a bit shocked by this turn of events.

"Maria, you were right to make me choose, and I made my choice. There is only you."

Those four little words again! Maria steps toward Linley and kisses her, long and deep and passionate, feeling each part of her body come to life, feeling more than she has ever felt before. An electric shock, the heat of fire. Linley moans softly in her arms. Maria wants so much from this woman and this life, from this world. But she pulls back now, for there is time. It will not be easy, this relationship. It must stay largely hidden. But Maria's world has just shifted on its axis, and suddenly the rewards of love are too great to dismiss. Love is not a precise science, but then again, neither is astronomy. Her life's work and worth—Maria's happiness—will always contain a degree of chance. But chance leads to possibility, upon which all great discoveries are made.

EIGHT DAYS AFTER THE FIRE
July 21, 1846

57

MEG

There is much to do but also nothing to be done. That is how every day since the fire has felt to Meg: hurry up and wait. Yes, Nantucket is a disaster. An island in need of salvation which has not yet arrived. Benjamin eats breakfast and goes off to "work" in town. But there is nowhere to work from and no customers to work for. He comes home exhausted from the sheer nothing-ness of waiting to begin again, with no colorful stories to share about his workday without color-ful customers.

This is of great concern to Meg, but as a new mother, it isn't quite her everyday reality. She lives with a newborn in a sphere outside of the world's basest realities. Hope needs to be fed every three or four hours, and so the baby has become her clock, her earth's rotation around the sun that is this new life. Morning blurs into afternoon which blurs into night, and although Lucy and Benjamin still seem to have a grip on when to eat each meal—with whatever they can put together from the garden—Meg doesn't even know what day it is. Plus, without school in session, days of the week tend to lose meaning anyway. Meg can tell time only by the fullness in her breasts and Hope's cries to be sated.

"What day is it?" Meg asks, coming from the bedroom and stretching her arms overhead. She can tell it's morning, but beyond that, not much else feels certain. Lucy is holding Hope while Faithful cleans dishes. She's been bringing the children with her most days so they can play together while Faithful helps Meg deal with new motherhood. "Good morning," she says, kissing the top of Lucy's head. "What a good big sister you are."

"Hope thinks so, too." Lucy nods.

"Today's Tuesday. Eighth day since the fire," Faithful says. "Why? Do you have somewhere you need to be?"

"I thought I might bathe," Meg says.

"Tuesday is a good day for that," Faithful says. "Good as any other, anyway. I'll prepare the tub for you after I finish in here."

"You don't have to do that, Faith," Meg says.

But Faithful looks at her with that similar, guilty expression that Benjamin has worn ever since the fire. "I want to," she says meaningfully, and the friends leave it at that. "I already had the girls fetch some buckets of water this morning for the washing up. We'll use it now for you and then do the clothing later."

The baby starts fussing in Lucy's arms, so Lucy hands Hope over to her mother. "I'm almost finished knitting that blanket, Mama. Jenny and I both made one. Today Mrs. Cole wants to teach us how to crochet the edges." She holds up the blanket as proof. "As soon as Jenny comes back from the outhouse."

"She's good with the needles," Faithful adds. "You know what? I'm going to pick some lavender for your bath," she says, heading out the back door.

Meg thanks Faith, and then turns her attention back to her daughter, who seems to want more praise now that baby Hope is around. "The blanket looks lovely, Lucy. Such fancy stitches! I know you are proud of your work, but please be sure you aren't getting too attached to the blanket. You'll donate it to the needy when the time comes, right? Not try to keep it?"

"Yes, ma'am, and no, ma'am," Lucy says, "But—" here she looks shy "—how did you know I wanted to keep it?"

"Because you talk about it like you have a crush on it. Like it's the cutest boy in the class," Meg says. Which makes Lucy giggle. "You get this look in your eye like you are in luuuuve," Meg teases her, which sends Lucy into positively hysterical laughter.

"Mommy, you're so silly. But you're right. And I think Jenny loves her blanket more than she loves Nicholas!"

"Who is Nicholas?" Meg thinks through the

boys she knows, pictures them lined up in their Sunday best at Zion's church at last year's communion service, and comes up with one in the year ahead of Lucy's. "Not Nicky Browne?"

"Nobody calls him Nicky anymore, now that he's double digits. Oh drat, I wasn't supposed to tell."

"Well, your secret is safe with us, Lucyloo," Meg says, cradling Hope as she feeds, and shifting herself a bit in her chair. She's glad to see her daughter acting like a carefree schoolgirl again instead of the center of a social and political drama. The summer months out of school playing and growing are as important as the ten others spent crouched over desks learning and memorizing, this year in particular.

Meg wonders now more than ever what will happen to Lucy's schooling in the fall. She has no idea what happened to her paperwork to sue Nantucket town over segregation. Did it burn up in the blaze? If it did, Meg's got to go back with Absalom and refile the lawsuit. On the other hand, if the paperwork somehow survived, will anyone care now about such a thing, when they barely cared to support it before all this chaos ensued?

"Mrs. Cole said the same thing, Mama, about having to let our blankets go. There's lot of homeless white girls in need of our charity, she 'splained."

"*Ex*-plained," Meg adds. "But yes, there most certainly are. And some Black ones, too."

Meg takes a luxurious bath in tepid water that Faithful prepares. It's chilly enough to cool down a body on another hot summer day, but not as cold as the ocean's shock. Faith puts Hope down for a nap and shoos Lucy out to walk with Jenny. "Let's give your mother a moment to herself," Faith whispers to Hope, as if the child will listen, taking the baby to the back porch with her. Meg closes her eyes in the metal tub in the corner of the kitchen and breathes in the lavender bath water.

She sinks her head under and washes her hair, takes a brush to her nails, and uses a washcloth on her skin, staying in the tub until her fingers get pruney. If taking a bath in a quiet house in the middle of a weekday morning isn't the sign that life is right, Meg doesn't know what is. She towels off and uses some beeswax on her lips and cuticles, massaging the extra into the dry skin on her elbows and knees. Meg is happy to see that her favorite yellow dress fits again, although only just.

There is a knock at the front door. Still barefoot, Meg goes to answer before the sound wakes Hope. It's a sight she never thought she'd see: Mrs. Eliza Macy, on her doorstep, looking nervous.

They exchange a pleasant although stiff

greeting. "I've never been to this part of New Guinea before," Eliza says, her eyes scanning Meg's house, taking in the second story and the big willow in the yard. "It's quite nice. And your home! Why, it's lovely."

"You seem surprised," Meg says.

"I didn't mean it like that," Eliza says, looking upset now as well as nervous.

Meg could invite Eliza in, make this—whatever *this* is—easier on the woman, who has clearly come for some sort of clearing of the air, or lightening of her own conscience. But only a week earlier, Meg had showed up on Eliza Macy's doorstep in dire need of real help, and Eliza had hesitated.

Eliza Macy is sweating profusely. She walked all the way from her house during this, the hottest part of the day. Meg dallies at the door a bit longer, asking after the girls.

"They are well," Eliza says, taking a handkerchief to her brow, damp under her wide-brimmed pink hat. The woman does have quite the collection of oversized accessories, and Meg has to give her some sort of credit for that. "Larson, though. He . . . well, the funeral is tomorrow."

"Oh, no," Meg says. She expresses her sincere condolences and asks if she might attend the service, if allowed. Eliza shares the details: the Unitarian church on Orange Street at ten in the morning.

"It's been quite a time. Alice is with child. She will move back home with me, with Larson gone. I think that will be a comfort to us all," Eliza says.

Life and death, living side by side. Meg thinks back to the night she gave birth and all that has happened this July.

"Congratulations on becoming a grandmother," she says, but Eliza flinches at the word.

"I'm delighted, of course I am. But, well, in truth the title of granny makes me feel old," Eliza says, drawing her face into an exaggerated pout.

Something softens in Meg, and she laughs despite herself. "By the time Henry's ship comes in, I'll be walking with a stoop!" Eliza says.

"My husband is on that same ship with Captain Macy," Faithful says, smiling as she enters the room, telling Meg that she put Hope into her bassinet. "The captain better bring them back before I become a granny, that's for sure!"

Eliza seems even more nervous now than she was when she showed up on Meg's doorstep minutes before. "Well, then you must be the one who shared the news with Meg about the good work they're doing."

Faithful nods but says nothing in response.

Eliza chatters on in the way society women must have been taught to, pretending one can smooth over life's blunders with inane chatter. As if Meg and Faithful won't wonder why in the world this woman has come to pay them a visit if Eliza continues to charm them with conversation.

"A woman can grow older gracefully, but I'll go kicking and screaming. In the end, I suppose I am quite vain." Eliza smiles as she concludes her diatribe, and Meg notices the small wrinkles around Eliza's eyes that give her appearance a touch of character. "It was nice to bump into you and Benjamin the other day when I was out shopping at Johnson's grocery."

Meg leans against the door frame and studies Eliza Macy as if she's an exotic bird, some rare specimen from far away that was once on display at the Atheneum. Faithful stands by her best friend's side, and together they fill the doorway.

"Eliza, why have you come here?" Meg asks.

"There aren't any other dry goods or grocers in town, you see, so I—"

"Yes. We know that. But why have you come calling on Meg?" Faithful asks. "Surely you must have had to ask someone for directions in order to find the house."

"Well, yes, I did. I asked at the barber's. And I didn't really need groceries today, not that there are really any left to purchase." Eliza's cheeks flush in the heat, or from shame, or some potent combination of both. "I came because I owe you an apology."

Church bells sound, punctuating the air around

542

them with three clear rings, lending veracity to Eliza's statement.

Eliza takes no heed of the bells, merely raising her voice to speak over them. "I want to apologize for my bigoted behavior—"

A bigot! Although Meg really wants to hear this apology and give Eliza time and space to explain, she's distracted by the bells, which shouldn't be ringing. She turns to Faithful. "But you said it's Tuesday," Meg says. "Right?"

"Oh, no, not again," Faith says, moving past Meg and stepping out into the street, her face turned up and out, waiting to hear any directions that might follow the bells.

Eliza suddenly understands. "Like yesterday, and a few days ago? Do you think it's another false alarm? Or, perhaps a real fire?"

There have been several of those over the past week, each one sending Meg into a paroxysm of renewed fear. The bell rings, the call goes out, and she's right back in that night, alone, her body aching, trembling on the wharf as she watches the harbor catch flame.

The church bells ring again. The whole of New Guinea braces itself. Carts in the street pause and horses' reins are pulled to halt by their riders. Faithful and Meg grip one another's hands, and Meg thinks of Hope, maybe jolted awake from the noise and crying alone in her cradle.

"To the docks, to the docks!"

543

"To the . . . docks?" Eliza asks. "Is that what he said?"

"That's what I heard," Faithful says.

"They've never called *that* one before," Meg asks. "Have they?"

Faithful and Eliza both shake their heads no, the three women exchanging worried looks.

Around them on Atlantic Avenue there is conversation, people asking their neighbors what they think it could mean to be called to the harbor in this way. The carts and horses continue on, unmoved by the call. "This isn't the Fourth of July, you know," an old man jokes, walking past with a silver-tipped cane that catches the sunlight as he moves. It's Luther Thomas, a long-retired silversmith. "Someone else go down and tell me about it tomorrow."

Is it an emergency, Meg wonders? Is it a command? Are they being evacuated? If so, should they pack belongings, and when will they return? The streets hum with speculation.

Meg feels a prickle of curiosity. She wants to follow the call to the harbor, to see what this is all about. Benjamin is in town already on Main Street, clearing out their shop and helping others do the same. She is sure he will walk to the docks.

"Let's go! Let's go!" Lucy and Jenny chant.

Faithful volunteers to stay with the baby and her son Daniel, who is playing in the back

544

garden. "When she wakes, I'll bring her down to town so you can feed her, if you're not back. By then it shouldn't be so insufferably hot outside, too. Better for me and her both to stay indoors."

Meg thanks Faith and puts on her shoes. Eliza is still there, standing on the threshold of her home.

"May I walk with you to town?" Eliza asks.

It feels somewhat like a parade, this procession of Nantucketers. It begins in New Guinea and picks up folks along the way, at Angola and York, at Orange and Flora and Union. Black and white and Pacific Islanders and Azoreans and Wampanoags who married into other families. Children skip along as if it is a holiday and there will be sparklers and ice cream waiting for them at the harbor. They will be sorely disappointed.

"You never told me your daughter's name," Eliza says, as they keep pace with one another.

"It's Hope," Meg says.

Eliza raises her eyebrows appraisingly. "We could all use a bit of that right now, couldn't we? And how is she doing?" Eliza asks.

Meg tells her, with a mother's pride, that the baby is not only a wise old soul with a strong and steady countenance, but seemingly brilliant and gifted besides. Eliza nods knowingly. "I remember you talking about another baby the night of the fire. Elliott, was it?"

"Elias," Meg says. She's been thinking about him a lot this past week, wondering whether he'd be jealous of the baby, whether at three he'd understand how to be gentle. She thinks he would pull on Hope's hair and make her cry.

"I lost a baby, too," Eliza says. "After the twins. Early on, though, not like you. I was only four months gone. I never told Henry about it, away as he was on a ship. Away as he always is. It must have been terrible to hold your baby and then lose him. I'm so sorry."

Meg nods as an acceptance of the apology, the two women walking side by side but not looking at each other, the crowd around them growing as they reach the port.

"Most of all," Eliza continues, "I'm sorry for trying to stand in the way of your cobbler shop. I said that my beliefs were purely economic, about commerce and competition. About what was fair and not. But, in truth, I thought you deserved less than me. I thought of you as less than me."

Meg stops walking, the weight of the words keeping her from advancing forward. Eliza pauses, too, and turns toward Meg. Each gives the other woman her full attention. The children run ahead.

"And now?" Meg asks.

"And now I know the truth."

"Which is?"

"That you are more than I'll ever be," Eliza

says. "And I'm so sorry for having caused you and your family pain."

Thank you would be the natural thing to say in response, only Meg doesn't thank Eliza. For although she is thankful for the words, she couldn't possibly thank someone for finally seeing her as human.

"Eliza, all I want—all *we* want—is to be equal."

"I'm coming to understand that. And I heard about your lawsuit. I wondered why you were at Hadwen House for the wedding and asked."

"I promise, I will never tell another soul about what I saw that night—" Meg begins.

"I know. And that's one more thing I must apologize for. I wasn't trying to bribe you for your silence, necessarily, but maybe I thought that money could repair the damage between us. I see now how wrong I was on that account, too. For some people—the best ones, really—their moral compass is not for sale. Which is why I went to town hall yesterday and inquired about your lawsuit. I submitted a letter in favor of it. It survived the fire, you know."

"I didn't know. Thank you for doing that."

"I believe in you, and I believe in school integration. And now that it's in writing, you have my word."

Meg nods to acknowledge this. "So now both Macys are crusaders, in word and in deed."

Meg sees Absalom Boston in the crowd, walking hand-in-hand with his daughter Phebe Ann, and waves. Then she turns back to Eliza, who, Meg notices, likes to walk at a brisk pace just like she does now that she's no longer pregnant.

"Mama!" a voice in the crowd calls. The harbor is visible as they turn onto Washington Street. Meg smiles as Lucy grabs hold of her waist. The pair of children are panting, out of breath.

"What do you think is going on, girls?" Eliza asks the pair.

"It's a ship!" Jenny says.

"A big one," Lucy adds. "We climbed up Jenny's roof walk a minute ago and saw it ourselves."

"Huge!" Jenny adds, pulling her arms as far apart as they can go. "It's coming round the shoal."

"How exciting," Eliza tells the girls, although her gaze seems far away and uncertain. She turns to Meg. "Isn't it?"

"I think so," Meg says.

"A whaling ship, you think? Or supplies?"

"I'm wishing for both," Meg says. "But supplies today."

Eliza nods. "Of course. We need supplies."

The Mitchell family arrives at the harbor at the same time, so Eliza waves at Maria.

Maria joins them, looking excited. "We're

saved!" she says, waving her hands in the air and laughing from the drama of such a proclamation. Meg and Eliza laugh, too, although the whole town is relieved by the truth of it.

Maria asks after Hope, and the three women talk about the baby, their families, the week since the fire. "This is a lovely reunion."

"We three are bound together now," Eliza says. "Oh—my daughters!" Eliza sees the twins and Alice in the crowd, so she calls to them. The girls push their way toward them, against the tide of people moving further north.

"I'm so sorry about your husband," Meg says to Alice. She then awkwardly congratulates her on the coming baby.

"It will be very hard raising a child without a husband, a father," Alice says. "But since my father is so often away at sea, that's what I've been thinking about Larson . . . that he's merely away on a long journey."

"Oh, Alice," Eliza says, sounding heartbroken.

It seems like denial to Meg, but if it brings the girl comfort in the coming days, who is Meg to judge?

"At least I can live and work at Mother's and now that she has taken in boarders, I won't have to worry about finances," Alice adds.

"The Macy House Inn," Maria muses. "We need one now that the Mansion House is gone."

"You have an inn?" Meg asks Eliza.

"I have an inn?" Eliza asks Alice. "And—you work for me?" Eliza asks Alice again.

"It's a good idea, isn't it?" Alice says hopefully, although her green eyes are hollowed and sad. "Now that the shop is gone."

Eliza looks stunned by the question, but also pleasantly surprised by it. "I suppose it is a good idea. Opening up my home this past week, seeing it filled with visitors—and family—that need to be fed and sheltered, makes me feel so useful."

And happy, too, Meg sees. Instead of agitated or angry or rude, Eliza Macy looks content.

"Girls," Eliza says to her daughters gathered around her. "Did you know that your father is a very good man?"

"You're not cross with him anymore?" one of the twins asks her mother. "For not explaining why he isn't coming home this July?"

"Oh, I'm still cross with him about that . . . but now I'm proud of him as well. All I had to do was gain a little perspective," she says, looking at Meg and mouthing a thank-you her way.

The crowd is moving them along. Maria waves at someone and says her farewells just as Eliza and her daughters get separated from Meg, who is keeping close to Lucy and Jenny.

Eliza calls back, "Stop by anytime, Meg. You're always welcome at my house."

Meg nods and keeps walking, thinking about how much has altered in the past week, and hoping that the tide of change keeps moving in the right direction.

Maria Mitchell is now walking arm-in-arm with that friend of hers, the pretty one with the long white-blond hair. The one from the wedding. Linley, her name is. They are deep in conversation, strolling without a care in the world and as if no one else around them exists.

Meg has heard that the Proprietors of the Atheneum have pledged a great sum of money and vowed to rebuild the library and museum quickly, and bigger and better than before. It must be that news which is causing the librarian to glow today.

Maria says something that makes Linley laugh, and both women tilt their heads toward the sky, as if searching for a meteor or comet, their faces positively radiant.

"Look, Mama," Lucy says, walking arm-in-arm with Jenny, copying the style of Maria Mitchell and her friend. "It's Papa!" Lucy lets go of Jenny and runs ahead to get Benjamin's attention. Benjamin scoops down and picks Lucy up, and she wraps her legs tight around his torso.

"Well, hello, my family," Benjamin says, his brow creasing in worry. "Where's Hope?"

"She's with Faithful," Meg explains.

Benjamin notices something out of the corner of his eye and a dark cloud covers his handsome face. He points in that direction "Hey! You!" He places Lucy down and calls out again. "You! Boy over there!"

He turns to Meg. "That's the little thief who took our merchandise and ran off with it in his wheelbarrow the night of the fire! When I get my hands on him, I'm going to . . ."

"Hey, mister!" the boy shouts back. "Mister over there!"

"You took my money!" Benjamin shouts. "And disappeared!"

"Papa, why are you mad at that boy?" Lucy asks, her elbow still linked with Jenny's. The small group pulls themselves out of the crowd and stops in front of M. Crosby and Sons Candlery, a spot Meg remembers vividly from eight days before. Lucy leans against the same barrel that Meg used to steady herself during a contraction.

Meg shushes her husband and places her arm on his. "Benjamin, please. You're making a scene." The racial balance in town is precarious at best. The last thing Meg needs now is for her husband to publicly harass a white boy in front of the whole of Nantucket. "Everyone lost something in the fire, and these items would have been taken by the blaze anyway. Let it go."

"Mister! Where'd you go?" the boy calls, waving his cap overhead.

"Here, son," Benjamin says, his anger diminished. "By the shop!" To Meg and the children

Benjamin says, "It's all right; I just want to talk with him, and clearly he wants to talk to me, too."

"You!" the boy says, pointing directly at Benjamin, his brown eyes filled with surprise. He has a neat bowl cut of sandy hair and an upturned nose. He seems perfectly harmless to Meg, almost comical even. "I've been looking for you everywhere! All week! Up and down New Guinea! I was awful confused as to your whereabouts, it being an island and all." The boy takes a deep breath of relief. "I have your wares."

"You do?" Benjamin asks. "Where are they?"

"In a safe location," he says. "You're the last one that I need to get settled with."

The boy tells Benjamin to meet him on the corner of Vestal and Grave after the happenings today. "Past the jail," he says.

"That sounds ominous, but all right," Benjamin says, warming to the boy.

The crowd begins to ooh and ahh and cheer as they get their first look at the ship. The boy walks away until he's swallowed up by the crowd. "And if anyone asks your business up there," the boy shouts, "tell them you're looking for Joseph Allen!"

"Well, I'll be," Meg says. Benjamin chuckles, thinking that Meg is referring to the boy's antics, but she's just caught sight of the boat herself. "Look."

Following a tide of Nantucketers, the Wrights walk out onto Commercial Wharf. Lucy asks for a piggyback ride, and so Benjamin picks her up and carries her on his back, making sure Jenny Cole has a clear view of the ship, too. They end up standing right beside Eliza Macy and her daughters on one side, and Maria Mitchell and her friend on the other.

Meg's bonnet helps shield the light from her eyes, but she blinks against the glare on the harbor. Coming toward them is a giant clipper ship, three-masted with six sails on each tall mast. Sailors are climbing the thing like ants on a tree trunk, pulling ropes and tying the sails down as the ship enters calm waters.

It's massive. And it's filled with supplies. The church bells clang and clang, a celebration of sound.

The boat is so big that it cannot dock close to shore, so it drops anchor out in the harbor. Smaller rowboats are lowered into the water and filled with goods. Meg's neighbors talk and cheer, laugh and clap as they watch. Sacks of what must be grain and rice. Large planks of timber. Bricks. Stone. Everything Nantucket needs to rebuild is there offshore, bobbing in the sea just beyond their reach. Sailors pick up oars and begin to row, coming closer with each stroke.

It has been eight days since their world was destroyed. Eight days since Hope was born. Elias only lived ten. Meg expects her baby will live longer than that, indeed believes that Hope will live so long that she will witness other changes in the world. But Meg doesn't know what the future will bring. No one does.

Something will happen with the integration of Nantucket's schools this fall, and something else will happen with the abolition movement and women's rights.

Something will happen to Eliza's new venture as a businesswoman, and with her new role as grandmother.

The Atheneum will be rebuilt, and the grocer's, and even the hat shop that started it all. Benjamin and Meg will stay and rebuild, or, Meg thinks, looking at the horizon line and the water and lands beyond it, maybe they won't. Maybe it's time they leave, as so many are doing—leave for places on the mainland with deeper harbors and growing opportunities.

Meg looks again out to the horizon line. Squints against the glare. Yes. Another ship is visible in the distance.

Next to Meg, Eliza Macy sees it, too, and gasps.

It's a whaling vessel, given the scale of it, with a red-and-white flag waving from its mast.

"I think that's Henry's ship," Eliza whispers to no one and everyone.

The sailors reach the pier and begin handing off their goods. Men from town come forward, roll up their sleeves in the heat and help. They place casks onto their side and unload them onto the pier. "What's this?" one local man asks, gesturing to a barrel near Meg.

"Oil," the sailor says, wiping sweat from his brow.

The wind shifts slightly and some clouds roll in, a quick and welcome change in the weather. *Finally,* Meg thinks.

And then it begins to rain.

AUTHOR NOTE

My family and I first vacationed on Nantucket during the summer of 1978, when I was eight years old. There were nine of us: my aunt, uncle and cousin, my grandparents, and my nuclear family of four. We rented a barnlike house called Equilibrium Stables (*Stable stables, get it?* my aunt pointed out) on Polpis Road for two sun-bleached and wonderful weeks, spending most of our days on Dionis Beach. There were gigantic dunes there then, and my cousin and brother and I would climb them and then roll down, climb and roll, climb and roll. We bought kites that flapped in the wind and shovels to dig in the sand. At low tide, my grandfather and I walked out and out and out in the clear water to collect tiny hermit crabs while my grandmother—fully dressed right down to her stockings—complained about the sand. We gathered scallop shells at Pocomo while being attacked by chiggers we called no-see-ums. We ate grilled cheese at the counter of one of the side-by-side town pharmacies, had malachite ice cream from The Sweet Shop and bought our newspapers at the Hub. It was magical. By the following summer, staying at the same rental house with the same cast of characters, Nantucket had become my favorite place on earth.

Forty some-odd years later, Nantucket is still my favorite place on earth. I am incredibly lucky to know Nantucket. I can tell you where to stay for a long weekend (Union Street Inn) or where to get the best lobster roll (Cru). I can tell you all about the Nantucket Lightship basket that my aunt had commissioned for me as a bat mitzvah present (made by Michael Kane, with a scallop shell top and a 1983 penny on the bottom). I can regale you with funny stories about the summer I spent on the island during college, drinking Rolling Rocks on the roof walk of a haunted house on Union Street. But until quite recently, I could not tell you anything about Nantucket's Great Fire of 1846.

I first came across a mention of the fire in Nathaniel Philbrick's wonderful history of the island called *Away Off Shore: Nantucket Island and Its People, 1602–1890*. And I sincerely mean just a mention. A whisper. Two paragraphs on page 13. But that's all I needed to get my imagination going, to wonder what might it have been like to witness such a thing as great and as terrible as Nantucket's Great Fire. To see my favorite place suffer so.

That tiny spark of an idea led me to buy up every book I could on the subject, which turned out to be . . . just one book. Doug V.B. Goudie's incredibly well-researched account, *ACK in Ashes: Nantucket's Great Fire of 1846* was invaluable to me as a writer, giving me every confidence that there was more than enough factual, historical information about the fire to help me flesh out a novel. (And, furthermore, V.B. had compiled it all in one place, which meant that I didn't have to go searching for first-person accounts and archives, since he already had. Score!)

Now that I had my setting clarified, I needed characters. Maria Mitchell (whose name is pronounced "Mariah") is a real historical figure who I *did* know a bit about, thanks to the observatory that bears her name and the portrait of her that hangs in the front entrance of the Atheneum. The Atheneum was the first building rebuilt after the fire, a pledge the Nantucket town trustees made and kept, and Maria received gifts of books from around the globe to help restore the library's lost collection. America's first female professional astronomer, Maria discovered a comet in October 1847, winning the coveted medal from the King of Denmark, earning fame for what is now called "Miss Mitchell's Comet."

Once I decided to make this historical figure a character in my novel, I read *Maria Mitchell: A Life in Journals and Letters*, edited by Henry Albers and *Among the Stars* by Margaret Moore Booker. Deputy director and curator of the Mitchell House, Archives, and Special Collections Jascin N. Leonardo Finger's book *The*

Daring Daughters of Nantucket Island gave me great insight into the independence, strength, education, power, and control that women on the island held, in terms of personal freedoms, civic action, and business acumen.

As the character of Maria evolved, however, I found myself pulling away from what was known into what I decided as an author to create. Maria and her family really *did* burn all their papers shortly after the fire, which meant two things for me as a researcher and writer: 1. I couldn't draw upon actual documents, since none survived from that period, so, 2. Suddenly, I was free to invent an entire backstory for Maria, one which might pose an answer to the burning question, *why would someone destroy all her correspondences?* This lack of evidence also allowed me to broach the hotly contested issue of *did she really help keep the firemen from blowing up the Methodist church?* And, further, as a woman who never married, did she ever fall in love? In these ways, I have been able to invent my version of this historical figure.

Meg Wright is not an historical figure, but I have based much of her story on the true accounts of two Nantucket women who lived around the same time, Eunice Ross and Phebe Ann Boston. In 1840, Eunice Ross took the entrance exam for the high school and passed. However, because she was Black, the local school board members did not let her attend—an issue that controlled much of Nantucket's politics for the next six years. In 1845, Phebe Ann Boston, daughter of Absalom Boston (the famous whaling captain whom you see glimpses of in this novel) was also barred from attending the high school after passing the entrance exam. Because of the newly instated Massachusetts law granting equal access to education, Boston threatened to sue the town of Nantucket, which the town didn't want to have happen and which ultimately led to Nantucket's schools' integration once and for all. Although several events depicted in the novel concerning integration and segregation did occur on Nantucket, I have condensed the timeline to fit the scope of my story. Also, because Phebe Ann Boston died of dysentery at twenty-one and Eunice Ross never married, I decided to create a heroine of my own to better personalize the story for readers. To learn more about issues of race, education, and equality on the island, I recommend Barbara White's *A Line in the Sand*, Frances Kartunnen's *The Other Islanders*, and Kabria Baumgartner's *In Pursuit of Knowledge: Black Women and Educational Activism in Antebellum America*. I also suggest visiting the Museum of African American History, which has outposts in Boston and Nantucket. To learn more about the history of slaves escaping to New Bedford by ship, I consulted *The Fugitive's*

Gibraltar by Kathryn Grover and *Sailing to Freedom: Maritime Dimensions of The Underground Railroad*, edited by Timothy D. Walker.

And that leaves us with Eliza Macy. Oh, Eliza. When I began to write, I thought there would only be her, a whaling captain's wife, struggling with financial issues and loneliness. *Captain Ahab Had a Wife* by Lisa Norling is a great resource for the life of New England women and whaling. But then I realized that a woman like Eliza was part of a rich and vibrant community, and I had to give her dimension and depth and characters to have conflict with. (And a he's-at-home! Thanks, Nathaniel Philbrick, for that historical treasure! And let's not forget, a mild addiction to opium, thanks to J. Hector St. John's classic, *Letters from an American Farmer*.) Of all the characters in this novel, Eliza is the one who is the most fictitious of the bunch, and the one with the most to learn.

That being said, it was incredibly fun to find ways and places to weave Eliza into history. For example, when I read about the fire breaking out on Main Street just before 11:00 p.m. on a Monday night, with two unknown witnesses first on the scene, I thought, *well, one of them is going to have to be Eliza. But why is she there? And what happens next?* It was in this way, through a combination of research and imagination, that I created this historical novel.

Other books I turned to for the history of the island, its customs, and Quaker life include: *The Nantucket Scrap Basket* by William F. Macy, *The History of Nantucket,* by Obed Macy and William C. Macy, *Quaker Nantucket* by Robert J. Leach and Peter Gow, and *Talks about Old Nantucket* by Christopher Coffin Hussey. Interviews with Frances Kartunnen, Betsy Tyler, Barbara White, Jascin Finger, Lincoln Thurber and Jim Borzilleri at the Atheneum, and V.B. Goudie helped answer many of my questions.

And, although I wouldn't call it an interview, strictly speaking, I asked Nathaniel Philbrick for his blessing to tell this story, when I met him in the fall of 2019. Did I know enough? Had I done all the research necessary to write a sweeping historical drama set during Nantucket's Great Fire of 1846? And, as any writer who fears imposter syndrome, I wondered, who put *me* in charge? He smiled at me and said, "You've got this."

ACKNOWLEDGEMENTS

I like to say that I moved from New York to Rhode Island to be closer to Nantucket. While I jest, there is also truth to that statement, because in Rhode Island I met the community of people who would change my life and make this book about Nantucket possible.

First, I'd like to thank Robin Kall Hominoff, who found me on Facebook and said something like "You read a lot and live in Rhode Island? How do we not know each other?"

Through Robin I met author Jenna Blum, who said something like, "You write and live in Rhode Island? How do we not know each other? You must join my writing workshop in Boston." And through both Robin and Jenna, I met author Jane Green, who said—in her wonderful British accent—"I think I know the perfect agent for you," and promptly introduced me to Allison Hunter at Trellis Literary, who believed in me and this novel and made all of my publishing dreams come true.

To Natalie Edwards at Trellis, who championed the manuscript from the beginning and who, along with Allison, has been such a delight to work with. You two have been my ballast when the seas get rough in this challenging industry. (There are no other whaling metaphors in this note, I promise.) To my editors Kathy Sagan and Nicole Brebner at MIRA, and the entire HarperCollins team, for your enthusiasm in acquiring the novel and taking such good care of it. In particular, thanks to Magen McCallum for the lovely interior map. (Oh, how I love a book with a map!) Additional thanks to my publicity and marketing team, Laura Gianino, Ashley MacDonald, Leah Morse, and Lindsey Reeder. Special thanks to Ann-Marie Nieves at Get Red PR, who kindly said, "call me anytime you are feeling nervous or stressed out," and actually meant it. As a debut novelist, it has been wonderful to welcome my Nantucket daughters into the world with your expert guidance.

To my writing group, which began at Grub Street Writers and is led by Jenna Blum, the most encouraging and life-affirming person I know (and who also just so happens to be a *New York Times* bestselling novelist): you are my people, my extended family. Thank you for sustaining the most ridiculous and hilarious text chains, and for the support, advice, and encouragement about both work stuff and life stuff. You talked about my characters as if they were real, which helped me see them that way, too. Because of you, writing is no longer a solitary endeavor. Trisha Blanchet, Hillary Casavant, Mark Cecil, Tom Champoux, Chuck Garabedian, Kimberly Hensle Lowrance, Edwin Hill, Alex Hoopes, Sonya Larson, Kirsten Liston, Joe Moldover,

Jenna Paone, Jane Roper, Whitney Scharer, Grace Talusan and Kate Woodworth: I love you all, even when you say that my pages need to be totally rewritten and that creating an outline might really help. A special shout-out goes to Mark Cecil in particular, who helped shape this book and its characters in ways that were invaluable. No one loves a hero's journey like you do, my friend.

To the team at A Mighty Blaze, which includes many of those mentioned above, but also includes the incomparable Caroline Leavitt, Allison Adair, Rachel Barenbaum, Karen Bellovich, Gabbi Cisneros, Ellen Comisar, Rachel Levy Lesser, Margaret Pinard, Mary O'Malley, Laura Rossi, Hank Phillipi Ryan, and Michele Sloane. The work we do together makes me really happy. A Mighty Blaze has been such a force for good in the world as well as in my personal and professional life.

Other writers to thank include Annie Hartnett, in whose class I wrote the first forty pages of this novel, and Randy Susan Myers, who helped me write a terrific query letter. Also, for their support and friendship, authors Lisa Barr, Jamie Brenner, Serena Burdick, Jacqueline Friedland, Natalie Jenner, Pam Jenoff, Nancy Johnson, Alka Joshi, Christina Baker Kline, Lynda Cohen Loigman, Sarah McCoy, Annabel Monaghan, Zibby Owens, Renee Rosen, Nancy Thayer, Adriana Trigiani, Heather Webb, Sam Woodruff, and many many others. I have been so delighted by this community and how we lift each other up.

To my forever friends, Gabrielle Tullman, Julie Seifer, and Jeannine Votruba, and to all of the terrific friends who have been by my side all these years, your encouragement and friendship (while raising kids/drinking wine/shopping/ taking long walks) mean the world to me.

To my mother, Ronnee Segal, thanks for believing in me and taking my writing seriously. You have read this book more times than I can count, giving sound advice and crying at all the right places each and every time. Thanks for being on-call 24/7 for any crisis, from an existential one to a fashion emergency, and for completely understanding the need for Nantucket-specific outfits. I love you so much.

To my father, Dr Norman Medow, for his excitement about this novel, and for acting as its unofficial publicist, telling his patients and the entire staff at Montefiore hospital that his daughter has written a book and that they must read it.

Both of my parents are, in their own ways, avid historians, who imbued in me a love for history, including curiosity about and nostalgia for forgotten times and places and interest in beautiful objects from the past.

To my aunt JaJa, who also read the book a few times and also cried on cue, you have always been a kind support in my life and a good listener. Thank you for being the one to introduce us all to Nantucket, and for the gift of my Nantucket basket.

To my children, Andrew and Zoe, for growing into wonderful, smart and funny individuals that I love to spend time with and for becoming the beach-loving people your dad and I always hoped you'd be.

To my husband, Brett, who understands what it's like to be a creative person, as well as what it's like to be married to one. Thank you for giving me everything I always wanted: beautiful children, a wonderful home, a hypoallergenic and loving dog, the space and time to write, and a vacation every summer on Nantucket. I love you and the life we have built together.

Center Point Large Print
600 Brooks Road / PO Box 1
Thorndike, ME 04986-0001 USA

(207) 568-3717

US & Canada:
1 800 929-9108
www.centerpointlargeprint.com